Ilthyn Productions

Emperor of the East Slope

To: Doctor Kegler,

Best Wishes,

by John Warner

An Alberta Story

Library and Archives Canada Cataloguing in Publication

Warner, John, 1943
Emperor of the East Slope / John Warner.

ISBN 0-9737967 - 0-7

I. Title.
PS8645 .A765E46 2005   C813".6   C2005-902724-X

Ilthyn Productions
e-mail
website   warnerjohn753@gmail.com
               www.ilthynproductions.com

This novel is dedicated to
Derek McCartney,
who, fifty years ago, told me I should;
and to my wife, Laura, who told me I could.

Thanks to
Debbie Elicksen of Freelance Communications
and
Nadien Cole of Nadien Cole Advertising
for the technical assistance in getting this
novel published.

While I have strived for historical accuracy in my writing, anyone smart enough to pick fault has me at their mercy and I plead poetic licence. All other errors are mine and mine alone. Most historical figures depicted are gone before us and cannot plead their case, but are judged by history.

John Warner

On the 88ᵗʰ anniversary of the battle for Vimy Ridge, 9ᵗʰ April 2005

TABLE OF CONTENTS

THE ETERNAL SOLDIER

The soldier lay dead.

Most of his face was missing. His weapon lay beside him, impotent. His body lay on its back, head down into a depression. The overnight rain had soaked the corpse, increasing its miserable plight. Gases of decay bloated the trunk and limbs inside the confined clothing, and during the day, fat blue flies laid eggs. Maggots crawled. Vermin and night creatures feasted.

Soon, he would disappear, back into the soil from whence he sprang. But that had not been his purpose here. Lured by fate, he died for the purpose of politics and power-wielding leaders who sent him as a sacrifice to their ends. His family, his loved ones knew not his fate, and maybe it was as well. Hopes, dreams, and promise went with him, vanished in a moment of time, while his corporal remains mouldered briefly, as a reminder to all who passed.

Yet, still the soldier lay dead.

ONE

H.R.H. PRINCESS LOUISE CAROLINE ALBERTA

Fourth daughter of Queen Victoria and namesake of
Province of Alberta, when it was created, 1905.

Princess Louise, by all accounts, was a beautiful, impressive, and clever lady. For seven hundred years, English royal princes and princesses were only allowed to marry royalty, regardless of their nationality. Despite the strictures of the Victorian era, she engineered the first to a commoner in all that time by marrying the Marquis of Lorne (later the Duke of Argyll). When he became Governor General of Canada, she lived with him there. Such was his love for her that when new provinces were planned in eighteen eighty-two, he named one for her: Alberta. Soon, there was a Province of Alberta, a beautiful Lake Louise, and a town called Caroline.

They became fitting tributes to her personality.

Thursday, June 6, 1912.

With a snorting hiss of steam, the Canadian Pacific locomotive shuddered to a standstill at the south Edmonton station. Behind it, the series of carriages clanked couplings and were finally still, after the rocking and clattering that accompanied their progress across the prairies.

Their odyssey over, scores of people descended to the station under the brilliant blue June sunshine. They were a macrocosmic study of mankind in this tiny corner of the world, this embryonic city. Most of the train's passengers were immigrants who had journeyed thousands of miles to get here, lured by freedom and cheap land. For some, this was their terminus for journeys that had begun as escapes from despotic governments, taking them by foot, horse and cart, steamship and train. They carried with them their worldly possessions, often-pitiful bundles. Small children clung to mothers' dresses. Few spoke more than a word or two of English, words that were picked up in their travels. Poles, Galician's, Ukrainians, and other nationalities stepped onto the platform: many dressed in their national peasant costumes. Babushkas, decorative cummerbunds, baggy peasant homespun pants and soft steppe boots, tcherkeskas and gaily embroidered blouses mingled with the suits, bowler hats, and Stetsons of the locals.

Some families were met by friends or relatives who preceded them to this place and sent enthusiastic word back to join them here. The warm air was filled with the babble of greetings in half a dozen tongues, as reunions took place. Others, bewildered by the unfamiliar surroundings, tried to absorb the reality that this, at last, was their new home. Their strangeness disoriented them. They took pause, not knowing quite how to get started. Several were helped by prior arrangement with agents, who had contracted to escort the immigrants out to where land was available for selection. Sharp land traders, who frequented the train arrivals and homed in on the more affluent-looking families, like sharks sensing blood, approached others. Their sales pitches, augmented by sign language, added to the general activity surrounding the train's arrival.

Nobody took any notice of a young man who was one of the last to step down from the train. With no family, he was no candidate for the hawkers. All the others were caught up in their own momentous bustle. For a moment, like the others, he paused and looked around. So this was it! This was Edmonton! It looked no different from a dozen prairie towns the train had passed through. He wondered why he had picked this one to stop at. He shouldered his seaman's bag and began to pick his way through the crowd.

He spotted the sign for a hotel nearby, and it seemed an obvious place to begin. He had made landfall in dozens of places around the world and learned the first place to stop was always a bar. A large horse-drawn wagon rattled by, as he paused across from the Strathcona Hotel. The man driving looked incuriously at the young man waiting to cross Whyte Avenue.

He was dressed in seaman's garb, a slight, middle-height young man with light brown hair and blue eyes. His nose was straight and sailed foursquare in a longish face, accented by prominent cheekbones. His mouth was generous and parenthesised by humour lines above a strong jaw. Some young women would have characterized him as somewhat handsome.

The Strathcona looked quite accommodating: a large square building with cream-coloured horizontal wood siding and maroon window and doorframes. The main entrance was right on the corner. Stepping carefully over some muddy ruts, which were drying in the hot sunshine, Tom Edmunds crossed the road. Mounting the wooden sidewalk, he entered the cool interior of the Strathcona. Several potted plants and a broadloom carpet in the lobby made pretence of elegance. He skirted these and several sofas that were occupied by patrons. A door marked "Bar" swallowed him to the right, and he found himself in a typical prairie tavern.

The wooden floor was strewn with sawdust and a scattering of tables and chairs. There were quite a few patrons, farmers in town to shop, and the ubiquitous urban tipplers and hustlers. A long bar with a polished top drew him, and he found an open spot between groups of patrons. He dropped his bag on the floor, drawing a resonant ping from a strategically placed brass spittoon. A large bartender, sporting a ferociously bushy moustache and a highly colourful vest with a gold watch-chain, enquired of his pleasure. Tom ordered a beer and received a large foamy glassful, for which he paid with a handful of change. He then savoured the cool brew. After the long dry trip on the train, it slipped down his throat like nectar.

He was not sure why he was in Edmonton. Somehow, while his ship had docked in Montreal, he felt the urge for a change in his life. A conversation with a Western Canadian in a harbour bar had stimulated him with the Horatio Alger exhortation to 'Go West, young man.'

At the age of nineteen, Tom had already seen more of the world than most young men. He ran away at age fourteen, unable to stand his home life any longer. As a child, he was of keen imagination and mental quickness. His mother expressed strong maternal pride in him, more so than the other nine children she had given birth to. But her hopes for him were thwarted by their social circumstances and the ingrained ignorance of his father.

He was born in a house on Bewicke Street, in Howdon, on the very banks of the River Tyne in northern England. The row housing had been erected during the Industrial Revolution – crude Victorian slums built to house the slave labourers of shipyards, coalmines and factories, which were 'England's Dark Satanic Mills.'

His father had been born in the house and never strayed more than five miles from home in his life. He himself had gone to work where his own father worked, and in his father's mind, his own son would follow him. This was the final straw for Tom. When the time came to leave school and start his apprenticeship, his father, despite protests from his mother and himself, dragged him off to the shipyard. He was introduced as an apprentice candidate to the foreman of the boilermakers, Mr. Dobson.

Perhaps because the human animal is not a thoughtless beast of burden, Mr. Edmunds' subconscious frustrations at life had long since found an outlet in ways typical of his kind. He was a total dictator in his household. He defended his authority with bullying and a heavy leather belt. He arose each day at five in the morning, and after his wife, Mildred, served breakfast, he departed for work. He would invariably return late at night to terrorize his family, fortified by numerous ales at the local pub.

This terror extended to his marital rights. His frequent, drunken dispensation of sperm into his fertile wife had resulted in a dozen pregnancies, some of which had not gone to term. The growth of his family, coupled with his denouncement of his wife as being at fault, only served to heap more frustration on George Edmunds. It was a vicious circle and one that a man of his environment and temperament could not cope with.

When Tom's wish for further education was vetoed without discussion, the seed was sown in his mind to leave. He was the third eldest in the family and saw what had happened to his two elder sisters, Sheila and Doreen. They were yanked out of school at the age of ten and put to work at home, helping Mildred Edmunds in coping with her growing family. They were mere girls, therefore only good for homemaking and child-bearing, so they might as well learn early about the former and make themselves useful, until such time as some young man married them and put them to the latter use. It was this attitude of being reduced to a chattel that angered young Tom.

With the same attitude directed at his life and aspirations, Tom rebelled. After six months of apprenticeship, he became heartily sick of the treatment and the conditions he suffered. One night, George Edmunds came home late, particularly drunk, and began to noisily berate his wife. Pleading with him not to wake the children, she tried to lure him to bed where she knew a quick bout of fumbling sex would soon reduce him to a heavy-snoring unconsciousness.

It didn't work on this occasion. He swore at her, accusing her of deliberately getting pregnant, then he beat her. Although he didn't usually go that far in his abuse, George Edmunds had finally gone the limit for Tom's patience. Before the father knew it, his son was on his back, pounding with his fists. The outcome was inevitable, as George was a strong, mature man. With his wife screaming, pleading, and clinging to him, he dragged them both through the kitchen, into the back yard, where he had thoroughly beaten Tom.

The next morning, after his father's departure for work, Tom told his mother he was leaving. His face was heavily bruised. His lip was split, and he ached all over. Mildred Edmunds tearfully accepted his decision and told Doreen and Sheila to pack him some food. Tom kissed everyone and left. Two days later, after signing on a ship in the Tyne as a cabin boy, he was at sea.

Lying about his age, he soon qualified himself as an able seaman and spent the next five years on ships, plying his way around the world. Soon he had visited most of the major ports of Africa, India, Europe, and Australia. Once he even got back to Howdon and visited the family. They were all glad to see this handsome, sun-tanned young man who had grown up while away. All except his father, who refused to speak to him. Undaunted, Tom returned to his ship and studied for his mate's ticket, seeking promotion.

After five years, however, the itch to return to land and do something new had presented itself. Being at sea was a little like being a gypsy. There was no permanent home or family, other than his shipmates. The conversation in the Montreal bar was a perfect catalyst to make him sign off the ship. Coming to Edmonton represented a radical change, being hundreds of miles from the ocean. He thought of becoming a farmer. That might give him the permanence he craved. There was the attraction of owning land, something denied him in England. Then there was the matter of promotion. Although he studied enough and learned almost all matters pertaining to sea faring, he knew the rigid class structure of Britain precluded his ever becoming a master of his own vessel. It was thus time to move on.

The near endless journey across Canada, especially the prairies, was rather reminiscent of being at sea. The train rocked and jerked its way across the flat lands, where the horizon was far off and winds blew the grasses in wavelike motions. Finding himself in Edmonton was a little like Dick Whittington seeking London's streets of gold. Unlike Dick, he was not penniless. He did have some savings. This thought prompted him to think of accommodation, and he caught the bartender's attention for another beer.

"Where is a good place to stay in town?"

"Here is as good as any. Good, clean rooms. Reasonable rates. You alone?"

Tom nodded. "Well, if you don't mind sharing, you can get a really low rate on that."

Thus it was that Tom made his first friend in Edmonton, Mr. Timothy O'Hanlon. O'Hanlon was his roommate for three months in that year of nineteen twelve. Gifted with a great capacity for blarney and alcohol, Tim O'Hanlon was a panhandler, a confidence man, and a natural salesman.

"My family came to North America during the great Irish potato famine," he would claim in a broad Irish accent, "while I was just a little shaver."

Keen students of history realized Tim must have had a remarkably long childhood, since the famine was sixty years prior. But tall stories abounded in the West. It was discourteous to contradict a man's personal legend. It might also provide for fisticuffs. Anyway, through a series of adventures, O'Hanlon had come to bless the Edmonton scene. He was a swaggering braggart, a free-liver who secretly confessed to Tom he was much richer than he ever allowed in public.

"Get into land, boy-o. That's where the money is!" O'Hanlon was a short man with a circular, pixie-like face. His cheeks were round, ruddy apples. His nose was turned up and flanked by two sparkling, enthusiastic blue eyes. Dressed in a green suit, buckled shoes, and a top hat, he would have fulfilled everyone's idea of how a leprechaun should look. The Irish brogue was cultivated and a part of his act. In private, his speech regressed to his Ontario roots. "I need a likely lad to work with me. Would ye be interested now?"

Tom had to smile. He had been hustled by the best in ports around the world. O'Hanlon gave himself away every time he opened his mouth. When the sales pitch went in, the blarney came out. For the rest of the time, he came to learn, Tim was a shrewd, direct, and persuasive person.

"This town, Tom, is filled with real estate offices. It's the biggest game in town. There are more than thirty brokers in this city, over a hundred money-lending organizations, and three hundred agents. They try to say they're legitimate. That just means they have big overheads and make small dollars. Me, I am my own salesman, runner, and financial councillor. I buy my own lots, sell them at a good profit, and make them weep. See, I buy a lot for a dollar down from the city. Then I go down to the station and meet the new people and sell them the lot for a hundred or whatever they are willing to pay. Then I roll the money over into new purchases and sell them too."

"And this is legal?"

O'Hanlon's face crumpled at the implied accusation. "Of course it's legal. I operate in the open. Surely, would I not be in jail now if I was crooked?"

"What do you need me for?"

"I need someone to act as a runner. That's the man who takes the prospective client to the lots for sale and shows them off. You have to be able to read your way around the survey maps and be quick on your feet to close the sale. I waste too much of my time doing this when my real talent is in promoting. You seem like a bright young man who can project an honest image to people. With me selling and you running, we can more than double my present turnover. But it's the closing that's the secret, my boy. If you can close the sale, you've got it made!"

If nothing else, Tom had to admit O'Hanlon was persuasive. Over the next few days, the Irishman showed him around town, teaching him all he knew about real estate. He let Tom observe his technique of approaching prospective buyers, turning the conversation to property, and then closing a sale.

He was the consummate salesman. He knew when to speak and when to shut up. He hooked clients like an expert trout fly-fisherman. He was aggressive, wheedling, and flashy, inspiring confidence when needed. His instinct for a prospect's weakness, his greed, was unerring. From Tim, Tom learned all the great sales techniques, which would later stand him in good stead. After three days with the man, he himself was hooked. In that time, he watched Tim make three hundred dollars without any legal repercussions. Fulfilling the faith O'Hanlon had shown in him, Tom began to ply skills he hadn't recognized in himself. They became a formidable team in the three months following.

Two major symbols of Edmonton's growth and prosperity were nearing completion at this time. The High Level Bridge, over the North Saskatchewan River, a two-tier decked structure running almost half a mile from bank to bank, was almost finished and would carry the Canadian

Pacific Railway to the heart of the city. Hardly more than a stone's throw away, dominating all around it, the newly erected Legislature Building was having its dome topped. Tom, to Tim's applause, shrewdly routed prospective newcomers past these structures. These symbols of power and prosperity, coupled with the armies of carpenters erecting new properties, instilled confidence and positive vibrations in the hearts of buyers. Edmonton was vibrant with activity. It was a prime place for people eager to make it in life by dint of their own efforts. It was true pioneering.

Tom loved the buildings. Contrary to the brick and stone edifices of England, they were hastily erected from wood. Skilled carpenters built a framework up and boarded-in in rapid fashion. Often, a walk around its sides and rear to discover a dingy view could compromise the elaborate frontage of a building, but nobody cared. The city itself was a mélange of buildings and open spaces. Valued, corner-lot buildings would mark street intersections, while the adjacent lots on the block would be empty. Clumps of undisturbed brush marked lots that one day would be filled when the right buyer came along.

Some districts of the city were widely separated from each other: Calder, Groat Estates, Northcote, Eastland, Wellington, Kensington, and Rosslyn, for instance. A journey to these places from downtown was almost like an adventure. One could take a streetcar. The transition to large, downtown buildings, built close together and towering more than five stories, in some cases, was rapid and full of impact. The streetcar would quickly leave the paved streets and plunge onto barely graded dirt streets that were sparsely lined with buildings. At times, rocking and swaying along its tracks, the vehicle appeared lost in the great boreal forest. Its route closely resembled a narrow woodland trail.

Tom rapidly learned that Edmonton owed its expansion mainly to its choice as the provincial capital over its southern rival, Calgary, in nineteen hundred and five. Alberta had become a province that first of September day, named after Queen Victoria's daughter, Princess Louise Caroline Alberta. Its history, however, went back over a hundred years to the fur traders, who had penetrated this vastness of land via the North Saskatchewan River, seeking beaver pelts for the Hudson's Bay Company and the North West Company.

Tom found the river valley particularly beautiful. It was littered with the progress of civilization. Ruins of the old Fort Edmonton mingled with brickyards, sawmills, and coalmines, especially around the area of Ross

Flats. Away from there, the yellow-brown slopes of earth subsidence punctuated the heavily treed appearance of the valley. Dark stands of spruce interspersed by the ubiquitous poplar clothed the riverbanks. Bright strands of white marked the presence of birch trunks along tributary stream valleys. Perhaps the river's biggest attraction was the deep slash it had cut into the prairie. It offered a break in the monotonous flatness of the land, a contrast of eye-pleasing depth, a rare relief, both topographically and mentally.

Tim had an arrangement with Glidden's stables for a horse and gig to be at his constant disposal. They used this to convey their prospective clients. It was fine in dry weather, but a trip along rain-sodden "roads" was a muddy experience, which lent little to enhance any sale. Rainy days were thus usually "planning" days, spent in the bar. And so, Tom fell into the real estate business. Both he and Tim worked themselves hard. Every train was met, every lead followed up. They often did not finish up until the late evening. After dinner in the Strathcona's dining room, they went to the bar and drank, plotting strategy until the late hours.

This was when Tom learned most of the foibles of the buying public. The amazing O'Hanlon had tales to tell and ambitions to relate which were eye opening in their boldness and scandalous in their methods. Yet, Tim had a basic flaw. He was like a moth attracted to the flame of easy money. He epitomized the term "easy come, easy go," for he was a gambler. He would sometimes disappear for two days into high-rolling poker games, which he occasionally won but often lost heavily. He would cheerfully lose a hundred dollars on the flip of a coin and couldn't understand why Tom was loath to follow his example.

Tom came here to do well for himself. In light of the hard work they put in, he simply could not justify frittering it away. He arrived in Edmonton with a little over a hundred dollars after being paid off his ship. One of his first acts was to open a bank account. It was during this time that he had an unfortunate experience with a surly clerk at one bank, so he transferred his funds to the Imperial Bank's imposing brownstone structure on Whyte Avenue. Had the directors of the bank, from which he withdrew his funds, been given a glimpse of the future, they would have immediately entrained westward to Edmonton to personally horsewhip the clerk.

By August, Tom had almost a thousand dollars on deposit and was looking for an investment vehicle. Tim had all kinds of ideas for Tom's money, but since they mostly seemed to accrue to his own benefit, Tom listened but was reticent to act on any advice from that source. In September, he decided to find a place of his own. The high life at the Strathcona was wearing a little thin. Tim had an on-again, off-again arrangement with a lady named Alice McGee, who frequently showed up in his bed. After a suitable number of drinks, any current friction between them was resolved upstairs, noisily and without any regard for Tom's presence in the room.

When Alice began to give him the glad eye, Tom knew it was time to leave. He found a widowed lady, a Mrs. Adams, who ran a boarding house just north of Whyte. It was a better arrangement than at the Strathcona. He moved into a pleasant upstairs room that was accessible via an outside stairway from the ground. Room and board was five dollars a week.

Entertainment, thus far, was centred on their real estate activities with the late night drinking sessions. Now, Tom was freer to do what he wanted, once the last client of the day had been dealt with. In Tim's company, he made the acquaintance of several 'professional' ladies who served his needs. However, he was a young man and anxious to court a young lady in a more traditional manner.

There were clubs and associations that held dances, but these were closely chaperoned. Church suppers and picnics were ideal places to meet young ladies where the supposed umbrella of church respectability weakened the vigilance of some parents. They were thus prime hunting grounds for the young blades about town. Tom made some friends, both male and female, and enjoyed some good times. He liked to go to the Strathcona Opera House and particularly enjoyed the Pantages Vaudeville Theatre at One Hundred and Second Street, just on the corner with Jasper Avenue on the other side of the river. If he had a date, he would treat her afterwards in the American Dairy Bar, a favourite snack place in the same building.

The year nineteen twelve was a banner year for the new city of Edmonton. A record number of arrivals boosted its population to over fifty thousand, although a slight over-enthusiasm in the enumeration was discovered afterwards. Seemingly, hotel registers were copied and the guest names filed as tax-paying citizens.

Miles of lands were annexed to the city. The paved roads multiplied from five to thirty five miles. Graded roads escalated to one hundred and eighteen. The province had enjoyed natural gas heating for over twenty years. Numerous plans were afoot to bring the same to Edmonton from nearby explorations. University buildings were erected. Downtown Jasper

Avenue, a broad thoroughfare with dual tramlines down the centre, was built up with multi-storey masonry buildings. Some, like the Tegler and McLeod buildings, towered nine stories high.

Still, there were faint indications that all was not well. Rapid growth, the enormous expenditure of urban development, and the building of the railroads depleted much of the city's funds to keep up with the growth. O'Hanlon recognized there were a growing number of unemployed men coming into town, especially from the railroad construction crews.

"MacKenzie and Mann's Northern is in imminent danger of collapse. Ye must always remember, Tom, when prices and bank interest rates rise to a certain point, disaster is just around the corner. Money gets stretched thin and someone, somewhere, demands payment and upsets the applecart. Then, it is like a bunch of dominoes. Ye must watch and be prepared for it. The investment in the West has been oversubscribed for what is coming back out. It's a smart man who sells off the short-term chattels to the fools scrambling to get them. They become the victims, because with cash in hand, you can buy back later from a buyer that which you sold him in the first place, for a fraction of the cost."

Obtaining a modest loan from the Imperial Commerce Bank, Tom bought a three storey building on Whyte Avenue. A store took up the ground floor, a lawyer had offices on the second floor, and above that were two small apartments. The combined rent from these tenants fell just short of Tom's monthly loan payments, so he had to sink some of his earnings into the venture to keep up with them. Tim approved, since the businesses were secure, and the income was assured.

The following year brought a decline in everything. The real estate market began to tighten up. They had to work harder to make sales for a smaller profit margin. Tom also bought a share in one of the many coalmines, which were tunnelling galleries under the north bank of the river. With a minimum capital investment came an agreement, in which he would put in twenty hours per week hauling coal up Grierson Hill with a huge cart drawn by four Shire horses. So now, he became a teamster in his evenings.

The majority shareholder was Harry McInnes, a huge slab of Scotsman with long red hair and bushy whiskers, invariably powdered black with coal dust. All the partners were reliable and hard working. It was just as well since it was backbreaking work loading and off-loading bags of coal from the cart. Getting up Grierson on a wet day was almost impossible in the mud. Tom's pay was thirty cents per hour, only a general labourer's rate, and money he never saw. It was taken in balance payment on his share. Still, his equity increased, and since it was a good, solid business, he was determined not to relinquish it, no matter what.

It was after one such hard day in October that he returned to Mrs. Adams' place, dirty, tired, and ready for bed. He forgot he'd promised some friends he would go to a Thanksgiving dance, organized by one of the local churches. Somehow, when his friends arrived, he summonsed the will to clean up and go. It was a night he would forever remember.

The dance at the Orangeman Hall on Fraser Avenue was typical of the times. A trio comprising drums, piano, and fiddle punched out a round variety of waltz, quickstep, and polka, popularised by Edmonton's Ukrainian element. Every once in a while, groups of men left to gather behind the hall for surreptitious quaffs at various bottles brought along. This provided a certain fortification to approach the demure young ladies who lined one side of the dance floor. In the early evening, quaffing took precedence over invitations to dance. After a while, the number of trips outside proportionately numbed the spectre of failure: being refused a dance. The dance hall became a little livelier as a result. The band was attuned to such procedures and threw in some faster polkas and the odd Gay Gordons.

By nine, the small hall was bouncing. Fifty couples bobbed around the floor to a lively polka. Tom danced a couple of times with different young ladies and was getting pleasantly sleepy after his long hard day. He was talking to one of his friends, Ed Slater, when a movement through the crowd caught his eye.

A young woman with dark blonde hair walked to her seat. She had a coltish gait as she moved. This caught his attention. She sat down with a visible bounce and turned, laughing to her neighbour. Her face was animated and vibrant, heart-shaped, yet with a firm chin and broad forehead. Beneath the mane of straight blonde hair, her clear eyes were light brown and elongated above high, striking cheekbones. Her mouth was as straight as her hair and too big for her face. She wore a pale blue dress that looked to be of good quality. As Tom watched, fascinated, the girl said something out of the side of her mouth that sent her friend into gales of laughter. Even across the floor, Tom felt he shared the joke.

He could not take his eyes off her. It was some time before he plucked up the courage to ask her for a dance. She seemed friendly, yet a refusal would have seemed to him, right now, a vast defeat. Perhaps it was better to worship her from afar and never know her than to suffer rejection! He waited. Tantalizing glimpses of her appeared between passing dancers like the jerky animation caused by the uneven process of frames on one of the early movies. Here, her head was thrown back, laughing; there, she was sombre, staring at the floor. In a matter of minutes, Tom's casual sighting of her had become an obsession to know her. He slipped outside and took his turn at a fiery bottle of rum before resuming his seat. Resolved now, he prayed for a waltz. The band obliged right on schedule.

He was on his feet in a flash, hurrying to get there before some other man beat him to her. Sensing someone rushing to his right, he accelerated and embarrassed himself by his precipitous arrival in front of her. She looked up, startled and amused at his sudden appearance. Her eyes and the corners of her mouth expressed her amusement. Slightly off-balance, Tom thought he was going to fall right on top of her. Somehow, there were no words. They merely stared at each other. A friend tittered at his clumsiness, but the girl continued her amused, cool appraisal of him.

"A dance...would you care to dance?"

Her smile became a little brighter before she rose in acceptance. Tom followed her on to the floor, realizing she came up to his nose in height. The blond hair filling his gaze became a face. She'd suddenly stopped and turned. Clumsily, feeling ridiculous, Tom bumped into her. Her mouth tightened into a straight line, but the laughter in her eyes spread, and the lips parted again, further confusing him. Even though she was staring at him directly, Tom was now confused as to the colour of her eyes. They seemed to be light brown but appeared to change with her mood. They were indeed almost almond shaped, the upper outer edges turned down in a hint of permanent amusement. At close range, her nose had a slight bump in the middle of the bridge, as if it had been broken at some time.

He took her hand, feeling the warm dryness of long, slender fingers, while his right hand slid to the narrowness of her waist. The bottom of his wrist brushed against the swell of her hip. He felt a surge of belonging run through him. Touching her was a new feeling, yet seemed as familiar to him as his own face. They ploughed off around the floor, endeavouring to accommodate each other's style. The silence grew long. Tom was grateful when she spoke first.

"It took you a little while to ask me!"

"How? How did you…?" Tom stuttered.

"I knew you would dance with me when I saw you at the beginning," she said. Such directness was unfamiliar to Tom. He retreated into a further bout of tongue-tied contemplation. This girl was totally absorbing! He already felt that he had known her for years, and he didn't even know her.

"My name is Jeanne."

"Jan?"

"No, silly, Jeanne. J-e-a-n-n-e! C'est Francais, Monsieur."

"Ah...you are French?"

"No, only half. Mon Grand-père, il etait un voyageur."

"If that was a proposal, the answer is 'yes'."

"No. You really are silly. I was telling you about my grandfather."

"Oh! Anyway, I'm Tom." He smiled the warmth of a person who had just revealed a close personal secret and then promptly felt foolish at his silliness. Close up, her face had a freshness to it which complimented the slightly blemished sum of its parts. Perhaps it was the beauty of her soul that shone through, he thought. It must escape like starlight through that sprinkle of freckles across her nose and inner cheeks. At all events, she was jolly nice looking.

"Penny for them!"

Ah, so she wasn't a mind reader after all. "I was just thinking what a good dancer you are," said Tom.

"No you were not!" She smiled a frank, open smile, not at all like the demure coyness of her contemporaries.

"I will answer it: 'I am too bold; 'tis not to me she speaks. Two of the fairest stars in all the heaven, having some business do entreat her eyes.'"

Jeanne stopped dancing and was holding him at arm's length, gazing up at him quizzically. "Methinks, sirrah, thou hast quaffed too long behind the hall!" She gave a curious breathy chuckle that charmed him immeasurably. They both broke out laughing. With the ice now well and truly broken, they continued around the floor, oblivious to the other dancers.

"Nice young ladies do not discuss such things," said Tom.

"Huh! What makes you think we girls only go and powder our noses?"

"Let me smell your breath!" asked Tom. She leaned closer and exhaled. Her breath was warm and sweet.

"Ah-ha! You had coffee last Tuesday, laced with cream and sugar."

Jeanne fluttered her eyelashes and tilting her head back, gave him a wilting stare. "Nevah, nevah coffee on a Tuesday, Lord Thomas!"

"Well, how about some fruit punch right now, since the dance is over and we're the only couple on the floor?" laughed Tom. With an embarrassed gasp, Jeanne turned and headed for the table in front of the band, where an elderly lady from the church committee was dispensing punch and goodwill smiles with equal fervour.

"Mmm, pretty good."

"But a little thin, right?"

"Well, a little whisky is nice," said Tom. They found seats in the corner, a mutual retreat in which to get to know each other. "So you are a Shakespeare enthusiast?" he asked.

"Is that what it was? No, I am more into romantic novels, especially those of the days of chivalry: King Arthur and the Knights of the Round Table, that kind of thing."

"Have you lived in Edmonton long?"

Jeanne told him, "All my life. On my mother's side, the family has been here for years and years. My grandfather was a French voyageur until he settled down to farm about thirty years ago. My father was Scots, so I am quite a mixture."

"Was?" Tom wondered.

"Yes, he was returning to the farm about ten years ago, and something went wrong with the wagon. While he was trying to fix it, it slipped. He was pinned under it and froze to death," said Jeanne sadly.

"I'm sorry."

"Yes, well, I was old enough to love him dearly and have missed him ever since. Mom moved into town with me soon after selling the farm. Ever since then, we have lived a few blocks from here. It's not much, but it is home. Mom is a seamstress and manages to keep us together on what she makes."

Tom asked, "Do you work?"

"Yes, I work at McAllister's millinery store over on Whyte. What do you do?" Jeanne replied.

Tom gave Jeanne a quick idea of what he had been doing. She was impressed with what he had accomplished. Her enthusiasm for his ambitions endeared her to him even more. They talked on, dancing occasionally but feeling a growing closeness. Tom thought she was the easiest girl he'd ever gotten to know. She seemed to have an empathy, which warmed him, and an energetic interest in all around her.

While it would have been considered forward to escort her home alone from a church dance, they managed the same by mingling with the crowd that walked down towards Jasper Avenue to catch tramcars home. Carrying her promise to see him again, Tom rode home to Mrs. Adams' in a rare euphoria.

****

Late June, 1914.

Just after noon on a warm June Sunday, Tom walked into Mrs. MacDonald's house. It was a ramshackle cube situated on a lot on Athabasca Avenue, just north of Fraser. It had once been whitewashed, but the boards were long since exposed and weathered dark grey by the Alberta climate. Canted and rolling like a long ocean wave, a stretch of wooden sidewalk boards led past the weeds and assorted trash that blew in amongst them up to the front door.

The theme was preserved on the inside, for long use and little care had brought the little place into disrepair. It was basically a three-room dwelling. The main workroom, with a bed in one corner, was screened off by a length of drapery supported by a rope. Four feet by four feet, a tiny kitchen that was also the bathroom, hovered inside the back door. Jeanne occupied the other tiny corner room, the original bedroom. Inside the main room, one wall was covered with sagging shelves that conformed to the warped nature of the building and made precarious the heaps of patterns, material, and boxes poised on them. The effect was of a cascade of items, frozen by some magical means. Across another wall, three long ropes supported completed, and semi-completed garments. A large pot-bellied stove sat on a concrete pad, but an enormous table swamped in dressmaking material and equipment dominated the room. At one end, a treadle-operated sewing machine squatted like some greedy monster waiting to gorge itself on the contents of the table. Behind this, Tom knew, Lillette MacDonald spent long hours, squinting with the aid of what natural or weak electric light she could obtain.

She glanced up, seeking to identify the visitor who entered. "Hello, Tom. How are you today?" Lillette MacDonald was a tiny woman with fine, sharp features and dark brown eyes like pools. Her face was a fine pattern of lines, etched by a hard life. Her light brown hair was fluffy and medium length. It always looked freshly washed and combed. Her accent had a decidedly French flavour, inherited from her mother.

"Fine, thank you, Mrs. MacDonald. I see you are very busy." Tom replied.

"Yes, there is so little money to be made at this that I sometimes believe if I stop for a minute, we shall starve."

For a moment, Tom caught a flash of what this woman must do to support herself and Jeanne. It was a grinding existence, trying to cope with the repairs and finicky requirements of women too rich and disdainful to be bothered with the trivialities of caring for their own wardrobe. He was sure Lillette must work with gloved hands in the winter. The place was so run down, it probably leaked cold air like a colander.

"Where are you off to today?" asked Lillette.

"Oh, off along one of our favourite walks, over by Mill Creek, I expect. It's such a beautiful day," Tom said, happily.

"You will be careful with my little girl, won't you, Tom? She is all I have." Lillette stared directly at the young man before her. Tom shifted uncomfortably and flushed. The little woman had made it quite clear she knew he and Jeanne were lovers. It was a very direct conversation for the times, where sex was never even hinted at by ladies.

"You know I care about Jeanne very much, Mrs. MacDonald."

"I know that, Tom," she smiled. "However, there are certain circumstances that can occur in a young girl's life, which society pretends not to understand or condone. A young man can be easily swayed by them and evade his responsibilities."

To Tom, this turn of the conversation was even more disturbing than before. He stared back at this serious woman who was looking him right in the eyes. He heard tales about Lillette around town. Her name was linked with many men, although none had become a husband to her. It might be said that Lillette enjoyed a bit of a reputation, yet there was no substantiating evidence. Her remarks to him were made without any rancour she might have felt for her own experiences. She was obviously on the watch for Jeanne. She, herself, was under pressure to keep a good reputation. Many of her customers were denizens of Edmonton's social morality and could put her out of business in no time should they boycott her.

She smiled again after a short silence between them. "It's all right Tom. I believe you are a strong and loyal person. Just remember what I said."

Tom was saved further embarrassment by the entry of Jeanne from her room. She had prepared some bologna sandwiches for a picnic and was anxious to be off. They both felt slightly guilty leaving Lillette to work while they went out, but this was rapidly replaced by selfish and youthful enthusiasm for their afternoon.

They walked down to Jasper and took a streetcar west. Crossing the High Level Bridge, they boarded a Kernan Lake streetcar and got off at the east end of Strathcona. From there, it was about a mile to the secluded part of Mill Creek, a place they had come to think of as their own. They walked to the top of the stream that was fed by a slough and made a circle around the water, coming back down on the other side. It was a walk they enjoyed, and it had become a habit. The creek dropped quickly into a ravine. It was fed by several minor streams and surrounded by stands of spruce, birch, and poplar. In late June, it was a bright, green idyll, effectively removed from the city.

They lay down in the warm grass and tried to ignore the few mosquitoes that were around. The sandwiches were good, washed down by sodas Tom had brought along. After that, they turned to each other, kissed, and cuddled. This shortly led to other activities. Tom had just exposed a pink-nippled breast, when Jeanne squirmed away from him, and much to his annoyance, covered herself again.

"I have to go to the ladies' room," she said.

Disgruntled at this interruption of his rising passion, Tom rolled away with a snort. Jeanne grinned at his annoyance and deliberately brushed against his hardening groin as she rose. They were screened from the faint path, which followed the creek by some willows and buffalo berries. Jeanne disappeared through a gap in these to tend to her needs. Left to himself, Tom slapped at a persistent mosquito and lay back to gaze at the sky. His stomach growled briefly at the spicy bologna he had eaten.

"Tom! Come and see!" Jeanne called.

"I already have! But I'll look again!"

"Not *that* silly." Jeanne said, huffily.

"What do you want then," Tom called back.

"Come and see, I have something to show you!"

Rounding the willows, Tom found Jeanne crouched down behind a thick-trunked poplar, studying something on the ground. Looking over her shoulder, he saw, nestling in the grass, a tiny spruce tree only two or three inches high. "A tree." Tom's disappointment was evident.

"Not *a* tree! *Our* tree!" Jeanne was excited.

"Ah!" said Tom without enthusiasm.

"We must move it," said Jeanne.

"What for?"

"Because these young thistles will outgrow it and choke it," replied Jeanne.

Irritated by this continued interruption to his needs, Tom was negative. "Spruce trees have been growing up between weeds for millions of years. If you move it now, chances are you will kill it!"

Jeanne was adamant. "No, we must transplant it in our special place. It will be our special tree, and we can watch it grow though the years." The promise inherent in that statement broke down Tom's resistance. Besides, Jeanne would not consider doing anything else until this matter was out of the way.

A pause. "You didn't go potty on it did you?"

"Almost," Jeanne giggled. "That's how I came to find it!"

With a couple of sticks and at the cost of a broken fingernail, they raised the spruce seedling with a suitable ball of earth around the roots. It was borne with due ceremony to their little trysting place. Like a mother hen, Jeanne fussed over its proposed planting site. Properly coached, Tom made a small excavation. They firmed the tree in its new home. Rushing back and forth to the creek, Jeanne cupped water in her hands to moisten the roots until she was satisfied it would survive.

Finally satisfied, she rocked back on her heels, squatting with pride beside her project. "One day we can come back here and it will be huge. *Enormous*! It will always be ours."

Jeanne's maternal gestures reawakened both their desires. They made love, leaving on most of their clothes in deference to the mosquitoes. The mosquitoes were forgotten after a short while. Later, Jeanne rolled over and looked at the tree. She reached between her thighs, fumbled a moment, and then extracted her fingers – slick and slimy with their collective love juices. Carefully with concentration, she wiped her fingers on the mossy top of the spruce's root-ball and repeated the process all around the tiny trunk. Still engrossed, she plucked out several offending blades of grass. "Now, it is truly ours. It will be nurtured, fertilized by us in the act of creation."

Such was Jeanne's seriousness that Tom did not find it ridiculous in any way. Their consummate lovemaking was like a pagan dedication to some woodland spirit, lending solemnity to the occasion. It was only right that the fruits of their obeisance be offered up.

" 'I think that I shall never see, a poem as lovely as a tree'."

"Who said that?"

"Kilmer. It is a new poem, just out this year."

"How appropriate and timely."

They left not long after, walking down the creek to the Saskatchewan and then along its shore to the Low Level Bridge. They were warmly and vitally alive – in love with the whole summer before them. They could not know that on the previous day, an event happened far away that would change their lives.

Returning home the following evening from work, Tom's attention to the Edmonton Journal was taken mostly with the acrimonious city council proceedings concerning police corruption. On the front page, beneath a cartoon on the subject, a story header on international news had little impact on him: 'Martial Law Proclaimed as Result of Shooting of Archduke Franz Ferdinand.'

****

Early in nineteen fifteen, events in Europe were still too remote for Edmontonians to realize the world was slipping into war; after all, they had more immediate concerns of their own. The city had over-expanded in the boom years of nineteen twelve and nineteen thirteen. Over-speculation, aided by the efforts of promoters, such as Tim O'Hanlon, began to reap its inevitable recession in accordance with the immutable laws of financing. Tom carefully noted things went almost exactly as Tim had predicted. There was creeping unemployment, and the swelling rank of men roaming the streets was fertile ground for the militant labour organizers.

As a result of this, Tom and Jeanne witnessed an IWW parade in January nineteen fourteen. The IWW was an organization born outside Canada, the 'International Workers of the World.' This had rapidly been dubbed the 'I Won't Work' or 'Wobblies' organization. It was a social unrest era that would later be characterized by cloaked anarchists creeping around, cradling round black bombs with hissing fuses.

The well-attended parade by the IWW marched through the Edmonton streets. Numerous bystanders jeered at the marchers, who comprised mainly Anglo-Saxons and Irishmen, supported by many non-English speaking minorities. These people particularly, treated with considerable discrimination and contempt, had their militancy fuelled by open suggestions that unemployed aliens should be sent back where they came from. Since to many, this meant a return to despotic governments that would surely persecute them, their choice of sides was evident. The lines of eventual confrontation were irrevocably being drawn.

Most of the people involved saw only an idealistic solution to an eternal human problem. They were unaware that the IWW was founded on the Marxist platform, namely: *The working class and the employing class have nothing in common. There can be no peace, so long as hunger and want are found among millions of working people, and the few, who make up the employing class, have all the good things of life. It is the historic mission of the working class to do away with capitalism.*

The last sentence, of course, was an open inducement to revolt. Thus, the reactionary theories of a European socialist, born of the evolution of modern feudalism, were being foisted on the whole world. By Sunday, February first, the IWW militancy escalated to bloodshed in the United States. An Edmonton parade invaded McDougall church in downtown Edmonton, demanding the right to speak from the pulpit. Amongst resistance to this, several participants refused an offer of employment for thirty dollars per month with room and board, reinforcing the 'I Won't Work' image. A police scandal was filling the newspapers at that time, weakening the force, and making the situation more serious. Now, a year later, the IWW was still a large element of social unrest and concern.

Tax revenue was falling around Edmonton. People decided to renege on paying them, abandoning ownership of lots that were no longer re-saleable. In May of nineteen fourteen, Calgary discovered oil at Turner Valley. In Edmonton, a stock-buying frenzy had erupted. Some of the stocks went from twelve to two hundred dollars, and in the usual process of kerb-side trading, the presence of crooked dealers robbed many people by trading worthless paper.

Finding better prospects in oil stocks, entrepreneurs such as the real estate dealers, had long gone south, Tim O'Hanlon amongst them. Numerous other events piled up, deflecting the population's attention from a conflict so far away. Besides, European turmoil was not their concern. Yet, it was, as the headlines in the Edmonton Journal began to tell them. A complex arrangement of treaties and alliances forged by European history had determined that any conflict would automatically align certain nations while dragging others in.

The bellicose Kaiser Wilhelm II and his Prussian generals were spoiling for mischief. The next step was proclaimed on July twenty-eighth. Princess Patricia, who was shortly to be married, visited Edmonton with the Duke and Duchess of Connaught. The reporting of their enthusiastic welcome had to share front-page honours with a declaration of war by the Austro-Hungarian Empire on the Royal State of Serbia.

Two days later, huge headlines declared: 'Slightest False Move Will Set Millions of Soldiers in Action.'

Germany arrogantly gave Russia twenty-four hours to declare her intentions. Serbia was already being invaded. The 'Triple Entente,' comprising Britain, France, and Russia swore to 'stand by their friends.' In response to this, on the evening of August fourth, wild scenes in Edmonton resulted. Crowds of Russians, Frenchmen, and Britons marched arm in arm through the city, singing all three of the national anthems. A Scottish pipe band led a thousand volunteers and reservists in a patriotic demonstration of solidarity. The sabres were being rattled. The grim reality of the sabre's obsolescence was still mercifully unknown.

Within days, Colonel Jamieson and Major Griesbach mobilized the Nineteenth Alberta Dragoons, most of them South African Boer War veterans. They and their comrades in the Hundred and First Fusiliers were already inspired to loudly perform patriotic songs at their weekly luncheon at the Gregory Café. Their departure was no surprise.

Meanwhile, the odious, ominous news mounted. Naval forces sailed. Blockades were imposed, and armies marched in an irretrievable slide towards war. The Germans invaded Belgium, sharing local headlines with the momentous news of the opening of the Edmonton Exhibition. The newspaper expressed its sentiments by publishing a large cartoon on the front page, showing participants in the 'Ex' trying to push a soldier-figure labelled 'War' off the front page.

It was to no avail. On August thirteenth, 'Citizens Day' during the Exhibition, the predominant headline declared, 'Most Fearful Clash in History of Humans Will Start Any Hour.' Three hundred men of the Princess Patricia Canadian Light Infantry left the same day. By the next day, the first casualty was reported when one of their number died on the train, less than a hundred miles away.

The focus was on Brussels. An enormous German Army threatened it. After twelve days silence on the matter, the British government admitted its Expeditionary Force had indeed landed in France. Inside the paper, a Rand McNally advertisement exhorted readers to purchase their twenty-five cent 'European War Map' as 'European war news cannot be read understandingly without a good reference map.'

The Germans were denigrated as barbaric. A special correspondent to the London Daily Telegraph, Dr. E. J. Dillon, wrote from Belgium: 'One could see masses of soldiers - a vision of hell, which only Dante could describe.' Dillon was already into superlatives; what was to come would defy even Dante's efforts.

Even while the Belgians, French, and British were dying in the thousands, arresting the German advance at the Battle of the Marne, men volunteered in droves. Some walked great distances to enlist, lining up outside recruiting offices in the early hours of the morning, anxious not to be excluded. Patriotic fervour was lit overnight and Albertans swarmed to the colours. As in all wars, the reaction of the womenfolk was mixed. Many pragmatic ladies were willing to ignore the war and keep their men folk at home. Others, stirred by the glamour of uniformed marching men and the glorification of combat, were driven to sending white feathers to beaus who were reluctant to risk their lives in a foreign conflict.

Jeanne belonged to the former group and made her feelings clear to Tom right from the start. It was easy at first to agree. Tom's business required his daily attention. However, the reduction of the male population made able-bodied men a little more conspicuous on the streets, and the odd look from passers by made Tom very self-conscious. Major Griesbach, promoted to lieutenant colonel, returned from England to raise the Forty-ninth Infantry Battalion. Recruiting commenced on January fourth, and Tom went down the next day to enlist.

"I'm going. I don't think I have any choice." They were sitting over a soda at the Owl Drugstore. He had just broken the news to Jeanne.

"But why?" She was shocked and angry. "If they want to fight over there, what the hell has it got to do with us?"

"Everything. I got a letter yesterday. My brother is already in France. Boyhood friends and relatives are going. If the Germans conquer Europe, our lives here will be irretrievably affected. If the British are prepared to stand up to this bullying and keep the Empire free, why not me?"

Jeanne's face took on the stubborn, no-retreat expression he knew as trouble. Her eyes narrowed, and her lips were pursed. "You're a fool, Tom Edmunds!" She glared at him, furious in her resolve. "You'll only succeed in getting yourself killed, and I...I'll..." Her voice trailed off. A tear trickled down her cheek.

Tom knew, in that moment, this might be the closest he would ever come to receiving a deep declaration of love from this mercurial girl. Hopelessly smitten by her, his heart soared absurdly with the endless futility of understanding her. He knew that despite their physical attentions to each other, the real allure was the continual mental fencing, her ability to elude his understanding.

Their minds were like two mutual-polarity magnets, cast on a collision course by the power of love, yet the closer they got, the stronger the force of repulsion. The tangled force lines between them were the sweetness, the fruit of the relationship.

"I'm going." He said it softly, firmly, and took her hand. She tried to remove it, but finally left it as more tears welled. Tom knew it was not the end of the matter.

TWO

MADAMOISELLE FROM ARMENTIÈRES

4:30 a.m., June 23, 1916.

God! How I hate these night sentry duties! The thought echoed in his head, by now, an old, familiar theme. He was twenty yards out from the front trench, crouched in a fortified shell-hole known as a 'sap.' All night long, he had lain up to his waist in slimy mud, taking turns with another man – an advance warning post against a surprise night attack. In the event of such an attack, they were supposed to use their field telephone to advise the company command post. In reality, the Germans would likely crawl to the lip of the hole before they knew a damned thing, so their real purpose here was to die as noisily as possible.

The sun was coming up, a red, yet indistinct smudge through the ground mist that hovered above the surface, making visibility quite poor. In a few minutes, there would be enough light to pick out the individual landmarks. If the 'Alleyman' came today, it would happen any minute now. One of the soldiers' nicknames for the Germans was the 'Alleyman,' derived from the French 'Allemagne.' Reaching out with a booted toe, Tom wriggled it in the ribs of his companion. He awoke with a start. He was reassured to note that Nobby Clarke's first instinct was to seize his rifle.

Silently, Tom gestured at the sky and looked knowingly at the telephone. Nodding, Nobby reached over and cranked the handle to raise the Command Post. It was their duty to phone at this time and report their readiness to warn of any German movements that may tell of an impending dawn assault. Not only did this call reassure their superiors in their turn, but also the need to make the call ensured wakefulness on the part of the lookouts. The penalty for sleeping on sentry duty was court-martial and death. Sometimes, the Germans saved the need for the court-martial.

Command would not call them for this reason, since the ringing of the field telephone would give away their position to the enemy. This particular post had been heavily mortared just two days prior, but this did not deter the senior officers from maintaining the facade that it was still secret from the Germans. "Dumb sods!" Tom turned away and resumed his careful left to right search of his front. He was always very careful and attentive on these duties. They were eerie and scary. He already had seen too many dead men who paid the price for a moment's inattentiveness.

In a way, he dreaded more light from the sun. True, it meant relief from the night and danger, but there was a negative factor. Twelve yards to his front right, a dead soldier lay sprawled over a tangle of barbed wire. The man belonged to a Highland Regiment they relieved in the Line four days prior. He was caught by machine-gun fire while returning from a 'Black Hand Gang' night mission out in 'No-Man's Land.' The wire held his head high enough that his dead, starting eyes looked back towards his own lines with a look of intensity, almost accusation. In as much as it could be said they were focused, his eyes stared directly at the observation sap. The corpse had become something of an albatross around the neck of the battalion. Every man coming off duty at the sap spoke of it. It spooked them to the nerve-weakened stage that the officers openly talked about mortaring the body to be rid of it. This all seemed a little unfair and not quite 'the done thing,' but certainly, a better prospect than risking lives to remove the spectral figure.

Tom could see the hump which was the Highlander, getting more distinct as the sun crept ever higher, picking out the tangle of wire, picket poles, and the edges of adjacent shell craters in the moonscape around him. He fell to wondering, trying to shake the too well remembered image of the man's face from his mind. Behind him, the whole battalion, brigade, division, would be 'standing-to,' in case of any assault. It was a daily chore. When the threat was passed, breakfast would come along, and everyone could 'stand-down.' Tommy Evans! For no good reason, suddenly, Tommy Evans came to mind!

Dear old Tommy: the drink-besotted Welshman who was chief engineer on the 'S.S. Teresa Belmont.' It was Tommy who took Tom under his wing, years before, when he'd first signed on ship after running away from home. The fat little Welshman had had four passions in life: his ship's engines, full bottles of Scotch, sex, and books, in any order or permutation but preferably as rapidly as they could occur.

The man from Cardiff started his career under sail, went over to steam, and of course, stayed there. He began reading in his spare time on the high seas. He was well past fifty when Tom knew him, but his omnivorous and voracious reading habits could have qualified him as a literary professor at any university. He was the most widely read person Tom would ever meet with a boundless and encyclopaedic memory for quotations and facts.

It was he who introduced Tom to literature; and sex! During one of their endless chats, Tommy unearthed the fact of Tom's virginity. "Good God! Look-you boy-o. You wouldn't know about a China woman's pookay then, would you? Mounted sideways they are! And easy to find, see, because they've got no hair!"

Tom had well guessed what a pookay was, but was unable to refute the description, since his scepticism was founded on ignorance. The thought, however, produced a familiar stirring. He readily agreed that once they were across the Indian Ocean, Tommy would take him to Leung Lee Wan's brothel in Singapore, a treat on him.

How clearly Tom remembered that night! After a fiery fortification ('fortification before fornication' the Welshman chuckled) from Tommy's stock of whisky, they tramped down off the gangway of the 'Teresa Belmont' onto the Singapore docks. Butting his way along assuredly through the tropical night, Tommy led him through a maze of narrow, smelly alleyways that clustered the area. Each street teemed with life; hawkers, beggars, rickshaw men, handcarts, and uncountable Chinese bustled past the bewildered eyes of young Tom. The Welshman dragged him along relentlessly, pausing only to seize his jacket and tug him away from any particularly persistent seller along the way. Low, dimly lit doorways gave mind-tingling glimpses of opium dens, brothels, mysterious stores, and bars.

Chinese banners hung over the upper half of each street, proclaiming the virtues of carbolic soap for all he knew, but definitely adding to the mystery of the journey. And at the end of it – sex! He already had grave misgivings about that, despite Tommy's administered 'Dutch courage.' The kaleidoscope of bewildering experiences stopped as Tommy yanked on his arm and propelled the pair of them through a narrow doorway. The intrigue of the red lantern-lit Chinese characters sashaying down the doorpost went for nothing alongside the carelessly scrawled English word 'brothel' on the wall.

The noise and smells of the street were suddenly cut off, replaced by a dimly lit passageway. A subtle, yet tantalizing perfume of joss sticks and opium drifted towards them, drawing them inexorably along, like fish on a line. Nodding and chattering in pigeon English, a wizened little Chinese man backed up the passage before them, genuflecting a welcome. He directed them to a table in a small room, surrounded by half a dozen others, before extending an arm towards a bar in the corner, well stocked with liquor bottles.

Three doors led off this inner room, to where Tom could only guess. The room was decorated with dark, lacquered walls, hung with banners in Chinese characters. Several hanging lanterns cast an atmosphere redolent with promise. Men occupied two of the other tables. On a deep couch, an Asian girl in a white robe was conversing intimately with an elderly man. The walls were decorated with murals depicting various explicit sexual positions, most of which were beyond Tom's limited experience to appreciate. One particularly caught him, when a soft voice beside him suddenly asked, "Whisky?"

Whirling in surprise, he almost buried his nose between a pair of naked, pert little breasts. Smiling down at him, the young girl waited for his reply, but his mouth just hung open, gaping. Tommy came to his rescue.

"Give him a whisky, unless he's going to settle for milk!" The fat little man slapped his thigh, delighted with his joke, and cackled anew at Tom's embarrassment. He turned and addressed the departing girl. "And hey, look-you! Two of them, and make them real scotch, not that bloody piss-water you try to pass off as real whisky. Johnny Walker, nothing else! You hear?"

"Okay, okay, Jo-nee Wor-ha." The girl shrugged and went on her way.

"Close your mouth boy-ho! You'll make that little darlin' think you want to bite on her tittee or something, and then she'll get all embarrassed!" Tommy went off into another paroxysm of laughter, further discomforting Tom. Three other patrons turned around to discover the source of the noise.

The second whisky was just beginning to work on Tom when a fat Chinese of middle age hustled into the room towards them with forced obsequity.

"Ah! Tommee E-wans!"

"Lee Wan, you old prick! How's business?"

"Business wery good. How many gir's you wan' fuck this time?"

"Are you jesting? I just this minute got out of hospital! Three months getting my stomach pumped out from your cheap booze. Almost had to have my cock sawn off from the clap I got here! I wouldn't touch one of your girls if you paid me!"

"Cheap We'sh cocksucker or'y wan' low plice!" Lee Wan was obviously not too concerned about customer relations. "You have dlink on me, then fuck gir'. Lin-Lin ask for you aw time. She rike Tommee!" The Chinese man gleamed a twenty-carat smile. The sales pitch was in!

"Well, Lee Wan, to tell the truth, I'm here to fix up my young friend here. This is Tom. What have you got for him? Something special to please me!"

Lee Wan's beam became twenty-two carat. He inclined his head to Tom in greeting. "How 'bout new gir'? A'most wirgin! Got nice tight cunt and nice tittees! Owny one pound, short time!"

"One pound! Why you damned Chinese bandit! For one pound, I could have the Queen of Sheba exhumed and fuck her back to life again!"

"Queen Sheba not a'most wirgin! Fifteen shiwings!"

"Piss off!"

"Twe've!"

"Two bob!"

"That plice ownry buy cheap Cardiff whore! My gir' ten shiwings!"

This, of course, was the real psychological barrier, one that Tommy Evans had had to break. He would lose face with Lee Wan if he paid too much. So, with a further barrage of insults, interspersed with a fine melange of epithets plus Chinese and Shakespearean asides, Tom's first sexual exploit was valued at four shillings and three pence. Honour satisfied on both sides, the two protagonists separated, Lee Wan to his back room and Tommy Evans to his fresh scotch. Five minutes later, a tiny girl, not even Tom's age, came out. Taking his hand, she led him through one of the doors.

"Wait for me here and enjoy yourself," was Tommy's parting shot.

By that time, Tom felt like a man about to have a tooth removed with a hammer and cold chisel and no anaesthetic. He was terrified he would not get an erection. The cubbyhole the girl led him to contained a tiny bamboo-framed bed with a straw palliasse and a broken-down, battered nightstand. There was barely enough room to stand up in the place. After the dirty blanket fell across the doorway, he found himself in embarrassing proximity to the girl. Quickly, without guile, she shed the robe she wore and stood before him, naked. She was thin, lithe, with narrow hips and skinny shanks. Above her flat smooth stomach, her upper body widened and his eyes fell upon brown-tipped, upright tiny breasts. She smiled encouragingly at him, her dense long black hair cascading over her shoulders. He spied more downy wisps nestling between her thighs – another story laid to rest!

He'd felt dryness in his throat, but the apprehension partly dissolved before his rising male pride. She indicated that he, too, should undress and moved to help him. Her soft cool touch on his belly excited him more. He'd reddened when his partial erection popped into view, an appearance never shared before. He had a moment of anxiety, a thought of failure, before she made an approving sound. Her knowing hands brought him to full throbbing readiness. He ran his hands through her hair and down her back, reaching around her buttocks, and up to her breasts again. Muttering something encouraging in Chinese, she'd sank back onto the bed and sought to penetrate herself with him, while he naively tried to kiss and fondle her. God almighty! She must have been all of fourteen years old, yet so worldly, so experienced!

The few seconds of fumbling by the girl became too long for his rising male dominance. With a thrust of his buttocks, he naturally achieved what once seemed an insurmountable quest. He remembered little else. It had been a warm, moist experience that lasted only a short time before he found himself back in the waiting room with the girl's 'good fuck!' ringing in his ears. Somehow, he passed muster but didn't know his grade. On the way back, he went by a half-open door and saw fat Tommy, naked as a jaybird, wrestling unashamedly with two Chinese women. Judging by the noise, a good time was being had by all.

Often since, Tom wondered about that young girl. Wiser now, he knew she had likely been sold into prostitution at a young age by her family. Now, six years later, she was probably an old hag, pox-ridden, genitally crippled and on the junk pile of life, lucky if she was riding an opium-filled relief from pain in her last few years. The only English she knew was the parting, 'Good fuck!'

A glint of sun off a piece of equipment brought him out of his reverie. It was almost five! If the Germans were coming, it would be now. If not, then both sides could stand down for breakfast. Somewhere, perhaps only fifty feet away, some poor Fritz was crouched, like himself, scared shitless and hoping he'd live to see breakfast.

The light grew quickly; objects became more distinct. The orb of the sun became visible through the mist. Lips of shell holes came into focus, their edges rounded by the glutinous mud, which had oozed down their sides and set like warm toffee. Involuntarily, Tom's eyes crept back to the now apparent hump, the dead Highlander. With more relief than revulsion, he saw the cause for fear was gone. During the night, a rat came along and ate the soldier's eyes.

June 25, 1916.

"Mademoiselle from Armentières, Parlez-vous.
Mademoiselle from Armentières, Parlez-vous.
Mademoiselle from Armentières, with lily-white
tits and golden hair, Inky Pinky, Parlez-vous..."

It was good to be bawling out the lusty words of the song this fine June morning. The sun was rising higher with the promise of a warm day. Birds were singing in the fields beside the dusty French road. The shuffle and tramp of the battalion's booted feet provided the beat for the leaving-the-Line song, and Gordie White, with a bloodstained rag around his head, led them through the verses in fine voice. A very faint rumble of artillery, far behind them, served as a reminder that the Front was miles away, and they were still alive.

Relieved by the newly arrived Canadian Fourth Division the day before, the Third was marching out of the Line, fresh from its tour of duty in the Ypres Salient. God, but he was tired! Tom reflected. He glanced around at the faces surrounding him, faces he would forever be proud to know. Ray Scott limped along on an especially bad case of trench foot, a filthy field dressing covering one side of his face. René Dumont from Morinville tenaciously clung to John Phillip's webbing, shuffling along blinded. Dan Williams sported a sling around his right arm. His left hand was blistered from holding a hot rifle. Filthy dirty, lice-ridden, half-starved, and semi-lame, the Forty-ninth proudly wound its way through the peaceful rural lanes.

It was a different group of men than those who marched this way only four eternity-long months before with an apprehension blunted by naivety. The physical make-up was different, since many had failed to return. 'Wounded in action,' 'missing,' and 'presumed dead' were succinct euphemisms for the suffering, terror, agony, starvation, hope, valour, and death that relatives could never know. Swinging down the road those months before, they had all been happy to finally get to fire their guns in anger at the Germans. Canada disappeared behind them more than a year before on June fourth, nineteen fifteen. Months spent in training in England were followed by frustrated hopes during four months of inaction in France when they served as railway and supply troops.

The eventual formation of the Canadian Corps and their own Third Division had come to pass on Christmas Eve, nineteen fifteen. With the Royal Canadian Regiment (fresh from Bermuda, poor sods), the Princess Patricia's Light Infantry (the 'Pats'), and the Forty-second Battalion, the Forty-ninth constituted the senior and Seventh Brigade of the proud new Canadian Third Division. Despite the morbid but proudly told tales of the already battle-tested 'Pats,' the patriotic fervour of the untried troops disallowed credence of conditions at the Front. It was inconceivable to them. Now, they knew! Oh God, how they knew! The Ypres Salient or 'Wipers,' as they knew it, was used by the High Command as a kind of baptismal experience for new formations. Only two miles south of the town of Ypres, the front lines of the Allies bulged into the German-held positions. Only about ten sections of land over which the Germans could lob a shell at will, the Salient had not been created by one of those glorious feats of arms with which journalists loved to regale their readers. It was created in nineteen fourteen when the invading German armies were fought to a standstill. The temporary foxholes, dug to repel counter-attacks, had grown into the present siege-warfare earthworks and fortifications thrown up by two mighty forces caught in a deadlock.

When their advance became stalled, the Germans realized it now behoved the British and French forces to attack them in order to try and throw them out of Northern France and Belgium. Thus, given the choice of ground, they retreated a little here and there and dug themselves in on the best topographical features, namely the ridges and higher ground. This gave them strategically overlooking, nice dry trenches, by and large, while simultaneously condemning their enemies to the lower, waterlogged ground. Ergo, 'Wipers!'

Thwarted of their military college concepts of a 'fluid war,' the generals approached the static nature of trench warfare with strategies involving massive, set-piece battles, where a mere few yards of insignificant mud was bought at the cost of hundreds of lives. The Ypres Salient, with typical disregard for strategic value, was occupied more through stubbornness than military advantage. The Germans wouldn't have wanted it, even if the Allies had pulled out. The never-briefed, never-consulted infantryman knew it, but the generals didn't, which made it all the more senseless. As the company wit Alf Foster had said, "The Wipers Salient sticks out into the German lines like the Allied arse waiting to be kicked!"

With great thoroughness, the Germans carefully sighted in their machine guns and artillery observation posts above their enemies. From Whyteshaele Ridge, overlooking the Salient, they were able, by observed as well as random fire, to inflict most of the two thousand casualties per month. That was considered *normal* merely for *just occupying* the Salient and reserve positions! The Canadians grimly realized that when an assault was launched, it was always, always uphill to the German trenches, through a sea of clinging mud and obstacles, laden down with over sixty pounds of equipment that slowed their advance to a snail's pace in the face of withering machine-gun fire.

Tom glanced silently at his marching partner, Alex MacFarlane. MacFarlane quit in his second year of law at the University of Alberta in order to join up. He could easily have been an officer, but instead, chose to fight as a private soldier. The decision was not predicated on the short life expectancy of a 'Lone Star' first lieutenant, but on MacFarlane's own personal reasons. Tom already knew it was not his courage. Chalk-white with exhaustion, Alex gamely struggled on.

Tom knew from their endless discussions that Alex's mind, like most of the other men, was filled with a sense of relief at having survived the ordeal. He thought with sadness, yet pride of the men they left behind. The Forty-ninth held up well in the Line, but they had to find a better way of doing it. The attrition of good men and materiel to support them showed clearly that unless one side or the other got the upper hand, this war could be fought until both sides were prostrated – the flower of their national manhood ploughed like common fertilizer into the fields of France.

Ordinary daily life, (which translated as mere survival at the Front), transcended most thoughts of actual combat. Abject boredom under the most primitive and dangerous conditions imaginable was their daily lot.

The moonscape of mud, which was their home, offered little shelter from the elements. Hot meals were virtually unknown at the Front, since lives could not be risked for transporting hot food along the communication trenches under fire. Mostly, the men ate their 'last hope' or iron rations, consisting of bully beef, hard army biscuits, cans of 'Machonochie' stew, washed down by foul-tasting tea brewed over communally-owned spirit stoves. A stale loaf of days-old bread was a Godsend.

Although proper procedures were laid down for sanitation, they also could not risk lives disposing of cans of human waste. And so, in the forward trenches, a man mostly relieved himself wherever he could. Feces, unburied corpses, abandoned equipment, and barbed wire littered the landscape in every direction, often submerged in yellow-scummed water, which drowned the wounded. The sucking mud could rob a man of his boots at every step, and as if all of these things weren't bad enough, the 'Alleyman' was ever ready to shoot the brains out of any man who foolishly raised his head.

These, Tom reflected, were only some of the delights awaiting the eager Canadians when they arrived in the Salient in April. Four days before their arrival, the British Fifth Corps exploded several mines under the German trenches after weeks of tunnelling to place the charges. (The impasse of the trenches was such that miners were an integral part of the army's ranks. Tactics reverted to the mediaeval practice of tunnelling under enemy fortifications.) On arrival, the green Canadians were ordered to occupy the huge craters that had ensued, along with a mess of minor craters and trenches. In the gelatinous moonscape of the Front, with geographical features shelled to oblivion, it was not until ten days later that it was realized the wrong craters were occupied. The Germans held the desired ones!

This blunder focused the irascibility of Commander-in-Chief General Douglas Haig upon the Canadians. To him, miles behind the Front on a neat clean map at headquarters, these craters were clearly marked. He was already displeased with the Canadians for other reasons. Since the only mud he ever saw was promptly removed from his boots by his personal batman, he had no grasp of the monumental difficulties involved in map reading at the Front.

Forced by political niceties to withhold his hand, he was eventually able to remove General Alderson from command of the Canadians. Alderson was a popular and cautious officer. His replacement, one General

Sir Julian Byng, was received with the enthusiasm reserved for a wet blanket. It was a shameful beginning for what was to be an illustrious relationship, but to the Canadians, an ex-cavalry officer who had helped evacuate Gallipoli was not, on face value, as good as Alderson. To add to the green troops' misery, as if suffering the 'Wipers' Salient was not enough, the Germans mounted an attack that culminated in the Canadians becoming seasoned in both defensive and offensive tactics.

The first day of June, on a beautiful morning, the worst artillery barrage the Front had ever seen broke over the Canadians. Major-General Mercer, their divisional commander, was killed at Armagh Wood in the shellfire that lasted until one in the morning. With rapid success (the regimental diaries described it as *almost leisurely*), the Germans then advanced against little opposition along Hill Seventy, Mount Sorrel, Observatory Ridge, Top Tor, and Armagh Wood. The forested and mountainous flavour of these place names was deceptive, since they referred only to blackened and twisted stumps of trees, long destroyed by artillery fire, clinging to higher ground maybe a mere fifty feet or so above the surrounding land.

The German tunnellers exploded mines beneath the Fourth CMR Regiment, killing all but three officers and seventy men of the seven hundred-strong unit. Two eighteen pounders of the Fifth Artillery Battery fired over open sights into the attackers, resorting to pistols as they were overrun. In the Line, the 'Pats' lost four hundred men, fighting a desperate flank defence that fortunately held.

Only one day out of the Line on relief, after nine days of constant shelling, the Forty-ninth was immediately called back in to counterattack. Trench-wise veterans grabbed up every scrap of food they could find. Blackjacks, knuckledusters, and knives were slipped into webbing and battledress. Hand-to-hand trench warfare demanded weapons not issued by the army. A long, bayonet-tipped rifle was unwieldy for close combat, impossible to swing around in a narrow trench. The man who got the first lick in survived.

Colonel Griesbach was delegated overall command of the attack, so Major Weaver took over the Forty-ninth. He was wounded by shellfire moving up through the trenches, and Captain Hobbs assumed command. Passing through the traffic-snarled bottleneck of the Lille city gate, the Forty-ninth was under constant bombardment. A real *hate* came over. 'Coal Box, Woolly Bear,' and five point nine shells exploded everywhere, illustrating their descriptive nicknames. The Germans tried desperately to negate any Canadian efforts to form up a counterattack.

With casualties mounting steadily, the Forty-ninth finally reached its jump-off position, about six hundred yards from the beleaguered 'Pats' who were at the other end of a communications trench called 'Warrington Avenue.' The battalion from the Ninth Brigade, promised as support, never showed up. They had been shelled to pieces back in the reserve positions. Delayed by the lack of support and a further German attack at Hooge, Colonel Griesbach finally ordered the attack in at seven a.m. A fortifying slug of rum did little to dispel the discomfort of helplessly lying in the mud of a collapsed trench for six hours, while being severely shelled. As the green rockets flared and whistles blew, with friendly artillery adding to the 'hoo-ha,' the Forty-ninth went 'over the top' for the first time.

Dazed, confused, and ill-briefed as to their objectives, the men plunged forward, most relieved to be moving at last and free from the nagging fears of incipient cowardice, which gnawed at them for hours. The fear of letting down one's comrades was one of the greatest hurdles for the infantryman. Waiting for hours in the cold wet was fertile ground for fear to grow. Reminders of what happened to men in battle were ever-present around them.

Tom only remembered showers of dirt and mud and the screaming rattle of machine gun fire. He vaguely recalled his platoon falling, literally, into a trench full of Germans. There was smoke and screaming, still more showers of dirt, and the deadly whine of bullets and shrapnel. The horrible slap of these deadly fragments into human flesh was a sound he would never forget. He finally came to sensibility in a shell hole with ten others with whom he had repulsed two German counterattacks. He found himself desperately trying to scrounge ammunition for his rifle. When it wouldn't fit, he discovered he was holding a bloodstained German Mauser instead of his own weapon.

They were relieved in the wee small hours of June fifth, creeping away to lick their wounds but proud to have been the only formation to make any substantial gain against the Germans. Thirty-two comrades were dead, two hundred and sixty-five wounded, and sixty-nine missing. The Seventh Brigade lost over a thousand men in three days fighting.

They learned from their experience, though. In the past four months, they had been through almost all phases of modern combat. They manned the trenches defensively, executed nightly 'Black Hand Gang' operations into No Man's Land and now, counter-offensive operations. They knew, too, it required tremendous manpower behind the battlefield to support operations. Extracting a wounded man from the battlefield to a field dressing station could take as many as six men several hours.

The tenuousness of life's thread was brought home to them. In their several sojourns into the Line, most of the old hands who joined up in nineteen fourteen were gone: dead, missing, or so badly wounded, they had been repatriated. In their frequent 'bull' sessions, the men seriously discussed the conduct of the war. Gone was the 'Berlin-by-Christmas-and-then-home' mentality. Submerged in mud, with death inches away, the realities of the situation were quickly brought home to the dullest infantryman. Modern arms had now completed a centuries-old trend. The days of the aristocracy or the rich being viewed as the ruling class already seemed to be numbered. Gone was the age-old and cherished prerogative of the armoured knight galloping around with impunity, braining helpless peasants with his mace. It started with the cloth yard arrow and the crossbow bolt. Now, the machine gun reigned supreme, for with it, a common soldier could arrest the advance of an army of aristocrats. The machine gun bullet of this war had become the great leveller of society. It killed with indiscriminate finality, both the high and lowly-born.

One topic that interested Tom was the great wave of emancipation that soldiers felt would follow this war. This had often followed periods of warfare throughout history. The magnitude of this conflict and the numbers of people involved guaranteed some change in the aftermath. For instance, no longer were civilian populations insulated by distance from the armed clashes. Zeppelins were now roaming over London and dropping bombs. This was total war.

The Canadians also considered themselves more emancipated than their British Regimental counterparts. Merely by deciding to imigrate to Canada in the first place, the seventy-five percent of British immigrants in the battalion had shown themselves to be more freethinking, more enterprising than their contemporaries. Any man willing to homestead in the forty-below-zero winters of Alberta was nobody's yes-man. All of the seventy-five percent British-born returned to fight in Europe, not because of Canada's automatic involvement at Britain's declaration, but because they believed it was their war too.

The British still believed in the 'few leading the many' concept with the frequently displayed ignorance of the 'few' rarely questioned concerning the validity of their decisions. Nowhere was this more evident than in the present conduct of the war. Militarily ill-equipped to cope with modern warfare, the High Command was responsible for thousands perishing in wasteful, repetitive attacks, which were ill-conceived and often foolishly telegraphed to the enemy by the stockpiling and movement of materiel and troops days before an attack. The Canadians were different. Their lifestyles made them think for themselves. They were more resistant to regimentation, asked questions, and improvised to overcome problems. This inherent farmer's ability to cope would inevitably make them better troops. Had they realized it, their agrarian background placed them squarely on the traditional paths of such great 'shepherd warriors' as the Hyksos, the Assyrians of Ashurbanipal, the Macedonians of Alexander, and the Roman Legionnaires.

Tom smiled. He eased the straps of his pack and re-slung his rifle. Alf Foster came to mind with his outspoken comments about the Generals: "You can't keep putting men into a meat grinder like this and expect sausages out the other end, unless you add a membrane of common sense to wrap them in." Like many of the soldiers, Alf hated General Haig. "Bloody Scotsman!" He would mutter, "Thinks he's at the Battle ·of Culloden!"

"Eh? Is that in Flanders?"

"Culloden Moor, you numbskull! Thousands of Scottish clansmen charging the English redcoats. Only trouble was, they had claymores and the Duke of Cumberland's English had cannon, loaded with grapeshot! You should visit the place sometime. Thousands buried in long communal mounds. Saddest place on Earth!"

"See! I said it was in Flanders!"

Tom remembered Alf's exasperated eyes turning skywards. He knew what Foster meant. He was one of the most critical of the High Command. He was careful to keep his opinions within his own close circle. It was not insubordination; it was a quest for an improved method of defeating the Germans with minimal losses. Everyone accepted there would be losses; the present ones were just unacceptably high. The officers felt it, too, and were just as shocked at the size of the casualty lists. Tom felt a hardening of resolve about what he would do with the rest of his life if he were spared. The daily problems of Edmonton life shrank into insignificance alongside Ypres. When he did get home, he proposed never to waste another moment of his life. Now, he truly appreciated how precious it really was.

Not for the first time in considering the future, his thoughts turned to Jeanne. A wave of hope flooded through him. He would marry that girl when he got back! He wrote often and received desultory replies, but he was not daunted. With her at home waiting for him, he could make it through the most desperate circumstances! A shaft of sunlight suddenly beamed out between a stand of Lombardy poplars beside the road. As the heat in the rays warmed him, he wished with all his being that he could share the simple joy of that sunbeam with her, right now. It was a sacred moment. The aches and pains, the chaffing of his webbing fell away. Taking a deep, life-loving breath, he joined in the next verse of the song his friends were singing:

> *"I don't want to go to war,*
> *I'd rather stay at home,*
> *Around the streets to roam*
> *And live on the earnings of a well-paid whore.*
>
> *I don't want a bayonet up my arse-hole,*
> *I don't want my bollocks shot away,*
> *I'd rather stay in England..."*

Summer, 1916.

By route march and train, the Forty-ninth made its way to the vicinity of St. Omer, about twenty five miles from Calais. They were always tickled by the stencilling on the side of the French railway wagons: 'Chevaux 6. Hommes 40.' To all the Allied soldiers, the trains became 'Hommes Forties.'

It was good to give up the old, soiled uniforms, delouse, and take a bath. For a short while, they could relax and unwind from the tensions of the Front. The war was a million miles away. They could indulge themselves in the simple pleasures and entertainments offered in the rest camps. They were housed in rows of 'Amiens shelters,' canvas and wood-frame contraptions, clustered around an old farmhouse that became their headquarters. The officers stayed in the farm outbuildings. While drafty and susceptible to leaks in the rain, the abominable Amiens huts were like palaces, compared to the trenches.

In these warm summer days, they wrote letters home and set up their own entertainment for the evenings. There were soccer and boxing matches, inter-battalion and division. Someone could always play a piano in the Red Cross or YMCA facilities to get a singsong going. A man might even get a glass of beer, some cigarettes, or a plug of tobacco for a faithful old pipe. A crazy bunch of amateur dramatists from the Third Division achieved immortal fame as 'The Dumbbells,' putting on many popular shows. Relief sank into each one of them like the warmth of a hot tub. Spectres past and future about the war shrank away.

Besides poring over Jeanne's few letters, seeking between-the-lines messages, Tom communicated with his mother who wrote regularly. George Edmunds died in late nineteen fifteen. Tom managed a couple of days' leave, while the Forty-ninth was in England. But his father's reception of him had, in no way, mellowed since he had gone back as a seaman. His father died unrepentant, unforgiving, stubbornly voicing betrayal by a son who would not follow in his footsteps. Without reconciliation, now that he was a man himself, Tom deeply felt the loss. He realized a man could only truly go forward in life with the approval and love of his father. Suffering a heart attack, George Edmunds took to his bed and succumbed to a bout of pneumonia. Fortunately, his young brother Bert was still fully employed at the Vickers' works, making war materiel, so the family still had an income. His sister Sheila was now engaged to a Tommy in the Tyneside Scottish Regiment. God grant he survives!

The Forty-ninth was issued new equipment with the usual stern admonitions regarding its care. The Ross rifle, to the relief of everyone, was withdrawn and officially replaced by the standard British Lee Enfield. Although a good target rifle, the Ross was unsuitable for warfare. Despite numerous modifications, the ejector mechanism on the bolt continued to jam, endangering Canadian lives. The rifle was the brainchildren of Sam Hughes, the redoubtable, bumptious, irascible, and conceited Canadian Minister of Defence in the Borden Cabinet.

At the outbreak of the war, Sam defied the government's recruiting procedures and raised his own standard. It was a fine piece of patriotism, become tarnished by events. Many of Sam's cronies, appointed by him for procurement of military supplies, were now under investigation for profiteering and pocket lining to the tune of millions of dollars. The Ross rifle wasn't the only questionable item on Sam's record. Cardboard boots and dud shells early in the war, along with his continued backing of the Ross, made him roundly hated by the men whose lives had been jeopardized by their presence on the battlefield.

The final official ruling on the Ross was academic, since Canadians were picking up the superior Lee Enfields from battlefields for months. This was done with the tacit approval of their officers. Colonel Griesbach was heard one day to ruminatively remark that, "...a lot of Commonwealth rifles were lying around..." after an engagement. Griesbach, himself, had a long history of condemning the Ross, having ordered courts of inquiry into its performance as far back as nineteen hundred and one and again in nineteen ten.

Food would forever be the making or breaking point of their morale for idle men. The sameness of army rations drove many of them to seek the 'eggs any style with chips,' offered at the local 'estaminets.' French refugees, torn from their homes by the war, invariably ran these establishments. These squatters, who then set up the estaminets, seized any premises not requisitioned by the army. They were a present-day manifestation of camp followers.

In the St. Omer area, an older woman, Madame Fronteneau, and her daughter, Michelle, ran the favourite of "B" Company. Typically, they were the only survivors of their family after being caught in the Battle of the Marne. They worked long hard hours, seeking out the potatoes and eggs to serve the men, along with the rotgut 'vin-ordinaire.' Despite the advances of half-drunk and lonely men, they did their best to maintain their dignity and morality. It was significant, however, that in the last analysis, they could still sell their womanhood for favours. It was reported, for the right price, Madame Fronteneau could be persuaded to share her rather aged charms with the occasional soldier.

In the rumour-rife billets, the story was told of Michelle once fellating five unscrupulous medics in fifteen minutes as the price for some medicine when her mother had been sick. The story itself was probably apocryphal, but like many others abounding in France, along with the availability of 'dirty pictures' and abundant tales of ready sex, a picture of French sexuality was being created that they would never live down. The army was unsympathetic to men who contracted venereal disease, docking their pay for time spent under treatment. The treatment itself was an uncomfortable process and also subject to soldierly exaggeration. For a man chancing to be daily blown to smithereens in the Line, such deterrents were of no consequence. Only the virgins wavered. Basic needs loomed even larger in the shadow of imminent death. The men attended the 'Maisons de tolerance' in droves.

The atmosphere in these red-light establishments did not cater to any romantic notions a soldier might hold. Rather, they existed purely to make money by removing both a man's need and his erection, the two being synonymous. The men waited in line before paying the Madame, whose assistant would escort them upstairs when an awaiting paramour became free. These ladies, inevitably unattractive in nature but possessing the necessary and required orifice, would be sprawled, often semi-clad, on a bed or couch. In this position, they expected an immediate attack and rapid enough retreat to ensure a steady flow of customers between their thighs.

Most of the women were blowsy country girls, anxious to make a quick-enough dowry, unavailable by any other means and thus enabling them to return to their village and find a willing husband. It was their only chance. Numerous bawdy stories circulated about the capabilities and willingness of these ladies to perform certain acts, most obscene and of questionable possibility, but making them more fabled. As the wag Alf Foster had said, "If *they also serve who only stand and wait* has meaning, then *these ladies also serve, who only lay to mate*." One of these harlots might accommodate nearly a whole battalion of men in a matter of weeks before taking an early, if tender retirement. Foster also concluded: "It's a piss-poor world when a man has not only to dig in the same battlefield as his comrades, but also the same woman!"

Swimming in the canals was also popular. The men preserved modesty by wearing sandbags with holes cut in them. In earlier days, it was common to find dozens of soldiers swimming nude in the canals. That was terminated when a senior officer came along on one such occasion to find a host of appreciative French women viewing a scene of cavorting, naked Tommies swimming in their canal.

Tom became a rather unwilling lance corporal, inheriting the rank mainly because of the depletion rate of experienced men. He would have been a full corporal, but a fracas with some British soldiers near Salisbury Plain blotted his service card. He was just as happy, since greater risk seemed to attend promotions. Subalterns and non-commissioned officers were expected to be active leaders. The lifespan of a 'Lone Star' in the great frontal assaults was measured in days.

Ambitious men were often dead men in this business. While he didn't necessarily consider himself less brave than others, Tom was worldly enough to grasp at greater survival. A number of officers still subscribed to the traditional old drills of warfare, exhorting them with such gems as 'Push on at all costs and get in there with the bayonet!' While such action threw panic into the hearts of backward tribesmen throughout the Empire in the past, modern warfare had very unsubtly changed this method into a highly dangerous practice. The infantry manuals of India, the Sudan, and the South African campaigns had no place here.

The modern infantryman, before going into action, probably crouched for hours in a muddy trench, numbed and shocked under a barrage and counter-barrage of high explosive shells, watching the casualties mount before he went 'over the top.' The suppression of his fear was the hardest – to try and not show cowardice amongst comrades. It was their biggest fear. When the time came to attack, it came with relief from the helplessness. It was a hard slog through the mud, carrying a debilitating pack in sodden clothes. The effort of struggling on overwhelmed a man's attention from the moment he mounted the palisade of the trench. The hail of machine-gun bullets and shrapnel cutting down comrades on every side was lost in the struggle to move forward. If they did reach and gain an enemy trench, they were too exhausted, bewildered, and inadequately briefed to know what to do next. The sacrifices were for nought.

Numerous successful penetrations of key positions failed to produce a break-through because the men were trained to 'consolidate every advance.' This removed any initiative to seize a strategic point a few yards further on. This simultaneously negated possible gains and committed men to poor defensive positions that the Germans soon over-ran in counter-attacks. These thoughts went through Tom Edmunds' head as he sat in the estaminet with his mates, drinking vin ordinaire. They went there together after visiting one of the 'Maisons de tolerance' in St. Omer. Now, they were reliving the experience over a plate of food and some wine at Madame Fronteneau's. They also had other news to discuss: orders were posted that morning, ordering them back into the Line.

"Do you think it will be any worse than Wipers?" John Silas asked Alex MacFarlane.

"Ah dinna ken, laddie. Ye know what we've all heard." What they heard was there was going to be a big push. What they understood from that was a lot of them were going to die.

"Maybe the British will get through, just leave us with a mop-up job." Bill McIntosh was always the optimist, but his voice fell off as he said the words. Poor Bill. He was as huge as the side of a prairie farmer's soddy and twice as soft. A replacement from one of the reserve units, he walked eighty miles to a recruiting station to volunteer for this hell. Despite his easy-going nature, Tom had him marked as a real tiger once the action started.

"They say they've lost over twenty thousand dead so far." Blonde-headed Bernie Robinson had a head for facts.

"Where is this Somme place, anyway?"

"Up the road, aways. It's an eighteen mile wide frontal assault, and that can swallow a lot of men."

"Hell, Scottie, they're saying it's the worst defeat the British have had since Hastings! If they've lost twenty thousand these first few days, it must be a real losing cause!"

"The Newfies' Regiment lost twenty six officers and nearly seven hundred casualties, just moving through the support positions."

"Good Christ, Bernie. Where did you hear that?"

"One of the fellows I know from a Field Ambulance Unit in St. Omer. He said they'd had over forty thousand casualties through there with Blighty wounds, and *they* were just on reserve status! The whole mess of them were caught in a counter-barrage while they were moving up, like the Newfies. It's the same old story, you know. The Fritzes know we're coming and sit up high with their artillery zeroed in on everything!"

"The Australians are supposed to have taken Pozières," chimed in McIntosh.

"Yeah, sure, with most of them left lying out there now, feeding the rats."

"Jesus!"

"They say some of the troops were committed three, even four times."

"Jesus!"

"Well, I hope they make some progress before we get there. This training we're going to start tomorrow had better have something more effective to it than what the British Regiments have tried!"

"When do they say we are going in?"

"First few days in September."

"Jesus!"

"Maybe the whole thing will be called off!"

"Don't be fucking daft, lad!"

"Jesus!"

"They say Lloyd George and that Winston Churchill fella are getting a little dubious about Haig's methods. Maybe they'll get rid of him!"

"You dull bugger! Moving Haig out will make no difference! They'll just find some other stupid bastard who'll fill us with Machonochie's, beans, and navy rum before presenting us to the Fritzes, who'll shoot the shit out of us like nothing has happened!"

"That's what you're full of!"

"I should be, that's all I get fed!"

"Jesus!"

"Hey, Michelle! Voulez-vous nous prenner un autre bouteille de vin, s'il vous plait?"

"Thank God for an educated man who can bring upon us the finer things in life!"

"I know what I'd like her to bring upon *me*!"

"Arse-first!"

The table talk degenerated into the second favourite topic of the trench-bound Tommies. The others got caught up in the ribaldry, and Tom's mind, as it mostly did whenever sex was mentioned, slipped back to a past scene. The trees in Mill Creek ravine were at their most lovely. Filigreed by the leaves, the sun's rays became a pale green wave of light sifting down before him. Partly dammed behind a fallen tree, the creek bubbled sparkling clear to fan out into their favourite pool. Every stone on the bottom was visible, three feet below the cool surface.

Facing him on the far end of the tree trunk, Jeanne sat with her bare feet plunged into the water, the silvery swirl darkening the long hem of her cotton dress. She smiled at him, secretly, knowingly, throwing her head back and allowing the warmth of the sun to strike her face, while the cool waters around her legs brought her to a balance with nature.

That chuckle of pure joy he had grown to love rose from her throat. Even now, after so long, Tom could see it well up through her graceful neck, to float forth and encompass him in her happiness. "Come on." She was pulling the dress over her head, removing the shift beneath. Underpants fluttered to the bank and soft, shapely blonde nudity flitted across his memory before she slipped into the water. Tom needed no second urging to join her.

THREE

THE VIRGIN OF BREBIÈRE

September 16, 1916.

The sucking passage of the five point nine and its erupting arrival nearby pierced his exhausted sleep only enough to make him twitch. The detonation of the second, closer by, brought forth a grunt. The mud-caked figure stirred in the gloom of the dugout. A glutinous river of mud flowed through the door, frozen in time like the encroachment of solidified lava, half submerging his inert body. He felt stiff and cold, totally beat. Rolling over, he gasped at the pain and discomfort. Sodden through, his woollen clothes pressed down on him like some grim second skin. The tears in his flesh from barbed wire glowed hotly and re-opened under the stress of his movements. Combat instinct found his rifle, caked like himself with mud, and useless. First on the list!

Another shell arrived with a slamming, earth-shaking roar. A trickling sound came from the rear of the bunker, as soil slid down to the floor. Would this hell never cease? Distant shouts came from outside, whether in English or German, he couldn't tell nor barely cared. A faint light filtered in through the hole leading up to the trench, making the time of day indeterminate. The heavy timbers shoring up the dugout were carved with letters barely discernible as Gothic. So this had once been a German position. Whose now?

His hands encountered something soft, a uniform. Nobby Clarke! Nobby Clarke! It must be! It started to come back! How many hours had it been since they tumbled into this German bunker? How many hours since they faced that murderous enfilade of machine gun fire and exploding 'Toads' to buy these few yards of advance in the mud of the Somme battlefield? Five hundred lives! Just yesterday! Had it been two or three counter-attacks by the 'Alleyman'? God, the blood and carnage! They took the same shell hole three times in an hour to get here. Each time, the hole grew smaller, as the dead heaped higher in it. He spat out a mouthful of mud and grimaced at the gritty texture. To go home! To stop this! He survived the previous day, could he survive another? "Godammit! Get a grip of yourself!" Lately, he had begun to talk to himself.

Nobby was not responding to the shaking he was giving him. Groping between the webbing straps across his chest, he got his numbed hands in a pocket and pulled out his matches. Movement caused the spread of cold up his body like a rising tide, robbing him of body heat, siphoning off his energy. Fumbling with stiffened fingers, he peeled the piece of waterproof oilskin off the box of matches. Fighting to steady himself between shivers, he wrestled a match to the striking patch on the side of the box.

"Bryant and May, give me day!" The match, reluctant at first, finally flared. He held it aloft. With an exclamation, he tried to shake it out. Fickle match! Now it would not go out! Finally, he dropped it. The morass beneath him greedily swallowed the light with a sizzle. It was Nobby Clarke all right but not Nobby Clarke. The corporal's tapes were there but not the head.

Tom retched and gagged. Ten hours since eating and only the foul taste of bile would go halfway towards bringing relief. He started to curse. The sight of his friend brought it all back in brilliant colours. The last, desperate defence of the shell hole, stumbling over the bodies! Jock MacDonald was standing back against the rim, run through by a German bayonet and screaming as he watched his bloodied guts slither through his fingers. A faceless Heinie stood prodding his rifle blindly in every direction until he became too much of a nuisance to someone and was shot down. Teeth and jawbone shattering and spurting blood at him, a face shrank away from his rifle butt as he reversed the weapon, frantically levered a round into the breech and shot a grey-clad infantryman about to throw a grenade into the hole. The 'Toad' exploded under the man, splashing Tom's face with unmentionable wetness.

Turning from Nobby, Tom received a jolt of remembered pain. He took his hand to his shoulder, where he discovered a deep flesh wound. Back in the memory, a wave of grey figures loomed out of the smoke and cordite, then withered to crumpled heaps. His Lee Enfield grew too hot to handle. They were leaping forward themselves, counter-attacking and gaining this stretch of trench, only to lose momentum to exhaustion. Nobby was right behind him. He had just slithered into the dugout, when something had gone between them like a thunderclap. A dud shell, fired at too close range and unarmed probably, but Nobby was in its way! Despite being knocked out, Tom was the lucky one.

He rolled onto his back and looked up at the dim patch of sky. He felt no urge to get away from the hideous mess that had been his friend. There were corpses everywhere. It was an everyday fact of life. For two days at Ypres, he slept on a firing step with a human leg protruding from the trench wall only inches from his head. With their stench constantly on the air, you simply got used to the dead being around. It was the rats he couldn't stand. Well fed on corpses, they grew as huge as jackrabbits and were known to attack helplessly wounded men.

The shouting outside grew louder. He could recognize the hoarse tones of Sergeant-Major Jones. Even through the relief of knowing they still held the trench, he wondered; wasn't there, somewhere, a German bullet or grenade with that bastard's name on it? He hauled himself to his knees, using his rifle as a prop. Reluctantly sucking at him, the mud gave him up. Lurching, he got to his feet, groaning, as his boots attacked his feet. There were so many patches of trench foot on them that the sodden wet leather felt like a school of piranha biting. He had a pull-though and piece of two-by-two somewhere to clean his rifle, but he first must get Nobby's paybook and dog tags. Identify the soldier as dead! Tom found the red dog tag and left the green in the hope a burial detail might find his friend's remains. He was not very hopeful. Groping in Nobby's battledress, he found the paybook and a wallet.

Leaning against the doorpost, he held the wallet to the light. "Mrs. Frederick Clarke, General Delivery, Wetaskiwin, Alberta. We regret to inform you…" Shit! The telegraph company must be making a fortune! A partly faded photograph showed a dark haired woman and three children posed proudly but self-consciously outside a farmhouse door. What would that rather horsy-looking woman and her three little ponies think to receive this photo back from their dead father's body? Would they be able to sense any spirit vibrations left from a pair of sad, dark eyes, perusing them longingly in quieter moments of this living hell?

Shoving the articles deep into his grenade pouch, Tom slithered up the river of mud and disappeared. Sergeant-Major Jones caught him almost immediately. "Edmunds, you lazy little whore's bait! Lyin' down on the job then, are you?"

"No Sar'nt-Major! Corporal Clarke is dead."

Jones was a solid individual with a barrel chest and a beer gut that constantly strained his webbing belt. A purpled potato-nose was mounted crookedly above a Lord Kitchener moustache. He was a good non-comm with a long service record. Tom's news brought a flicker to the keen blue eyes. For a moment, Tom thought he looked to the depths of Jones' tortured soul. The recovery was fast. "Well then! Get your 'orrible little self down about thirty yards! Lieutenant 'iggins is h'arranging a little reception party for the Fritzes wot are showing certain undesirable h'intentions! And clean up your rifle, lad, a squirt of mud when you pull the trigger will only h'encourage the barstards!"

Tom lurched away in the direction of the jerked thumb but was arrested by the booming voice behind him. "Corporal Edmunds!"

"I'm only a Lance-jack, Sar'nt -Major!"

"Not now, you h'ain't, son. Clean up your dirty face and rifle, and let's see what you can do with two tapes on your arm!"

Refusing promotion in the field under fire was tantamount to mutiny. Not wanting to risk a court-martial, Tom hurried away before Jones could promote him to sergeant and put him further at risk.

A rotted plank in the duckboards trapped his foot. He sprawled headlong in the mud. The seeping cold of the water was renewed down his legs. He could feel his boots being refilled as his woollen socks and puttees, not removed for days, soaked up the moisture like eager blotting paper. This bout of trench foot was easily the worst he had ever had. The only cure was to wash and dry his feet frequently, replacing his socks with clean, dry ones. Dry! What a word! A Nirvana in this wilderness, this paradise lost! His only pair of spare socks were in his pack, probably just as wet and useless by now. It was almost as if the Germans, unable to kill him, proposed to pin him down until advanced trench foot would do the job for them.

A troublesome nit attacked his left armpit. Slinging his rifle, he scrubbed furiously through his battledress, the pain of scratching bringing temporary relief from the itching. Angrily, he got to his feet, cursing the war and all responsible for it. Give them one day's experience in the trenches, and for sure, the politicians would soon sue for peace. Being alive was the only, minimal plus in this almost-existence.

As he trudged along, he tried to visualize where they were. He thought they were in the Fabeck trench system, near Courcelette. The firebay part of the trench was completely caved in by shellfire striking the parados. Bits of equipment and human remains protruded everywhere. Tom fervently hoped they would not have to perform the grisly task of digging in here. A pile of equipment atop the parados gave him some cover to look towards the German lines. Over to his right, less than a quarter mile away, was the village of Courcelette. Courcelette! In reality, the 'village' was a clump of shattered, blackened tree stumps, surrounding piles of rubble with occasional ghostly fingers of old chimneys protruding like impromptu tombstones.

The killing had been horrible! The Canadian Twenty-second and Twenty-fifth Battalions carried the village in a bayonet charge, catching the Germans unprepared in the middle of a relief. The carnage was so terrible the commander later wrote: "If Hell is as bad as what I have seen in Courcelette, I would not wish my worst enemy to go there."

No less than eleven counter-attacks were repulsed. Tom saw that the position was *still* unsecured! Courcelette! The name would go down in history as the site of the first ever mechanized tank attack! General Haig, trying to conduct the battle from twelve miles behind the Front at the Château de Valvion, was desperate to achieve some measure of success. In the face of huge losses and small gains, he squandered the great secret of the tank in an ill-advised first engagement. Although their effectiveness was lost in the mud, the tanks demoralized the Germans and helped take Courcelette. Had they been committed on firm ground, these terrible new weapons would have virtually ensured the desired major breakthrough, which the Allies were striving for.

British Prime Minister Lloyd George later said, "And so, the great secret was sold for the battered ruins of a little hamlet – Courcelette!"

Still short of their objectives with over seven thousand casualties in a week, the Canadians found it difficult to move the Germans, except where they willingly retreated to even better defensive positions. The battles at the Somme were even worse than the Ypres Salient. Hundreds of thousands of men were sacrificed in wave after wave of attacks that were ill-planned and ill-starred. It was beginning to emerge as a cold-blooded fight of attrition. The artillery barrages were impressive but impotent. They were generally haphazard in nature. The Germans merely sat them out until it was time to emerge from their deep concrete bunkers and fire lethal hails of machine gun bullets at the hapless attackers. Row upon row, they plunged forward through the mud with desperate faith and blind loyalty, only to be gunned down. Often, the German gunners didn't even have to aim.

Ahead of them were names like Thiepval Ridge, Mouquet Farm, Zollern Graben, Stuff Redoubt, Hessian Trench, and Regina Trench; names to be burned into the memories of Somme veterans. Later, they would be proudly embroidered on battalion colours, to gather dust in church stanchions, noticeable only to the bored eyes of a disinterested churchgoer during a dull sermon.

It was taking four hours for some 'body-snatchers' to get a wounded man to the field dressing stations at Poisières. Too often, they dumped the contents en route and returned for someone not beyond their help. Only yesterday, the wounded situation got so bad that German and British stretcher-bearers worked side-by-side, tending casualties, enemy or friendly, and exchanging hopelessly wounded prisoners. Strongpoints lay yards apart, taken and retaken several times over until the grey and khaki uniforms were piled like strata in some grim geological evidence of the history of ownership. No demarcation line could be drawn between the combatants; they were completely intertwined, almost homogenous to an outside observer.

A stream of bullets suddenly ricocheted off the metal by Tom's head. He allowed himself to slide to the bottom of the trench. A flurry of 'Flying Pigs' came over, and he realized the Germans were getting ready to mount their first attack of the day. He frantically stuck his pull-through cord into the muzzle of his rifle and tying some two-by-two onto it, grabbed the weighted end at the breech and sawed it backwards and forwards to swab the mud out of the barrel. Quickly, he replaced the filthy rag with another dipped in oil from the supply in the butt of the rifle and pulled it through. He glanced quickly through the barrel, and prayed he would not blow his face and hands off with the first round he fired.

A real 'hoo-ha' had now developed. The air rained explosives. Hearing English shouted in the next traverse, he grabbed an ammunition pouch from a dead body and dashed around the corner. A dozen men were crouched readying themselves against the trench wall. Tom jammed rounds into the rifle magazine as fast as he could, bolting the last one into the breech to give him eleven shots. He filled a spare magazine and stuck it in his top pocket, ready at hand. He eased the long Solingen knife he'd lifted from a dead German in its sheath. Slumping sideways, he grabbed his bayonet and attached it to the rifle.

"Block the trench here!" A sergeant from the Princess Pats screamed at him. The din increased and shells began to fall perilously close. Tom knew what he wanted, nodded and grabbed a row of grenades off the firing step. The fighting trenches were not excavated in straight lines. If they were, an attacker could fire from the parapet from end to end, raking them with enfilade fire and killing the defenders. To avoid this, in plan form, the trenches were castellated or zigzagged. The line closest to the enemy was called the firebay. About ten feet back, the more rearward connecting trench was called the traverse.

Because the Canadians had captured this trench, they were defending it facing towards what had been the German rear, so the firebays and traverses were in reverse. The parapets were at the *back* of the trench, the parados at the front. Similarly, the firing steps were now on the wrong side, so the new inhabitants lost some of the advantages of the defences. Because of their limited numbers, the dozen hodgepodges of infantrymen with Tom could only hold a short length of the trench. They would be all right if they were able to stop the Germans from this position. Should the enemy make it into the former firebay trench to their immediate rear, they would become very unwelcome neighbours.

The Colt machine gun mounted on the parados began its rasping, metallic cough of death. The cry, "Here they come!" was superfluous. Three men were detailed to accompany Tom. He moved quickly to the bend in the trench from which he'd arrived and made one man mount the firing step.

"Concentrate on the Fritzes trying to get into the firebay! We'll go around and stop any who get through!" The man nodded and placed a spare clip beside him. Tom and the others ducked around the bend into the corner of the firebay, about twenty feet from where Nobby Clarke lay. Lieutenant Higgins' plan was to sandwich any Germans who got into the trench between his own men and those with Sergeant-Major Jones who were in the adjacent firebay. Tom's task was to forestall German occupation of the trench by being ready to shoot straight down the trench and kill any who might get in. He knew Jones would have men one trench-length away, doing the same thing. Any Germans who survived would be outflanked on both sides when the attack petered out.

"Up there!" One of the men nodded and jumped up in the corner, ready to bolster the efforts of the man around the corner. Tom and the remaining man waited, hand grenades ready. The rattle of small arms fire increased. They could hear spent rounds slapping into the sandbags above them. A 'Flying Pig' exploded in the empty trench, whizzing shrapnel past them, and showering them with dirt.

The man above them suddenly yelled and began to fire as rapidly as he could. Without looking, Tom and his comrade pulled their pins and lobbed their grenades in the direction the private was firing. A light mortar shell exploding just above them followed their twin explosions. Greasy yellow smoke and debris spattered them. Tom felt something metallic ping off his steel helmet, making him glad he had it. He remembered how they had first been issued at 'Wipers.' There were insufficient supplies for everyone. "How come there ain't enough for all?" someone asked. "There will be after you've been in the Salient for a month," came the macabre reply.

Hoarse shouts were heard nearby. Half a dozen grey-uniformed men of the Kaiser dropped into the trench. Tom and the other man pitched more grenades and immediately opened fire, but more figures tumbled from above. Their fire was returned. The man on the firing step grunted and slumped down, shot through the chest.

"Back around the corner!" Desperately, the two men scurried away from the superior number of Germans and lobbed a couple more grenades over into the firebay. A couple of 'Toads' were returned, but they went astray. A courageous but misguided German appeared round the corner. Tom's companion shot him. Two more appeared but were quickly despatched by the ready bayonets of the two Tommies.

A quick glance around into the traverse trench told Tom that too few Germans had made it to resist the hand-to-hand combat taking place. They were in no position to secure prisoners, so none would be taken. He tossed another grenade into the firebay and heard a cheer from the traverse. The German attack began to falter. The other man, Peters, Tom now remembered his name, was wounded in the arm but gamely picked up two more grenades and stood ready, as Tom changed his magazine.

Bolting a round into the breech, Tom took a deep breath and nodded. Peters threw the two grenades as quickly as he could. Tom was around the corner the moment the second exploded. Pulse racing, heart in his mouth, he pointed his rifle down the trench, peering through the shrinking fountains of dirt. There was no resistance. Almost a dozen Germans lay dead and mortally wounded from the close-quarters explosions. There was one doughty soul who sat up suddenly and pointed his Mauser. Ready, Tom got his shot off first, but just as he saw the grey figure jerk, a slamming smash in the left arm threw him back to the trench wall.

The desperate will to live overcame the pain and shock. His right hand threw the rifle over the crook of his bent and screaming left arm, clumsily and frantically working the bolt. Again and again he fired into the grey mass of uniforms sprawled in the trench. He was still working the bolt and pulling the trigger on an empty magazine when Peters and another man came to his aid. He stood, shaking like a leaf in a strong wind, understanding the shock, the reaction, understanding not the pain-shock but the killing-shock, the raw horror of kill-or-be-killed.

The German attack had failed. With a sentry posted, Tom was helped back to the traverse, waves of pain and nausea washing over him. Fortunately, cutting open his battledress sleeve revealed only a deep flesh wound in his upper arm. The bone was not broken. One of the men bound it tightly for him. He began to feel a little better. With sighs of relief, the men in the traverse fell back to rest, glad to be alive. The traverse was pronounced secure and further sentries were posted. Four men were killed and seven wounded in the encounter. Tending their wounds and fatigue, the soldiers lit up their cherished Woodbines and slumped to the bottom of the trench, which for once was dry.

It was a close call. Cautiously peering over the parados, Tom could see dead enemy soldiers only a foot from the edge. Here and there, further away, he could see slight movement from some of the wounded that were unable to crawl back to their own lines. Unless a well-marked body-snatching crew came along, such men were invariably doomed. Tom found himself selfishly hoping they would soon die, not from compassion, but to save the anguish the wounded often caused. They cried out in the darkness of the night, imploring aid. To shoot a man was one thing, to have to listen to him die for hours afterward was almost unbearable, barbaric. Critically injured, in shock, and exposed to the cold and wet, many would become victims of the mud today. Standing orders forbade rescue attempts. Not only could such good Samaritans get themselves shot, but their mere presence in No-Man's Land might well start an artillery exchange and kill hundreds more. One of the great ironies was that such an event might advance the enemy's cause, making the initially wounded soldier's sacrifice worthless.

Dropping back, Tom watched as the dead were removed. The fighting area was made ready to withstand the next attack. Don Meadows of "A" Company nearly had his arm torn off by a mortar fragment and was heavily bandaged. Conscious and cheerful over his mates' assurances, he had certainly 'copped a Blighty one.' The continually spreading stain on the bandages boded ill for his chances, however. A ragged volley of rifle fire slapped into the upper sandbags, reminding them that evacuation was impossible.

The haggard, filthy faces around him made Tom realize they were almost finished. This trench was going to be 'here or never' for all of them. Five days in this meat grinder was just too long. Military formation had long since been lost. He counted seven different battalion patches amongst the men. Lieutenant Higgins stood to the side, anxiously discussing the critical state of their ammunition supplies with the 'Pat's' sergeant. With no supplies or relief, they would find their position untenable at the first strong German sally.

"Standby, coming in!" Sergeant-Major Jones' voice rang out. He appeared around the corner, accompanied by six men. Imperturbably, he snapped a parade-ground salute at Higgins and cast a professional eye over the scene. "Word from above, Sah, they plan to 'old us 'ere today, and the word is that the Fourth Division will relieve us after nightfall."

A muted cheer went up at the news. The end was in sight!

"Thank God!" Higgins' dirty face grinned at the news. "Any of you men got the means of a brew to celebrate?"

"Right here, Sir, if someone will get the water." Tom levered himself to his feet. The army did not supply spirit stoves, but they were essential for brewing the soldiers' cuppa. Usually, they clubbed together and bought one between them, forming little 'tea societies.' It just happened to be his turn to carry the stove.

"Good, good! I think we could all use some right now. Sarn't-Major!" Higgins turned aside to discuss some matter with Jones.

Tom's arm hurt like hell, but he was glad to be doing something to keep busy. Although over the initial shock of being hit, he didn't want to think right now. He remembered a book about the Vikings which had described a 'beserker,' the almost insane out-of-mind killing urge in battle. It seemed he had been there. To the veterans, it was obvious the Germans might have spent the last of their available reserves. They should get a brief respite, maybe until they got out of here. Now, with watchful sentries posted, they settled down to a bull session.

"What's the first thing you're gonna do when you get home, Chalky?"

"Fuck myself daft, lad or rather back to sense again, I must have been crazy to volunteer for this lot!"

"What are you gonna do second?"

"Put my kitbag down and close the front door!" Chalky White eyed the tatterdemalion group surrounding him, pausing with the hung timing of the natural comedian. "Later, I'll buy a house with a big yard, and when my 'fornifications' have born natural fruit, on the little bleeder's fifth birthday, I shall take him into the garden and make him dig a hell-hole like this, flood it, and make him sit in it for an hour each day, so he knows not to volunteer like his old man did!"

Tom thought it a splendid parody of this 'war-to-end-all-wars.' Somehow, this muddy-sided trench was not the glamorous notion they all had entertained when they'd signed up to fight the Kaiser.

"Maybe you should dig the hole in the local cemetery, Chalky. Add some realism!" Jack Wilson jerked his thumb at some dead limbs protruding from the caved-in trench.

"Aye, and maybe you could give him some of this piss-water to drink too! Oh! Sorry Tom, no offence!" Peters grinned at Tom, still brewing tea one-handed and in limited quantities.

Peters' reference to the tea was not a criticism of Tom's brewing ability, more a comment on the source of the water. The only fresh water available to troops in the Line was transported in old petrol cans, which tainted the water horribly. Here, right in the Front, no such luxury was available. They usually scooped their water from the nearest shell hole. Since these invariably contained: mud, rusted equipment, gas residues, chemicals from high explosives, not to mention excrement, it was not too palatable, or healthy. Nobody cared to dwell on how many corpses might be lurking, rotting beneath the scummy yellow surface.

To combat disease, contagion, whatever, Tom was careful to see the water was thoroughly boiled before skimming off the top scum. He then added the prescribed quantity of chloride of lime provided by the army. Defying the King's regulations, the lime did not sink obligingly to the bottom of the liquid, but rather hung suspended, adding its own noxious personality to the brew. Not to be outdone by nature's despoliation of the water, the army added a further torment for its tea connoisseurs. Tea and sugar were 'conveniently' packaged, ready-mixed together, so anyone shunning sugar in his cuppa was out of luck. The tea, nonetheless, was enjoyed as the first hot thing any of them had taken in days. They were used to making do with cold food, but a nice warm drink really hit the spot.

Sometimes, as a desperate measure, they had been known to crush the packets of rock-like hardtack biscuits and stuff them into an empty sandbag with handfuls of sultanas. Boiled for a couple of hours, this mess produced a kind of pudding, which was hacked up into slices and distributed, bag and all, amongst eager, starving recipients.

"Who's got a Woodbine, then?" A packet was produced and the singly voiced request grew a half-dozen hands, decimating the remains.

"My last bloody ones, you bunch of thieves!" A blue haze began to fill the trench from the lighted cigarettes. Dick Turner went and relieved one of the sentries.

"How much longer you reckon we're gonna be here?"

"Until Kaiser Bill personally strolls over and offers his surrender, son."

"Very funny, you stupid bastard!"

"Jesus Christ!"

"First thing I'm going to do when I get out of here?" Alf Barnes interrupted, and in the silence, he looked them all over. "First thing I'm going to do is get down from the train in Edmonton and kiss the ground. And, if I don't make it, I expect whoever does to do it for me!"

The pact was sealed by a long and thoughtful silence as they all thought of that new city out on the prairies. They were remembering that less than half the original volunteers were still surviving in the Forty-ninth. Many were dead, more were wounded and the others' fates unknown. None of them would have been surprised to learn that history would never be able to accurately detail the casualty figures here at the Somme. Several of those present wore the little gold arm stripe signifying the wounds they received were not serious enough to qualify them for a medical discharge.

"Did you hear John Kerr is up for the V.C. for tackling that machine gun the other day?"

"Yeah, if his mom had only had twenty kids like him, the rest of us could all go home!"

"First thing I'm gonna do?" Chalky had obviously done some re-thinking. "Very first thing I'm gonna do is borrow a field gun and shoot down the bloody Virgin!" The Virgin! They had all forgotten her! High atop the church of Notre Dame de Brebières, the Hanging Virgin figure was seen by all formations of troops moving up to the Front through the town of Albert. Damaged by shellfire, she listed at a precarious angle. Legend was that when she toppled, the army holding the town would win the war. Fate was held in check by a party of Canadian engineers who had cabled the statue securely to the steeple.

Tom finished brewing the tea and turned out the stove. Leaning back, he then took a sip from his mug. Reaching into his pocket, he pulled out the now dog-eared little book of Shakespeare that Jeanne gave him before he left Edmonton. King Lear, Act Five, Scene Three, seemed anticlimactic after the past couple of hours.

The Forty-ninth was relieved as promised later that evening. They originally moved up through positions occupied by their fellow Seventh Brigadiers, the Forty-second Battalion. Events of the past few days cemented a relationship between the two. Henceforth, they both knew they could trust and respect each other. Neither would have to look to their flank in battle. They were in the Somme for a full week, in combat at close quarters for an eternally long two days. Five officers were killed, twelve wounded. Thirty-eight other ranks were dead, nineteen missing, and one hundred and seventy-seven, besides Tom, were wounded. They had taken about one hundred and forty five prisoners of war. Communications with the rear were nonexistent for the past twenty-four hours. Only heroics removed those desperately wounded who survived the battlefield.

Classified as walking wounded, Tom stayed with Alex MacFarlane and the rest until they reached the rear echelons. Amidst expressions of regret that he had not sustained 'a Blighty one,' his comrades took leave of him near a field hospital. They could not know it, but before he returned to active duty in the New Year, the Forty-ninth would return to try and take the Regina and Kenora trenches near Courcelette. It was a disaster. Many of the men who wished him farewell on the seventeenth had but weeks to live. Forty more were killed, one hundred and eighty wounded, and sixty went missing.

By late fall, these engagements of attrition, henceforth known as the nineteen sixteen Battles of the Somme, were terminated. Well over a million men were engaged in the bloody process. During the few months of their involvement, the Canadians had advanced four thousand yards on a three thousand-yard front, enduring two thousand four hundred casualties. This equated to one casualty expended for each five hundred square yards of mud and devastation. Twenty-four thousand people spread evenly over an equivalent area of four sections of Canadian prairie would be only sixty-three feet equidistant from the next person. That was the price, in human loss, of this pathetic mud.

This specific series of frontal assaults gave birth to the infantry dog tags, a mute acknowledgment of casualty accounting in modern warfare. The steel helmet was born. Not long after, during a parliamentary debate, David Lloyd George rose to speak at Westminster. *"No amount of circumspection can prevent war leading to the death of multitudes of brave men, but now the generals are not partaking in the personal hazards of a fight. They ought to take greater personal risks in satisfying themselves as to the feasibility of their plans, as to whether the objectives they wish to attain are worth the sacrifice entailed, and whether there is no better way of achieving the same result at less cost of gallant lives."*

The terrible, unrewarded slaughter of the Somme was finally recognized. At one and the same time, this speech was a thinly veiled criticism of the General Staff's handling of the Somme offensive, while warning future military leaders of their obligations to the House, the Nation, and the Empire.

FOUR

LADY LUCK ON VIMY RIDGE

"Gentlemen, it's Vimy Ridge." The dapper figure of Lieutenant General the Honourable Sir Julian Byng, Commander of the Canadian Corps, studied the men before him. Behind his straight nose and full moustache, the full-faced General Lipsett of the Third Division remained impassive, like his fellow divisional commanders. Only Arthur Currie of the First, touted as Byng's eventual successor, stirred in his chair. With their adjutants, operations officers and other aides, the Canadian staff met at Lille to find out their next objective in the war.

"This assault will be carried out by a purely Canadian force, namely us." Again, Sir Julian paused to gauge a reaction, smiling as if he were the bearer of good news. This time, he had the satisfaction of seeing them all stir and exchange looks. "Not being Canadian myself, and strictly between ourselves, I see this as a political decision, prompted by recent high level consultations." Byng deliberately played down the true nature of the firm protest Robert Borden, Prime Minister of Canada, made to the British.

Black-edged casualty lists had descended across Canada like some grim blizzard. Posted on prominent public buildings, the long bulletins hovered like buzzards over the fate of departed soldiers. For the first time, a public awareness of the internecine nature of the conflict occurred. A groundswell of protest followed. Borden was forced to question the British government about the conduct of the war. Arrogantly told to mind his own business, Borden threatened to withdraw Canadian troops. In response, he won some command autonomy for his soldiers.

The macabre loss of life on the Somme came home to roost. Rising pressure in Britain also prompted the search for a better way of defeating the Germans without such high human losses. A cynic might have said the British had merely made a bureaucratic decision, whereby they appeared to give way to the Canadian demand, while absolving themselves of any future accusation of squandering Commonwealth lives. At the same time, they were bolstering nationalistic pride in the Dominions, by letting them accept the full responsibility of undertaking whole segments of an action.

In future, any failures would be directed at national, instead of imperial commanders. That also may be said to let the British off the hook.

Now, looking at the men before him, Byng was certain they were all fully cognizant of the responsibility they were facing. Their only salvation was to win. He could read both satisfaction and apprehension in the eyes of those before him, and he was satisfied in turn at the reaction. All the officers present knew that a cover-up had prevented any enquiries from causing the gravest public revolt against the terrible losses on the Somme.

"Gentlemen," Byng called them from their reveries. "This move is designed to ensure the Canadian Corps gets a chance to prove it can do its stuff or be caught lacking! Now, for some preliminary background! Since nineteen fourteen, the Germans have held Vimy Ridge. The British and French armies have expended almost two hundred thousand men against this highly important strategic point. I believe that over seventy thousand failed to return. The name 'Cavalry Rouge' was given to our friends in the excavating business that are constantly digging up the still-occupied red trousers the French wore in their attacks in the first year. I am not mentioning this horrid aspect to provide a negative or depressing note, now that it is our turn, but rather to underline to you all that I do not propose a similar fate for us. In light of our now abundant experience, this operation will be planned and executed properly."

All minds present digressed back to the Somme, where supplies had been stockpiled to support the assault of three-quarters of a million men, during daylight hours, right under the noses of the Germans, for a long period of time. General Haig may as well have personally briefed the German General Falkenburg on his battle orders.

"I have in mind two main aspects to the plan, which I believe will give us an edge no previous assault has enjoyed. First, we will achieve the complete subjugation of the German defensive front, including trench and communication networks, by artillery fire. General Morrison's artillery will comprise nearly four hundred heavy and over seven hundred medium calibre pieces and over eighty thousand tons of ammunition. These will be exclusive to Canadian operations. Saturation bombardment will commence seven days before the attack goes home with the intent of complete disruption of their supply lines. Nothing, nothing must get through!" Sir Julian smacked his fist into his palm for emphasis. "Nothing!

"Accuracy of fire and observation will be assisted by night ground reconnaissance and aerial photography that the Royal Flying Corps has promised. The latter will be of particular value to our intelligence in determining the effectiveness of our artillery on the other side of Vimy Ridge. At the time of assault, a rolling, progressive barrage will be utilized behind the protection of which our men will advance. Bunkered enemy troops must not be allowed time to mount an effective defence once the barrage is past. Our men must be well-trained, indeed, thoroughly-trained, to stay close to the barrage and be about the Germans' ears the moment they try to emerge.

"The second aspect I wish tended to is the complete briefing of every man involved. I do not mean every lieutenant or every sergeant or corporal, I mean every last *private* is to know *exactly* what is expected of him."

This time, Byng got a general stir in his audience. He knew this was what they were waiting for. An observer of these modern, set-piece battles would note that the grand plan devolved into a general melee in which shell-shocked, exhausted, and disoriented men performed actions little-related to the objective thrust intended. Without the 'feel' of a battle being available to them, generals committed their men and awaited the outcome. To commit them without proper briefing, as had been the practice, was gross mismanagement, especially to the minds of the self-sufficient Canadians.

Byng continued. "I have given orders for a complete model of Vimy to be laid out between Estrée Cauchée and Les Quatre Vents. This model is to be constructed from aerial photographs. This will also provide basis for amendment to the model, as time goes by. Divisions, by rotation, will train there vigorously until everyone knows his part and can perform it under any condition.

"Orders will be drawn up and distributed in a couple of days. Broadly, I anticipate an assault by all four divisions, each utilizing two brigades, with one in reserve. Troops will move into holding areas on April eighth. Most of the assembly points will be in extensive tunnels and underground caverns presently being completed at my orders. This is being done to keep cohesiveness to all elements right to the forward areas. There will be no disorganization from either the weather or possible German barrages. The men will be launched fresh and ready, from the immediate advance areas.

"Gentlemen, at dawn on April ninth, the Canadian Corps will carry Vimy Ridge with a well-organized, well-executed, and irresistible assault! Divisional staff will meet here tomorrow at ten to discuss other details and file each unit's status. Thank you, gentlemen!"

At this, the massive wheels of planning were placed in gear. The logistical considerations were staggering. The organization and deployment of hundreds of thousands of men, horses, trucks, and railroad movements, ammunition, guns, food, water, field dressing stations had to be determined and fitted together. For every man who would appear at the Front, more than three others had to labour to equip, move, and supply his needs and replacements. Telephones, boots, and the new 'bangalore torpedoes' (long pipes stuffed with explosive to tear large gaps in the barbed wire defences) had to be shipped, positioned, and made ready. Roads, light railway systems, and four miles of tunnels had to be engineered and constructed. Easily cut through the chalk beneath the surface, the tunnels provided shellproof routes to the frontal areas, where the men could remain under cover until they jumped off.

Food and hundreds of other diverse items were stockpiled. Even items most insignificant, yet vital to combat troops were tended to. As the word came down through planning stages, the Canadians discovered the closer details of their task. The broad frontal attack would stretch from 'The Pimple' in the north, to 'Farbus Wood' in the south. Their role was only part of a major Easter offensive. British units on both sides would flank them. The Fourth Division would be at the north end, advancing on 'The Pimple' and 'Hill One Forty-five,' two German strongpoints.

Third Division would be to their immediate south, delegated 'Bois de la Folie.' Second and First Divisions were at the south end. Although their task seemed easier with less strong points and a gentler slope, they had to advance the most distance, almost three thousand yards to attain the crest of the Ridge. Under Field Marching Orders, the Seventh Brigade would be one of the two committed by Third Division. The Forty-second Battalion would be on the left with the Princess Patricia Canadian Light Infantry in the middle and the Royal Canadian Regiment on the right. The Forty-ninth Battalion was assigned a 'mop-up' role. This was not as easy as it sounded, as with the rolling barrage, advancing troops had to keep close behind it, leaving the possibility of safely bunkered Germans popping up in their rear. Since they could not spend time neutralizing such pockets of resistance, the task devolved onto the 'Mop-Up' Battalion. The Edmontonians had a vital and possibly dirty job.

Reinforcements, stretcher parties, communications, and supplies would be included in their tasks. In addition to the usual four companies, the battalion added a headquarters company. Lieutenant Colonel Palmer, Major Weaver, Captain Chattell, and Lieutenant Nolan, with forty-six other ranks, would direct the efforts of the Forty-ninth from the rear. One of their fears was they could be called forward to reinforce a situation already gone badly or to counter-attack any German retaliation.

Corporal Tom Edmunds, sporting a gold 'wounded' stripe, was assigned to Headquarters Company as a 'duckboard runner.' Being a runner was an unenviable task in some ways. They were favoured targets for snipers. The need to move rapidly from command posts to field posts with vital orders came secondary to personal safety. The bobbing head of a runner traversing from one point to another, contrary to the general flow of an assault force's movements, betrayed him to an experienced sniper. For the same reason, only experienced men were utilized – those who knew their way around. Becoming a casualty to an alert sniper ensured a runner's message did not get through and might easily turn the tide of a battle. To combat this eventuality, two were normally despatched, each with a numbered, written message. They travelled at intervals to avoid simultaneous casualties and were required to thoroughly memorize maps of the battlefield – a further need for experience. All units were under standing orders to relieve any incapacitated runner of his message pouch and forward it with another man. Due to the importance of their task, runners could not be counter-ordered to execute any other task, including helping the wounded.

For weeks, the Canadians laboured with the rehearsals for the action. As General Byng dictated, a model was laid out near Quatre Vents. Officers on horseback moved forward on each flank, simulating the imaginary line of the rolling barrage. They trained until they knew everything thoroughly, then went back and did it over again. Byng himself was frequently at the scene, observing their proficiency. Occasionally, seeing some anomaly, he would group the soldiers around him and use his swagger stick to scratch diagrams in the dirt. This personal touch did a lot to endear him to the common infantryman.

At Vimy Ridge, the sub-surface chalk enabled the trend of burrowing to reach new frontiers of development. Locked head-to-head and immovable, the opposing armies, unable to flank left or right, reverted to the ancient art of tunnelling under the enemy's defences. As the Forty-ninth had learned in occupying 'Wipers Salient,' sappers on both sides determinedly undermined each other's excavations and set off massive explosive charges beneath them.

In the Flanders mud, this was extremely hazardous, but the chalk at Vimy was easily worked and resistant to subsidence and cave-ins. Even before the Canadians' arrival, British sappers won the underground battle and freely constructed tunnels, some of which actually emerged in No Man's Land. Since October nineteen sixteen, the Canadians improved on these subterranean endeavours. Grange Tunnel, for instance, was seven hundred and fifty yards long and lay twenty-five feet below ground. Numerous side galleries extended off, comprising stores, hospital facilities, water reservoirs, and command posts. The Seventh Brigade worked diligently on it for months. The infantry, as a result, were better heeled than their cousins, the gunners, who lived in terrible squalor and semi-starvation.

One company of artillery was dug-in in the Neuville Ste. Vlast cemetery. Corpses protruded through the walls of the gun emplacements. The men hung their helmets and equipment on ready pegs provided by thighbones. One pit had the head of an internee with long blonde tresses. The men stroked it as a mascot as they went about their tasks. This grisly humour was their only morale builder. The winter had been terribly harsh, alternating between deep-freeze and melt. While the cold was unwelcome, the warmer periods brought the stench of the dead on the breezes. The quarters were rat-infested and supplies difficult to deliver. Often, a tin of bully beef and a frozen loaf, cut with a wood saw, served ten men for a daily ration. Snowmelt provided water to try and soften the hated Huntley and Palmer Number Four biscuits.

The overall picture, the impending assault on the German lines, was influenced by several factors. The main attack was planned southeast of the Canadians, through Arras and the Scarpe Valley. Imperilled by the course of the war and the need to also fight the Russians, the German morale sapped to the point where surrender was a popular option for their infantrymen when pressured sufficiently. To counter this, better defensive positions were constructed behind the old ones. A measured withdrawal was accomplished in the early part of the year. The area between the new Hindenberg Line and the old positions was then totally devastated to impede the Allies' progress.

The German plan was well monitored by the Royal Flying Corps, whose pilots suffered grievous losses, while lumbering around over the lines in defenceless biplanes at the mercy of such German aces as Baron Manfred Von Richtofen. In trying to take immediate advantage of the withdrawal, the Allied generals discovered, to their dismay, that after such a long trench-bound stalemate, their troops were unable to sustain a rapid advance. Nor had they learned to hold in reserve units trained and equipped to exploit any breakthrough and flood any opening the Germans might yield. The well-planned and executed ambushes by the Germans returned the General Staff's thinking to siege mentality.

The Canadian task of taking Vimy Ridge was thus a minor part of the whole plan. No 'Masse de Manoeuvre,' the means of exploiting success, was arranged; the conditioned thinking was that Vimy Ridge was impregnable. Yet now, the preparations, the dispositions, were complete. Tomorrow, the expenditures of planning would be reduced to individual acts of heroism and death. The hush of expectancy settled over the continuing shellfire, hanging like a cloak over each individual as he felt his mortality and gauged his chances of survival on the morrow. Personal equipment was cleaned and checked. Rounds were inspected, polished, and magazined. Bayonets were sharpened, and straps adjusted on packs. Food and water bottles were packaged, boots dubbined, and puttees adjusted. The men completed their checks on April eighth. Everywhere, a feeling of being ready, of being adequately prepared, suffused everyone. Letters were written to mothers, wives, and sweethearts, each with a suppressed knowledge that it may be a man's last communication with loved ones.

The night was silvery. The long columns of men swung down the road from Neuville Ste. Vlast. A low, frosty moon illuminated the land. Films of ice shone on the water in nearby shell holes. It seemed like a good omen for the morrow.

The western slopes of Vimy Ridge were turned to a moonscape in the previous three years by German shelling. With their long tenancy, and success in repelling other assaults, the Germans seemed remarkably quiet

– perhaps over-confident. Overhead, shells moaned through the sky, keeping up General Byng's bombardment that commenced two weeks previously. The troops could not know it for sure, but true havoc had been wreaked in the German rear lines. Over forty thousand tons of shells were stockpiled since January to pour on the Germans occupying Vimy Ridge and its support positions. More ammunition came forward each day with the well-oiled system. Within a few hours, the play of field guns would increase, as the rolling assault barrage commenced. Stage one had been effected.

Although confidence was in the air, older hands were apprehensive as to whether the amount of shelling would really prove to their advantage. Too often, they followed pulverizing barrages of heavy guns, which nothing should have survived, yet determined Germans still came out of their burrows and killed many a friend. Still, the slightly frozen ground would enable them to advance a little easier in the morning.

A soft whisper of marching feet seemed to come from all around. Thousands of men moved up, a swelling movement of might, assembling in the night, ready to strike at dawn. Breaking step, the men disappeared, rank-by-rank, down into Grange Tunnel and a dozen other such assembly points. Within minutes, they were gone like ghosts into the ground. A piece of coloured marker tape attached to a signpost stirred in a new, slight breeze. High in the sky to the west, a moonlit and silver-edged rampart of cloud began to swallow the stars. A blustery frontal system was moving in wetly from the Atlantic and before first light, the weather was destined to change.

The Early Hours. Easter Monday. April 9, 1917.

The waiting, the worst time, was upon them. Snug in Grange Tunnel, the men handled it in various ways. The air was thick with tobacco smoke and a fug of wet clothing, body smells, mineral oil, leather, and latrines permeated everything. As it was a Sunday, padres of various denominations moved amongst the men, holding impromptu services and hearing confessions. Some rechecked weapons. The click and scrape of rifle bolts came from everywhere. The perennial card games were in evidence. Some hardy souls even slept.

Tom slipped away from Headquarters Company for a while and sought out Alex McFarlane. They found a place near a ventilation shaft, and with their packs for pillows, sat with their feet up on the rails of the light railway track that ran through the tunnel.

"Well, Tom. What do ye think?"

"It looks well organized this time, Alex. We may just carry it off."

"Aye, the only problem, laddie, will be keeping up with the rolling barrage. If the Fritzes pop up before we are on their positions, it could be a long day. Still, ye'll no be having that problem, eh?"

Tom was grateful for his friend's subtle way of eliciting his personal fears about being a duckboard runner. They discovered months before that a fear discussed became less a problem than one unvoiced and festering inside.

"Yes, but I don't favour all that running around I'll have to do."

"Maybe the phones will stay intact and save that."

"Do they ever?" They both fell silent for a second. After their long experience in the army, they both knew Murphy's Law often prevailed; the Germans were its willing helper.

MacFarlane took out the short-stemmed briar he favoured and filled it with shag, cut off a plug from his pocket. Watching him light it, Tom hoped his friend would make it through. Alex was a constant source of quiet strength and reassurance to him. In their many long chats, Tom grew to deeply respect and care for this perceptively intelligent man.

"Are you still going to finish your law degree when you get back to Alberta?" Talk of the future was always a bolster at such times as this.

"Aye, business law, I think. Criminal law is the obvious public image of a lawyer, yet business is growing faster than crime right now. There will be good opportunities after the war for a good business lawyer." The remark was shrewd. Newspapers from back home voiced the growth of the Alberta economy, and many more settlers would be arriving after the war ended.

"Maybe I can retain you then?"

Alex smiled. "Ye still determined to start the transportation business?"

"Sure, look at the experience I picked up here when we were supply troops! Railways, the new motor trucks, the coming modes of transportation, and the army gave me a free course in how to handle the logistics of moving materials. Back home, the demand for the shipping of grain, beef, and farm materials will grow, and I will be one of the few people with the expertise to do it."

"There certainly seems to be an opportunity there."

"Would you care to invest some of your high legal fees?"

"Heh! It will be a long time before I will be accused of being rich!"

"That's just your canny, skinflint Scottish ancestry showing!"

MacFarlane laughed. "Maybe I'll just ride to riches on the back of my millionaire transportation friend, getting his ass out of legal tangles."

"You've got a deal, counsellor!" They grinned and shook hands on the joking prospect.

"What about that woman you have back there?"

"Jeanne? Well, that is a matter I look forward to pursuing when I get back!"

"Aye, but there was never a woman born who did not want a house with pots and pans in the kitchen. Where is all the money to come from?"

"Love will find a way!"

As the time ground around to three in the morning, a sergeant began to make the rounds. "She's cold outside, boys. The wind is up and blowing sleet in the face of the Fritzes." The news was welcomed. Partially frozen ground would be easier to negotiate than the mud, and with the weather in their faces, the Germans would be handicapped.

At three-thirty, bread and meat were distributed, followed by the traditional tots of rum. The 'Lone Stars' grouped their platoons and delivered last minute instructions. Short exhortations and morale-building speeches went up and down the ranks. Every officer became a Henry Fifth at Agincourt. Tom shook hands silently with Alex and made his way back to Headquarters Company.

At four-thirty, the men were moved up to the final assault positions. Precisely at five, a growing rumble came down the tunnel. The earth began to shake. The Allied *Hate* began as hundreds of field guns and mortars came into play. Already saturated with artillery fire, the German front, communication and rear-support trenches, were subjected to a horrendous rain of high explosives. The whistles blew. The men rose and went out into the open and formed up. For better or worse, the battle for Vimy Ridge had commenced.

Vimy Ridge, 8:55 a.m.

"Well done, Edmunds! Have a cup of tea there in the corner and I'll have another job for you in a minute." Lieutenant Harry Nolan, Alberta Rhodes Scholar, waved across the bunker and disappeared into an adjacent space in the bunker off the sally port of Grange Tunnel.

Crossing the floor, Tom slumped onto a crude wooden seat and grabbed a tin mug from a table. A pot of black, stewed tea simmered on a spirit stove. He poured himself a cup. It tasted great. The sight of the stove caused him to wonder how the one he had carried for so long was faring. Chalky White had now carried it safely through a couple of engagements. The time was nine a.m. Good signs of the battle had already come in. Tom just returned with verification that the Seventh Brigade, with the Forty-ninth now deeply involved, reached its first Black Line objective twenty minutes ago. They were right on schedule and doing better than anyone ever had before. He took another pull at the mug, savouring the warmth of the strong liquid in his stomach. It was cold and miserable outside. His body was wet from the waist down. His boots were already biting him through the coarse woollen socks. His puttees were caked with mud.

Telephones rang incessantly in the bunker. Aides bustled to and fro as Lieutenant Colonel Palmer kept pace with the news and issued necessary orders. Most of the other divisions were making good progress. Only the Fourth was held up in subjugating Hill One Hundred Forty-five and The Pimple. These two strongpoints were proving more difficult than expected – too much of a hornet's nest to merely bypass and mop up later, as had been the plan. A small cheer went up as First and Second Divisions' positions were advanced on the map to Red Line objectives. It now appeared that at least the southern half of the Ridge would fall to the Canadians.

A sudden bustle arose around Palmer's door and Captain Chattel strode out with some message forms in hand. "Where are the runners?"

"Here Sir!" Tom and a man wearing the shoulder flash of the Forty-second stood to attention.

"Very well, here is a vital message for Forty-second Battalion Headquarters. They should be..." Chattel's finger circled and then stabbed down on the map. "Right here at this trench and shell hole. I'll tell you quickly what it's all about, in case you have to pass it verbally. The Germans are proving a problem at Hill One Forty-five and The Pimple. We are afraid they may be able to enfilade the crest of the Ridge and launch a counter-attack from there. They have to be stopped. For now, Forty-second is to provide a flank defence from the furthest point of advance, that is, Bois de Folie, back to Black Line. This is to thwart any German attempt at counter-attack. Four Lewis guns are on their way to reinforce. We expect a white rocket when these orders are received and implemented. Do you both have that?" The two men nodded. Chattel paused and eyed them both hard. "This is absolutely vital! Any sortie by the Germans without this counter in place could lose the whole battle for us!"

The proffered messages were tucked safely into message pouches attached to their webbing. Since they would have to travel much the same route, they staggered their departures, the man from the Forty-second going first.

Outside, the weather had not improved. The wind was blustery and drove sheets of wet snow and rain across the landscape. The noise from exploding shells had receded slightly, now that the barrage crept almost to the crest of the Ridge. Pockets of men were spread all over the rising ground ahead. Some were resting, or guarding groups of prisoners, while others tried to root out the more determined pockets of German Resistance. Many were involved in extracting the wounded from where they had fallen. German infantry rocket signals were still bursting over the high ground. The enemy frantically tried to call down artillery fire on the Canadians, but by now, the massed guns of the Canadians had them beaten. Only a few desultory shells were coming over. They had no ranging information. Dust and smoke added to the snow to block Tom's view of how General Currie's men were doing to the south.

Keeping his head low, Tom set off along the communication trench, turning right after about fifty yards. This took him towards the Ridge. The bottom of the trench began to slope upwards. Due to a curve in the Front, he would have to go a little closer than he would have liked to Hill One Forty-five, but it could not be helped. At least the trench covered him better than being out in the open. He knew the consequences of that route. Just as he was about to turn the next bend, he heard the dull thump of a German mortar explode ahead. Reaching the point of impact a minute later, he found a bloody shambles. A group of the Forty-ninth stretcher-bearers were caught trying to pass an ammunition mule and spotting the melee, the Germans had loosed a round on them with deadly accuracy.

The mule lay split open like a side of beef, its insides splashed over the trench wall in a tide of red and white. Around it, a dozen men suffered varying wounds. Some of the dead were on stretchers; wounded men escaped the field with 'Blighty ones,' only to be caught here and killed. Three of the men carrying them were dying, horribly mutilated, and beyond help. Boot prints in the trench floor filled with blood. A man nursing a shredded arm, one of the stretcher men, clutched at Tom and screamed for help. "Duckboard Runner!" He screamed back, shrugging the man's hand from his arm.

He heard another curse him as he stepped over the dead, biting through his lower lip with intensity. He slipped and stumbled and suddenly saw a familiar object. It was a despatch case like his own. Stooping, he grabbed it from the ground and opened it, dreading, and reading at the same time, the same message he carried. He quickly glanced around. Somewhere here was the runner from the Forty-second who set out before him. It was hopeless. He had a sobering moment's thought that it could easily have been him if he left first. There was nobody here to take over the duty, so Tom stuffed the extra pouch in his webbing and continued on his way. He was conscious now that he alone had the message that must get through. If he failed to make it, many more Canadians would die, just like the ones he had just passed. He shuddered to think of the carnage if the two armies wound up sharing the Ridge at close quarters.

Reaching what was the most forward of the trench system, Tom climbed onto a firing step and peered cautiously out from between two sandbags. The only movement he could see for the next fifty yards were several wounded men trying to crawl back to the safety of their own trenches. Some of them had been out there for hours, cold, in pain, and desperate. He shut the thought from his mind and checked the terrain again.

Due to the lay of the land, his next piece of progress would almost be right under the noses of the Germans on Hill One Hundred Forty-five. He could crawl over the intervening space, but he would be heading the wrong way to be mistaken for a casualty and thus make himself a prime target. Running was no better, but it was quicker and seemed to be the only way. He carefully plotted a series of shell holes proceeding in a diagonal towards the east. After about the fifth one, a fold in the ground would afford him cover from direct observation and fire. Taking a few deep breaths, Tom hauled himself over the parapet. Moving in a series of mud-sucking leaps and stumbles, he tumbled headlong into the first shell hole.

So far, so good! Trouble was, if they'd spotted him, they'd be trained on the hole and waiting for him now! Another deep breath and he was over the slippery edge of the hole. He scrabbled madly, found a footing, and then crouching low, scuttled into the next depression. His precipitant arrival was arrested by a tangle of rusted wire and two feet of scummy, icy water. Drenched to the skin and gasping, he cursed himself free of the wire. It tore at his clothing and lacerated his arms and legs. He slithered to the edge of the crater and got to his knees. And that is when the sniper hit him.

He heard nothing, saw nothing, only a kick in the chest like a mule that flung him back into the shell hole. A searing, burning pain spread across his chest. He felt himself go numb. A picket pole stopped his slide to the water. It was only when he reached out to grasp it that he realized he was not dead. Reaching into his battledress, he found the wound where the bullet had skated across his ribs from left to right. Fumbling in his left breast pocket, he found Jeanne's 'Pocket Edition of Shakespeare.' From spine to edge and angled halfway through the pages was a deep furrow. The round struck the book first and was partially deflected. Had it struck him one more inch to the left, it would have gone behind the book and through his heart. He shuddered and felt a cold wave of shock run through him both with the simultaneous realization and his body's reaction to the gross abuse.

Rolling over, he grimaced at the pain but bit deep into his already bloodied lip, determined to move on to the Forty-second command post. He was the only runner with the vital information. A Maxim heavy machinegun opened up over to his left. Trusting the Germans were otherwise occupied, he darted back to level ground. The lurching through the mud aggravated the pain intolerably as his chest heaved and twisted. It felt like a burning iron was searing the torn flesh. He was sure one of his ribs must be caved-in.

He made two more shell holes without event. Only one more to go and he would be safer. Halfway to it, a great gout of mud and fire arose in front of him. For the rest of his life, he would swear he actually saw the arrival of the 'Woolly Bear.' Time seemed to stand still in the microseconds that followed. He was like an actor, frozen on an exposed, timeless stage, waiting to be struck down. A black, acrid cloud of smoke erupted. There was a hiss of death. Shards of steel flew by him. A mighty hand plucked him up, dashed the wind from him and dropped his rag-doll body to the ground. Gobs of mud rained down on his face and torso. Everything went black.

Then it was cold. A great stiffness seemed to pervade his body. In the first glimmer of returning consciousness, he thought that this was surely his release from the army. If a man took a direct hit from a shell, did that not qualify?

Good God! He was alive! The matter certainly seemed to demand some attention! He opened his eyes. Through a layer of mud, he blinked at the greyness that was the world. How long had he been out? The grittiness of the mud on his eyeballs caused him to reach to brush it away. Mistake! A torrent of pain shot through his shoulder. It was echoed by similar pain from his legs that seemed to be a long way away. He was content to leave them there. His fingers found oozing blood under the front rim of his helmet. His chest raged. He had all the immediate pain he could cope with. A warm trickle down his right arm into his armpit told him of copious bleeding. A continuous high-pitched whine went through his head, and in a calmness he couldn't believe, he told himself the explosion destroyed his hearing.

He carefully began to examine his wounds. The blood coming from under his helmet was only an oozing amount. His worst affliction seemed to be his right shoulder. It had obviously taken a piece of shrapnel. Although his torso yelled trauma, it did not seem life threatening. Down below, he found his trousers shredded and numerous patches of angry purple flesh seeping blood.

Tom lay back for a moment, actually rejoicing in the wounds. Release from this hell was now at hand! He would live to see Jeanne again. Suddenly, he realized how he had been deliberately ignoring that thought. But there was something else! There was something he could not fathom. He could lie here. He didn't feel cold at all. He could lie here and wait for a body-snatching crew to haul him off, but there was something else. He had it a few minutes ago. He felt himself sliding into torpor and shook his head. It came in a flash! "Flank defensive against Hill One Hundred Forty-five!" The casualties if he didn't! He must get on!

Groping around, he found both despatch cases gone. Rolling over, he began to crawl towards the next shell hole. His legs were aflame, but he willed them to work. He pushed forward on his belly. He was committed now to staying exposed on the surface. It might be fatal to enter another shell hole; his body would never get him back out, and then he would fail! "Ah. I don't want to be a soldier...ah...I don't want to go to war..." The song seemed to help, even though he could only hear it inside himself. The fold of ground grew closer. He screamed with the pain. It felt good. He screamed again, hearing nothing. The sucking in of air revitalized him. He felt like some savage being, screaming defiance at the elements.

The thought emboldened him, demanded he rise to his feet and scream again. He got to his knees and then his feet, swaying. He could still walk! He stepped into a yielding snowy mound and howled. A great belch of putrescence arose from the rotting corpse beneath. The world canted crazily. He found himself on his face again. He was cradled in a glutinous mass, a melange of clay, both earthly and human. The gritty particles of sand and glacial flour, dumped through the eons and mingled with animal remains formed the soil, the building block of life in the eternal cycle. 'Man is but clay.' The sonorous words of the Anglican burial service echoed through his deafened head.

Blended beneath him was the compost of thousands of battle-fallen: Crècy, Châlons, Waterloo...Vimy. The endless cycle of the soil! 'Ashes to ashes, dust to dust...' Sad, the soldier who could not die and join the glorious fallen; join the blessed cycle! Here he was, doomed to slither through the primordial slime of his forebears, shut off from their eternal and blessed relief by an undiscriminating epidermal layer, unconscious of its own environs! He writhed in the mud, the taste of Henry the Fifth, Charlemagne, Attila, Napoleon, and Né upon his lips. Yet not their victories! Only their decay!

He found his feet once again. The pain was receding, fading into an awful numbness he feared more. A line of wire passed him on his left. He stared at it malevolently, hypnotized by its erratic, swaying movements. "Plum and apple...ah...all we get is..." A violent, unfelt crash into his side tumbled him into a shell hole. He sensed someone falling with him. Oh, hell! Now, he had been captured by the goddamned Heinies!

He looked up and saw a 'Lone Star' bending over him, giving him heck as usual. He smiled slightly. The singing whine made him oblivious to every word, yet he could lip-read quite easily. "...in my life! The bastards were shooting at you! Are you stark raving mad, man?" The lieutenant paused for breath and then started with realization. "Runner?" Tom nodded weakly, an idiot grin of satisfaction spreading over his face. "Where's your pouch?"

"Gone." Gosh, it was hard to talk when you couldn't hear yourself!

"Set up flank defence. Essential. Forty-second east of Pimple from Folie." Oh shit! The world was going grey now. "Folie to Black Line...four Lewis guns coming...white flares acknowledge orders." There! He had done it!

The 'Lone Star' was sharp. "Four Lewis's coming to help us flank defence Bois de Folie to Black Line. White flares to acknowledge, am I right?"

Tom nodded. "S...sorry, Jeanne darling. I...I just have to get back, I...I...couldn't..."

"Crispin! Stretcher party here, *at the double!*" Roaring the command, the lieutenant's voice was almost audible now but fading. Flashes of white-light pain penetrated a growing darkness. Tom could hear his own voice, unclear in his deafness, moving away from him into the darkness. He followed it.

The lieutenant was scribbling furiously in his map case. "Brown! Take this message to the Brigadier! Hurry! You did well, Corporal. Corporal?" He leaned down and turned up an eyelid of the man he had knocked into the shell hole. "Hey, stretcher party! Move sharp!"

Vimy Ridge, 12:00 noon.

What a lousy ship! Never had he sailed anything that rocked and pitched the way this one did! He felt liable to be thrown from his bunk at any moment and was reminded of a typhoon the 'Teresa Belmont' once weathered in the South China Sea. There was no fluidity such as in water, more of a solid jarring, as if the ship were aground – on the rocks! Tyneside's Black Middens! Goodwin Sands! Sable Island!

Alarmed at the thought of these nautical graveyards, he forced his consciousness to the surface. The wind was whining in the rigging. He could hear its keening. A faint greyness was appearing, and he could hear muted thunder. Was it thunder or the roiling surf they were aground in? No, not thunder, shellfire! He was still on Vimy Ridge! The stretcher bumped to the ground. A grimy, mud-spattered face appeared above him.

"Still wiv us den mate? Wanna Woodie to smoke?" Tom shook his head. "Offer you a fuck, I would, but dere's none to be 'ad. Besides, you ain't fit enough like." The friendly Cockney face split into an even wider grin.

"Haark! Gulp!" Cough, cough. "How it...going?"

"The battle mate?" Nod, nod. Jesus! That hurts! "Got it won then, ain't we me old sparrer! The lads were on the Ridge by ten. Got 'Ole Kaiser Bill by the short and curlies, mate. Damned Fritzes were running so 'ard our lads scarce 'ad time to turn their own guns on 'em before they wuz out of range. Only trouble wiv the action is, nobody available to charge on to Berlin!"

"T...time?"

"Twelve noon mate and the first day of the rest of your life!"

God! It was over two hours since he was hit, and they still hadn't reached a field dressing station! He looked around at the body snatchers who carried him. Exhausted, grimy, and mud-caked, the four of them were struggling all this time to get him to medical attention. Heroes!

"'Ang on now, matey; I 'ave to loosen this tight bandage on your leg to circulate the blood some. It may 'urt a little."

Pain flooded through his right leg, as blood returned to the muted nerves and set them screaming anew. He twisted in pain on the stretcher. "Okay, okay, 'ang in there, mate! You're doing famously! Only another ten minutes, and we'll 'ave a pretty nurse billing and cooing over you. You'll be fine, mate. Blighty one if ever I saw it! Now, just tighten the bandage, and we're off to the races." There was a fumbling at his thigh. "Lucky 'ere, though, coupla inches 'igher, and you'd be addressing your Mum in a squeaky voice!"

"Bye 'ole son!" Light flooded back, and Tom suddenly realized he'd blacked out again. The snatchers were off to find another victim. He scarce had time to smile and raise an arm in thanks before they were gone. He knew he would probably never get the chance to thank them properly.

The field dressing station was busy. Two lightly wounded men, detailed to help, took his belongings and put them in a 'Blighty bag,' carefully marking his name, rank, serial number, and unit. They whistled with amazement when they saw the pocket Shakespeare. A good-looking nurse with curly brown hair and intense blue eyes bustled up and gave orders to another man who started to remove Tom's clothes, cutting them off with scissors. Quickly and efficiently, seemingly undisturbed by the carnage, the young woman circled the stretchers and the walking wounded, testing a bandage or a tourniquet here and probing a wound there.

They were in an area screened off from the wind by canvas walls. The main hospital area was underground. This was a sorting area where the wounded were classified. Those requiring urgent attention were taken first. The man undressing Tom took off what he could and then covered him with a blanket. For the first time in hours, he felt warmth stealing back into his body.

The nurse bustled back. Her uniform was streaked with blood and smeared with dirt. Close up, Tom could see the blue eyes were glazing with fatigue. She whipped the blanket off him and looked him over. Despite her bustle, her fingers were gentle as they checked his shoulder. He winced. She brushed against his rib wound and nodded imperceptibly. There seemed no point in embarrassment as she further gently explored and probed just below his naked groin.

"Number two, Jenkins." She waved to her aide who began to cover Tom again. She quickly scribbled on a notepad, tore the sheet off, passed it to Jenkins, and was gone. The aide fished a safety pin from his apron and pinned the note to Tom's blanket. "Have you out of here in about twenty minutes, soldier." Jenkins scampered off in pursuit of the nurse.

It was two hours before a doctor finally saw Tom. Fortunately, with no internal wounds, he was allowed some hot tea and a small canteen of soup. He was exhausted, not just because of his own mental and physical state but also by those around him. Many men lost limbs or had taken bullets through their bodies. Some were blinded. The war was over for them, but the real fight was about to begin when they tried to resume the threads of life with the burden of physical disabilities.

Down in the seemingly endless labyrinth of tunnels, Tom was washed clean and his wounds irrigated with saline solutions and iodine. The medical people were more careful of cleaning up wounds. Too many cases of gangrene cost too many limbs and lives. Gas gangrene developed in numerous cases, where horse manure used on the fields, entered open wounds. In view of the numerous corpses, contagion through open wounds was another risk.

A doctor spent some time sewing up Tom's larger gashes. He was told he had a broken rib on the left side. The sniper's round skated across his ribs from left to right, nicking his breastbone. It now ached intolerably.

His shoulder had some severed tendons from a piece of shrapnel, which the doctor removed and saved for him. He was told there might be permanent damage. His legs were peppered with numerous small pieces of metal. The doctor optimistically forecast they would "work themselves out in due course." A couple, however, would require surgical removal in England. The last was what he wanted to hear. Two years of this, and now, hopefully, he was out of it. Within two hours, he was in a 'Hommes Forty' rattling towards Calais. About four hundred wounded fellows embarked on a Channel steamer, and after a choppy passage, they landed in Dover. By the following evening, Tom had had his operation and awoke in a hospital in Canterbury. He was told to expect two weeks of convalescence before being repatriated to Canada. An officer came around and filled out the necessary forms to process his medical discharge, to take effect on his recovery.

Tom took the opportunity to send a message to his mother. She arrived on April eighteenth by train. They sat together in the warm sunny garden of the hospital, catching up on family news. Mildred Edmunds had aged considerably the past few years. Her life was one of hard work, providing for the family needs. New lines marred her clear features. Tom always remembered her as being younger, but once the deterioration of a hard life set in, the onset was rapid. Mildred's hair was totally grey and lifeless. She stooped slightly. She wore a cheap, thin overcoat, and although Tom said nothing, he suspected she had come down with tuberculosis.

The meeting was a strain for both of them. They belonged to different worlds now. They were tongue-tied once the family news was out of the way. They hugged each other with relief that his ordeal was over. He could now plan his future. He told her of Edmonton, which she could not imagine, Jeanne, and the proposed business. They promised to write. Too soon, visiting hours were over, and she had to leave. After a restrained parting, he watched her slight figure walk to the exit, stiff with repressed emotion. He knew instinctively he would never see her again.

FIVE

MARGARET

Edmonton, July 1917.

Tom's bed was one of twenty in the high-ceilinged ward of the new Colonel Mewburn Pavilion of the hospital. Bright light streamed through the tall windows, casting squares of sunshine on the floor and the beds. Tom lay propped up against his pillows, waiting for visiting hours to begin. After leaving France, his right leg became infected. He had to battle with a doctor, who at one point, insisted it should be amputated. The veins became visible as red, angry lines, creeping inexorably up towards his trunk. Somehow, he didn't know how, he had beaten the poison and was now recuperating. For a while, he was sick with diarrhoea and delirium. His body fought against the insidious advance of the infection. The poison showed itself aboard the ship coming home, and two days ago was the first time he had been on his feet since he left England.

His shoulder gave him trouble too. A further operation was necessary. It was stiff and sore from the stitches. One thing that was a source of strength to Tom was the knowledge he was out of the conflict. He did his part and was finished with it. His dreams of what he would do with the rest of his life were firm enough to sustain him. He still had nightmares, where waves of grey-uniformed men swept towards him; his Lee-Enfield grew hot between his hands, and his shoulder felt jellied by the recoil of the rifle. Jubilant waves swept through him when he awoke to find it all now behind him. During his fevered delirium, however, it was a terrifying experience. His relief at being free was always reduced, his thoughts saddened, by the memory of those who would not be returning.

His eyes moved around the room and stopped on the starched figure of Nurse White sitting at the centre table. A couple of the guys tried to joss her a little, but she reacted with stern rejection to their advances. She was considerate in her ministrations but aloof with her womanhood. Not for the first time, Tom wondered what two days in the Flander's trenches would do to White's protected sense of propriety. Amongst the death, degradation, and dangers, she would revert, as they all had, to a primal sense of survival.

A quick flash of White, shucked of her clothes and copulating at will with the roomful of men went through his mind. It was a silly fantasy, yet he heard of French and Belgian women who were reduced to just that state in order to provide sustenance for their children. The ripples of wartime suffering lapped their way into places not comprehended by women like White. A few minutes' disgust and degradation to trade for a bowl of soup for a child, and damn the allegiance and nationality of the man! Nurse White would be no different in those circumstances!

While most civilians regarded the soldiers as heroes, Tom encountered some with no comprehension or appreciation for the sacrifices that were made. At times, he told himself he was over-reacting, but the aloofness, almost disdain with which Nurse White behaved, brought his anger to the surface. White was the first female in years who had a semi-permanent place in their lives. Other than a few sloppy embraces in a 'Maison de tolerance,' nearly all the men had been deprived of female company. Most of them longed daily for the sweet embrace of a good woman but forgot how to even talk to one. White's aloofness crushed their clumsy attempts to readjust. She fractured their confidence.

All here had cheated death. Some of them were crippled and were poor prospects for a woman now. Some poor devils were no prospect at all. The first woman they were able to have a decent conversation with, to form a relationship, however distant, had been White. White did not seem to understand this. She seemed to lack the necessary empathy to aid them in rehabilitation.

But today was Jeanne day! Today, he did not need to dwell on White. Jeanne promised to come by. This brightened him immeasurably. He sent word of his return as soon as he could, but Jeanne had been busy for a few days. Now, today, in this very room, she would walk back into his life, and the world would stand still! For the hundredth time, he turned to the large clock that hung above the door. He seethed to speed up the pendulum as it swung back and forth. He knew it wasn't slow. The old janitor climbed onto a chair only yesterday and meticulously wound it. Yet, he knew it would be called upon to stop the moment Jeanne entered the ward.

The man in bed five broke into a wrack of coughing, heaving, and tossing. His tortured lungs sought relief. White moved unhurriedly to hold a bassinet for him. Mustard gas or chlorine? It made little difference now; thousands like him would not survive much longer. The national death rate over the next few years would increase as the deprivations and injuries took their toll. White wiped the man's bloodied chin and took away the bassinet.

Ten more minutes! He tried to count the squares of light on the floor and lost count at fifteen to the image of ivory flesh, dappled by moonlight filtering through Mrs. Adams' hand-crocheted curtains. A pair of elongated, narrow breasts, sweeping apart in perfect symmetry, swayed before his face in the rhythm of love, and then they were gone. Seven minutes! Oh God! The clock was in hospital! Maybe it was sick too!

A faint stirring came from the corridor and White, returning to her desk, frowned at the undisciplined disturbance. Outside was a gathering of friends, wives, and family, anxious not to miss a minute of the strict and meagre one visiting hour allotted each day. Was Jeanne out there now? She must be on her way or she would be late. He tried to trace her progress: a five-minute walk to the streetcar down Fraser, ride along Jasper Avenue, change to cross the High Level Bridge, and then another five-minute walk here. The longing for her was killing him! If he did die now, could he possibly hold his breath long enough for one last heart-flutter, so he could smile as she approached his bed? Five bloody minutes!

The man in bed seven babbled in a drug-induced sleep. Only this morning, surgeons removed more shrapnel from him. A glass tumbler on his bedside table contained jagged steel fragments. There was *his* parlour conversation piece! Faces appeared at the double glass doors. Tom recognized the wife of bed seven – no conversation for her today! At the sound of a distant bell, White rose reluctantly and beckoned them in. Cries of joy and reunion rose. The invasion fanned out to the individual beds under White's stern eye. The bedside chairs were all commandeered and positioned as the room settled down to a steady buzz of endearments and family news.

With the chairs all gone, where would Jeanne sit? It was unthinkable that she should not come. Finally! She was there, hovering at the threshold, uncertain of herself. Tom couldn't call her, only gape. He waved, but she missed him and then spotted him. His eyes welled tears as she came towards him, her open, lovely smile lighting up the room. The blonde hair was a little longer, flowing from under a perky little hat that matched her dark blue coat. She still moved in the same coltish manner he well remembered.

"Hello Tom!"

"Hello, Jeanne! You look lovely!" She stood awkwardly at his bedside. " Don't I get a kiss?"

She stooped and offered him her cheek. Oh God! Something was wrong! This wasn't how he had imagined it! White! That was it! That goddamned White with her cold disapproving stare was inhibiting Jeanne's reactions! But White was at the far end of the room.

"Are you getting well?"

"Yes, my leg is healing quickly now, and I'm starting to walk on it. Like I told you in my letter, the doctors say I may always limp, but I'm working on that too. They were wrong about the amputation, so I shall prove them wrong about the limp also. Maybe you can come for some strolls with me along the banks of the Saskatchewan and help me." He felt like he was babbling inconsequentially, like a man at the end of a plank, awaiting the prod of a buccaneer's cutlass to drop him into the shark-infested sea.

This direct appeal to the heart of their old relationship caused Jeanne's face to slip. She cast her eyes down. There was a long pause, while she contemplated his blankets. He gazed in apprehension at her. "Tom, you know I've always cared for you. There is something I have to tell you that has to be said to you face to face for that reason. I am getting married next month."

The world lurched and went grey. Jeanne's voice, eager to placate, to rationalize, went on fading in and out like a bad telephone line. "Know you'll like him...John Williams...so interesting...alive...concerned about...people...world..."

She always had this mercurial ability to change, this girl. She would fervently throw herself into some pursuit only to suddenly abandon it and pick up another with equal relish. Was that why he cared for her? Was her attraction her continued freshness? And how did you cope with it? The woman who was his torrid, clinging lover now stood before him ready to formally shake his hand as if nothing had ever happened!

"The IWW parade we saw in nineteen fourteen? One of the marchers... respected leader now...explained it all to me...so exciting...new way of life." She was still trying to rationalize it to him.

He'd carried the memories and pinned the hopes of a lifetime on this woman through two years of war and desperate circumstances. Surviving to return to her, his whole elevation of her as a standard, a cherished dream was suddenly toppled. A great emptiness overwhelmed him. A dark realm of vacuum and cold seized his heart.

Jeanne's words faltered to a stop. His face was unable to maintain any kind of facade.

"Is your mother happy?" Somehow, he found words.

"She has needed...needed some persuasion."

"Well, you'll pardon me if I don't attend." He waved at the bed, not caring if she took his true meaning.

"Of course, I understand." She had taken his hand at some point, but he couldn't feel her touch. He wanted to blurt out his love, yet knew it was hopeless. He knew her too well. She would be too unreceptive, too taken up with this damned fellow. Perhaps on the bank of the Saskatchewan or up Mill Creek, he might sway her, at least call a temporary halt to this madness. However, not here in this sterile environment, not with White looking on. Only some of the men in the other beds would understand.

Another long silence had fallen. He felt her relinquishing her grip and felt the awful finality. "Goodbye, Tom."

Goodbye? Such a word of finality. He didn't, couldn't reply. He never saw her leave. The ward blurred. His face went slack. The clock on the wall stopped for him, yes, but the pendulum had not swung up on a wave of delirious happiness. Instead, it swung down like some vengeful scythe, ridden by demons, slicing and maiming right to his very soul. The sniper's bullet, all the efforts of the Germans to kill him, all had failed. Now with a few words, Jeanne had destroyed him.

He refused supper that evening, never hearing White's admonition. His mind fell into a continuum of torpor, while his body, abetting his mental plight, greedily ingested a pneumonia virus. The onset of such infections were known to the medical staff and recognized as a risk inherent in long bed-rest cases, where the lungs were not exercised. Within two days, his temperature was one hundred and four and the staff fought for his life. They did so alone, for seemingly, Corporal Edmunds had lost the will to live.

Only the deeply rooted sense of survival brought him out of it. His body was barely recovered from his wounds before it was battered by this new affliction. The doctors began to recognize the symptoms of acute melancholia, which seemed to suddenly strike veterans of the trenches for no apparent reason. There seemed to be a level of tolerance, varying with the individual, at which a soldier's mind would snap under the depredations and horror of warfare. The most recurrent was shell shock, a condition that was treated generally as cowardice and cause for a court-martial. The sheer numbers involved, however, eventually convinced more rational leaders that the condition could not be rectified by the King's Regulations. It was, indeed, a natural result of the soldier's experience. Doctors only now began to grasp the reality of post-battle stress syndrome: a combat affliction that could strike after the fighting was done.

Reliving the dangers, the nightmares, and recurrent fears after the event wasn't easy to deal with. It was an unnatural mode of life: to exist in a rat-infested muddy hole, half-starved, lice-ridden, and afflicted by trench-foot, while a similarly plagued individual, only yards away, tried to kill you. The mental effects did not simply dissolve the moment you stopped doing it.

Similarly, modern citizens did not hang their hats, boots, and paraphernalia on thighbones protruding through the wall of their living rooms. Nor did they have to entertain putrefying corpses in their dwellings. These were constant reminders to the soldier of the frailty of his condition. One minute alive and viable, the next a heap of bloodied rags and corruption. All of this was bad enough without adding the moral implications of killing, often face-to-face. It took an individual of extraordinary immorality and low intelligence to shrug off the stress involved.

So, with the vague, first awakenings of understanding, the medical staff tended to the physical needs and the deliriums of the occupant of bed six. They were rewarded after a few days with a gradual drop in temperature and almost a week later, Tom opened his eyes consciously for the first time.

"Hello, Corporal Edmunds, I'm Margaret Thomas." A demure young woman swam into focus as she leaned forward. She had dark brown curly hair, cut fashionably short, and a long face. A white blouse was fastened protectively at her throat by a large brooch. She smiled at him nervously. "I've been reading to you for several days, but I'm not sure you've been listening." Her smiled broadened at the daring of her remark, but as an icebreaker, it failed. Tom looked at her as if she were crazy. Her eyes dropped, and she wilted visibly under the brooding stare." I...I'll...go get

Nurse White. We've been expecting you to wake soon." Defeated, she beat a hasty retreat.

"Ah, Edmunds! You are back with us." White hoved into view, crisp and starched as ever. Tom stared at her dully. What was wrong with these stupid bitches? Couldn't they leave a man alone? His stomach growled at him. He'd lost fifteen pounds off an already lean frame, and his body was sending messages, urging restitution. "You must be hungry. How about some nice soup?"

"Take your food and shove it up your ass! And take Mother Goose here away with you!" Tom was pleased to see the genteel Miss Thomas, hovering in the background, disappear rapidly. White, however, fixed him with a baleful glare and leaning in close, eyes slitted in fury, hissed at him.

"Listen, you snivelling, popped-up little bastard. That girl comes in here voluntarily three days a week to try to bring comfort to some of the *real* men in this place. She just spent two days by your bedside, reading to you to assure you there was hope for a sick man. Leave her alone! As for me, it's my job to clean up your shit and wipe your ass when you won't get off it. We've fed you, supported you, and now you're awake, you're on your own. You speak to that girl again in that fashion, and I'll personally throw your fucking ass out of this ward!"

For a moment, Tom was nonplussed by the starchy White's choice of terms. Then he slowly broke a smile. "All right, White, you really are a treasure. Thank you. I do believe I would like something to eat." An expression briefly crossed White's face that he'd seen before on another unlikely countenance. As she bustled away, Tom realized apologies to her would be totally wasted. Then he remembered the other face: Sergeant Major Jones' when he had told him of Nobby Clarke's death. It was that momentary window through the facade of professionalism where the stress of caring, the tortured personal price of war, was laid naked to the eye.

Brought back from the brink, the sense of survival taught him by the war helped Tom look forwards and upwards. In the days that followed, he finally got out of bed. His physical wounds had healed. He exercised his shoulder, despite the severe pain and won back some respect from Nurse White for his stoicism in getting it to work, despite the doctors' declarations to the contrary. Starting with immediate interests, he scanned newspapers daily, avid for news of the Forty-ninth. His attention to the printed details spread through the whole paper until he had his finger on the pulse of Edmonton once again.

The war had brought a new prosperity to some, yet it was only in the supply of war materiel. The real estate industry was in the doldrums. Edmonton expanded quicker than its population. Many people let their land go back to the City, after seeing it accumulate unpaid taxes for several years. The City had land up to its elbows that it couldn't sell. Tom gave a silent blessing to Tim O'Hanlon for advising him to get out of the lots he owned.

Women now had the vote both in the provincial and municipal elections, thanks to the likes of the redoubtable Emily Murphy and her cronies of the Women's Canadian Club, Edmonton Branch. Conscription had only recently been enacted to provide manpower for the Canadian Corps. This was put in place due to the lack of volunteers. It was a sop to a continued resistance to provide men from Quebec, who claimed no interest in the war. Prohibition was still in effect, and now for the first time, with the prospect of getting out of hospital, Tom was to experience its onerous effect on the life of a drinker.

He was assured by the prim Miss Thomas, to whom he apologized, there were certain people in Edmonton known to bootleg illicit liquor; although, she personally was not acquainted with them. Out in the bush, up One Twenty-fourth Street, illegal stills were set up and doing brisk trade with 'certain elements' in town. Margaret appeared to genuinely forgive him for his rudeness. He was pleased with her company. They found a mutual interest in reading. She kept him well supplied from the Strathcona library. Somehow during his coma, his brain filed the problem of Jeanne away, and a platonic woman friend like Margaret was a good new beginning for him.

Margaret's father was the owner of Thomas' Store, a Jasper Avenue business boasting three floors of departmental shopping. It was very successful. Since she was an only child, it also made her a local heiress of some consequence, although she did not play on the fact. Margaret was a head shorter than Tom with an angular build and introverted brown eyes. Her nose was straight, like his, where it should probably have been turned up to soften her features. She was very shy. Since her features were a little severe, she tended to put off any potential suitors. Her skin was unblemished and pale, where a few freckles or a dimple might have enhanced her looks.

Eventually, the day came when Tom was released from the hospital. He said goodbye to White, who was as starchy as ever. Margaret came to see him off, but she hesitated a moment as they parted company. With an abrupt gesture, she proffered what was obviously a book, wrapped in brown paper. Her shyness forestalled whatever she might have wanted to say. They parted with vague and insincere words of maintaining contact.

Tom boarded a tram along Whyte Avenue, carrying his small bag from France. Mrs. Adams made sure his old room was available to him. Since his trunk of old belongings was in her attic, it made sense to return there. He looked out as the tram rattled the few blocks, noticing new buildings and minor changes since he left in nineteen fifteen. It felt strange to be back with only this little bag and his scars to show for the two years of turmoil. The war was far, far away, unable to directly touch this place. It was now a closed chapter in his life.

The motion of the streetcar reminded him of a 'Hommes Forty.' He hummed a few bars of a song they had always sang coming out of the Line.

> *"I don't want to go in the trenches no more*
> *Where the whizzbangs and the shrapnel whistle and roar.*
> *Take me over the sea, where the Alleyman can't get at me..."*

Well, he was over the sea now, where the 'Alleyman' couldn't get at him. Reaching his stop, he climbed down and limped along the street to the boarding house. Mrs. Adams had kindly visited him in hospital, so she was already caught up on his recent history. She greeted him fondly with a kiss on the cheek and a freshly brewed cup of tea. She thanked him for his contribution to the war, a gesture not lost on Tom, who, like warriors returning throughout history, had experienced strange and contradictory behaviour from those they left behind.

Finally, he was back in his room, trunk retrieved from the attic. He sat for a while, gazing out the window at the birch tree with its green leaves. Now that he had reached this, the beginning point of his life again, he was lost. The army ran his life for two long years, deciding his every move, feeding him, moving him, and housing him, albeit in 'Amiens Huts.' Now, he had to adjust to making his own decisions. He desperately missed all his comrades: Alex, Chalky White, even Sergeant Major Jones! The camaraderie and excitement they provided was gone. He was alone. More alone since Jeanne had deserted him! He looked at the bed. One night, he snuck her in here without Mrs. Adams knowing. The risk of being discovered added spice to their lovemaking. He would never forget it. Now he had to live with the memory.

He opened the package Margaret had given him. It was Homer's Iliad. On the fly leaf, she had enscribed a brief message: 'To Tom Edmunds. Best wishes. Margaret Thomas.' He knew she meant more, but his senses were dulled with the loss of Jeanne. He sat, unthinking, his eyes unfocussed on the book in his lap.

It was a half hour before he stirred. Life was going to go on with him or without him, so it may as well be with him. Turning to his trunk, he opened it, and began to unpack, neatly laying his things in the old chest of drawers.

SIX

JEANNE AGAIN

Lillette MacDonald died on November ninth, nineteen eighteen. She was one of the last Edmonton victims of the great influenza epidemic that swept the world, killing millions. Soldiers who had survived the deadly perils of the trenches returned home only to fall to the dreaded disease: a terrible irony. Tom Edmunds would not have known about Lillette if the list of the dead hadn't been published each day in the Edmonton Journal. He caught her name on November tenth.

It came as no surprise that the frail little woman had become a victim, living as she did in that ramshackle little house with its cold draughts and insufficient heating. He went over the same day and enquired of a neighbour what arrangements had been made for the dead woman. He was told the authorities contacted Lillette's daughter in Winnipeg. Jeanne put Gabriel and Arseneault funeral home in charge of arrangements, and she would be coming out for the funeral. Tom arranged for a wreath to be delivered to the funeral parlour in his name.

Back home, Tom sat down and thought carefully. Jeanne was submerged in his mind the past while. A subconscious defence mechanism to save him pain suppressed the memory of her. Despite this block, his longing was as strong as ever, the unobtainable desired by the unforgetting. He also had Margaret Thomas to deal with. Their relationship had slid, predictably, into an engagement for marriage. While his seeing Jeanne again might lead to possible jealousy problems with Margaret, he was more concerned about how his own feelings might surface and muddy the waters. Still, he could not avoid paying his respects to Lillette MacDonald by attending her funeral.

His relationship with Margaret was a curious one. She was interested, as most women were, in finding a presentable husband. His recent success placed him in that bracket. For his own part, the courtship began in a casual fashion, a chance meeting downtown that led to a soda on Jasper Avenue. This led to a social dance, which in turn, led to a picnic, and subsequently, serious courtship. They came to their present state almost like a mutual surrender to circumstances, a metamorphosis, as he was absorbed into her family.

Tom had no illusions about Margaret's attraction. On the Edmonton scene, she was a good catch because of her father's wealth. Most men would overlook her rather plain looks in favour of the power she represented. Tom wryly admitted that his sometimes-disappointing reception by bankers in the past had been enhanced by his association with Margaret. As a member of the Thomas family, his financial clout would increase enormously. In a very real sense, Tom realized that seeing Jeanne again would sow a seed of dissatisfaction with Margaret. That could have a devastating effect on his relationship with her. He couldn't nor shouldn't expect Margaret to be like Jeanne. It would become an exercise in frustration and doom their marriage.

Yet, Margaret was an unknown quantity. She had demurely resisted all his attempts to seduce her. Sex before marriage was out of the question, although he considered it a key factor in a relationship. What would happen to them if sex was largely proscribed by the ignorance imbued in her by her mother and current social mores?

The thought of a mother's influence reminded him of Lillette's admonishing him long ago to 'take care with Jeanne.' This one thing, this expression of trust by this woman, who must have guessed they were lovers, had endeared her perpetually to him and demanded his attendance at the funeral. Lillette MacDonald had been his friend.

His mind went back to those sun-drenched days, long ago and worlds away in pre-war Edmonton. Everything was larger than life because he was in love and Jeanne's soap-scented, fragrant limbs were his, along with her willing lips and yielding body. He happened upon a bar of the same soap recently and the scent pitched him into a mind-spinning fantasy that she was still nearby. Reality was brutally frank. He hurled the soap as far as he could. The enormity of the vision's impact scared him. He had to bury her image under that subliminal defence mechanism that stored her memory just beyond his conscious thought. Now, shrugging fatalistically, he penned a short, formal note of condolence to Jeanne to be attached to the wreath. Let fate fall where it may!

The very next day, he received an urgent message to rush to the Thomas residence. Alfred Thomas had suffered a stroke and was admitted to hospital. For three days, Alfred remained unconscious in a private room.

Margaret saw enough suffering at the hospital in her volunteer days, so she was prepared for the ordeal. Not so Irene Thomas. She went to pieces. A dumpy little woman who had fussed and bustled her way through life, devoting three times the energy needed for simple tasks, she was not equipped to handle this. All her life, she made mountains out of molehills and her manic insecurity thrust her into acts of martyrdom at the slightest occurrence.

She gave a command performance of total panic. She cried on the first day. On the second, she declared her inability to survive, and cast herself on the goodness of God. By the third day, God did not exist. Seemingly, nor did her husband. At a time when the poor man might have found consolation and strength from her presence at his bedside, she deserted him in favour of indulging her own selfish histrionics. On the only occasion she was persuaded to enter his room, she broke down in the doorway and set up such a wailing, the alarmed hospital staff escorted her out. It was left to Margaret to keep vigil day and night.

Tom could not be bothered with Irene. He disliked her from the start. She was the opposite of all he stood for, a Jonas in this land of hopeful pioneers. Alfred Thomas was brainwashed into protecting and coddling the woman. Somehow, he still found the means to succeed in business while saddled with her. Perhaps, Tom reflected, the old man did so well because he found it a better life spending long hours working, away from his wife.

Irene was not fond of Tom because he refused to indulge her histrionics. If Alfred died, his stuffy, unobtrusive, but pleasant refereeing between them might well be missed. Meanwhile, Margaret was galvanized into a frenzy of mother-care, drawn into the old lady's vortex of panic. Irene even denounced Margaret's time at the hospital as being wasted since it wasn't being spent on her.

Although he felt bound to help out of a sense of duty, Tom avoided Irene and took some shifts at the hospital instead. Alfred awoke on the third day and the doctors were conducting tests to see what damage had been done to him by the stroke. So far, it was promising that aside from some restricted mental functions, he might be in fairly good shape. Returning home after one of these bouts of duty, Tom found a note under his door bearing familiar writing. His fingers trembled as he opened the envelope. He sat in the old stuffed chair by the window to read.

Dear Tom,

Thank you for your kind note regarding Mother. The funeral is at St. Anthony's 97th Street at 3:00 tomorrow afternoon. I hope you can attend.
J.

He was seized by an emotion of such intensity it frightened him. His heart and soul swelled together like an explosion, growing with the enormity of an exploding star cluster. The universe lay before him. He was poised on its brink and ready to launch at dizzying speed across its vastness. A dazzling light streamed from behind him, radiating with the power of the total happiness accumulated by mankind. The rays pushed him, urged him, and then were suddenly gone, attenuated by reality.

He stood by the window for an eternity; his eyes focused on the old tree outside. He would go, of course. The problem lay in organizing his thoughts, tending to his propriety. His guilt distorted the scene every time he thought of the happiness of Jeanne's arms around him. Instead of beauty, the pair of them became naked and lewd, sprawled across Lillette's coffin.

A low grey nimbus swept across the city, spitting rain and sleet at the ground. Under the implacable menace of the weather, the weak wintering sun had already succumbed and was lowering toward the western horizon. Tomorrow would be a miserable day for anything, yet perhaps, appropriate for a funeral. A few flakes of snow brushed the windowpane, and the last of the tree's fall leaves committed suicide onto the lawn.

****

Tom entered St. Anthony's Catholic Church close to three in the afternoon the following day with excuses made to the Thomas family. A clapboard erection, dating back fifteen years, it reflected the poverty of the neighbourhood. The sill plates were laid on grade and rotted, heaved by the rain and frost. The whole of the small building was out of plumb. Its saving grace was an exquisite painting of the beatitudes behind the altar, done by an unknown artist. Lit by various supplicants and others dedicated to Lillette, candles gave yellow light within and threw an encompassing warmth to combat the flurry of cold air and snow, which shepherded Tom inside. The weather indeed, was miserable.

A bier supporting a coffin stood before the altar. The lid was open. He slowly moved down the aisle past the half dozen people in the pews. Lillette's animated features were frozen in a look beyond sleep-like repose.

She reminded him of a dead infantryman he had seen at the Somme: wounded and left alone, his life force sapped by the clinging, treacherous mud. He had surrendered his life in a dream-like trance of incomprehension. Other dead faces sprang to mind, a hundred of them, jammed into eternity in a combined rictus of pain and horrible slaughter. The Highlander on the wire at Ypres Salient glared at him. This time, there were no rats. He shuddered slightly and was glad for Lillette, glad that she was at peace.

Delinquent in his religion, but training for a Catholic marriage to Margaret, he bowed his head and stumbled through a "Te Deum" for Lillette's soul. Then he felt *her* presence.

Jeanne approached him from behind. He paused and then turned his head. She stood close to his left shoulder, staring down at her mother, a pink lace handkerchief dabbing at one eye. The glow of the candlelight caught her hair and in that moment, she turned her eyes to him. His heart slipped. A wistful, tender smile suffused her pale lips, contrasting her reddened eyes. In that moment, he knew he would love this woman forever.

"Hello, Tom." Her voice was husky with emotion.

"Jeanne, I'm sorry. These aren't the circumstances." He trailed off as she smiled anew, cutting off anything more he had to say. She offered her arm. He took it and led her to one of the front pews. A couple more people entered, perhaps a dozen now present to commemorate Lillette's memory.

They sat together, remote from the meaningless Mass. The priest's words, sympathetic and inadequate, were out of touch with the waves of emotion he felt coming from Jeanne. He burned to hold her but she was untouchable to him.

In no time, they found themselves at the main door. He stood back, while she graciously received the condolences of the people filing out. Tom had borrowed a car for the day and told the funeral director that Mrs. Williams would ride with him to the cemetery. They followed alone behind the hearse. An inch of snow had fallen in the night and a cold penetrating wind sliced across the cemetery. With a thick topcoat under his robes, the priest said the final rites, possibly with some haste. After a few comforting words and a handshake, he left with the funeral hearse, tucking Jeanne's payment under his vestments. A scud of grey cloud skimmed the trees as a pair of gravediggers appeared. They hung back out of respect as Jeanne continued to stare down at the already half-frozen flowers and the scattering of dirt that had been tossed on top of the coffin.

Finally, Tom took her arm, and she reluctantly turned away. He was proud of the way she had borne herself and reflected that by now, Irene Thomas, in Jeanne's position, would probably be down in the grave, grovelling in anguish atop the casket. For the first time, he wondered, where was John Williams at this time of need?

They wound their way between the gravestones of long-dead Edmontonians, shuffling through the snow until they reached his car. Handing her up, Tom tucked a car rug protectively around her. Settling in his seat, Tom turned to face her. "Where are you staying?" She sat silent behind her black veil. He sensed a sorrow much deeper than just her mother's death.

"Sorry?"

"Where can I drop you?" Tom asked.

"Oh. At Mother's place, I suppose. I have to pack up her...things."

They drove off in silence, with their thoughts a million miles apart. He could sense the dam of her emotions cracking and crumbling behind the facade of decorum. He knew she would eventually break down and cry uncontrollably. Should he be there to take her in his arms? Damn John Williams and his absence! He wanted to take her into his arms. God, how he wanted that! But, she was a married woman, untouchable. She was danger to him, a downfall. She rejected him. She was not his! He dared not give in! He turned towards her, impulsively, his mouth trying for the words, 'I love you,' but she hadn't noticed.

"Tom, would you please get me some brandy or something?" Her voice was small, her gaze straight ahead. He nodded mutely.

Braking at the house, Tom helped Jeanne down. They went inside. The shack was even more depressing with the stove out and Lillette's indomitable presence missing. Garbage and uneaten food, relics of Lillette's illness, littered the place. The worktable and sewing machine were as she had left them: cluttered. Material, half-finished articles of clothing, and patterns still cascaded from the shelves. Tom gathered kindling from outside the back door. Striking a Swan's Vestas, he started a small blaze in the big pot-bellied stove and piled on some logs.

"Back in a few minutes." He knew a bootlegger a block away and quickly returned with a couple of bottles under his coat. The chill of the place had dispersed a little. Still wearing her heavy coat, Jeanne worked rapidly, pitching out the garbage and throwing most of the mess into one corner. A couple of wooden chairs were pulled up before the stove. Jeanne reopened the door of the stove so it drew better. The flickering redness of the flames lit up the inside of the place, causing shadows to dance on the drab walls.

"I've brought you something we used to drink in France. You'll like it." Tom grabbed an old pot and placed it on the stove, pouring in copious amounts of a cheap red wine and brandy. Very quickly, the vapours filled the shack. Finding two old glasses, one badly chipped, Tom poured out warm portions. They both sat gazing into the flames and sipping at the potent brew. A long time, a settling time, went by. Jeanne put out some dry bread and an opened can of meat. They picked at the food, dipping the hard crusts into the wine.

"This place is worse than an Amiens hut!" Tom remarked.

"What?"

"This place, it's worse than an Amiens hut. They were canvas and wood frame contraptions they put us in for accommodation behind the lines in France. They leaked like a sieve and kept the cold *in*! Still, they were paradise compared with the trenches!"

She smiled and was serious. "We never did talk about France, did we Tom?"

"There was no time," replied Tom. "Here, have another drink."

"Thanks. Just like old times, eh?"

"Except, we are older?"

"Do you have to spoil it?" Jeanne asked wryly.

"No, Jeanne, but I don't want to compromise you." She threw back her head and laughed. He glared at her, hurt.

"I never could talk to you, could I?" He put his glass down and rose. "I had better go!"

"No! No Tom! Please, please stay." He turned and saw her breaking down like a sand castle attacked by the tide. Tears flowed down her cheeks. "Oh God, I'm so unhappy!"

"But Jeanne, everyone has to die sometime!"

"It's not just Mother, it's my whole life!"

"Then why don't you come back here?"

"And do what?" She threw out an arm, indicating the shack, her weeping stopped by indignation. "Support myself and my daughter, just like Mother? Work myself to death in poverty to be buried on a miserably cold November day with only two graveside mourners?"

"Daughter?" Tom's mind reeled. He could not have guessed this! A child! The shackles went brutally back on the soaring hopes Jeanne's words had brought him. In his mind, she had been ready to leave John Williams, come back here and be with him. Now this! A marriage without consummation, without children, is without substance. It may be broken up. A marriage with a child proves consummation, love, fecundity, and the existence of a family unit! A child was a permanent personification, tangible evidence, of the joining of two people and proof against his wildest hopes!

"A daughter! You...have a child?" The words almost choked him.

"Why yes. Her name is Jennifer, and she is four months old." The wistful smile on Jeanne's face faded as she saw Tom go chalk white.

He tried to mask his discomfiture, rising to pour more of the heady brew from the stove. "I just never thought...I..."

"It happens in marriages, Tom." Her voice was low and the hand on his arm gentled the words. "I am sorry. It is a shock for you."

"Yes, well, I should have thought."

A long pause ensued, while Jeanne gazed at Tom, who stared into the fire. "I let you down, didn't I Tom?"

"What?"

"When you returned from France, I let you down."

He shrugged. "You had your life to lead."

"Perhaps, but that doesn't mean I have to stop caring about you. I realized some while ago that I was hasty. I think I could never love another man the way I love you."

She had never, ever before, said 'I love you.' Appended to the odd letter received in France had been the careless 'Love, Jeanne,' which was a mere greeting, not the declaration he craved. It was typical of her mercurial nature that she would throw it at him now, protected from his willing love by a wedding vow.

A knife twisted in his heart. "What kind of game is this? You have a husband, a child, six hundred miles away, and you torment me with a statement like that? I think I had better go!" Tom's buttocks left the chair, but his feet would not move. He knew he couldn't leave, as did Jeanne. She too rose. He turned to face her. Her face streamed silent tears.

They were in each other's arms a moment later, she sobbing as her reserve finally broke. She cried like a child, her whole being racked. She cried in sorrow. She cried in despair. Finally, she cried in hope. They clung to each other until she drew back and looked him in the eyes. Her face was a sodden, reddened mess, yet her eyes sparkled with a ferocious hope, the first step forward after desperation. A rueful, knowing smile creased her features. She leaned into him and brushed his lips with hers. She pulled back to gauge his reaction, and then their lips met in a mutual frenzy. One of the chairs crashed to the floor as they swayed, crushing against each other.

Possibly the only thing of real value in Lillette MacDonald's shack was the enormous duvet she made and once shared with her husband. Now, it was put to its proper use again, dragged to the floor in front of the cherry-red stove. They fell upon it, devouring each other. So great was their urgency, they tore at each other's clothes, finally becoming contemptuous of the need to be totally naked, and coupled. She was still in her blouse and stockings and he in his shirt and socks. Long after their shuddering release, they remained clinging together, the uncertainty of their future together palisaded from them by their encircling arms. Reality was pushed away. For this time only, fantasy would prevail.

Finally, Tom withdrew from her liquid warmth and stood above her, refilling their glasses. The stove was now belching great waves of heat. In the light from the opened door, Jeanne watched him. She knew what she said earlier was true. She loved this man and thoughtlessly deserted him when he was terribly vulnerable, thinking only of herself, awash with new dreams.

Tom turned sideways. She could see scars, terrible scars, on his legs. There was white, livid scar tissue on his arm. She ran her eyes over the rest of his lean frame to where his penis stood out, glistening with the juices of their lovemaking. Then he removed his shirt, and she gasped at the wound over his heart, a purplish splash of devastation on his smooth body. She knew now that this scar, on the surface, was less than the one she inflicted beneath.

Tom crouched over her, leaning close, and offering the replenished glass. "I'm sorry, I..."

Jeanne placed her finger on his lips. "No, Tom. Kiss me." Again their lips met, softly this time, contrasting the earlier tumult with a tenderness that spoke a million thoughts. She patted the duvet beside her. "Tell me about France."

It was a catharsis to their relationship, the dissolving of a barrier. Tom spent so long bolstered by thoughts of Jeanne while in extremis in France that she acquired an almost ethereal persona, like a guardian angel. Telling the story to her would return her to a human entity he could relate to.

He talked for over an hour. Jeanne's fingers lovingly traced the living evidence of the hardships and danger. Tom had never spoken to another being, not even Alex MacFarlane, with the depth of feeling, almost confession that he now brought to Jeanne. The experience had been bottled up, suppressed not only by some manly code of non-admission, but also by a reluctance to face and accept all that had happened. As he spoke, Tom felt ghosts slipping off his shoulders. He felt instinctively that he would have no more nightmares about the war.

He told Jeanne of the misery, the depravations and death, his eloquence close to foundering but for the gift Tommy Evans had brought him. He told of the humorous, the ridiculous, and the gratitude for the simplest things. At the end, he told of the sniper's bullet. It was only proper that Jeanne's slender fingertips were in the puckered edges of the wound when he described how her gift saved his life. He promised he would show her the bullet-furrowed Shakespeare that was safely stored in his trunk at home.

This brought them to the present. They became aware of each other in another way. They stripped each other of their remaining clothes and lay back, revealing all in the light from the stove. Jeanne found his tumescence with hands then willing mouth, while he discovered, with wonder, the new heaviness to her breasts from childbearing. Her nipples were larger, the aureolae enlarged with usage. Her belly was slacker and deposits of fat, not unwelcome, lay upon hips he remembered as leaner.

"I never knew what you went through. I'm sorry."

"It's all right, my darling, it's all right."

She wept openly. He entered her again, slowly, and reverently. This time, they were careful with each other, rising from wave to wave of mounting awareness. She cried out at the end, her rhythmic sharp intakes of breath and moans taking him back to their early years of lovemaking. She gripped him tightly as if she would never let him go again, legs tight around him, drawing him and his offering deep inside her. He stroked her, caressed her, taking them both carefully down. They were wet with sweat, a mutual sheen of consummation. She felt the wetness running out of her, coursing between her glistening buttocks.

"Stay with me." The words came sibilantly from his lips, soft against her earlobe.

She shook her head. "It's impossible..." She squeezed him, suddenly, urgently, suppressing his squirming objection. "I am married. I have a child. You don't know how much I would like to Tom! Not just for you but to escape. My life is miserable. We live with his mother, and she hates me! She is a miserable old witch, for whom I can do nothing right! She nags constantly. John is gone half the time, and I am at her mercy! God knows I expect little. Look what I was raised with!" For the second time, Jeanne's arm indicated their humble surroundings. "But for my little girl, I cannot. She is a little angel, yet she is not *mine*. *'She is like her great grandmother'*." She mimicked the words sarcastically. "The old witch lies about me constantly, trying to poison John against me. And he is completely in her hands, divided between us both! She's mean, vindictive, and horrid! I think her husband dropped dead just to be free of her!"

Jeanne drained her glass angrily and handed it to him for a refill. The stove, like their ardour, cooled to a dull glow. The room was darkening. Tom could not reply. He stroked her hair and tried, in vain, to transfer to his brain the texture and roundness of her breasts. He wanted to store the feeling forever. At this point of losing her, he needed memories he could retain. His man's mind, he knew, would betray him. Men's minds were incapable of delivering such sensations at a future summons. In minutes, it would be a poor memory; in days, an elusive fantasy. Reluctantly, Tom withdrew from her, becoming an individual again. He reached up, took the pot, and poured the last of the fortified wine into their glasses. "Can we drink to love?"

Silently, they toasted each other. Only parting remained. "Do you want me to stay with you?" Her head shook with a smile, heavy-lidded eyes fading on him. He couldn't resist running his hands over her once more. She shivered sleepily. Her breasts swelled to him. The fat on her belly, above the matted pubic hair, fascinated him. Was there no way? He knew the answer.

Outside would be dark and cold. He stoked the stove before leaving, banking it for the night. As a last gesture, he lifted her to the bed, wrapped in the great duvet. She was limp in his arms, drunk, satiated, and totally exhausted emotionally. He brushed her lips with his and hushed an unintelligible message of love.

The streets were dark and deserted. He drove home in no time. Dawn crept over his windowsill before his vigil with the remaining brandy ended and he slept until midday. His subconscious kept him under until it knew her train had departed.

SEVEN

MRS. THOMAS EDMUNDS

Winnipeg, January 2, 1919.

The silence in the Williams' kitchen was profound. The sheer tangibility of the wait weighed heavily on Jeanne as she awaited her husband's reaction. She had just seized the opportunity to break the news of her pregnancy while Mother Williams was out.

Part of her reasoning was the natural instinct for a young mother to have her husband be the first to know. Yet, she had to admit, her main reason was need for solidarity with him. John had made it clear to both her and Mother Williams that he wanted no more children, for a while, at least. He placed the burden of contraception squarely on her. She knew the first thing Mother Williams would do would be to represent the pregnancy as an act of defiance, incompetence, disloyalty, or worse.

She had to get John on her side before the old witch tried to influence him against her. If she could get him to accept the baby before the old woman found out, his loyalty to her would forestall interference. She hated all this manoeuvring over what should be a simple thing, but with that old harridan, peace was impossible. Jeanne also had another, bigger problem. She was convinced the child's father was Tom Edmunds, not her husband's. She prayed she could handle this without betraying herself.

"How can you be pregnant, woman?"

"I...I don't know, John. I just don't know. I thought we had been careful."

"*We*? It's *you* who has to be careful!" he cut in sharply.

Jeanne gulped and hung her head, a move he took as guilty acknowledgement. In fact, she was triumphant. His remark was exactly what she'd anticipated and hoped for. *Men*! In their male ignorance, what did they know about menstrual cycles? The period of fertility was nothing to them. They only knew there was a *disgusting* time to have sex and the rest was okay, if the woman was willing. They would blithely spurt their seed into a woman, and if she got pregnant, it was her fault! Then, should she not conceive when a child was desired, well, it was still her fault!

She was pretty sure John's ignorance would help conceal the fact he wasn't the father. It was another reason to keep Mother Williams in the dark for as long as possible, as she watched Jeanne like a hawk. She had been menstruating a week or so before the news of Lillette's death arrived. (Despite her avowed adoration of Jennifer, the old witch complained about having to look after her, while Jeanne took time to attend the funeral). Then John went away for two weeks to a conference in Ontario. She was gone five days to Edmonton. Such mathematics were beyond him but not his mother. She thought she had the problem beaten, but his next remark floored her.

"Anyway, it is probably somebody else's."

She gasped and felt the flush of scarlet guilt rushing up her neck and face. Had John Williams looked at his wife at that moment, he would have seen the naked truth upon her face. But he was already ashamed of his outburst. He knew it was only intended to hurt. Eyes averted, he rose and placed his supper plate in the sink.

"I...er...I have work to do." Awkward, still not looking at her, he left the kitchen.

Jeanne sat for some while, silent tears streaming down her face. She rose to tackle the dishes, wiping her cheeks on her rough apron. She knew, despite his mean remark, that John still loved her in his way and would apologize. The remark was based on a need to reject the child he didn't want. She astutely reflected his remark would help her, for any suspicion he might have entertained would be quashed by the guilt he now carried for the accusation.

Soon, she would take him a cup of coffee, and they would be able to discuss the problem more rationally. Jennifer was asleep and would not disturb them. Once again, she knew everything would be all right if she could straighten it out before Mother Williams got into the act. They would somehow cope with the extra mouth to feed on John's union salary.

Her real dilemma lay in the future. She still loved John, but the conception of the child she now carried had been an expression of love for Tom Edmunds, not just some quick sexual exploit. Her regard for Tom in the early years was girl-like, fun tempered by the torrid physical relationship afforded by youthful sex. Now, as a mature woman, she discovered him for what he really was. She was careful to separate the guilt she felt for deserting him while he was in France. Now, she saw him freely as a courageous, motivated man, whom only her maturity could appreciate.

She would rob Tom of his fatherhood if she were to continue this charade. She knew intuitively that Tom would take her gladly if she went back to Edmonton, along with Jennifer. But then, she would be robbing John of his fatherhood of Jennifer. She cursed herself for a fool, yet regretted nothing. Stirring the required two spoonfuls of sugar into John's cup, she resolved to let sleeping dogs lie and await events. She carried the coffee to his study.

John was not at his desk. The huge stack of papers she witnessed while dusting that day still littered its top. Normally, he devoured paperwork voraciously, pencilling notes and flourishing signatures on directives at a speed few could equal. She loved to watch him work when he was unaware of her attention. Now, he stood at the window, brooding at the dark sky.

"Coffee?"

He didn't hear her enter. He turned with a look in his eyes. It seemed like hurt to her. 'Cuckold' sprang to her mind. He ran a hand over his bushy eyebrows and receding curly hairline, then vigorously scrubbed his large square jaw. He peered down at her from his six-foot burly frame, and as if suddenly noticing them dangling from his other hand, mounted his horn-rimmed glasses on his nose.

"I'm sorry, Jeanne. I didn't think what I was saying."

"It's all right, I guess." Eyes downcast, toe shuffling at the pattern of the carpet, she knew she was playing him like a fish, but she had to do it.

"I suppose, I was concerned how we could cope on my money." He shrugged lamely, oozing guilt. "The federation cannot pay me any more, but I guess we'll get by."

"We'll do our best. I'm going to have a nice bath and go to bed." It was her normal way of initiating sex between them. He looked up and perked slightly. "I won't be long, then. I just have one more pile of stuff to do."

Feeling slightly soiled, Jeanne left him and went upstairs. Several months later, her options were made plain to her when she noted in the Winnipeg Free Press an announcement of the recent engagement of Miss Margaret Thomas of Edmonton to Mr. Thomas Edmunds.

****

Edmonton, late March, 1919.

It was homecoming time for many units of the Canadian Army. Amongst them, months after the conflict ended, Edmonton's own Forty-ninth Battalion was finally entrained. A general fever of preparation for the homecoming of the battalion ensued. The Forty-ninth was one of the few units to remain intact throughout the war. Most battalions that went overseas were broken up as replacements for other units and lost their identity.

An enormous civic reception was planned with the whole city involved. As veterans, Tom and Alex, (who had also been repatriated with a wound), were invited to march in the honour ranks and proudly looked forward to the event. Around noon on Saturday the twenty-second, businesses around Edmonton blew their whistles, warning people they had two hours to congregate for one of the biggest events in the city's history. The Great War veterans fell in and marched from the MacDonald Hotel, behind the Edmonton Journal Newsboys Band, escorting a large number of dignitaries. They formed up outside the Canadian Pacific Railroad (CPR) station at Jasper and One Hundred and Ninth Street. Close to two in the afternoon, two trains rumbled over the High Level Bridge, bearing five hundred men under the command of Lieutenant Colonel Palmer. The Journal Boys struck up 'Hail, Hail the Gang's All Here' and every horn, siren, whistle, and voice in Edmonton was raised in salute.

Only a brief few minutes were allowed for family reunions before the Forty-ninth fell-in in company formation, facing the veterans. It was a stirring moment. Old comrades and unfamiliar faces sharing common bonds faced each other. Tears were shed. Bishop Grey said a prayer of thanksgiving for safe return, and Lieutenant-Governor Brett invested Captain Norman McEachern with the Distinguished Service Order.

Mayor Joe Clark recited a typically impassioned speech, welcoming the men back and touching on such things as their first moments with loved ones, the desperate struggle they had returned from, and Edmonton's desire to honour them. The parade proper commenced after Joe called for three cheers. The steel-helmeted Forty-ninth fixed bayonets for the occasion and marched eastward along Jasper Avenue.

About thirty thousand citizens assembled to witness the homecoming. Each and every organization involved had a position along the route.

Bunting and flags were everywhere as the rhythmically marching soldiers passed. Organizations, such as the Boy Scouts, Girl Guides, Masonic Society, Sons of England, United Commercial Travellers, YMCA, Knights of Columbus, Orange Association, Red Cross, St. John's Ambulance, Northern Lights Lodge Five Hundred Thirty-nine Ladies Auxiliary, and the Brotherhood of Railroad Trainmen fell in behind them, their unlikely names and associations joined as one in the event.

At One Hundred and Second Street, a choir of four hundred schoolchildren sang, 'See the Conquering Heroes Come.' Swinging south on One Hundred and First Street, the parade passed under a specially constructed 'Welcome Arch,' which comprised a major arch, flanked by two smaller ones. The giant word 'Welcome' was emblazoned across the central arch and topped by Brittania bearing aloft a huge Union Jack. At one end of the flat-topped arch was a sailor figure, and at the other, a soldier.

Arriving at the armouries, the Forty-ninth halted. Lieutenant Colonel Palmer ordered, "Dismiss." With a turn to the right and a heavy stamp of feet, the battalion stood down. With that simple act, the Great War was over for Edmonton.

Demobilization would begin next morning, but it was merely a formality now, as a mass of humanity swept down on the ranks. Men, gone for years, found grown boys for sons instead of the infant they remembered. Many of those boys marched homeward, buried under their father's helmet and dragging a rifle too heavy to lift. Following behind them, clinging to each other tightly, their parents gazed longingly. The fear of loss through all the years of separation was now broken. Tears and laughter broke loose at a familiar touch.

Yet, there were others who looked on with only pride and loss.

Edmonton became one big party, unrestrained by prohibition. The last official activity of the day was a brief concert at the armouries at eight. After that, dozens of parties started, similar to the one Tom and Alex attended at a private hall. The veterans stockpiled illegal booze for weeks, and the denizens of prohibition were sensible enough to keep to themselves this night.

The old cronies talked the night away, while old ghosts walked the streets; ghosts that had marched at their elbows that day and sat and listened to their stories. Their comrades and families would forever remember those who had not returned. One of the Great War Veterans Association's prime functions was to provide support for the dependants of the war dead. Edmonton and environs raised twenty thousand men to fight in the war. Four thousand and fifty served with the Forty-ninth Battalion. Of them, nine hundred and seventy-seven were dead, missing, or presumed dead. Two thousand two hundred and eighty-two suffered one or more wounds. Eighty-one percent had been casualty listed.

Two Victoria Crosses, eight Distinguished Service Orders, thirty-four Military Crosses, twenty-seven Distinguished Conduct Medals, one hundred and seventy Military Medals (one worn proudly by Tom Edmunds this day), and eighty-four other distinctions were awarded the battalion. Battle honours from a dozen campaigns were officially listed on the Forty-ninth's colours.

In the purplish twilight, as lovers loved and stories were embellished up and down the streets of Edmonton that night, there came a faint stirring breeze, almost from nowhere. It set up a faint soughing hum, like distant voices raised in a snatch of song:

"Plum and Apple, Apple and Plum,
Plum and Apple, Apple and Plum,
There is always some
The Service Corps get strawberry jam and lashings of rum,
But we poor blokes, we only get Apple and Plum..."

****

On the Wednesday morning following the Forty-ninth's return, a Canadian Pacific train stood gently spurting steam, as the engineer readied it for departure. The guard stepped out and was preparing to wave his flag when a backward glance revealed three young men approaching around the corner of the station. They were walking with a collective cadence that he could not quite place. Just before reaching him, they turned left and stepped onto the tracks.

"Here! You can't...!" He broke off in amazement as all three stooped to the ground and kissed it between the ties. Without a backward look at the nonplussed guard or any sound, they turned on their heels and disappeared the way they had come. Alf Barnes had not made it back from

France. At their reunion, Tom, Alex, and Chalky White recalled Alf's wish. They had just fulfilled the responsibility he had placed upon them.

Two months after the Forty-ninth came home, Tom and Alex began a tradition that lasted many years. They sat down in Tom's living room, in front of a warm fire over drinks and tobacco, to discuss and analyse their world. Sometimes, they ate out together, but they always repaired to Tom's study. It became a usual Thursday night ritual. One had a cigar and brandy, the other a cherished pipe of Balkan Sobranie and scotch. As the smoke wreathed blue around them and the liquor mellowed their mood, their frank analyses and mutual trust brought forth a march of progress, which served them well. Down the years, they toasted first the memory of friends, followed by a short pause. It gave them a kind of peace, a time to collect thoughts, and continuity in all things.

On the first of all these evenings, in a quiet moment, Tom sighed. "Well, it's over. At last!"

"For now, Tom laddie!"

"What do you mean, for now?"

"Until next time. I've talked to some people. Captain Ansover, who was with the One Seventy-eighth Battalion, has a degree in international law and figures the Versailles Treaty is an invitation to future trouble. Also, because of some of the terms, it was the German government that surrendered, not the Imperial Army, so it is spunky for another fight."

Tom looked at Alex with disbelief and growing alarm. "You mean we might have to do..." His voice fell huskily. "Do *that* again?" Alex nodded. "Then you could be right, Alex. I hadn't thought of it that way."

They stared at one another for a long while. After reaching for their individual drinks, their gazes turned to the coal fire burning brightly, the very depths of the coals built like a labyrinth of glowing caverns. There was a beckoning to the fancifully inclined in the red, orange, and yellow walls, an encouragement of images, real and imagined, of recollections sweet and sorrowful. And every once in a while, a softly snorting release of flaming blue gas gave life to the entity, reality to their concerns.

****

Winnipeg, August 20, 1919.

David Karl Williams was born on August twentieth, nineteen nineteen, a child of Libra. He was a sturdy man-child, a second and easy delivery for his mother. He suckled at Jeanne's breast. The look of contentment brought a long-needed peace to her. Mother Williams, refusing to yield an inch, huffed and snorted at every opportunity during the pregnancy. Usually, it was regarding the inconsiderate nature of the conception, sometimes, thinly veiled comments hinting at infidelity. It was almost like the old witch could read Jeanne's mind. John showed some lack of enthusiasm for his son, whether out of solidarity with his mother or his own choosing, Jeanne was not sure. Her own guilt prevented her calling him on it.

While bearing all of this stoically, Jeanne often wondered if this cantankerous old woman actually shared any female characteristics. She was fairly confident that her mother-in-law had not dared voice any of her thoughts to John. It was necessary not to incite her by arguing with her in any way. A major part of Jeanne's relief stemmed from the fact the little boy didn't bear resemblance to anyone. He had not popped into the world looking like a miniature Tom Edmunds nor did he carry a sign protesting his birth certificate. In fact, he was such a cute little guy that, surely, even Mother Williams would have to take him to her heart.

The now christened David Karl was given two strong names. 'Karl' was John's idea, and he would not be swayed. Jeanne didn't want her son named after Karl Marx. Although, one of John's heroes, he was not one of hers. Mother Williams was all for it, just because Jeanne was against it. Outnumbered and despairing, Jeanne gave in.

****

Edmonton, December, 1919.

Tom and Margaret originally scheduled their wedding for early January nineteen twenty, with a suitably long and fashionable engagement. However, Alfred Thomas suffered another, massive stroke in late September and it looked like he might die. Initially, they discussed pushing the wedding back to the middle of the following year. Alfred, however, recovered sufficiently by the end of the month and in the euphoria following, they brought the wedding forward instead. This was a risky gesture. Such action invariably had the local gossips branding the bride as pregnant. Should their count from one to nine be interrupted by a birth, then tongues would wag and heads would nod.

While they had unimpeachable moral justification on their side, Tom and Margaret had their minds decided by Alfred's doctors, who declared he might well suffer a final, fatal stroke at any time. He had permanent partial paralysis of his right side. It was difficult for him to talk. His mouth would droop and flop uselessly, frustrating him. He was also incontinent and confined to a wheelchair.

Everyone, including Alfred, agreed he should be given the joy of giving his daughter away at the ceremony. The circumstances brought Tom and Alfred even closer. They spent a great deal more time together, discussing the future of business. This was only accomplished from Alfred's side by laborious and frustratingly difficult note writing.

Tom and Margaret were married on December sixth, nineteen nineteen. They decided to make it a fairly small affair because of Alfred's condition. There was nothing to be gained by making Alfred a spectacle at the reception, so after the ceremony at St. Joseph's, they were taken by a procession of cars to the Macdonald Hotel, where selected guests attended a limited but lavish reception. Irene made sure the reporters got the story straight regarding the rushed ceremony date. She seemed to have a good day, casting only very few motherly sniffles. Since the Thomas family was Roman Catholic, Tom was required to undertake tuition to be confirmed in the faith to sanctify the marriage. A healthy donation to the church repair fund expedited Tom's acceptance in time for the new wedding date.

Alfred held up very well at the ceremony and looked delighted with the whole affair. He didn't seem to mind that the constant urge to smile kept a nurse busy wiping drool from his chin. Margaret, as most brides do, managed to outdo her beauty and looked radiant.

On the steps of the 'Mac,' one of Margaret's young cousins from Ontario caught the bridal bouquet, and they were off for a quick honeymoon in Calgary. It was hardly an elaborate honeymoon. Tom's business pressures, Alfred's illness, Irene's needs, and Margaret's newly-enforced involvement with the Jasper Avenue store precluded a more sustained and traditional destination. They promised themselves a proper honeymoon later: something to look forward to.

They would have opted for the famous Canadian Pacific hotels at Banff or Lake Louise, but heavy early snows meant unreliable travel, especially if they had to return quickly. They stayed at Calgary's Palliser Hotel, where Margaret gave herself to Tom for the first time, a little demurely and apprehensively.

For all that, the few days in Calgary did what they were supposed to do: break the ice on intimacy. They went on long walks and rode horses for miles towards the foothills, admiring the Rocky Mountains perched across the western horizon. With Christmas close, they purchased gifts with a Calgary flavour for friends and relatives then returned heavily laden from their shopping expeditions.

****

In late January nineteen twenty, Alfred Thomas suffered a terminal stroke and died after lingering several days. His death was reported throughout Western Canada due to his wide business interests. All parties were urged to continue association with Thomas' store through his daughter and new son-in-law, who would be overseeing the business.

For Irene, it meant a release. The reality of Alfred's incapacity proved almost as fearsome as her many imagined problems. She seemed to attain a state of peace with his passing. After the funeral, she showed little inclination to be involved with the business. As long as she could live comfortably, she was content to let Margaret and Tom handle everything.

This, in turn, gave Tom the financial clout he required to expand Edmunds Transport. At the Imperial Bank, the manager, Bernie Caulfield, suddenly became available without appointment. He rated an offer of a cigar from the cherished box on the inner office desk. Striking while the iron was hot, Tom increased his fleet of trucks from two to six and employed eight more men. A special advertisement in the Edmonton Journal declared unabashedly that 'With the recent expansion of its fleet of highly roadworthy trucks and enhanced warehousing facilities, Edmunds Transport now stands ready to serve the multifarious needs of Western Canada with routes also to the United States.'

In the meantime, Tom's staff at Edmunds Transport came to him to ask if they might unionise. He was against the idea, but his comradely ideas derived from the war swayed him. They assured him they would be co-operative and were enrolling in a small union called the 'Western Canada Transportation and Associated Workers' Brotherhood.'

Unbeknownst to all of them, the Brotherhood was in the beginning phases of voting itself into the Canadian Labour Federation, which in turn, was a scion of the International Brotherhood of Workers belonging to the 'One Big Union,' created in Calgary in the early part of the year. Had Tom been able to see through this smokescreen, he would have vetoed the idea. The IBW was rooted in the International Workers of the World, the 'I Won't Work!' marchers of nineteen fourteen. They were bad enough back then, but now, new influences were at work, primarily Bolshevism. That ensured the more radical elements amongst them garnered power to create harm.

In early March, Margaret snuggled up to Tom in bed. "Guess what?" He guessed immediately, but let her play it out. "We are going to have a baby." She was wearing such a smirk of complicity and accomplishment that Tom laughed and took her in his arms. It was indeed happy news, if a great surprise to him. They practiced no birth control and barely even talked about children coming along, assuming they would one day, like a new dining room table or bedroom suite.

Now the reality was with them and suddenly, too. They were really still honeymooning, although working twelve hours a day at their respective businesses. Too busy at work, surfing the enthusiasm of her newfound sex life, Margaret had not considered the consequences of their frequent and vigorous actions.

They were staying in the Thomas house. It was convenient to downtown. Irene complained of being alone in a big silent house, even though it had almost always been that way. Still, they decided they should have a place of their own. They bought a lot at the eastern end of Jasper Avenue, where it terminated as a narrow lane just short of meeting Ada Boulevard. The house they contracted to build sparked another possible endeavour, further prompted by the rapid expansion of the city. Peter Carson was a carpenter with big ideas but small capital and even smaller business sense to carry them through. Sitting over a few shots of illegal rum one evening amongst the lumber skeleton of the home, he and Tom agreed to partnership in a construction company.

The slight trickle of wounded returning from the war began in nineteen sixteen. It was so slight that only the occasional amputee was seen. Such men were regarded as heroes. By the time the Armistice of nineteen eighteen occurred, the trickle became a flood, but the people were now inured to the sight. It was regrettable that at the time most needed, sympathy for the larger numbers was not forthcoming. Such had been the plight of soldiers throughout history.

Although public knowledge was suppressed, Canadian troops rioted in Britain when they learned they could not go home immediately at war's end. It was a sign of the mental stress of warfare, a clear indication of how close to breakdown the armies had been. The Germans were in worse condition. Many riots took place when the Kaiser abdicated and fled into exile in Holland in early November nineteen eighteen. The German Navy mutinied when the admirals wanted the fleet put to sea to scupper the Armistice talks. In the following year, the left-wing Sparticists fought openly on the streets of Berlin for government control. This rebellion was bloodily suppressed and merely became a precursor of the social and political upheavals to follow.

While events never reached this pitch in Canada, a private soldier's pay of one dollar and ten cents per day and twenty dollars per month for his family made none of the veterans wealthy. Indeed, their pay had not increased since the beginning of the war. Formed in nineteen seventeen, the Great War Veterans Association (GWVA) hounded the government, mainly on behalf of the physically disabled. The greater tragedy was the overall disregard for the mentally disabled. Shellshock was observed but not acknowledged by the military medical people, who declared it 'a manifestation of childishness and femininity.' Thus was written off the serious psychological trauma of thousands.

'Most of the men come back with sluggish mental action,' was the simultaneous judgment of the Hospitals Commission, which blamed this on the soldiers having been totally cared for by the army for so long. At the same time, the government was quick to cancel wartime contracts. Thousands of civilians were thrown out of work at the same time as veterans were seeking employment. A federal plan through the Soldiers Settlement Board enabled veterans to borrow up to seventy five hundred dollars to establish themselves as farmers, but post-war prices still left most of these men on the wrong side of the financial scales.

There was a general air of frustration and delusion as the twenties approached. The banks waded into the economy by calling in higher risk loans and raising the interest rates. Prices fell back to mid-war levels. In nineteen twenty-one, a mini recession was to occur, which would have an adverse effect on jobs. As Tom Edmunds learned from O'Hanlon, the perpetual swing of the economy was predictable. A wise man sold at the top of the swing and bought at the bottom.

Although he hated the idea, Margaret made Tom join the Edmonton Club, 'the stratosphere of Edmonton society,' as Margaret liked to call it. This was a closed-club membership for the wealthy and a major sphere of influence in the city. He also joined the Freemasons, which further enhanced his position in Edmonton's hierarchy. While he was busy building his plutocratic ties, he was unaware that John Williams would pay him a visit. John was one of the delegates to the 'One Big Union' conference. After suffering defeat and a quick term in jail for being involved in the Winnipeg General Strike, he would soon visit Edmonton as a union regional secretary.

****

On the night of February tenth, nineteen twenty, Eldred Connaught engaged in a sweaty, though uninspired, bout of sex with his wife. Although possessing an elegant name, Eldred was not a man gifted with intelligence or even the basic niceties of civilization. His wife was little better. They lived on a small farm about eighty miles southeast of Edmonton and subsisted at a level of mostly self-imposed poverty and isolation.

The only mutuality they achieved was no particular love for each other. They tolerated each other with the surly ill grace and churlishness, which only the very ignorant can achieve. They rutted occasionally when it suited them with little technique or caring. The son they would bring into the world would be quite bright. But reared in this environment, he would become, to some observers, an emotional cripple.

At all events, after a series of grunts, Eldred rolled off his wife. Not long after he began to vibrate the room with his steady snores, the wondrous yet indiscriminate act of fertilization was completed. The life cycle of Nathan Eldred Connaught had begun.

EIGHT

FLAPPERS

The experience of the army taught Tom Edmunds some important lessons. Motorized transport would be the coming trend. The army proved that a business had to be in full control of numerous job trades and support organizations in order to not only function, but to function efficiently. Infantrymen, truck drivers, muleteers, mechanics, railwaymen, cooks, and clerks: all these people came under the control of an autonomous management system, which had no need for consultation or bargaining to achieve its ends.

The latter was a most important fact, since if a company owned woodland, cut the trees, milled the lumber, hired the carpenters, built the houses, and then marketed them, it achieved a flow-through ability guided by one concept, free from external interruption. Not only construction but transportation, too, was pliable to this idea. If a trucking company was allied with a vehicle sales and mechanical repair company, it could cut its costs and achieve economical advantage. As he had sat with Peter Carson amongst the clutter of lumber of his new home, swilling rum, Tom had visualized all this in his mind's eye.

Tom formulated his business plans in his weekly meetings with Alex. He still had money from his share of the coal business and ownership of the building on the south side, which, with full occupancy, was paying off handsomely. Edmunds Transport, while taking up most of his time and energy, was quite successful. He could see that, soon, John Homolka would be able to take most of the load off him. He had the financial strength of Thomas' Stores to draw upon for help. Thus, as promised, he became a financial partner in Carson Construction Limited. Peter Carson had great ideas concerning production, and as long as someone else gave him the organizational backing he needed, he was able to do a fine job. Edmunds Transport started to haul lumber into the city and deliver it to Carson Construction jobsites. In the negotiations of the partnership, Tom brought in Alex, who put in several hundred dollars as an investment.

A huge black-haired man with body hair like coiled barbed wire; Carson thought the arrangement of a one third each partnership was a fine and fair idea. He only wanted to direct his considerable genius and energy to putting up buildings. Any means to serve this end was fine with him. He was not sophisticated enough to see that if his two partners ganged up on him, they controlled two thirds of the company.

There were two further pieces to the puzzle Tom Edmunds formulated. First, he needed a lumber company to supply Carson Construction with raw materials. Edmunds Transport would, of course, deliver these materials. Second, he needed to cut out the middlemen in his purchase of trucks. The use of trucks in France and their innate advantage over horse-drawn vehicles had not been lost on him. By nineteen twenty, the number of cars on Edmonton streets multiplied twelve times since his arrival. There were now over thirty five thousand vehicles plying the roads. They were a rapid growth industry, and by becoming a dealer, he could purchase vehicles for Edmunds Transport a lot cheaper.

It took an extreme amount of persuasion, but eventually Tom convinced Margaret to agree to mortgage the Thomas' Store against a loan of fifty thousand dollars to set up a Ford dealership. They purchased property on Jasper Avenue and One Hundred and Twelfth Street, just west of the CPR station. Carson Construction swung into action. By September, a magnificent structure was created. It contained a splendid showroom plus a repair depot with rows of doors. On October twenty-seventh, the first stock of cars and trucks were just being delivered when something else also arrived: Elizabeth Rose Edmunds.

She was a sturdy little baby with strong lungs, 'like a steam whistle,' Tom used to say. Born in the middle of the night, as he held her for the first time and looked down at the solemnly steady gaze she gave him, Tom felt something beyond words. This little creature was a creation of his and Margaret's. He swore her total and eternal love.

This love he would have to share, because only three months later, Margaret announced the advent of Robert Alex Edmunds, who bounced into the world on November tenth, nineteen twenty-one. By this time, Edmonton was going great guns. The businesses were doing extremely well. The debt on Edmunds Ford was half retired, and sales increased daily. The mini-recession of nineteen twenty-one was behind them, as Tom had predicted. His boldness was being rewarded. The car dealership's construction contract kick-started Carson into erecting commercial buildings as well as homes. They struck a deal to start up a sawmill out near Edson.

By the end of nineteen twenty-two, Daniel Alfred Edmunds would arrive, coinciding with the final building block of Carson. That year, they signed up another partnership that would be the realty end of the business: buying the land and selling the final product. Now, they did everything from cutting, sawing, shipping, assembling, and finishing, to selling. Tom also thirsted after a hardware business to supply all their needs but would have to wait until nineteen twenty-four to get it running when James Henry Edmunds would be born. It seemed like business opportunities were directly related to baby making, but James would be the last child.

The other pregnancies were normal, but for some reason, James was a problem. Margaret was sick almost right from the start. She was listless and tired. At first, they put it down to the fact she was working too hard keeping Thomas' Store running. She suffered pains, and in the second trimester, became toxic. The doctors were at a loss to explain this sudden departure from her normal pregnancies. They ordered her to bed. Bloated and suffering, she remained there through the balance of her term.

They needed a nanny as soon as Beth (as Tom called her after the 'Little Women' character) arrived. Mattie Goodpenny would have her hands full for ten more years around the place. Tom always thought her name was right out of a children's storybook, but her services had to be augmented by a maid to care for Margaret. They hired Gladys Smith who had some nursing training. She basically became Margaret's companion upstairs.

The birth was horrible. It took twelve hours of labour fraught with suffering. At one point, Doctor Jacobs, their family physician, seriously considered a Caesarean section right there in the room. James was breach-birthed and arrived with the umbilical cord around his neck. Margaret was torn and bled badly, barely surviving the ordeal. Afterwards, Doctor Jacobs told Tom that Margaret would require an operation, since she was so badly torn up inside. There should be no more pregnancies, he warned.

The event was a turning point in the Edmunds family. After the ensuing operation, Margaret turned in upon herself, spending most of her time upstairs with Gladys. She still maintained an interest in the store, but it declined with the years. Far from adversely affecting her relationship with James, the ordeal seemed to work the other way. As the baby of the family, he unquestionably became her favourite. Yet, the ordeal pushed her beyond some mental limit. The operation seemed to rob her further. While they still occasionally visited each other sexually, she and Tom maintained the separate room status that pre-natal confinement had imposed on them. Down the years, he was to often reflect that her mental regression was an inherited trait from her mother, Irene, a dormant problem sprung by the stress of James' difficult birth.

The whole era of the 'Twenties,' the years of the 'Flappers' was a period of growth and presented new ideas to exploit. Tom Edmunds often worked sixteen hours a day. Only each week's evening with Alex provided light relief, even though at such times, the topic was often business. A third member was, by self-invitation, added to their soirées.

Beth and Alex formed a relationship of mutual adoration. Alex doted on the elfin-child and could always be counted on to produce a 'wee sweetie' from his pocket to tempt her taste buds. The candy was augmented by little gifts. No sooner would he arrive in the front hall of the house, a small hand would slip in his and a pair of pale brown eyes would gaze up at him adoringly, waiting for their reward for such devotion.

From the age of three, Beth joined them on most such nights. Bathed by Mattie Goodpenny and dressed in her flannel nightie, she would tiptoe in with her special teddy bear and climb into Alex's lap. She loved his man-smell, the odour lingering in his tweedy clothes of pipe tobacco and the faint whiff of the soap he used. She would climb onto him, wriggle down, and lay perfectly still without interrupting them. She had no idea what they talked about; she just wanted to be there. Within an hour, she usually fell asleep, thumb in her mouth, and later, Mattie, with a soft apology would steal in and take her off to her bed.

As she grew older, Beth would screw her tight buttocks hard against Alex's lap, finding some totally unknown pleasure in the closeness. She became bold enough to join in the conversation occasionally but eventually began to miss the odd evening to other pursuits. By the time she was fourteen, Beth was an infrequent visitor, but each time, she somehow ended sprawled across Alex as she sank into sleep.

While Tom and Margaret had been building their family, the men at Edmunds Transport attained membership in the Western Canada Transportation and Associated Workers' Brotherhood. For several months, there was no noticeable change. But by mid nineteen twenty-one, a creeping list of 'safety concerns, procedural wrangles,' and 'attitude problems' began to haunt the company. Tom had not opposed the unionising of his employees but now found himself spending more time sorting out these problems instead of getting on with the job itself. He realized after one half-hour meeting with a union representative that he had lost the 'one concept' ruling rights. He was now forced to consult with others when he wanted to do something. It offended his ownership pride. Then, when several things went wrong and caused customer complaints, he knew he was in for trouble. Although minor, non-attributable errors by his employees caused Tom to believe a mild form of sabotage was being performed on Edmunds Transportation.

Soon after, consultations (which quickly became demands) were opened concerning wage increases, shorter hours, and 'more employee input into company affairs.' It was the final straw. Tom gave them a flat 'No!' The union finally threatened a strike, and Tom called an employee general meeting to try to avert that possibility. It was a recessionary year. As the autumn drew on, business was poor and overheads high. They were already struggling to make ends meet.

On a Thursday evening after work, Tom went back to the yard to meet with his employees. So far, it had been a futile job trying to convince them there was little to be done towards providing raises and shorter working hours, in view of the recessionary times. Three of the men, Tom Schocter, Alf Dupuis, and Edward Standard became more and more difficult to deal with. Tom suspected that some of the yard problems, such as missing or overdue freight and repairs not undertaken on the trucks were retaliation for his unwillingness to give them what they wanted.

Someone had already opened the gates and let everybody in when he arrived. For some reason, this gave Tom a twinge of insecurity. The least amount of sabotage would destroy what little business he had left. He greeted the men, who were clustered in a tight little knot of discussion, and went into the office building. John Homolka sat waiting for him. Homolka, a rugged-faced Ukrainian, justified Tom's faith in hiring him by becoming an able manager. He still had some problems with the English language but typified the hard working ethics of many immigrants. Tom preferred such people in his employee ranks and was not above hiring anyone who had promise.

"Well, John, what are we going to do?"

"Mister Edmunds, every man want more money for less work. Only thing, where money come from? Work not get done."

"That's very true, John. There is little enough work to be had without cutting down on our efforts and raising our overheads at the same time."

"You want I speak to them?"

Tom shook his head. "No, thank you, John. I have to make sure they understand my position, and the only way to be sure, is to speak to them directly myself."

"You must tell them *no money if no work!*"

"You are with me then, John?"

The grizzled Ukrainian nodded his head. "Sure! You give me work when nobody else will. I work for you."

They went outside and it was obvious that Standard had been stirring them up. Nearly all twenty employees were present; some looked accusingly at Tom, while others shuffled their feet and looked at the ground, embarrassed. Glancing over at the gate, Tom spied a figure he recognized as John Williams hovering. He knew immediately that this meeting was going to be more difficult than he'd figured. While he had not yet met Williams, he had been pointed out around town. Tom would have hated him anyway because of Jeanne. The fact he was trying to meddle with Tom's dreams was further cause to despise him.

"Okay, fellas. I've asked you to come here tonight so we can get everything out in the open. As I understand it, you want a ten cent per hour raise and a guaranteed forty five-hour week with double time for overtime and two weeks holidays, paid."

There was a murmur of affirmation, almost as if they believed by saying it, Tom was approving it.

"Well, I'm afraid all of that is not possible." The mood of the crowd changed again, becoming sullen and intractable. "As you know, we are in something of a recession, and business is slow. We have to work hard drumming up business; there is little enough of it to allow for such increases."

"What about all the profits you made two years ago?" Standard was certainly spoiling for a fight.

"That was two years ago, Edward. The money was reinvested in various enterprises. You may care to note that one of those was the purchase of two trucks, which led to my ability to hire you. Furthermore, the financial plans of this company are none of your business." Out of the corner of his eye, Tom saw John Williams dislodge his shoulder from a gatepost and casually stroll towards the group.

"But we work here; we have a right to know!"

"You may work here, Edward, but you did not found this company, sacrifice financially to get it going, and you are certainly not suffering losses like I am, trying to keep it running, and incidentally, also keeping you employed!"

"If times are so hard, how come you're building a new house?" It was Williams, softly interposing the question from the edge of the gathering.

"Who are you?"

"I am John Williams, Regional Secretary for Western Canada of the International Brotherhood of Workers." The introduction was made with a haughtiness intended to intimidate.

"Well, *Mister* Williams, this is a private meeting called by me and is only open to employees of this company. Your kind are not welcome here. Kindly leave the premises!"

"Let him stay!" "He's helping us, Mr. Edmunds!" A half dozen voices protested.

"You men wish to be guided by a jailbird? You want to be taken down the paths of Bolshevism by this shit disturber? If I am not doing business with the world, I'm not earning money, and if I'm not earning money, I can't pay you."

"Bullshit!"

Tom began to lose patience. "I can prove in the books that Edmunds Transport is losing money, and I'm carrying four of you right now. As of this moment, I don't believe I shall continue to do so. Who wants to be laid off?"

"Don't listen to him!" It was Williams again. "The employers are always crying poverty! Poverty to them is when the roast on the Sunday table is less than five pounds, and they are one penny short of paying cash for a new car." He snorted derisively. "They have never *been* poor! They don't know what it's like! They just want other people, namely the poor, to suffer, while they grow richer and richer!" A small ragged burst of approval came from many of the men, but some still looked downright sheepish about the whole affair.

"Tell us what you can offer, Mr. Edmunds." It was Harry Block, a young, hard-working fellow with a wife and three kids Tom knew he could barely support.

It was time for a straight pitch to the likes of Harry. "There is not much to offer, Harry. I can let you have more time off, but it will be unpaid, since there is not enough work to go around. As far as the raise goes, I can stretch to two cents per hour, but that is it." Block dropped his eyes, disappointed, while a low growl came from the men. They all got involved willingly in the trade union movement, seeing it as an easy route to higher wages and better conditions, yet few saw the politicking and financial whys and wherefores involved.

"Not good enough." Williams was quite emphatic and could scarcely control his delight. He and the three ringleaders clustered together for a minute, Williams gesturing furiously and counting off points on his stubby fingers. There was obviously some reluctance to the cajoling. Tom saw Alf Dupuis take a step back and make little effort to re-establish his place in the group.

"We have decided to call a strike." Standard made the announcement with ill-concealed delight and defiance.

"Very well, when will it start?"

"Immediately!"

"That would contravene the agreement between this company and the union. It was tacitly agreed that any strike would be preceded by forty-eight hours notice."

"In view of your negative and intractable view towards our rightful demands, we consider that agreement void."

Tom thought how much Standard had come to sound like Williams. He turned to walk back into his office then turned at the last moment. "If you do indeed strike now, it will be illegal, and I shall sue the union for breach of contract. Anyone wishing to continue to work, please show up tomorrow, as usual. In the meantime, this meeting is closed, and John will lock the gate in five minutes."

Back behind his desk, Tom slumped into his chair in anguish.

"What happen now, Mr. Edmunds?"

"God knows, John. Half of those men out there can't afford to be away from work more than a day. I can't give them something I don't have. Unfortunately, as long as they believe in that Bolshevik Williams, they're going to be caught between the devil and the deep blue sea."

"Maybe you fire all of them!"

"The idea sure appeals, John, but there is an agreement with the union. They have broken it now. That puts them and the union in the wrong, and I don't think the union will appreciate the show of bad faith."

Outside, the men moved slowly to the gate and clustered around John Williams, who was obviously inciting them to more mischief. To Tom now, it was academic. If his outfit were shut down, just for two days, the damage would be irreparable. Produce would spoil, contracts would be broken, and other companies anxious to step in, would supersede Edmunds Transport. The irony was that the others paid less, and some of the men outside would find themselves working longer hours for less money if they found new employment with them.

"Go down and lock the gate, John. Ask first if any of the men can be counted on to come in tomorrow."

The gruff Ukrainian was back in a few minutes. "Nobody, Mr. Edmunds. Some guys maybe get to think tonight, come back tomorrow. I not know. Some not like, but Williams say 'lock-out' or something."

"Yeah, he'll try to twist the facts. Say the capitalist locked the poor under-paid, over-worked, workers out of their jobs. The poor are being downtrodden by the rich again! Sonofabitch! What am I going to do now?"

There was little else to do except go home. Tom took the books home with him and searched through them again, anxious to see if he could find a way to satisfy the men. He didn't know why, but he felt guilty, like he was letting them down. The next day, the newspapers printed stories about the 'illegal lockout at Edmunds Transport' with following paragraphs of drivel, which Williams obviously fed some reporter to try and justify his actions. By the end of that day, Tom was cornered. He fended off numerous clients with excuses, knowing they read the real reason why he could not perform his contracts. By noon next day, he knew his company would be on the skids with no salvation. At six that night, the telephone rang. Margaret answered and passed him the instrument.

"Mister Edmunds?" The caller was hesitant, unsure. "Mister Edmunds, this is Harry Block."

"Hello, Harry."

"Mister Edmunds, there is er, something I would like to tell you."

"Yes, Harry, go on."

"Well, while I wish you could give us some more money, I er, don't agree with what some of the men are talking about."

"Like what?"

"They, um, er, they are talking about doing harm to some of your equipment, Mister Edmunds."

"Who is plotting this?"

"I'm sorry, I don't want to say, but there are a couple of us who don't agree, and I wanted to warn you to watch out. You've always been good to me, Mister Edmunds, and I personally would mean you no harm."

"Harry, who else doesn't agree with this?"

"Well, er, Alf, Robbie Baines, Fred Thompson and the little guy, er..."

"Dave Lefrenier?"

"Yeah!"

"Harry, do you want to work?"

"Yes Mister Edmunds!" The reply was emphatic.

The idea came and gelled immediately. "Very well. Carefully now, ask these other fellas if they can meet me tonight at, er, let me see...the corner of One Twenty-fourth Street and One Hundred Seventh Avenue at about eight. Can you do that?"

"Yessir!"

"Very well, see you then, Harry." Tom hung up. "Ha! Got you, you goddamned no-good son-of-a-bitch!"

"Tom, really!" Margaret glared at him.

Darkness crept over the sky when the men met as planned. The street intersection was in an undeveloped section of Edmonton with stands of poplar and scrubby willow. They were not seen. Tom detoured and picked up John Homolka. Tom outlined his plan to the men and recruited them to his cause with a promise of jobs.

"Just like 'Wipers' and 'Black Hand Gang'!" chuckled Harry Block. They all shook hands.

Piling into Tom's car, they drove off to the Edmunds Transport freight yard. It was deserted as expected. There were no picketers in evidence. Only a strike sign and a barrier across the gate indicated the situation. Removing the barrier, they drove inside.

Alf and Robbie quickly went around the trucks and started three, backing them up to the loading bay. Since there was not a great deal of freight, they were able to load it speedily, making two round trips to a piece of property Tom owned about ten blocks away. A narrow, winding trail reached a fairly large clearing in the trees. Everything would be hidden from view. With that done, they moved out all the office equipment, maintenance tools, and other company items. In four hours, they stripped the place bare. The remaining trucks were started up and driven to the new premises.

Tom already briefed Alex McFarlane, who now burned the midnight oil preparing incorporation papers for the new freight-hauling company, while terminating the assets and liabilities of Edmunds Transport. By noon the next day, all debts would be paid, and the company would have disappeared overnight. By three in the morning, the group of conspirators unloaded the last of the trucks and sat around drinking throat-burning bootleg navy rum, chortling over the coup they had pulled off.

"So, what are you going to call the new company, Mr. Edmunds?"

"How about 'Midnight Express'?" Someone chimed in.

"How about 'Black Hand Transport'?"

"'Phoenix', the bird that arises from the ashes."

The next morning at seven, the first picketers arrived and noticed nothing. Their sign and barrier still sat in the same place. Nobody bothered to interpret the fresh tire marks in the dirt. Morosely, they clustered at the locked gate, wishing for a cup of coffee. At nine, a young man arrived from a real estate company and began to affix a large sign to the fence.

"What do you think you're doing?" Edward Standard was there in a moment, suspicious.

The sign read, 'This valuable property for sale. For enquiries, phone Ephraim Jacobs, Edmonton Properties Inc 2-4675.'

"You can't put that up here! This is Edmunds Transport!"

"Not any more", the lad exclaimed triumphantly. "It's being sold!"

It was then that the various overnight differences, the tire tracks, the hush of silent buildings became apparent to the men. Standard immediately dispatched a man post-haste to John Williams' hotel. He tore down the real estate sign in a rage. When Williams arrived an hour later, he was speechless with anger when he saw the situation for himself.

On that day, Tom Edmunds attained great notoriety as a captain of industry. Even people who might have evinced some sympathy for the strikers' cause had to laugh at the way they were so easily outwitted. 'Go picket a for-sale sign!' became a derisive catch phrase throughout the city for many years afterward. As for Tom, he was rueful about the money he lost in the scheme, but he figured he had no choice. He also knew it would not be so easy next time. John Williams would be more determined than ever to get him. The vendetta had only been cranked up a notch.

New men were hired, and by the next day, the new company, "Trans-West Transportation," did greater business than ever, thanks to the free publicity. In press interviews, Tom was careful to point out the illegality of the strike, which union officials grudgingly conceded when questioned. The strikers didn't have a leg to stand on and could only watch helplessly. John Williams disappeared and left them to their fate.

Tom also learned a lesson he would adhere to the rest of his life. He vowed that never again would he allow any of his companies to unionise. Conscious of two-way communication, he installed liaison committees, employee incentive programs, and profit sharing. In the years to follow, he would eventually bless the experience he gained in saving the ghost of Edmunds Transport.

****

"Tom." Tom Edmunds looked up. He recognized that serious tone to Alex McFarlane's voice. They were ensconced in Tom's den, tobacco and spirits to hand. Beth was asleep, sprawled across Alex's lap. His fingers stroked her hair. "Tom, do you remember in the war, how many men you killed?"

It was a horribly direct question, one that neither man had asked before. It was a question only outsiders, such as children, might innocently ask. It was not a question veterans put to each other. Only the closest of friends could hope to impose such a question on each other. It was so private and personal.

"I don't rightly know, Alex." He spoke slowly, drawing out the words, hoping for some kind of enlightening sign from his friend or even a dismissal of the question. "I do know I killed some Germans, usually when they were trying to kill me."

"Yes, that is the point, Tom. How many times did you kill anyone who was not trying to kill you?"

"Well, I suppose, never. Unless some of the rounds I fired towards their lines hit somebody."

"That is so impersonal, isn't it?" The conversation took a creepy turn, and Tom shifted in his seat. "What I mean is, if you can kill somebody without looking at them, there is no real conscious blame attached to the act."

"What is this, Alex, some kind of philosophical view of war?"

"In a way, I suppose, but do you remember after we were near Courcelette, and we found all those loaded rifles – German and British –

lying around abandoned? We asked ourselves at the time, how come there were so many fully-loaded rifles found in the middle of such a fight?"

"Yes, but there were a lot of troops. There was bound to be lots of equipment."

Alex shook his head. "I spent a lot of my time shooting over the enemies' heads, Tom. Not only that, but a lot of men around me either didn't fire at all or else merely loaded rifles and handed them to those of us who were willing to pull the trigger. I knew men who didn't raise a finger against the Germans even when their lives were threatened."

"What are you saying?"

"I am saying that many soldiers, on both sides, had no desire to kill, whatever the circumstances." Tom looked at his friend, aghast at the consequences of what he was saying. He had no argument to offer. He saw it himself but failed to admit it. In the spirit of comradeship, no blame was attached to a man who did not kill the enemy. No fingers were pointed. The shared danger bound them in a vow of silence regarding another man's behaviour.

"I do not believe this is a matter of cowardice. It is more a matter of morality, ethics, and a code deeply imbued in people by their upbringing: 'Thou shalt not kill'. "

"Did you kill anyone?"

"Yes, God forgive me. I killed when I had to but more, I feel, to protect my comrades than myself."

Tom nodded slowly. "I know what you mean. If all those rifles were aimed and fired to kill, how could any army have survived? Millions and millions of rounds expended. They had to go somewhere."

I have always felt badly about this, like I did not do my duty." The soft-spoken Scotsman gazed into the fire, tortured by his thoughts.

"How many do you believe did not fire to kill?"

"Probably half."

"God! But I have to agree with you, Alex. I feel that is indeed the way it was. Please don't blame yourself. In fact, I don't know what you are blaming yourself for."

"Nor do I. It is just that now, in retrospect, one wonders if it would have changed anything."

They smoked on in silence, deeply moved by what were two different confessions. They knew the subject would never again come up between them.

NINE

LIM WUK WAN

Wing Pei Luang sat on the loading dock. It was lunchtime. He opened a bag of dried noodles and munched on them reflectively. He was busy all morning, loading a truck bound for Lloydminster and helping with other routine tasks. He pushed ten wheelbarrow-loads of gravel around the yard, filling potholes around the place. Luang worked for Tom Edmunds at the transport yard for eighteen months and proved himself a conscientious and reliable worker. He suffered some teasing, but it had not been as bad as some of the pure racial hatred he experienced elsewhere in the community. Tom Edmunds had seen to that.

Today, however, Luang's mind was thousands of miles away, and since he stopped working, the object of his distraction rose to the front of his mind, like some dreadful spectre. He took a well-thumbed bankbook from his pocket and opened it at the last entry. The balance, with no withdrawals shown, was slightly over two hundred dollars.

He took two pieces of paper from another pocket. One was a tattered rice-paper letter written in Chinese characters. Another was an official-looking letter from the Canadian Department of Immigration. He placed them on the wooden floor of the dock, side by side. He gazed at the three items, one covered with the copperplate entries of a bank teller, one with the dark ink of some professional letter-writer in Shanghai, and the other a typewritten bureaucratic sentence of doom. He gazed off into the distance, eyes misted, as if seeking divine help.

Luang was twenty-seven years old, a stocky little man with straight black hair and a strong, intelligent face. He did not have the cheeks and eyes that typified the Western cultures' idea of Chinese looks. He had thin lips and a relatively long face with a straight nose, which decried his Asian blood. His hands, turned inwards on his thighs, were long and tapered, coarsened only by the labour he performed. Born in Vancouver, he arrived in Edmonton two years earlier, living with an uncle who offered to take him in.

In his contemplation, Luang missed the dog. Mudd was the yard watchdog, not at all aggressive, a ferocious-looking mongrel that was well liked by all the truckers. Attracted by the rustling lunch bag and the treats he had come to expect, Mudd crept up behind Luang. He whined and shuffled his front paws expectantly but was ignored. It was the tearing of the paper bag that alerted Luang to the dog's misdemeanour. Turning quickly, he found Mudd with his snout in the noodles. He reached over to swat the dog. In the process, he scared the animal into stepping onto his papers. A horrible scream came from his throat as a couple of muddy paws ripped and stained his precious documents. A torrent of Chinese abuse poured out of his mouth. He leaped up to kick the dog and pursued it along the dock.

Unused to such treatment, poor Mudd yelped, and tail between his legs, he cut left and leapt off the dock. Unable to reach the dog, Luang's frustration reached a fever point as he grabbed a box of apples bound for Grande Prairie. Yelling, he pitched the fruit after the dog, scoring one lucky hit, while the rest went wildly around the compound. With a burst of frantic speed, Mudd retired out of range, while Luang continued to harangue him.

"What the hell is going on out here?" Tom Edmunds appeared out of the office door. Luang was now crouched over, retrieving the dirty and torn paper off the dock.

"Luang, I'm talking to you!" To his astonishment, Tom saw the young man burst into tears. A stream of Chinese came from him, all unintelligible. "Get in here!" Sullenly, the young man completed gathering the papers and shuffled by Tom into the office. "Sit down! Now what in the Sam Hill are you doing trying to murder Mudd and destroying customers' property?" Luang shook his head, desperately trying to compose himself. He was still futilely trying to organize the papers in his hand. It was bad joss to look so wistfully at the papers. Now he had lost face with his employer.

"Look, Luang, Mudd is a good dog. You and he get along." Tom decided to try for the conciliatory approach. "For the past few days, you have been a screw-up. You put the Athabasca stuff on the Vermilion truck. You lost the gas cap on unit six and broke a bunch of boxes. What is going on? Is something bothering you?"

"I sorry Mister Edmunds, I do better now on." He rose to go.

"Sit down, Luang! Do you know the saying 'a problem shared is a problem solved'?" The Chinese man shook his head. "Tell me the problem.

There is one isn't there?"

There was a long pause. "The government..." his voice trailed off.

Tom waited with decreasing patience. "Look, the government is responsible for a lot of our miseries, but we don't all go around trying to kill friendly dogs and throwing apples at them! Now, what the hell is wrong?"

"They not want Chinese here! Try to stop Chinese coming! Chinese build railroad, but no good!" The words, goaded by fury, tumbled out.

"Luang, this is not right. I know many people don't like Chinese, but you are here. You are Chinese. You belong. You are a good worker."

"You know Jones family? Arrive last week?" Luang was referring to a prominent English family that arrived in Edmonton the previous week. "They pay money to come? No!" He shouted the word, furious again. "Canada not want Chinese, make pay to come. English not pay. Chinese pay."

The tirade began to make sense to Tom now. He recalled the Canadian government instituted a head tax of five hundred dollars each on Chinese immigrants after eighteen eighty-five when most of the coolies working on the CPR were laid off. It was an unjust system, but he never had reason to consider it before.

"Well, they cannot send you to China, Luang. You were born in Canada!"

"They raising head tax. Now will be too much money." The young man's head dropped.

"What will be too much?"

Luang looked up, his pride allowing him to compose himself. "I have been promised hand in marriage of Lim Wuk Wan. She is distant cousin living in Shanghai." The formal declaration stiffened the young man's resolve, and he stared at Tom, as if daring him to repudiate the statement.

"So when is she coming?"

"Never!" The facade collapsed again into desperation.

"Never?"

"They raise tax. Soon one thousand five hundred dollar. I never afford to pay!" A sadness of great enormity grew over Luang. Anguished, he cried out, "Now, I never have wife. Never have children. Canada not want me."

It was obvious to Tom that to come up with that amount of money would be impossible for the young man. He began to grasp the enormity of the problem. "How do you know they are raising the tax?" For his answer, Luang held out the torn letter, his face still turned to the floor. Tom scanned the ragged contents. "Bastards!" He was astonished and repulsed by what he read. "It does say you have three months before this new tax comes into force. Do you have any of the five hundred dollars you need now?"

For answer, Luang proffered the bankbook. Tom's eyes snapped up to the young man as he saw the list of deposits. He could tell at a glance that almost all Luang's money earned from his employment went into the bank account. There was a total of two hundred and sixty-five dollars and eighteen cents. The deposits and lack of withdrawals told a mute story of dedication and sacrifice. He would not have five hundred dollars within the allotted three months.

"How will you get this young woman over here?"

"It already taken care of but not matter now."

Tom nodded. He was deeply moved by the dilemma the young man was in. "You love her?"

"It is arranged marriage. Canadians not understand. We wait for nine years. I write her, she me, all time." Luang held up the tattered remnants of the rice-paper letter. "She wait make good marriage. I wait make good marriage." He reached into his pocket and withdrew a worn wallet. He produced a cheap photograph of a young woman. The print was worn, faded, and thumbed to the point of disintegration. It showed a young woman of indeterminate looks posed self-consciously for the camera. In a flash of deja vu, Tom remembered pulling out the picture of Nobby Clarke's family in the greasy mud of a dugout.

"Just a minute." Tom reached into his drawer and scribbled for a minute. "Here, Luang, take this." He held out the cheque, made out for two hundred and thirty-four dollars and eighty-two cents. "She is a beautiful young lady. Send for your wife-to-be today."

"But I cannot take this!"

Tom was ready for this. He knew that Luang had already lost face because of his loss of temper. The subsequent confessions of his problem didn't help. To take money now would bring dishonour on his marriage in the young man's mind.

"This money is a loan, Luang. It must be paid back with interest."

A flicker of involvement cracked the dismay on Luang's face. "But how much interest? It take many years repay such loan."

"You must repay me the money when you can. The interest shall be that you will make me godfather of your first child."

Luang's face suddenly shone with gratitude. "Ah, thank you, Mister Edmunds. My family never forget this you do!"

"Very well, now get the hell out of here. Clean up the mess you made, and then take the rest of the day off to arrange for her to come. Go on! Out with you!"

A minute later came a voice calling out softly, tantalizingly, across the yard. "He'ya Mudd, good dog! Come get nice noodles! Good Mudd! You come, boy!" Luang was trying to entice a very wary dog from behind a truck.

Long after Luang had left, Tom stared at the patch of light through the doorway. He knew about racial discrimination. He knew the immigration laws were a human disgrace. He learned in his life that a man's worth did not depend on his skin colour. That was why he had many ethnics working for him. After a while, he composed a very strongly worded letter to his Member of Parliament. He expected no change, but he had to register his disgust.

His view of the matter was not improved when a fussy bank clerk telephoned to confirm if it was all right to cash his cheque. It had been presented by 'some Chinaman.'

****

Germany revisited.

The Treaty of Versailles, signed between Germany and her enemies at Compiègne, stipulated the handing over of weapons and withdrawal from areas of occupation. Reparations were demanded by the Allies, which were intended to reimburse them for the expenses of the war and to pay for civilian losses. The ancient method of reparations, that is to say, plunder, ransom, and slavery were considered barbaric in the modern world, so simple repayment of costs was determined as more civilized. This did not mean the exaction of payments was less onerous on the people concerned.

Alsace-Lorraine was returned to France. Germany lost her overseas colonies. Belgium and Poland received land formerly under German control. This weakened the German purse. The Allies occupied the

Rhineland for a fifteen-year term, and the new army, the Reichswehr, was limited to one hundred thousand men, no submarines, and no military aircraft.

It was the sheer exorbitance of the reparation payments that held the genesis of future problems and misery for the German people. One hundred and thirty-four billion gold marks was the total payment demanded, to be collected on the backs of a nation and people in economic and physical ruin. People were jobless, ill fed, cold, and desperate. The situation led to political events bordering on anarchy. Very quickly, by nineteen twenty-one, with interest accruing rapidly due to the tardiness of payments, threats from the Allies resulted, underscored by their occupation of Dusseldorf and Duisberg. Annual payments of two billion gold marks with additional percentages of German export funds were demanded.

By nineteen twenty-three, the situation had reached the pitch where France unilaterally occupied the Ruhr to demand reparation payments. The result was a massive devaluation of the German mark. Runaway inflation commenced. Within weeks, the mark was worth only one eighth its value. In this ruinous state of affairs, where inflation outstripped wages, people became desperate.

It was with keen interest that Tom and Alex followed these events. The economic and political consequences of events in Europe coloured their plans and opinions.

As with all forbidden fruits, prohibition enhanced the lure of liquor beyond its natural level of appeal to the average citizen. Although Edmonton was a little too parochial for the 'speakeasy' pleasure houses found in major cities, it still had its places where women 'of easy virtue' gathered to offer fun. The pressure of easily obtained liquor, its attendant problems, and people's basic needs finally had prohibition repealed in Edmonton in nineteen twenty-three.

There immediately sprang up a great many 'beer parlours,' establishments that jammed in the maximum number of people. They served up a maximum flow of beer during the legal open hours in true frontier style. Hard liquor was only obtainable through government vendors, so the bootlegging trade survived reasonably intact and thriving. To protect the morals of inebriated men from the temptations of women, the government decreed that women who might attend such establishments could only be served in a separate room, whether accompanied by a man or not. This segregation of unaccompanied men was designed to discourage sexual fraternizing. As a consequence, most men who felt a stirring after a couple of beers tended to gravitate to one of the establishments boasting the time-honoured activities of whores.

There were several such active houses in Edmonton, most of them out in the undeveloped areas, where their activities could go unremarked by the virtuous. They were also more discreet. One night in nineteen twenty-four, Tom found himself escorted to one by the redoubtable Peter Carson. The separate sleeping arrangements with Margaret frustrated him to the point where other women became attractive to him.

Compared to the 'Maison de tolerances' of France, which he enjoyed meagrely during the war, Tom found this more entertaining. The girls were younger, better looking, better dressed, and seemed genuinely out to have some fun. They wore silk clothing with shortened skirts, revealing more leg than had been seen in Edmonton for years. They liked to dance, prancing around the room to the new electric phonograph music, flapping arms and legs in a whirl of aggressive sensuality most wives would swoon at.

Instead of the line-up, quick coitus, and out, Tom found himself entertained, teased, and treated attentively. That he awoke next morning with two young women in the bed, one snoring like a buzz saw, detracted not at all from his enjoyment. He did, however, realize that gossip would catch up with him, so he never went back again. The following year, after a brief affair with a young woman he met, he launched a longer-term relationship with a young widow he met through the Great War Veterans Association, who sported a lively disposition in the bedroom. He found her an apartment and kept her for the next three years.

The radio station, CJCA, was launched in nineteen twenty-two. People throughout the city and the north listened to music and news that bound them together. Movies, which only a few years before were silent, became 'talkies,' removing the need for the musicians who played in the orchestra pit. The cultural side of Edmonton grew fast. The Edmonton Grads, a group of young women basketball players, went to Paris for the nineteen twenty-four and twenty-eight Olympics and won all their games in the demonstration events. The Grads were one of the winningest teams in the history of sports and world famous. From nineteen fourteen on, they were only narrowly defeated once in their entire careers. Tom was happy to make donations to their expenses in sending them on their tours.

A meeting of extraordinary concept took place in Edmonton in nineteen twenty-seven. Where the idea began was obscure, but the driving force came from the substantial union membership in the city. For six months, a steady campaign of pressure was exerted towards the business establishment to hold a public meeting for welding together the disparate purposes of the unions and business.

The theory proposed that common ground could be reached in discussion, which would unite all efforts, reach a new accord, and enable the Edmonton economy to march forward to brilliant new horizons. The efforts to promote this utopian scheme were met by stony silence from the business leaders, who merely saw it as another effort to raid their pockets to enrich the common worker. After all, where else was the magical 'wealth for all' to find its source?

Amongst others, Tom Edmunds saw it exactly in that light. He likened such a meeting to 'appearing naked in a pit of poisonous and starving serpents.' Yet the pressure built. A couple of clergymen took up the message from the pulpit, and a groundswell of public opinion grew, spurred on by articles and letters in the newspapers. 'What harm could it do?' and 'What have we got to lose?' and 'We have everything to gain' became fertile slogans for the liberally minded majority of the public. Continued silence from the city businessmen was viewed as an unreasonable conspiracy of oppression.

The writing was on the wall when certain members of the Provincial Legislature spoke out. The Edmonton Chamber of Commerce quickly caved in, if only to appear reasonable. The Edmonton Club was made of sterner stuff. A secret committee produced a narrowly voted and thoroughly cynical decision to recommend member involvement for appearances sake only, but reserved subsequent action to the choice of individual membership.

Committees from both sides met to produce a list of agreed participants and a format for the meeting. It was agreed that a short speech from two of each side would precede an open debate between two principals, prompted by a question and answer session. Bills appeared all over town, urging the meeting and exhorting union membership to 'make sacrifices' as an example of willingness and solidarity of purpose in this grand endeavour.

Tom Edmunds was approached to partake as one of the people on stage. The Pantages Theatre was chosen as a suitable venue for the 'Forum of the Future.' He was one of those who re-christened it the 'Forum of

Failure.' His reluctance to be a business representative became iron determination when he learned that John Williams was travelling from Winnipeg to be a major representative of the union side.

On the night, there was an electric air of expectancy throughout the packed theatre. Everyone settled in their seats. People stood at the back and packed the foyer, unable to gain entrance. Others stood in the warm fall evening, out on the sidewalk. Technicians hurriedly ran out speaker wire to bring them sound of the proceedings. Newsmen and photographers dominated the first row, ready to record this historic meeting for posterity. Flashbulbs lit up the scene, as the principals filed onto the stage and took their seats.

Tom Edmunds and Alex MacFarlane occupied seats on the end of the third row, a block reserved for 'parties of primary interest.' Never shy of appearing in public, the stage group was salted with politicians, including representatives of Mayor Bury and Premier Brownlee. Recognizing a political hot potato, these worthies avoided attendance, deputizing senior lieutenants of their regimes to give speeches of vague hope and non-committal content to open the meeting. And thus they did. Having established such a vague political legitimacy, the politicians sat down and the real meat of the evening began.

In alternating order, two speakers rose from each side and gave non-inflammatory views on 'co-operation, common cause, and sharing of purpose.' It was obvious this careful stepping around the minefield of specifics did not provide any cue for the gathering to get down to brass tacks. At the end of the first rather boring hour, the audience waited with intense expectancy as the two men chosen to debate the issues went to their respective lecterns.

James Harris was a property-owning landlord and held shares in several businesses. He was chosen for his lawyer's ability to quickly seize a point and expand upon it. He was a forthright individual, impressive in a three-piece grey suit, tall and lean with a long, yet handsome face. When John Williams stepped forward, Tom Edmunds felt his ire rise like a poisonous tide in his body. John had put on weight. The dark blue suit he wore did little to detract from the fact. He now wore horn-rimmed glasses. His dark curly hair, while still long, succumbed to age and was rapidly turning prematurely white. His bulk and his reputation made him an impressive figure on the stage.

They started with polite rejoinders of welcome then opened the floor for questions. It was previously agreed the Press could ask the first three questions. This was done to exclude initial inflammatory partisan questions from either side but failed to recognize the innate ability of good reporters to provoke reaction.

"What exactly is each side willing to give the other to accomplish full co-operation to the betterment of all?" The speaker sat down, and the moderator turned to James Harris to indicate the floor was his.

Harris was immediately at a disadvantage. He had no proxy to speak of commitment on behalf of the businessmen. Although he knew he would have a chance of rebuttal, Williams would cut him to pieces. An unmistakeable restiveness spread through the crowd at Harris's weak references to 'committees – possible investment opportunity – joint ownership of some ventures – profit sharing.' It was patently obvious his answer was not direct enough. As he ceased speaking, a voice at the back shouted "Not enough!" and this proved the catalyst for change of tone of the meeting.

John Williams paused with the seasoned timing of an experienced speaker. Unlike Harris, as Secretary of the Canadian Brotherhood of Workers, he could speak authoritatively for his membership and deliver on any kind of statement he cared to make.

"I have been a unionist for more than twelve years. I believe totally in the need for unions and what they stand for: the betterment of the lot of the workingman. Mr. Harris, regrettably, has offered nothing here. What strength of voice on *committees* would the workers' representatives have? What numbers on a committee would they constitute? Where would the funds come from to invest in *joint ownership?* Who would have *last* word on their disbursement? I grant Mr. Harris that further negotiations are needed." Williams paused, confident that having uttered it first, he had managed to skilfully defuse Harris's only possible rejoinder. "We need more commitment, more on the table to deal with from the owners."

In his rebuttal, Harris could only weakly repeat what Williams had already disarmingly granted. Round one went to the unionists. The moderator called for the second question but was called on a point of order by the original questioner. "Mr. Williams has responded to Mr. Harris's comments, but has not expounded his own statements in response to my question. Could we please have a specific answer?"

The moderator turned to John Williams without comment. Everyone in the place, including Williams, knew the journalist was right. Embarrassed, he climbed to his feet again.

"The unionist movement will grant its full co-operation in any enterprise, which will benefit everyone, but this must include more favourable working conditions, pay, and treatment for the workers. It is obvious that a happy and satisfied worker is more productive. This not only helps the business he works for, but raises his self-esteem, making him even more valuable. Given a say in how things are done, being included in the daily operations and planning of a business, can only be a positive step for all concerned.

"In my experience, the business leaders duck this commitment. They count on a continuous cycle of replacement employees to water down the combined, accumulated expertise, and dedication of long-term personnel in trying to resolve differences. One of the first needs is for business to enshrine the principal of long-term employment."

Properly, the moderator again gave the floor to Harris, who finally had something to work with. "The cost of *enshrining* long-term employment is prohibitive. Can loyalty and dedication be purchased? What kind of dissatisfaction do we create when we *buy* a man for life? Does he not feel as equally trapped then as he does now? Has he become a blind commodity with no reasonable choice of seeking new employment?"

The debate was heating up. There was a murmur of varied opinions through the crowd. The moderator called again for the second question. The journalist designated rose. "What do you regard as the main stumbling blocks to making progress?"

This time, it was Williams' turn to go first. He rose to speak. "As I have stated, the employer usually seeks to avoid these issues. They reserve unto themselves final say in everything, rarely taking advantage of the employee talents residing in their businesses. Rewards for special efforts and dedication are rare."

"Horse feathers!" It was his turn to be heckled. The colour rose up his neck. Normally, union speeches were made to partisan audiences and any interruptions were usually of praise.

"Some employers would rather shut down their businesses than negotiate with legitimately constituted representatives of the workers." Tom Edmunds, in turn, felt the colour rise in his own neck at this veiled reference to himself, but moments later, joined in the common laughter when a cry from the back of the theatre loudly voiced the old "Go picket a for-sale sign!"

The taunt caused Williams to explode. "The employers have garnered wealth to themselves on the sweated labour of their employees for centuries. It is time in this modern age to forge a new alliance where the worker is given full recognition of his worth."

"Communist!" This time the heckling came from closer to the front of the theatre.

"I am not now, nor have I ever been a Communist!"

"Then why is your firstborn named Karl, after Karl Marx?" This time, it was Tom Edmunds who called out.

John Williams turned in rage towards him and pointed his finger like a lance. "Karl Marx had many admirable ideas but not all of them practical in this modern world. I do not cleave to many of his ideas, but the rights of the worker loom supreme in my own visions. Many of our workers went to Europe in the Great War to further the lot of the common man. Now, avaricious, ruthless, and grasping employers, *such as yourself*, have denied the rights they fought for." In fury, Williams advanced to the edge of the orchestra pit and yelled directly at Tom, who now stood and began to shout back.

Anxious to keep order, the moderator urged Williams to return to his place and keep his peace, while signalling to several burly off-duty police constables, who were hired as bouncers in the event the meeting became rowdy. Two of these men strode down the aisle, intent on removing Tom from the premises, but a growing cry of "Let them speak! Let them speak!" came from the audience, who were finally getting their reward for attendance. In the interval before the moderator reluctantly waved off the bouncers, both men had time to take a breath. It was John Williams who got to speak first.

"I am not now, nor have I ever been a card-carrying member of the Communist Party. A lot of people believe I called my son Karl because I admired the teachings of Karl Marx. This, to some extent, is true. However, I do not believe in everything Marx said, and certainly little of what has been made of his beliefs in modern Russia. I made what I would like to think was my own intelligent selection of his more worthy writings, which are substantive in our society. For instance, I believe in freeing people from oppression. In our society, this does not necessitate revolution. I do not condone revolution, even less now than I did then, having seen its effects.

"Karl Marx wrote 'Das Kapital' in England. His teachings, therefore, do not reflect theories derived from Russian but rather British influences of repressive capitalism. They are, perhaps, thus more pertinent to us as a Dominion than some of us might think. Marx wanted the emancipation of the proletariat, the modern serfs who serve capitalistic masters.

"Is there anyone here who would criticize the efforts of another author, Charles Dickens, who championed the freedom of youngsters from child labour in the mills and chimney flues of Victorian England? Would you condemn William Wilberforce, who had slaves in the British Empire emancipated a century ago? Would anyone speak against Emily Pankhurst and other women who worked for women's right to vote?" Cunningly, Williams included the few women present.

"The unions of the world work towards the same honourable and reasonable goals. There should be a common committee of workers and employers, tasked with sharing the wealth. Thank you." Williams took his seat to a wave of applause.

"Mr. Edmunds, would you care to come on stage and respond?" The moderator sat back with sweat beading his brow.

"I will answer from here, thank you." Tom stood in his place and turned to face the crowd. "This country was built by men and women, who were prepared to sweat and labour for little reward other than achievement of their dreams. That is a concept I don't expect *you* to understand." Swivelling, his finger jutted abruptly at Williams, sitting on the stage. "As for the men who went to war, they did not go for the twisted reasoning you have ascribed to them. Yes, they fought for freedom, but it was freedom from the tyranny of another nation they fought for, suffered and bled for. How dare you usurp their memory, their suffering, and sacrifice for your miserable propaganda ends!" Tom's voice rose in a storm of indignation.

"Amongst others, *I* did not go to France to promote *your* Communist principles. I went to fight for *our* country! It makes me want to puke to think that while we were making such sacrifices for you, you lurked here, exercising your miserable, cowardly, and vile treasonous lies, safe from physical harm. We succoured our nation's progress. You habitually bite it!

I came from a background of poverty. Canada has allowed me to be successful in my dreams. The opportunity is there for all men, but not all want it. Some, like you, would rather leech off the producers, the true leaders of progress. I killed better rats than you in the Flanders trenches!"

Even if the speech had been spoken in private, it would have been grossly insulting. The white fury on John Williams' face showed that he had been stripped to his soul. He leaped to the edge of the stage, screaming a response, only the orchestra pit stopping him from leaping down. Even then, one of his supporters hauled on one arm, in restraint, as the theatre went into an uproar.

The moderator pounded his gavel, screaming the meeting was closed. A dozen fistfights broke out. In moments, what had been touted as a major civilized breakthrough in relations had become a minor war.

Williams was hustled out the back door of the theatre and taken to his hotel. Tom and Alex took a half hour before the crowd cleared sufficiently for them to exit. Rocks were thrown at Tom's car, and two windows were broken. Although he hired watchmen, more minor damage was recorded at several of his business establishments. The newspapers had a field day. The meeting made national news on the radio networks. Letters of support and accusation flew. Alex cautioned Tom that the vocal threats to sue coming from John Williams might prove dangerous.

In the end, political expediency ruled. A survey of opinions revealed a strong feeling of insult from veterans who did not believe their wartime experiences were motivated by a wish to further union agendas. After a few weeks of rhetoric, the great experiment fizzled like a damp squib and was relegated to history.

If there was any lasting outcome, it lay with the depth of hatred between John Williams and Tom Edmunds. Where before they had merely despised each other, their relationship now was one of open enmity and hatred.

****

In his eighth year, Robert Edmunds was tall for his age. He had the lanky kind of build that would always make him appear head and shoulders above all around him. His first few school years had not proven him an outstanding student but did satisfy the demands of his teachers and his parents enough to keep alive the hope of his one day going to university. He looked very much like his father, except a thinner face and long fine blond hair, which flopped boyishly over to one side of his features. His priorities were much the same as all young boys, fun before academics until the first handful of days of nineteen twenty-nine.

That year, Edmonton became the focus of worldwide attention due to a heroic mercy mission. An outbreak of diphtheria occurred at Little Red River, a tiny settlement near Fort Vermilion. This was over five hundred miles as the crow flies, north of Edmonton, on the Peace River. The resident doctor cabled urgently for antitoxin, but Northern Alberta was in a deep freeze. Besides the hazards of the winter journey, the durability of the antitoxin through the extreme cold was questionable.

Dr. Bow, Deputy Minister of Health, fell back upon two recent innovations of the modern world to get the medicine to Little Red River. First, he called Wop May, a World War One flier who was part owner of the Edmonton Aero Club. Bow persuaded him to attempt a flight to deliver the antitoxin. The rapid spread of radios throughout the North linked people together. He got CJCA radio station to broadcast news of the attempt and request assistance from along the way. The radio enabled the public to keep abreast of events, one of the earliest occasions where news was up to the minute, not printed later in a newspaper. Clustered around their 'cat's-whiskers' radios, everyone felt they were a part of this great adventure.

In temperatures around thirty-three below zero, May and his fellow pilot, Vic Horner, delivered the antitoxin safely and days later, returned to Edmonton. The open-cockpit plane arrived back to a welcoming crowd of ten thousand people, eager to cheer the two heroes. Standing amongst the crowd was the Edmunds family, and on the spot, young Robert decided he wanted to be a pilot.

The historic flight turned around public apathy to spending funds for a proper airport at Blatchford Field, on the northwest corner of the city. Very quickly, Wop May, Punch Dickens, Stan MacMillan, and other like-minded aerial entrepreneurs forged routes into the far North. Aircraft reached Aklavik, in the Mackenzie Delta, later in the year. Soon, Edmonton could boast four smooth grass runways thirty-five hundred feet long and obtained Air Harbour Licence Number One from the authorities in Ottawa. The demonstrated usefulness of both the airplane and the radio were not lost on Tom Edmunds.

******

Towards the end of the twenties, with his children growing around him, Tom Edmunds felt that fate had been kind to him. Everything was flourishing, and in a time of economic growth, the construction, automotive, and transportation industries were strong performers. It was easy to forget the tougher times and look forward to the future. Then, in early March nineteen twenty-nine, he received a letter from Tim O'Hanlon in Calgary, right out of the blue. His Irish friend complimented him on his success and went on to try and panhandle two thousand dollars for what Tim described as his 'last bid to hit the big one.' The letter finished by promising to cut Tom in on a share of the success.

Tom took the letter to the window of his office overlooking Whyte Avenue and reread it, pausing at the end to stare down without taking note of the busy scene below. The money itself was nothing. It was the subliminal message it contained that was all-important. He pulled on his winter coat and told his secretary Molly Hines that he would be gone the rest of the day. Boarding a tram eastward, at the terminal, he climbed down and trudged off on a walk he sometimes took at times of stress or great contemplativeness. It was, in essence, a pilgrimage to the tree he and Jeanne transplanted so long ago. It now stood almost twenty feet high, a proud and healthy young spruce that promised to grow to full stature.

Taking the usual route, Tom threaded his way through the starkness of the denuded deciduous trees. It was cold, but clear, with snow still on the ground. Regular strollers through the area had left an easy path through the snow. He went over in his mind the ramifications of Tim O'Hanlon being short of money. Of course, he could easily have gambled away his poke, knowing Tim, but there was something else to it. Times were *too* good, right now. Inflation was up and expansion in every area was running at a high pace. By the time he came to the tree, he reasoned it was time for a readjustment in the financial marketplace. The dilemma was whether there would be a mini-recession, like nineteen twenty-one, or was he faced with a major collapse, such as O'Hanlon taught him could happen from time to time. He would send Tim the money. That was a given, but what should he do about his own interests?

The tree was healthy and ready for summer. After tweaking a few dead deciduous leaves from its branches, he snapped off a tall poplar shoot, threatening to chafe the lower branches. He probably would not visit it again for a few months. Continuing down Mill Creek to the North Saskatchewan River, he sifted through the information available to him.

The moneylenders were almost in a state of runaway. Bad sign! Employment was good, indicating a break was not imminent. What he had to do was more research on the state of the money markets and find out what the bankers truly thought. He knew Bernie Caulfield was not the man to ask. He was merely a cog in the machine with little economic shoulder to the main wheel. Still, close contact with Bernie would forewarn him of local ripples. He needed contacts close to the money markets and the stock exchanges down East.

Most of the economic indicators were good, as far as he knew. Vehicle sales ran high and construction was at a steady pace. The newspapers were enthusiastic about the state of the West. New electric appliances, such as radios, iceboxes, and other household gadgets were selling fast at Thomas' Store. By the time he reached the Low Level Bridge and boarded another tram, he knew what his plan of action should be: research and layout of contingency plans.

In his letter, Tim described the arrival in the Turner Valley oil game of I.W.C. Solloway, a stock promoter from Toronto. The speculative game of oil stocks settled down since the initial Turner Valley oil finds, but the glow of gas flares in the southern Calgary skies was a constant reminder of riches to those smitten by the bug of speculation. Gambling, in some form, was an oddity of the Western nature. The adventurous spirit that made men emigrate out West epitomized the built-in desire to reach out that extra arm's length to grasp a greater reward. There was no shortage of men who fancied themselves as 'oilmen' in Calgary.

As a fringe player to the lawyers, doctors, politicians, and major wheels, who gathered in exclusive sequestration in the Calgary hotel suites, Tim O'Hanlon became a party to a stock manipulation fraud. Solloway set up an elaborate stock-trading establishment on Eighth Avenue, using his previously established practices to reel in investors. His huge stock quotation board, backlit to catch the eye, attracted investors in droves. At the same time, certain unscrupulous parties began to 'wash sales' – buy their own stocks at slightly inflated prices – driving up the value until it caught the public notice. Once this happened, it became a self-perpetuating spiral until investor interest gave out, leaving the late buyers holding over-inflated stock.

One of the techniques used by traders was the 'call loan.' This enabled buyers to obtain stock in their name for a down payment of a third-to-one half the trading value of the share. While they were liable for the balance of value on sale of each share or when it was 'called,' most speculators liked this method. They were thus able to buy twice as many shares for their dollar. By using the paper profits expected on the sale of their shares, speculators could use this 'credit' to buy even more shares. Money borrowed from banks to finance these sales was not secure, since the true value of shares was not reflected. A sudden shakeout in values could hazard the billions of dollars, which were diverted from normal commercial securities into stock trading. In this way, the old stable method of paying up front for a stock certificate at a price reflecting its true worth was undermined. Some stocks, such as electrical manufacturing giants Westinghouse and General Electric had tripled in value, their success in manufacturing sales cloaking the mostly speculative flavour of their asking price.

The inherent risk was should a buyer putting up only thirty cents on the dollar have that stock fall to thirty cents in trading value, he would make no gain and still be liable for the seventy cents he did not pay in the first place, payable as soon as he sold it. This was presupposing a willing buyer could be found at thirty cents. The stock could as easily fall to zero value if nobody fancied it. He would lose his total investment and still incur the outstanding debt of seventy cents. It was like a deck of cards built up as an inverted pyramid. Tom was aware of the practice. He dabbled in stocks and made money, but to him, risk-taking in businesses under his direct control made far better sense than putting his money in others' hands. He liked being in control. Placing the net worth of a company in the hands of speculators did not suit him.

****

To the brew of boiling speculation following Solloway's sortie into the market, the Calgary 'oilmen' now threw in a major ingredient on March nineteenth, nineteen twenty-nine. Home Oil, which traded in Toronto at three dollars fifty a share, announced the purchase of a United Oils lease in Turner Valley for a price of one million dollars. Solloway and the rest raised half the million through the 'oilmen.' Since Home Oil was a producing, successful company, the elevated interest in shares became a frenzy at this news. Activity was so hot on the Calgary Exchange that extra staff and a day of closure did little to allow a catch up with record keeping. In the middle of this mayhem, Solloway was supposedly guilty of 'bucketing,' an illegal manoeuvre whereby orders (and money) were accepted for buys, which were then not put through the Exchange. This was intended to protect him and his partners if the stock should fall and they should find themselves short of the four million dollars in stock they held.

Home Oil stock eventually went to twenty-five dollars in Toronto, realizing huge profits for early buyers who had then sold to eager speculators. There was some retrenchment of the prices in the succeeding months. Tom received a cheque for four thousand dollars from Tim O'Hanlon. The bulk of investors now sat dangerously on inflated value stock that they had paid short on. Many people were jittery.

The events in Calgary played no influence on what Tom Edmunds had planned. Wheat, the great staple of the West, was still steady between a dollar forty and a dollar forty-five per bushel on the futures. It took a dive in August, but a rapid recovery sent mixed signals. He first discussed the matter with Alex McFarlane that Thursday night. They agreed they had two options: total pull-out of all businesses that may be at risk in a major recession and reinvestment in more stable markets at an appropriate time, or hang in, gambling on a short period like nineteen twenty-one. Tom had a hunch this recession would be tougher.

Over the following months, into late summer, Tom Edmunds reviewed the strengths and vulnerabilities of his various companies. He hired a man in Toronto to watch the stock exchanges, both there and in New York. For other economic indicators, he felt he could handle observations himself. The telegraphs into stock offices in Edmonton were pretty quick and reliable sources of trends. He began to quietly attend for a half hour in the mornings, rising early and dropping in before he went to work. He subscribed to major eastern newspapers which came to him days old, but still gave him food for thought.

He had his hands full with various concerns. Peter Carson still did wonderfully at directing Carson Construction. Tom and Alex installed an accountant that reported directly to them to see the financial end was adequately covered. The ancillary industries, real estate, lumber, milling, and hardware could be made dormant and were under Tom's direct ownership. The actual construction operation could be shed, since in a recession, it would suffer greatly and become a liability.

At Phoenix Transport, John Homolka had things well under control. The Ukrainian was not an innovative manager, but he developed a real knack for dispatch, got on well with his staff, which he kept under firm control. His strong sense of honour gave customers the commitment to service they needed. The company grew under his management but could easily be downsized. Tom felt the vital movement of some commodities would still require servicing. Now, they had the mail contract and that would surely continue, even in tough economic times. A proposal to purchase three more trucks would likely be dropped and four of the present vehicles sold off.

Edmunds Motors grew so rapidly that an expansion was under serious consideration. A young man of boundless energy and talent named Grigor Kovaks had quickly risen from salesman to manager. Hungarian by birth, Grigor was an auto mechanic in the Austro-Hungarian Army during the war. His two passions in life were cars and women. His charming persuasiveness ensured he turned over both at a rapid rate. He was instrumental in Tom going into the gas station business, shrewdly pointing out the great demand for gasoline, and the fact that such an endeavour fell in line with Tom's 'flow-through' principle of business alliances. While very lucrative, the gas stations would also have to go. The proposed record order for new cars for nineteen thirty-one would require severe review. They had already paid a sizeable deposit against these orders and were committed to the nineteen thirty orders, which were due for delivery soon. An option on further stock of the nineteen thirty model should probably be cancelled. If sales did fall, the front-end financing would ruin them.

Regarding Thomas' Store, Tom had serious disagreement with Margaret. Sales were running at an all time high, so to her, it seemed unreasonable to consider selling such a lucrative venture that had proven a financial anchor to all their enterprises. She also had a great ingrained loyalty to the business, which affected her objectivity. With her mother in ailing health, it did not seem proper for her to consider such a move. She refused to even cut down on stock orders.

Peter Carson was floored by the idea of selling out Carson Construction. He got very angry, and since Tom had to keep his plans confidential, he was unable to persuade Carson to sell. Peter was not a financial person, and stymied by a two to one vote, he had to go along with the plan. He raised some capital and bought himself up into a fifty-one percent share, figuring that in future, he could stave off such treachery by future shareholders. The balance sold very quickly, takers encouraged by the company record, but also the announcement that Tom Edmunds was selling to raise capital to go into the radio business. Tom and Alex made a healthy profit selling their Carson shares.

For that was what Tom proposed to do. The Fort Vermilion mercy flight demonstrated the value of the radio. Now advertising was selling fast on this medium, generating profits. Tom once read that during the Roman Empire, ships due to carry corn from Egypt to Rome during a famine had their cargoes switched to sand. The sand was spread on the Circus Maximus arena floor, so the ensuing games would take people's minds off their bellies. Tom agreed with philosopher George Santayana's premise that 'Those who cannot remember the past are condemned to repeat it.' He believed bad times might be forgotten by a little entertainment. 'The Dumbbells' entertainment group did that in the Canadian Corps between stints in the Line during the war. The advertising effectiveness of radio also fitted within his 'flow-through' principle. His various companies could buy time at a preferred rate. A great deal of money was required to set up the radio station and procure staff and programs. A great coup was achieved in buying the broadcasting rights for the 'Amos and Andy Show' from the United States. One of the most popular radio shows of all time, it would keep many an ear tuned to Edmunds Broadcasting.

Edmunds Motors proved difficult also. Tom had to be careful not to give the impression he was doing a massive selling out. It would not only alarm customers but also drive down the selling price. Grigor Kovaks' handsome face went purple with rage when the idea was aired to him. He refused to be any part of it. He quit on the spot and stormed out of the premises. The next day, he was back, still angry, but willing to talk. They finally agreed to go halfway, cutting the nineteen thirty-one orders from Ford and selling off two of the four gas filling stations they set up around town.

Tom would not budge over the extra nineteen thirty models, for which they had guaranteed delivery. Their quota was greedily bought at a small profit by a dealership in Winnipeg. Grigor's strongest argument was loss of market share if they did not have the vehicles in stock to cope with demand. At this point, Tom felt he had made enough manoeuvres to begin attracting scrutiny of his actions, so let the matter go at that. He kept a few low-key negotiations going on shares in other companies he regarded as high risk in bad economic times. Even so, Grigor bought one of the gas stations himself, intent on staying in the game. Tom had to refuse to finance it for him, since this would have left him as vulnerable as if he still owned it. Grigor went to a bank for a loan, and the whole exercise left him in a state of mind which laid a question as to his continued loyalty and commitment to Edmunds Motors.

By early September, all of these plans were put in place. Tom sat back, nervously, as the economy ran on unchecked. Margaret was unmerciful, as she saw the cash registers ringing up ever-increasing sales into October. Although very reclusive, she pored over the business finances like a vulture picking over a carcass. This was not an entirely unwelcome habit, since she came up with diverse views on matters, making for a balanced overall determination of how things stood. Tom found some release from his nerves, however, in the arms of Annie Leblanc, the widow whom he had kept as a mistress the previous few years.

After Labour Day, there occurred several ripples that spread through the money markets, characterized by journalists and economists as 'shake-outs' and 'spasms.' On October twenty-first, a drop occurred. It was recovered the next day with a slight rally. The next day, there was a further drop and on the twenty-fourth, the Winnipeg Grain Exchange hiccupped mightily. Wheat dropped by eleven cents per bushel in twenty minutes. Wheat future speculators had automatic 'stop-loss' orders at two cents above their margin, but these were all subscribed to so rapidly that, with events outstripping the reaction time, many people were wiped out. By the end of the day, wheat recovered steadily but was still down by six cents.

The phone rang early on the morning of Tuesday, October twenty-ninth. It was Edward Wellington, the stock-watcher in Toronto whom Tom hired as a scout. "Big action in New York, Mr. Edmunds. Everything is for sale. Suggest you sell everything you've got."

Tom immediately phoned Alex to close the sales deals remaining and cash cheques from the purchasers. It was in the nick of time.

In the next few hours, twenty-three million, five hundred thousand shares were traded. The volume was so great that the stock ticker recording the transactions was four hours behind. Casual investors in Edmonton did not rise early enough to match the opening time of the New York market. The three-hour time difference, plus the ticker delay, jammed them out of the ability to make transactions. The information getting to them was too stale in the volatile market. Orders to sell were delayed, causing further losses. The stocks plunged below the sell value. As news spread, shocked crowds packed the stock houses to watch the boards. The short call loans now took a major part in the panic selling that took place. Investors tried to get out from under the debts they now found themselves responsible for. The value of many stocks dropped by sixty percent.

The Canadian newspapers, especially in the West, had different agendas to follow than a bad day on the New York Stock Exchange. Wheat was stable again and the Canadian stock issues had not plummeted the same way. The Edmonton Journal reported on an upcoming banquet in London for winners of the Victoria Cross, to be given by the Prince of Wales. Yet, only two days later, the paper headlined 'Mad Rush of Selling Sends Winnipeg Wheat Down Fourteen Cents.' It was the beginning of the end. With one side of the house of cards removed, the rest collapsed quickly.

Black Tuesday, October twenty-ninth, nineteen twenty-nine, had passed, but the residue of its events would smear the lives of people throughout the world as they endured 'The Great Depression.'

****

Vancouver, 1933.

The building was in Vancouver's Chinatown, up a narrow flight of stairs, next to a shabby restaurant. The place was redolent of memories of the Orient. Once Tom ascended the stairs, he might have been in Singapore again. They were here on an urgent appeal for money. The worsening times of the Depression had driven Tom almost to the wall and the banks, even good old Bernie Caulfield, had refused any further credit.

True to their bargain, Luang had made Tom godfather of his firstborn, six years earlier. Luang had remained immensely grateful. When word had spread about lay-offs and business closures, he had shyly approached Tom. "Sorry, Mr. Edmunds to make talk, but maybe Uncle Wan Yan Lee can help." While Tom had not been keen on dealing with what was probably a Chinese Triad, he had no other choices to turn to.

Now, he wasn't fooled by the twists in the narrow corridor and the rooms leading off to each side, giving glimpses of various small enterprises. Everything up here belonged to the Triad. Each room and twist of the way was a line of defence. It reminded him of the 'Wipers' trench systems. The inner sanctum was up ahead, but there would be two or three exits to this place, like gopher holes on the prairies.

They paused a moment in front of a shabby door before it was opened a crack. A face scrutinized them from within. Through the last defence, an outer office, they passed into a long narrow room with no windows. Chinese prints and screens decorated the walls, although they were indistinct in the semi-twilight of the room. Several chairs were grouped before a large wicker chair, almost like a throne. In the chair sat the hunched figure of a Chinese.

He was of indeterminate, yet ancient age, a wizened and skinny little man, wasting away inside a dark crimson robe stylised with dragon designs. He wore a matching round little hat atop his head. A cigarette smouldering between nicotine-stained fingers added to the room's poor visibility. As they approached him, he suddenly brought his hand to his face with a gesture akin to a slap and then drew on the cigarette violently, sucking the fumes as if they were life-giving oxygen to a drowning man. He blew the smoke out reflectively, eyes narrowed as he scrutinized the pair of them. Three other men stood around, ranged before the old man. Tom and Luang came to a stop about ten feet short of the group. Luang bowed his respects to the old man. He was acknowledged by a slow blink.

"This is Mister Thomas Edmunds. Mister Edmunds, this is my uncle, Wan Yan Lee."

Tom stepped forward, hand extended, but he was intercepted by one of the other men who took his hand and shook perfunctorily and without enthusiasm. The man was heavy-set with a round moon-face. The gesture was a slight, an insult. The apparent lack of acknowledgement by the old man momentarily annoyed Tom, although he quickly suppressed his feelings. Despite his previous experience with the Oriental ways and Luang's warnings, the act took him unawares.

The hand-shaker started a quick fire speech, his arm frequently extending towards Tom. Tom could understand very little, only the odd word of the Cantonese. It was obviously a diatribe against him. Luang took no part in the discussion. He several times took a deep breath and almost leapt into the dialogue, such was his distress. One of the other men was obviously the spokesman for Tom's case, but he managed little speaking time. Moon-face frequently cut him off. The arrogance of this man, his obvious hostility and self-righteous annoyed Tom intensely. He was lost on the actual words, but the body language was unmistakeable.

The old man paid no apparent attention to either of them, keeping his gaze on Tom and shifting it only long enough to steer a fresh cigarette to his hand and lighting it. One of the first Chinese phrases Tom had learned was: "How much?"

"My uncle wishes to know how much you want, Mr. Edmunds."

"Thirty thousand dollars."

Wan Yan Lee did not even breathe hard at the figure given him. He mumbled a few Chinese words, unintelligible to Tom.

"My uncle says it will be necessary to take part ownership in the business in order to secure the loan."

Tom was expecting this. He didn't want to give anything away. There was the concern about interference, so he had a ready answer. "Tell your uncle, although I like Chinese people, many white people do not. If they learned my company was part owned by Chinese, they might not do business with me. Then your uncle's investment may prove worthless."

There was a hiss of breath from Moon-face at this open insult. A certain chill crept into the room. Tom wondered whether he overplayed it. The old man pondered this with inscrutable features as it was translated to him.

The next question: "What then, was Tom prepared to do in return for the money?"

"Tell your uncle I will not give him an open promise to do anything that may prove outside the law nor anything that may prove detrimental in any way to me, my family, and my interests. Otherwise, I will repay his loan with agreed interest and assist his needs in any other way."

Moon-face began the arm-waving attack again. After about five minutes, the exchange finished with a torrent of Chinese, which Tom could not possibly follow.

The old man's voice was old and cracked.

"My uncle says there must be more talk, but he will tell us as soon as possible what decision has been made." Luang's voice was low, full of defeat. It seemed certain Tom was lost. The obvious diatribe against him had not been stemmed by any small means. He was not confident of the outcome and wary of causing embarrassment. However, it was worth the gamble he was going to take. If face was lost, so be it. Tom stepped forward and immediately, Moon-face interspersed himself between him and the old man. He stopped moving when Tom did.

"Honourable Father," he knew his pronunciation was terrible. There was a gasp of breath around him as those present realized he understood their language. Behind him, his antagonist hissed like a cobra with rage. The old man's eyes widened and then quickly became veiled. "Honourable Father, I have come to you as a worthless Quaylo. I would like your consideration in this matter. Thank you."

There was a long soundless pause. Tom could feel the animosity coming off the heavy man in waves. He hissed again like a serpent. He had been slighted, lost face, and the knowledge made Tom feel the sweat trickling down his back, where he expected to feel a knife thrust at any moment.

Wan Yan Lee had not blinked since Tom spoke and still regarded him with lizard eyes. Had he been too presumptuous? Had he caused them too much lost face?

The sound, when it came, was eerie, its source unknown. It was a high-pitched, lasting squeak, like a noisy door hinge being rapidly manipulated. Wan Yan Lee's face creased even more. Tom felt everyone's attention transferring to the old man. He was laughing! The squeak became a gurgling guffaw, filleted by age. He slapped his knee once and subsided into a mute shaking that threatened to become a paroxysm. Again, he slapped his knee and the keening began again, louder than before. Rocking back and forth, the old man began to howl with mirth.

The others joined in, at first hesitant and timid until the true hilarity hit. In moments, the room was in an uproar. Tom had to join in too. It was too much. After a minute, Wan Yan Lee began to recover and eyed Tom with a shrewd reappraisal. He fished in his robe and produced a fresh cigarette. Lighting up, he again sucked on it as if life depended on it. He nodded sagaciously and stared at Tom through the rising smoke.

"Give him what he wants," he said in fluent English. Tom started and then really laughed in earnest, pointing at the old man who began to wheeze and shake again. He slapped his knee, stomping his foot up and down in glee. Waving them out, choking and spluttering, he terminated the meeting.

****

Oddly, the great turning point, the revelation of his future, came to Danny Edmunds in a single event, just like his brother Robert. Whereas, Robert became embroiled in aviation, Danny took up geology. In the summer of nineteen thirty-four, the Edmunds family got away from the misery of the deepening Depression by taking a holiday in Jasper. They went on a train that was a big thrill to the younger boys, Danny and James.

The first sight of the Rockies looming like a wall out of the plain was an astounding sight to Danny. He rushed from side to side of the carriage, as the track wound around curves, getting the best view he could. Just after the train entered the mountains proper, a view above them held him totally spellbound. Amongst all these peaks, these giant fangs of rock, these immortal, everlasting monuments of might, one of them was bent, curved and twisted.

Long striations traced the bends, emphasizing them, and his only experience to compare them with was the sight of a man at the Edmonton Exhibition drawing striped candy that fell into similar shapes. But how did you bend a mountain?

"Daddy. What is the name of that mountain?"

"I don't know, son, but the one further in, I know, is Pyramid."

"That mountain is called 'Folding Mountain', son," said a man in an adjacent seat.

Danny watched it in fascination until it was out of sight, too overawed to question how it became so strangely shaped. His wonder was further channelled when other mountains had the same marks, sloping upward at various angles only to end in dizzying faces. The mountains looked dry and a whitish grey in colour, as if they bore no water. Yet some bore snow, even glaciers, as he was to discover.

They stayed two days in Jasper town site before heading out on horseback to a camp. There, they stayed for five days. Danny hounded his parents for the money to buy a book he found that told how mountains were formed and eroded. In a short time, he knew all the terms: strata, tilting, anticline, faults, folding, vulcanism, metamorphic, igneous, glaciers, limestone, malachite, calcite, granite, and fossils, until the family was totally bored.

James was his chief slave in hauling rocks, but he was not above pressing Beth, Robert, and his parents into helping out. They rode horses and hiked for miles, puffing up endlessly steep slopes until they reached vantage points, where they could see the mountains stretching for mile after mile. Danny returned each time with pockets full of rocks.

At night, while the others gathered around the campfire and told stories and sang songs, Danny would peer into the dim light at some fossil embedded in a rock. His books told him it was hundreds of millions of years old. At twelve, he could barely grasp the number one million, let alone hundreds. He finally returned home with fifty pounds of rocks and a firm determination of what his future would be. A grainy, poor black and white photo, shot from the train, showing a very distant Folding Mountain was framed and hung over his bed.

More books introduced him to further mysteries. He visited the Drumheller Badlands and excavated for fossils. Deeper and deeper, he dived into the fascinations of geology.

****

David Williams did well in school. He was, perhaps, brighter than any other student, but was lazy enough to squander the opportunity to excel. Despite this, by the time he was old enough, the atmosphere of his home was sufficient to prod him towards a university as far away as possible. There had always been a faint whiff of discontent between his parents. They never openly rowed, but rather tended to ignore each other with occasional flare-ups. The worst he remembered was when he was six years old. The very day after his grandmother died, all her pictures from around the house had disappeared. His father's rage at his mother was terrible, matched only by his mother's blithe disregard.

David himself did not care. He remembered little of the old lady. To him, she was a stern, unbending character that had shown him little kindness. There was something wrong with her that was unmentionable, and she spent her last couple of years secreted in an upstairs room. His mother ministered to the old lady, her posture and facial expressions, as she returned down the stairs telling chapters of her unwilling caring. The upstairs room itself smelled horrid. David and Jennifer avoided it, only being shooed in occasionally by their mother under some duress from the old lady or by their father. John Williams spent a lot of evenings with Mother Williams, as she was known. David had not missed the fact that friction between his mother and father was directly related to the amount of time his father spent with his grandmother.

Jennifer quit the home at eighteen, scurrying off to Toronto with a young man she quickly married, much to her father's anguish and annoyance.

In nineteen thirty-seven, with the prairies baking under the autumnal sun, David sat in a westbound train and watched the effects of the Great Depression first hand. The Williams family was not very rich. The money from his father's union employment did little to keep bread on the table. Unionism had not flourished where men desperate for work abandoned the brotherhood in favour of a day's pay. Jeanne Williams brought in extra money with some dressmaking, a thing she said she picked up from his maternal grandmother and sworn never to do.

David himself worked a few summers on farms around Winnipeg and managed to save a few dollars. When he announced his intent of studying law, his mother produced fifty dollars she saved towards his and Jennifer's educations. With Jennifer long-gone, his mother said, ruefully, it probably made better sense if he made good use of it all instead.

He picked Calgary as a university because, not only was it far away from Winnipeg and his parents, he was fascinated by the Rocky Mountains. From Calgary, according to a picture he saw, you could see the mountains most days. David had no vision of his future, no sturdy dreams of courtroom appearances in the manner of Clarence Darrow. Rather, it was something to get started on until some revelation showed him his true direction. He regarded himself, humorously, as some wilful Saul on the road to Damascus.

Not being very political and having little interest in current events, David was not particularly aware of the looming spectre of world war. His studies would be interrupted by four years in the navy. He would not finish his final year and commence articling until nineteen forty-seven.

****

In July of nineteen thirty-seven, a high school rugby team from Edmonton won the regional finals and was poised to go to Calgary for the provincial title. Most of the boys graduated that summer, and in the mad camaraderie of rugby-fest, they were awash in testosterone. They cavorted nude in the dressing rooms and smuggled beer in for a party. When their coaches left, several girls came in to join them. They really cut loose at having fun.

A month later, James Edmunds arrived home, staggering on his feet, bruised and bloody from a brutal beating. His mother, on a rare visit from upstairs, screamed at the sight of him coming in the door, bringing Tom at a run. James had a broken nose, two broken fingers, and his face was smeared with blood. His shirt was ripped, torn, and bloodstained. His pants were scuffed and grass-stained. He leaned against the doorframe, wheezing and gulping on blood pouring from two lost teeth. His only visible eye was wild.

They carried him inside and sent for Doctor Jacobs. All the time, Tom asked him who did this to him. It was a horrendous situation, with blood staining the carpet up the stairs and women behaving hysterically. They bathed his wounds while they waited for the doctor. He squirmed in pain at their ministrations. He said nothing, only gritting his teeth against the pain. His hair was matted with sweat and blood. The wild look in his eye would not abate.

When the doctor finally arrived, he shooed all but Margaret out. It was half an hour before they came downstairs. In the meantime, Tom called the city police. A constable waited to investigate what happened. James was an easy-going boy who rarely got in scrapes, so it looked like he was brutally attacked.

"What happened? Who did this?"

"I am sorry, Mr. Edmunds, but James will say nothing. He has a broken nose, two broken fingers, and lost two teeth. He has some nasty bruises, but apparently, no internal injuries. He will be sore for several days, but I don't think he has suffered any damage to the black eye. Hopefully there will be no concussion."

"But, what the devil is going..."

"I'm sorry!" Doctor Jacobs raised his hand. "The only thing I can tell you is that James wants to see Beth right away."

While the parents and family looked at each other nonplussed, Beth took the stairs and went up to James's room. She found him supine on the bed, battered and weak from the attack.

"James, what the..."

James held up his hand. "They...they told me..." His words came thickly through his puffed lips and injured mouth. "They told me that you had sex with them."

"What? Who? What are you talking about, James?"

"Three guys from the rugby team. I met them on the way home. They said horrible things about you." Beth's face unfolded in a display of understanding and horror, but James plunged on. "They say you had sex with all of them, that you lay naked while two of them did you. They said you sucked them, that the cum was running out of you, while you lay like a beached whale. I don't know what that all means, I only know it is too horrible. Not *my* sister, not *my sister Beth*! So I hit them! And kicked them!" James rose up in the bed in a fury of righteousness. "Then the three of them kicked *me*! Punched me!" He fell back, horrified by the guilt of admission in his sister's eyes. "Oh no! No! Not my sister! Oh Beth!" He screamed and rolled on his side away from her, screaming again as the writhing of his body tortured his injuries.

The door burst open to his parents who watched astonished, as Beth, streaming tears, fled past them. Doctor Jacobs rushed in. After fumbling in his bag, he administered an injection to James who soon subsided into a sobbing heap before sinking into a deep-drugged sleep for twelve hours.

Despite repeated questioning, James never revealed what happened. Beth was likewise mute. Although two boys were traced who also suffered injuries consistent with a fight, no connection could be made to identify them as James's assailants. The only manifestation of the event, barely obvious to the family, was a coolness emanating from James towards Beth, which never relented.

****

December 2, 1938.

Beth Edmunds dropped the long silk nightdress around her ankles and stood naked in front of the big wardrobe in her bedroom. The large mirror on the door revealed her image from head to toe. She regarded her form with a critical eye. So this was what Edward Sturdee Junior was going to get tomorrow! She shuddered slightly at the delicious anticipation of feeling Edward's hands and lips on her body.

Tomorrow was her wedding day. She threw herself at Edward shamelessly, yet thanks to his resolve, not totally wantonly. Edward's limit of carnal knowledge of her was limited to passionate kissing and fondling, since he had not provided the leadership she was anxious to follow. The bastard was a tease. That was it! Belonging to such a staunch church family, his natural desires were restrained by morality. She had intuitively known that if *she* had taken the initiative, he would have been shocked, and she did not dare lose him. Still, she knew the adequate size and hardness of him, and her eyes narrowed at the thought. Anticipation, they say, is part of the pleasure.

Her form was slight, her brown hair fashionably short and carefully curled. Her looks, she had long debated, were average. She had her mother's solemnity, her father's eyes and quick smile, which gave her mobility of features. Her shoulders were suitably narrow, ribs visible without being prominent. Her breasts were smallish but firmly rounded like upright dumplings. The dark red nipples had small areolae and erected readily, as they were now. Their peculiarity was that they appeared to be mounted on an extra prominence of the breasts, creating, as she observed from a sideways view, a lemon-shape. Also, her left nipple was set at the bottom edge of its areola instead of in the middle, a quirky imperfection she supposed was a family trait.

Her waist was narrow. Her navel was an 'inner' that lurked only half concealed, like a lecherous wink. She frowned as her gaze settled on her hips, which swelled appropriately, yet carried a ripple of puppy fat. She must diet! Swivelling, she looked over her shoulder at her buttocks. Just below a pair of sacral dimples, they were nicely pear-shaped without being too prominent and lined up with the widest swell of her hips. Her thighs were sleek, yet muscular, and she had been complimented on numerous occasions for her shapely calves.

She pirouetted one more time. Edward Sturdee was one lucky fellow!

TEN

MRS. EDWARD STURDEE

On Saturday, December third, nineteen thirty-eight, Elizabeth Rose Edmunds married Edward Clement Sturdee Junior. Beth made a beautiful bride in what was recognized as an Edmonton society wedding. As the Depression years dragged their way towards the end of the decade, any such wedding was a light on the horizon. This was more so.

Tom Edmunds had established himself as one of the entrepreneurial princes of Edmonton. His Ford dealership was still afloat despite the demise of others in the city. Trans-West Transportation maintained, if nothing else, a steady level of business. His entertainment interests prospered and were known to the general public. His name had become a household name.

Then there was the Sturdee family. Edward Sturdee Senior was a pillar of modern Alberta society, a doyen of the law fraternity and the Anglican Church. A scion of a well-heeled law family of Ontario, son of a High Court judge, Sturdee came to Edmonton in the early nineteen twenties and rapidly established himself as one of the city's pre-eminent lawyers. His massive mansion on Ada Boulevard was a centre of importance for influence in the province. Premier William Aberhart was a frequent diner there and a Sturdee intimate, even though their politics did not mesh. They should have been enemies, but their mutual thirst for power and strong church affiliations made them cronies instead.

Tom wondered how long the convenience of association would last. Until five years ago, former Premier John Brownlee was also a frequent dinner guest at the Sturdee mansion. Resigning amidst the scandal of a lawsuit against him for seduction of a young woman, Brownlee found out immediately the price of any hint of immorality in the eyes of Edward Sturdee. He became persona non grata overnight. It was noteworthy that it was not the immorality, so much as the loss of power that had influenced Sturdee. A successful defence and retention of the premiership would probably have ensured Brownlee's continued dining privileges, at least until the power was transferred to Aberhart. Sturdee dabbled in politics, fascinated by the power, yet never got his feet wet. He was a megalomaniac who saw himself in the behind-the-scenes kingmaker role rather than the public figure.

It was this particular wedding, between two of the most powerful Edmonton families that caught the attention of the socialites. The wedding was performed at the MacDougall Church with the reception afterwards at the Macdonald Hotel. In some ways, the wedding had proven a blessing to Margaret, who was bitten by the typical female hype over a marriage. She happily played the role of the bride's mother for months leading up to the ceremony. The actual day was a triumph for her. She looked almost as radiant as the bride.

William Aberhart himself read the lesson then characterized 'this marriage between two of Edmonton's premier families as an historic and portentous event.' By this time, his Social Credit policies were seen as no better, and perhaps as flawed as any other government's, but with a true politician's flair, he could not resist using the happy occasion to assure an audience that this was an indication of coming improvement.

A raw Edmonton Journal staffer, a short and skinny figure named Nathan Connaught attended the ceremony. He was instantly jealous of the handsome groom and personally offended by the lively beauty of the bride. The theme of his report was laced with innuendo about the sumptuousness of the reception, at a time when people were starving and working for a pittance. His editor, sensitive to the collective power of the families involved, made him clean it up, but the thread of disapproval remained. For a long time afterwards, Nathan fantasized about having sex with that desirable bride, surrounded by the opulent favours of her position in life.

Edward Sturdee Junior was a handsome young man, fresh out of law school and raring to continue the family tradition. Intelligent, but inclined to be a trifle grave, he had a bright future. He was squarely built, like his father, with a mane of blonde hair and straight, regular features. His eyes were a pale brown and partially masked the personality behind them.

Although she never considered herself a great beauty, Beth would always view old pictures of her wedding as special. She wore a long silk dress trimmed with gold lace. A long train, attended by four little girls, was topped with a helmet of shining white silk, embroidered with flowers. With the face gauze thrown back for the photos, her elfin features were framed to perfection and next to her, that Adonis figure of Edward Sturdee, resplendent in a morning suit and top hat in hand.

It was the family affiliation that swayed Tom Edmunds. He did not like Edward Senior and despised his social climbing. The marriage made sense from the viewpoint of power, hierarchy, and money. Tom extended his dislike to the son, whose stiff and formal embarrassment in asking for Beth's hand had somehow offended Tom's openness. Incomprehensible alarm bells sounded in his mind at the time, but they remained just as indecipherable ever since, achieving no particular form that he could distinguish.

The union was sealed however by Margaret and Beth. Typically, these women knew for months before their male counterparts what was to transpire. Edward Sturdee, as Alex McFarlane pointed out to Tom, was a great catch for Beth and the Edmunds family.

Now the wedding was over. Attentive to his bride, the groom was escorted to the bridal suite by well-wishing friends and abandoned to Beth's mercies. Edward was still a virgin. His hopeless surrender to Beth had begun almost a year before when, in the steamy heat of an aggressive kiss from her, he laid a timid hand on her bosom. His self-shame at such debauchery was further confused when she gave a deep sigh, and a covering hand pressed his more firmly to the soft mound. Over subsequent months, his awakened maleness led him to fondling inside Beth's clothing. It was done with such a degree of shyness, almost reticence that Beth wondered if he would ever get where she really wanted him to go. As he made slow advances, more of this indistinguishable, forbidden, and desirable fruit was made available to him.

On this, their wedding night, Beth was eager but cautious with him. She knew he was inexperienced and she didn't want to scare him off. The patience she required, coping with his inept fumbling almost destroyed her. Somewhere, the poor dear heard it was painful for the woman the first time. He used this as a reason to back-pedal from the issue, gallantly offering to wait.

Now that this gorgeous piece of manhood was hers, with her body screaming to be penetrated and lustily ravished, Beth was in torment. At this juncture, she almost felt like laughing hysterically, but the situation was too serious. She had to put all of her experience and wiles to work. With cunning hands and, eventually, her mouth, she primed her husband.

She was expecting a rebuke momentarily, but the latter technique was met with more reciprocated fervour than she had thus far received from him. With him fully rampant, Beth rolled under him. After some confusion concerning which orifice, she guided him and consummated the marriage.

The next morning, they were booked on a train heading east to Ontario to visit Sturdee relatives, show off the bride, and honeymoon at Niagara. A large number of well-wishers showed up at the station to see them off. A reporter and photographer from the newspaper were there to record the final stage of the nuptials. About twenty other Edmontonians gawked from a distance, some not quite sure what was going on.

Porters weaved between them with heavy barrows, loading enough baggage, it seemed, to sustain them for a year. Margaret stood to one side, dabbing her eyes in classical motherhood in synchrony with Mrs. Sturdee. Beside her to one side, Robert stood aloof. Danny was more interested in the locomotive and had taken young James to see the hissing steam.

Elbowed aside by a press of people, Tom found a quiet spot next to Alex MacFarlane. "Time flies."

"Aye, they make a canny couple, do they not?"

"Hmm, until you stay with them for five minutes."

There was never anything left unsaid between these two men. The quiet look returned by Alex merely spoke silent acquiescence. Even ignoring the rumours about Beth, the couple seemed entirely too different. His quiet, withdrawn handsomeness did not mesh with Beth's vivacity. She darted from experience to experience like a butterfly drawn to new blooms.

"Goodbye, Uncle Alex, dear!" It was Beth herself, throwing her arms around her favourite man. Had the long years and the familial taboos not surrounded them so, he would have been the man she would have turned to and loved dearly and solely in her life. But, the barriers were there, even though a deep love existed between them. Whether his feeling totally matched her's was of no consequence to Beth. For sure, he loved her with a fierceness that went beyond the avuncular, although stopped short of a lover's passion. She adored him. He was the quintessential man for her, with the right amount of her father, blended with a very special masculinity she found in no other man. Often, alone, she fanaticised about making love with Alex. As her hand crept up her thigh to the warm moistness, each time she knew, it became a little harder to be satisfied with just any man. Now she stood before him, mutely asking this final blessing from him to depart with another man.

"Goodbye Lize." It was his special, secret name for her. He pressed an envelope into her hand, while kissing her. Inside, she later found a short handwritten poem to her and a cheque for one thousand dollars. She kept the poem through the years as it grew ragged and faded. She shed more tears over it than almost anything else in her life.

With a crescendo of "goodbyes," the train started to pull away. The newly-weds scrambled aboard, laughing with nervousness and the humour of almost being left behind. Standing there, Tom couldn't understand why there was always this last minute rush, stretching the moment out, as if it were elasticised and could be preserved forever in the heart.

His mind went back to a train leaving more than twenty years before from this very platform. That time, the train was filled with men in khaki uniforms, hanging out of every door and window, wishing farewell to loved ones. That moment had been elasticised in the memory of all who had been there and stretched out to the fullest. It had to last many of those left behind for eternity. So many had not returned!

For him, too, the moment had been elasticised, permanently etched in his memory. He saw it as if it were yesterday. Desperately scanning the entire crowd that was there, his eyes had finally lit on a solitary figure, which arrived too late for a kiss or spoken word. Piqued by his refusal to stay, Jeanne relented only at the last moment, showing up too late to see him off with a touch. As the train chuffed away, she stood like a statue, tears streaming down her face, unable to pick him out. He was waving like a madman. "Love you! Write soon! Goodbye!"

"Goodbye! Daddy! Daddy! Pick me up! I want to see the train!" It was James. Tom stepped forward twenty years, scooping his son up high into his arms. He could not understand why James was crying. The tears fell like rain down on Tom's face and collar. A fourteen year-old boy was in his arms, crying like a five year old. But he had raised his son too late. The train was gone.

****

Late July, 1939.

"I'm sorry, Daddy. I didn't mean to embarrass you – make you and Mother look ridiculous in this town."

"I know, Elizabeth, but that part is already done."

She knew how angry he was by the use of her formal name; she was always 'Beth' to him. But not now, not when she finally admitted to marital infidelity several days ago and told Tom that Edward Sturdee, quite rightly, wanted a divorce. They were seated in the parlour together. It was not the heat of the fire that sent sweat trickling down between her breasts. "Will you try and help me?"

"Of course! What else? I shall see Sturdee this evening. A divorce, uncontested, seems the best way out. I cannot afford any further furore right now that might affect some deals I have on the go."

"I shall need something to live on. I don't want to move back home."

"Perhaps it would be best. We could keep an eye on you." It was not a serious suggestion, just a means to hurt. Tom looked at his daughter keenly. She hung her head. He wondered what made her do these things. "You may be disappointed if the Sturdees are fighting mad. You may just have to hold up your head and ride this out as gracefully as possible. Anyway, it is time I left."

"Are you sure they did not want me there?"

"No, you were not specifically invited. Probably scared you might jump the old man!" Tom saw the instant hurt cross her face, but didn't apologise. Beth had caused a lot of turmoil over this business. She had the comment coming. He rose to leave.

"Daddy. It...it's just that something was wrong. I'm sorry."

****

The study of the Sturdee residence survived from another era. Tom was not sure if it was Victorian or Edwardian, but the crocheted antimacassars, the deep dark furniture, flocced wallpaper, and the generally sombre formality of the place echoed another age. The brandy and cigar tasted good. As he sat back in the settee, facing the fire, Tom thought that, whatever else he was, the elder Sturdee was not a Philistine when it came to the better things in life. He didn't expect the courtesy under the circumstances.

The senior Sturdee leaned against the mantelpiece, looking down at Tom with the expression he wore when he'd just put an indisputable argument before a jury. The jurymen were about to fall over each other in the mad scramble to declare in his favour. Yet, as Tom noted, the stance was too stiff, too contrived.

Pompous and power-hungry men like Sturdee developed such attitudes until the contrived became the normal. Now the poise was gone; the pose looked gauche. Sturdee was scared! That was it! Tom's mind raced. It was not just that he could say 'no' to Sturdee's proposal. There was something more, some intangible at work he could not define. Actually, Tom's mind was already made up to say 'yes' and make a quick retreat before things got too complicated. But now, Sturdee was scared. Yes, he was scared!

Advantage was a word well understood by Tom from his business dealings. Sturdee had had this initiative, but lost it like an over-reaching chess move. The urge to score off him was a taste stronger than the brandy and cigar. Sturdee had just called Beth everything but a two-bit whore, leading up to his proposal for a settlement. Oh, it was done with eloquence and polite words, but somewhere in the dissertation, the honour of the Edmunds family was collectively impugned. That was when Tom's ear became unsympathetic.

He glanced across to where the younger Sturdee sat. Edward was nervous, tense, resigned, and looked exhausted. He also looked – guilty! Of what? Tom's eyes slid back to Sturdee, whose lips were still pursed with the righteous indignation, which demanded compliance to his wishes. Goddammit, the man was scared! It could not be because of the ramifications of Beth's transgressions. Surely, his church would not ostracize him? His reputation sullied then? Surely the scandal was not part of Sturdee's concern. Beth's transgressions had all been laid out; she had slept with a travelling salesman; she was mysteriously absent when a visiting distant-cousin was also not in evidence. The butcher, the baker, the candlestick maker, Tom mused.

He could not see this as seriously as the Sturdees seemed to be making it. After all, it was *his* rampant genes, hardly theirs, that would be paraded in front of the Edmonton society snobs. Come to that, it was as yet a close secret. Why should it be paraded at all? He wondered for a moment how many people might know about him and Jeanne; such things were never well kept secrets. Well, he had kept them on a string long enough.

"'Therefore the archer sends griefs against us and will send them still, unless we give the glancing-eyed girl back to her father without price, without ransom.' You are familiar with Homer, Mr. Sturdee?"

Sturdee made a noncommittal movement of his head regarding his study of the classics, but Tom could see he seized on the admission of Beth's transgressions. He gave him a moment to reflect on the part about ransom and price and then continued. "If young Edward is convinced there is no means of reconciliation, I suppose the marriage must be terminated." Relief spread through the room like an announcement of more lifeboats available on the Titanic. "It seems to me, however, such a short time, for two people to get to know each other." He paused for effect. Raw nerve! The smell of fear again! For some reason, he could not fathom the Sturdees *wanted* this marriage terminated! Now was the time to slide the knife in. "Of course, I think that Beth would be entitled to some kind of alimony to provide for her well-being and a home to live in."

"What!" Edward Sturdee almost bellowed, levering himself away from the mantelpiece and spilling half an ounce of Napoleon brandy. "You mean Edward should provide funds to her when *she* is the one who...who..." He stumbled for words. A wave of moral indignation swept over him. "She...she..." He sat down with a bump, completely failed for words. Half a dozen provincial court judges would have given their eyeteeth to see Edward Sturdee flat on his ass and speechless.

Tom was unrelenting. "That's exactly what I mean. Do you want the people around here to think that your family cannot provide for its own, even when they leave the family?" As Tom well knew, most people in Edmonton would pass a begging Elizabeth Sturdee on the street and feel the Sturdees had every justification in kicking her out flat broke. "Will they not then wonder about a marriage that did not work? So short a duration?" There it was again! Fear! A palpable ripple of apprehension greeted those words. Even a blind negotiator could have sensed it. *What* were the Sturdees afraid of? Was it the effect it might have on these pillars of society and the McDougall church?

"What have you got in mind?"

It was not a capitulation. Tom didn't expect that, but he had won negotiation. "I don't want to make things difficult." A pained expression came from Sturdee. "What I would suggest is a small allowance until Beth marries again. In the meantime, if you can afford it, I think I could persuade Beth to take an extended holiday. That way, you could get the divorce processed quietly, uncontested, and without any adverse publicity."

The glazed look was coming out of the elder Sturdee's eyes. He opened his mouth to start a protest. The enthusiastic nodding of his son's head stopped him. "I think he is right, Father. Elizabeth is stubborn, and it could prove awkward. Best remove her from the scene if possible."

"But this is blackmail!" Sturdee got his wind back.

"Listen!" Tom's voice cracked like a whip across the room. "I don't like this any more than you do! Still, it was your son who begged me for my daughter's hand. You were well quoted as being very happy about it. A few minutes ago, you said a lot of hurtful things about her, for which I am not willing to forgive you. You take this matter further at your own risk. I have offered the easiest and cheapest way out. If you are too stupid to take it, if you want this to be a public matter, then pay the consequences!" Tom stood up, ready to leave.

The word "stupid" seemed to do it. It had the right ring, the right kind of balance. Sturdee's pique collapsed like a pricked balloon. With a silent nod, he agreed.

ELEVEN

THE QUEEN MARY

Early August, 1939.

Beth's train journey across Canada was uneventful. The Sturdees agreed to fund her trip out of town, while the divorce proceedings were put in motion. She would join a cousin of her mother's, Helen Smythe, in Toronto. They would travel to Britain together for an extended visit. By the end of the first day, the sameness of the prairie scenery bored her utterly. She engrossed herself in a new novel called 'Gone with the Wind.' The trials and tribulations of Scarlett O'Hara occupied her sympathies until the train rolled through the more interesting Canadian Shield scenery in Northern Ontario.

The train rolled into Toronto, where Aunt Helen met her. Helen was in her upper forties and starting to resort to the artificiality of a woman going to seed. She had a comfortable-looking bosom and an obvious problem with her hips. She never married, having been engaged to a soldier killed in the Great War. Somehow, she raised neither the interest nor succumbed to the advances of anyone else and remained single. She was, however, quite vivacious and full of enthusiasm for the coming trip. Her blonde hair, obviously peroxide, was carefully coiffed. Though she wore an abundance of make-up, it was applied over a once great but declining beauty.

For a couple of days, Helen let Beth shake off the train journey's tedium by showing her around Toronto. The greater bustle of the larger and more cosmopolitan city was a change from Edmonton. This comparison was over-shadowed days later when they rolled into New York. There was nothing quite like it in Beth's book. They stayed for five days, visiting all the usual tourist traps. They saw the Empire State Building, Central Park, walked down Wall Street, and marvelled at the skyscrapers, viewed from the Statue of Liberty.

The Cunard luxury liner they were booked on to Southampton was the 'Queen Mary,' one of the largest ships in the world and holder of the

'Blue Riband' for the fastest North Atlantic crossing, both ways. This meant little to Beth, a prairie-raised girl, until the taxi reached Pier Ninety. She gasped when she saw the huge red and black triple funnels towering over the customs sheds on the pier. It was not until they cleared the boarding formalities and went out onto the quayside that she fully began to grasp the enormity of the mammoth ship. The immense black and white steel wall towered over her, dwarfing all around it. Twelve decks, stacked as high as the Statue of Liberty's hand, stretched high above, overshadowed, in turn, by the soaring great funnels, each large enough to drive three trains through. The eye didn't know whether to sweep up to the mast-tops, almost one hundred and fifty feet above the dock or roam side to side along the one thousand and twenty foot length of the leviathan.

At each stage of her journey so far, Beth's experience of man-made objects widened to new superlatives. The transition from Edmonton's High Level Bridge to New York's skyscrapers was a gradual one. This confrontation with the 'Queen Mary' was staggering. Even Helen was speechless, a rare event for her.

Taking in the graceful lines of the ship and its impressive, implacable aura of quiet reliability, Beth fell in love with it immediately. Going up the covered gangway, they were swallowed into the side of the ship and greeted by the purser and his assistants. They were cordially welcomed and assigned their cabin. A steward led them along endless bright and elegant corridors and opened the door for them.

They were bewildered by the miles of passageways and stairs, intimidated like most passengers at ever being able to find their way around. The steward smiled with pride at their confusion and pointed out the ship plan on the bureau in their room. "Don't worry, ladies. Everyone is a little strange at first." He spoke in a chirpy, Home Counties dialect.

Barely two hours later, announcements of departure filtered through the ship. Beth and Helen made their way up on deck. It was an eighty-degree day. Even the cool sea lay listless under the onslaught of the New York humidity. The steady activity of boarding gave way to the frenetic antics of non-passengers making last minute good-byes and streaming down the gangway. The business of departure crescendoed as the gangways were drawn ashore, like some giant last chance to opt out of this adventure. Huge hawsers were flung ashore like giant unwanted umbilicals. They both almost jumped overboard as the ship's mighty horn blared out above them, vibrating their whole world, swamping their senses with its amplitude.

A gaggle of tugs whooped replies and nosed in towards the liner, while a faint vibration underfoot bespoke the start of propellers. A throng of dockside spectators yelled and waved. Streamers flew like rainbows over the crowd. Imperceptibly, the gap between the ship and shore widened. The dock began to move past them.

Pier Ninety receded, as if it were motivated, not the vessel. Beth found herself afloat on a ship for the first time in her life. High up, they seemed suspended in space and time from the crowd ashore. She envied the heightened emotions of several honeymoon couples spread through the ship. What a wonderful, romantic way to depart on the journey through life with a man! She wondered if such an event would have helped Edward and her, then shrugged. That part of her life was closed.

The vertical architecture of Manhattan was now revealed from a new vantage point. The piers spread out around its feet like the giant roots of an oak forest. The ship was moving more rapidly. Staten Island and the Statue of Liberty slid by. The 'Queen Mary' trumped every other vessel in the harbour.

Shortly after, a slight turn pointed them at the open sea, and the tugs and pilot vessels departed. The vibrations increased. The ship took on its oceanic character as the swells of the Atlantic slipped beneath her keel. In half an hour, the ramparts of Manhattan sank into the sea and disappeared completely. An increasingly cold breeze from the ship's motion made their perspiration-soaked thin dresses uncomfortable. They abandoned their watch at the rail and went inside to unpack.

Over subsequent days, the 'Queen Mary' and its baroque splendour increasingly overawed them. Various proud crewmembers filled them in on comparative facts. The first class dining room on R Deck could accommodate eight hundred diners and was one of Beth's favourite places. It was even more elegant than any hotel she had been in with large fluted columns that rose to a recessed ceiling, with concealed lighting three decks above.

The tables were square with four comfortable dining chairs to each. Fresh flowers from the ship's own greenhouses graced each table daily. They entered the room through huge brass doors set in the bottom of an enormous mural depicting 'Merrie England.' At one end of the dining room was another mural of the North Atlantic with a stylised New York skyline at the bottom left corner. Between this and the opposing European coastline, a small, electrically controlled model of the 'Queen Mary' traced the daily position of the ship for the benefit of passengers. And there were reports of Hollywood movie stars dining here!

Beth was amazed when their steward told them the dining room could contain Cunard's original steamer, the 'Britannia,' plus the 'Nina,' 'Pinta,' and 'Santa Maria' of Christopher Columbus fame. The ship itself outweighed the entire Spanish Invasion Armada by twenty thousand tons. There were four thousand miles of cable in the ship and over ten million rivets in the hull. Victualling was of staggering statistics: fifty thousand pounds of fresh meat, two tons of tea and coffee, twenty-five thousand packs of cigarettes, over three thousand bottles of champagne, twenty thousand bottles of beer; the logistical items to cater to the individual needs of over two thousand passengers and eleven hundred crew were endless.

Near the dining room on R Deck, Beth discovered a sixty-foot swimming pool in ancient Greek decor, complete with fake palm trees. This was a stupendous thing to her, a swimming pool on a ship! She immediately hurried to one of the shops on the Promenade deck and bought a swimsuit.

The whole ship was so opulent that it was exactly like being in a floating luxury hotel. All the services competed with or surpassed the best hotels. The food was first rate and served on the best silver and English bone china by superior waiters. With smug feminine satisfaction, the pair of them settled in to be pampered for the next three and a half days.

"Excuse me, ladies. Per'aps, I may be of assistance."

Struggling with the deck chairs, Beth and Helen turned towards the voice. A bright sun beat down on the deck of the ship this first morning at sea. They were determined to sit and enjoy it. With the 'Queen Mary' making almost thirty knots, the breeze outside was not tolerable, so they were setting up the chairs behind glass.

A man with greying hair stood behind them, regarding them with a bright, inquiring smile. He was impeccably dressed in a charcoal grey suit of foreign cut. The neck of his silk shirt was open and sported a colourful cravat, secured with a heavy gold pin. He had a narrow, bird-like head with a prominent beak of a nose, which accentuated the impression, along with bright eyes. His hair was carefully combed back from a high forehead and parted arrow-straight.

"Zees tings, zey are per'aps difficile, non?" He tilted his head to one side, nodding at the same time. The effect increased his bird-like appearance, yet he kept a quiet air of assured authority. "Permit me?" He proffered a gold-knobbed cane for Helen to hold, and without further ado, quickly and expertly set up the two deckchairs. "Eh, voila!"

"Oh, you are French?" Helen gave a little simper.

"Oui, Madame, my card." Like a magician, he produced a business card engraved in gold lettering.

"Mister...er, Monsieur René de Fourquet." Helen was spellbound.

"At your service, Mésdames!" The man gave a formal little bow and retrieved his cane from Helen's nerveless grasp.

"Merci beaucoup. You are very kind!" Beth gave him a friendly smile and was rewarded with a penetrating gaze.

"Not at all. It was my pleasure. A bientôt, Mésdames."

"What a nice man!" Helen regarded the retreating figure of M. de Fourquet with a ruminative stare. Beth gave an inward chuckle. Aunt Helen was supposed to be *her* chaperone. Drop a few pounds and years and she would be an item on a shipload of men. Helen Smythe had a discriminating eye despite her staid outward appearance. The romance of a sea voyage seemed to have awakened dormant urges in her.

They saw the slightly built de Fourquet several times that day. Beth was struck by the same quiet assurance in him that she always admired in Alex MacFarlane. One or two people invariably accompanied him, obviously employees who travelled with him. In the dining room, he enjoyed a larger table of his own that entertained a procession of guests, including Captain Irving. All of this naturally increased the curiosity of Helen. She discreetly obtained a snippet of information here and asked a bold question there. De Fourquet, she finally reported to Beth, was a prominent and wealthy French industrialist. Not only that, he was a widower, an especially interesting fact as he had been caught staring at their table several times.

That evening, a bottle of wine arrived at their table with a note. Pulling out her pince-nez, Helen scowled at the message. 'I trust you will forgive the impertinence, but I see you have ordered the *Coq au Vin Toulouse*. I have always enjoyed this particular Medoc with this dish and hope you will accept and enjoy this bottle.' One of de Fourquet's cards was tucked into a ribbon around the bottle.

"Thank you!" Helen mouthed across the salon, waving to him. He bobbed his bird head in acknowledgement. Beth did not miss the way his eyes slid from Helen to her. She also did not miss his name on the label of the bottle. Whether it had come from the ship's cellars or his own private stock that travelled with him, she couldn't guess. One thing for sure, the wine was delicious, expensively delicious.

The women went to powder their noses after the meal. Helen, unused to more than a sniff of wine, was pleasantly tipsy. It was she who suggested they adjourn to the Veranda Grill for the evening. Being early, they found a table close to the dance floor. Gradually, the floor filled with dancers. Helen sat amused and happy, humming and swaying to the music.

"Good evening, Ladies. I trust you enjoyed the wine?" It was de Fourquet.

"Ah, dear Monsieur de Fourquet! It was so nice of you, but I am afraid it has gone to my head!"

"Not so far, I trust, that you cannot accept an invitation to dance?"

"Oh, I'd love to!" Helen was on her feet with a move that belied her bulk. After whispering a murmured excuse to Beth, the pair of them took to the floor.

Beth sat and watched them amusedly. She was not the slightest deceived by the roundabout way de Fourquet was taking to reach her. With his urbane charm and elegance, he was utterly destroying Helen's resistance. He moved ramrod straight around the dance floor and was flexible to the rhythm of the music and his partner. Helen did all of her part to make them a graceful couple. Beth's suspicions about her maiden aunt deepened, suspicions nobody else in the family might entertain.

She was concerned Helen not make a fool of herself. De Fourquet was a fascinating man, and once he got past this ritual dance of introduction, it would be interesting, provided Helen's feelings were not hurt. The man in question smiled at something Helen said and then transferred the smile to Beth over Helen's shoulder. They were gone around the dance floor before Beth could react to the shifted glance. Beth felt a familiar warmth stirring deep in her belly. It spread to her loins. She felt a slight flush on her cheeks.

The band took a break, and Helen took the opportunity to invite de Fourquet to join them. They made light talk, while he enjoyed a brandy. Beth left him on the hook. She was beginning to enjoy the whole episode. Her own anticipation was building, as she sensed him seething to communicate with her directly but restrained by social mores. He continued to work on Helen, complimenting and flattering her. Thus he managed to hide his intentions behind a marvellous aplomb, which she admired. Had she not felt she was fine-tuned to the signals, she would never have guessed his aim. When the band returned, de Fourquet, with a polite air of duty, asked her to dance also. He behaved punctiliously on the floor, a firm but well-placed hand on her waist. Strong currents flowed between them, and Beth marvelled at his self-control, while emulating his example. After one last duty turn of the floor with Helen, de Fourquet bowed his leave and left.

Helen babbled on about him in their room as they prepared for bed, probing Beth for her opinion about the man. Beth gave guarded replies and wondered if she should say something to her aunt and save her from embarrassing herself. They only had another day and a half before they would be in Europe. Still, it was not Helen's but her own opinion of de Fourquet that kept her awake half the night.

They received a bouquet of flowers the next day, accompanied by the ubiquitous gold card inviting them to his table for dinner. Helen replied in the affirmative and spent the rest of the day fussing to get ready. Beth finally dressed simply in an understated light grey dress, low-cut and off the shoulders with a string of pearls.

The meal was a delight with only one other couple to share the large table. They had Consommé Royale, Red Mullet Meunière, followed by Croquette of Duckling and Shoulder of Lamb. For dessert there was Macedoine de Fruite Chantilly or crèpes, flambéed at their table. Beth was entranced with the whole affair. The opulence of the dining room, and the formal elegance of the table, was the stuff of dreams for a prairie girl. Most of the men were in formal eveningwear with only the occasional but expensive dress suit in evidence. Many of the women were in gowns, although some wore simpler dresses, like Beth. She did not feel as out of place as she might have. It was a terrific display of the haughty grandeur of the British Empire (even though many present were Americans and other nationalities). Still it was the thought, the sheer mind-set of grand affluence that set the scene. Monsieur de Fourquet was in tails and bow tie and looked very handsome in this old-world uniform of class and distinction. He proved an attentive and knowledgeable host, dancing attention on the pair of them equally.

They moved on to the Veranda again to dance, but shortly after their arrival, Helen begged off with a headache. Carried along by the continuing ambience of the evening, Beth was disappointed it was about to end. She gamely rose to accompany Helen to their cabin. Instead, Helen grasped her arm in restraint. "No, dear. You must stay and keep Monsieur de Fourquet company. Please don't worry about me, I shall be fine in the morning."

De Fourquet had also risen, a concerned host, yet, as Beth sensed, secretly delighted at this turn of events. He summonsed a steward and insisted he escort Helen to their cabin and report back her safe arrival. It was all very gallant, but once left alone, they were like a pair of kids suddenly left alone with the cookie jar and each being afraid to raise the lid first.

The steward returned in short order and handed Beth an envelope. Tipped by de Fourquet, he withdrew as Beth looked inside at a piece of Cunard stationery. It contained but two words: 'Be discreet!' She almost choked on her drink. This provided de Fourquet with an excuse to take her wrist solicitously. Gathering herself, Beth crumpled the paper and dropped it in her purse. "Aunt Helen reports she is safely home." She noticed with some satisfaction that this good news did not cause him to relinquish his hold on her hand.

Now de Fourquet, or René as he insisted, changed his attitude towards her. He still maintained the same decorum, but the warmth he displayed melted any reserves Beth might still have felt. They talked about his family. There was a tragic drowning accident almost ten years prior. He lost his wife and four-year-old daughter. Disconsolate, he plunged into the family business to purge his life of the loss. With his two elder brothers dead in the Great War and only his mother and unmarried sister in Paris, the de Fourquet family enterprises were woefully short of hands at the helm. The workload made for a complex and convenient catharsis for his grief.

Beth discovered he must be very rich with several coalmines and steelworks near Douai and other properties throughout France, including a vineyard in Bordeaux, where the delicious wine from the previous evening had come from. He had been to America to cement some industrial relationships there and expected good results from his efforts. He was rueful now about his lack of a family on which to lavish his good fortune.

Beth responded by telling him of her failed marriage. She did not allude to the reason. She felt it would weaken her position with him. He did not probe but did pick up on her ruefulness being driven by propriety rather than regret. They danced several times, latterly with the lights low and his cheek brushing hers. Beth enjoyed the scent of his cologne and the brush of his breath on her ear. They danced well together. By the end of the evening, they melted into an unspoken relationship.

He did not detain her when it was time to go. They went up a couple of decks to one of the rear lounges and watched the great wide phosphorescence of the ship's wake, boiling up behind the stern. The thoughtful, if experienced crew turned the lights low for just such a rendezvous. They stood close together, René's arm encircling her waist. He whispered something French into her ear, which she didn't understand, yet the meaning was clear.

She hugged herself with a happy warmth and put her head on his shoulder. He turned her and held her chin in his hand, looking deeply into her face. She liked his eyes. They were deep, dark brown, comforting. His lips hovered tantalizingly close to hers and then softly connected. She sighed and returned the kiss, placing her arms around his neck. It was like rediscovering the old teddy bear she had had as a child. It had been a true and fulfilling friend, protecting her from the evils of a child's nocturnal fears. René's lips unlocked the warm familiarity of sensual trust and partnership. They were both captured by the peace of a burgeoning love.

The next day, René broached the idea of Helen and Beth travelling to France as his guest and staying at his château for a few days. The 'Queen Mary' stopped first at Cherbourg before backtracking to Southampton. It would be easy for them to disembark with him. From there, they could travel by train and car. He would pay their way to London later.

Anxious to convince them, he talked in glowing terms of the château, which had been in his family for almost a hundred years. Helen at first demurred, not wanting to commit them. When Beth had challenged her about the 'be discreet' note, she only said she was not a fool and knew what was taking place from the start. She also described her regret at never settling down to a love match.

Beth was in a stew of anticipation. She made her feelings clear to Helen, but recognized that the older woman had a responsibility as a chaperone. Their trip was precipitated by Beth's infidelity. To allow her now to make off and start an affair with 'some Frenchman,' as it would be termed, while the divorce was being processed, would be a gross abrogation of duty to the family. The only opportunity to accept the invitation lay in the fact that they were not required to show up at any particular place at any particular time. A telegram to Helen's relatives in Reading, saying they were staying in London for a few days, would allay any worry or suspicions. Another telegram to Alberta would serve the same purpose with no address of lodging.

There was romance in the air and their reasoning proved to be Helen's 'out.' Thus two cables were sent from onboard. Unable to mask his joy, René sent his own telegram to his staff to prepare for his guests. They were met in Cherbourg by representatives who had arranged for visas and cleared their passports before escorting them onto a 'Première Classe' coach of the train. As they passed through the station, the bustle of the busy place almost took Beth's breath away. People streamed everywhere, while porters threaded between them, pushing enormous barrows of luggage. Hawkers sold newspapers, roast chestnuts, and coffee from wheeled devices with dainty canopies.

The French countryside was more interesting than the Canadian train journey but took on increasing familiarity to Beth. She had grown to know these places from listening to her father and Uncle Alex. She thrilled to read place names where they had alighted from this very track.

A liveried chauffeur in a massive Renault car met them at the Gare Ste. Lazare. It had the classic inverted "V" across the grill and the most enormous headlights Beth had ever seen. It was mid-afternoon when they left Paris. They saw only a few of the famous sights. René told them they simply must make time to visit Paris. He would show them all the wonders. At mention of the Louvre, L'Arc de Triomphe, the Eiffel Tower, the Touilleries, they readily agreed they should do it.

They turned into the gravelled driveway of the château a couple of hours later. Nothing, not even René's descriptions, prepared them for the place. They gasped in unison, as the car crunched its way between massive iron gates and opened a vista of undulating yet carefully trimmed lawn. There must have been almost twenty acres of parkland before the house.

It was set back behind clumps of trees bordered by flowerbeds. A series of fountains played into stone pools sculpted with parapets and dotted with statues. Normally at this time of the year, the fountains would be turned off and the water lilies dotting the pools would be shrivelled and uninteresting. But René ordered them turned on for their visit. He was well satisfied with the result. The two women turned their attention to the house itself.

It was double-winged, forming a U shape. Within lay the main entrance and courtyard. The driveway swept around a final fountain pool to gain access to the courtyard. Like many such buildings, the chateau was built as a reflection of the glory of Louis XIV's Versailles. The inside of the building only increased their awe. For the next day and a half, they explored the halls, the rooms, the stables, and the farm behind. The gardens, although still very beautiful, would be breathtaking in the summer months.

The second night at the château, René simply showed up at Beth's room with a bottle of champagne. They made love, at first, like some reprise of an old familiarity. Then they became greedy, finding pause only a few days later. René was a good lover with a sense of timing and consideration Beth had never experienced before. He possessed great energy, mentally and physically, and had a lean body, which did justice to his almost forty years. Beth fell further happily in love with him each passing day, as he did with her.

René loved to strip Beth naked and view her in the firelight of his upstairs study. A large couch faced the fireplace. He would sit and swirl brandy in his glass and watch the fiery flickering lick at her body. When the sight of the subtle curves of her breasts and slender thighs grew too much for him, they would slide from the couch onto a tiger skin rug before the fire. More good brandy would be spilled. In a few short days, they matted the beast's fur.

Although the original plan was for them to stay for just a few days, it rapidly became a week. Fully aware of what was going on, Helen retreated during the day, developing a consummate interest in the local countryside, which the chauffeur drove her to daily. She visited several local Great War battle sites and doubtless reawakened some poignant, if painful, memories for herself. The week stretched into a month. Dragged into the conspiracy, Helen grew more and more guilt-ridden as more weeks went by. They were in a full-blown deception campaign, phoning back to Canada to pretend they were in England.

Helen was finally forced to fix a date for their departure. The relatives would be getting concerned. They devised a plan whereby they would both go to England, visit relatives to establish their alibi, and then Beth would return to France. The night before they were due to leave, René served a sumptuous meal. With great gallantry over liqueurs, he presented Helen with a beautiful bouquet of flowers. Accompanying it was a jewel box containing a massive amethyst brooch set in solid gold. Helen was overwhelmed. Tears streaked the makeup on her rounded cheeks.

Not long after, she excused herself and went up to bed. With a pause barely proper, they followed her up the long curved staircase. During her stay, Beth was sensitive to the feelings of the château staff. After all, she was an interloper, a foreigner, and a very young one at that. She was concerned there may be some resentment. The opposite proved true. Devoted to René, the staff recognized the source of his new happiness and responded accordingly. One of the elderly women actually drew Beth aside one day, and in halting English, blessed her for bringing sunshine back to the place.

They gravitated shamelessly to René's room after the first night and returned there now. Although René left special instructions for this night, the staff went one step further. Truffles were laid out with the brandy he favoured and champagne for Beth. Rocquefort cheese and fruit were laid out tastefully with a special vase of flowers. A note of appreciation to Beth from Albert the butler and his wife, Meurice, Marguerite, and the others, lay with a garland of flowers on her pillow. The expression enhanced the occasion.

They made love reflectively in the huge old bed, winding up lost in a tangle of bedclothes. There was an air of doubt, of unfulfilled expectations, finality, and hope to their mood. They knew they would have to part in the morning, but was it to be a permanent parting?

"Beth."

"Yes?"

"I love you."

"And I love you, René."

"Life has been wonderful these past days, but I have to tell you it is not always like this. Tomorrow, I shall have to plunge back into my work. It has been neglected the last while as never before. Usually, I am just a visitor here, but you have made it seem like a home again. I have always worked so much that now I'm not sure whether I can find the time for...for..."

"For me?"

"Yes, I want to marry you, Beth."

"You can't." His face fell. She wanted to burst with love. "Until my divorce comes through!" Her words momentarily perplexed him.

"You mean, you won't." His face beamed. " You *will*?"

"Of course I will!"

He seized her in a great bear hug of joy. Leaping off the bed, he strode purposefully across the floor, naked. He could not keep still; he was in such a frenzy. "Divorce! Yes! We will have to have that straightened out. As soon as we have a date, we can plan our wedding day." He was striding left and right, throwing out his words staccato as he went. Beth laughed. His naked buttocks flashed and twinkled back and forth. Changing direction wildly, he gesticulated with his hands in true Gallic fashion. "There will be lots to arrange!"

On another impulse, he swivelled suddenly and throwing open a closet, fiddled with the dials on an ancient-looking safe box. Grunting with satisfaction, he bore a leather case to the bedside. "This was my grandmother's." He produced an enormous diamond ring, and seizing her hand, drew it onto her finger. Beth was speechless at the size of the jewel.

"Hah! Too big! Eh bien, it is easily fixed!" Around the room he went again, his skinny shanks flashing, buttocks swaying and glinting whitely, while his flaccid penis bobbed. "Mother!" An incongruous exclamation and he stopped short. "We must tell Mother and Mathilde. They will be surprised!"

"You make it sound like it might be a problem, René. Will your mother not approve of me?"

"Approve of you? Mais certainment! How could she not? A thousand times, yes! But we must find a way and a time to do it. She still behaves as though Denise and Yvette were still alive. A new wife for me will surely shatter that illusion."

"But I still have to go to England for two weeks."

"My heart shall stop when you leave and shall not beat again until you return."

He returned to the bedside and smiled tenderly at her. Beth pulled the sheet up to her chin. He clucked reproachfully and drew it down, exposing her torso. He smiled possessively. Her nipples hardened in the cool air. She smiled back the same way and reached out for his rising manhood.

****

August 20, 1939.

"Get out of France!" Tom Edmunds could feel the high colour rising up his neck.

Beth's voice was weak and an ebbing and flowing hiss obliterated some of the words. "But Daddy, it is so wonderful here, and I am in love!"

"When your Aunt...no, *if* your Aunt Helen ever dares to come back, I shall strangle her with my own hands! She was supposed to chaperone you in *England*! Not sick you on some bloody Frenchman in *France*!"

"Daddy!" He could envisage her chin coming out in defiance. "Daddy, René is not 'some bloody Frenchman.' He is a gentleman, and incidentally, a businessman of whom I'd say you would approve of in every way. Please don't give me the jealous father routine because it won't work. I love the man."

"Young lady, you are not yet twenty-one! You will return to England on the next boat and then onward to Canada. Do you hear me?"

"No, Daddy. I am starting a new life here!"

"Beth!" Tom's tone took on a conciliatory tone. "There is a war coming! For God's sake, think of us worrying about you. Hitler has grabbed the Sudetenland, Austria, and is looking for an excuse to get his hands on Poland. Such a move will precipitate a war! I have been there, Beth! You must get out of France! When it is all over, you can go back, invite me over to meet him." Tom paused, feeling a victory imminent, his wave of confidence cresting over his daughter's intransigence.

There was a long pause. "Daddy, please understand." Her voice was low now, muted, and barely audible, yet quite discernible over the wire. "I will marry this man, I promise you. I shall be his wife, the wife of a Frenchman. I shall be a Frenchwoman, and here I shall stay."

"But the war..."

"You and Uncle Alex had this war slated for ten years ago and it never happened. The French Army is the biggest and best equipped in the world. The Germans would never want to attack!"

"The Germans may not want to, but Hitler will make them. For pity's sake, Beth, use your head. Come home. This fellow will follow you, if he cares enough."

"*This fellow* has a name, Daddy; he is René de Fourquet, future father of your grandchildren."

"Beth."

"I see no further purpose in this, Daddy. Please say hello to the boys and to Mother and Uncle Alex. Goodbye."

Tom was left listening to the crackle and static of a closed line.

In France, Beth kept her hand on the phone in thought. René told her for weeks that a conflict was on the way. He had all his foundries working overtime. They were producing armaments for the French government as fast as they could. Every day, signs grew more ominous, even as Chamberlain, Desladiers, and others met with Adolf Hitler to try to avert the inevitable. She still trusted in the feelings she vented to her father. Her place belonged where she placed her faith and love. That place was with René.

****

Edmonton.

For years since the famous diphtheria mercy flight, Robert Edmunds had trudged, hitched, or bicycled his way up Portage Avenue to the Northern Alberta Aero Club's premises, where he hung around, getting the occasional bit of work cleaning aircraft. He was awarded with the occasional flight for his efforts. That endeared him more to flying. By the time he was fourteen, he could fly, although his training had been entirely unofficial and could not be counted. He also caught the attention of Jimmy Bell, the hard-working airport manager who was to be a major proponent of the new air age in Edmonton. Both were associations well-suited for the young Robert.

At sixteen, despite the recession, he obtained his private pilot licence. Since he would have to wait two more years to obtain his commercial ticket, he filled in the time by apprenticing part time for his aviation mechanic licence. In nineteen thirty-nine, he got his commercial licence but had to put his proposed aviation career on hold, while he enrolled at the University of Alberta Engineering Faculty.

Days before classes started, Hitler invaded Poland and the long-foreseen war began. On September tenth, Canada followed Britain's lead and declared war on Germany. Amongst the entire hobbledehoy in the press, it was obvious many pilots would be needed to fight. Robert heard his father and Uncle Alex talk about the impending conflict long before reality set in. He read all the books about the first war's flying aces. Indeed, he now knew many of them personally. He also avidly read reports of Hitler's Condor Legion flying in the Spanish Civil War.

While Canada had no real air force of its own, Robert knew the role of the airplane in this war would be very important. He had watched the frail fabric and wire open-cockpit airplanes develop into the all-metal monsters that roared around at nearly four hundred miles per hour. He knew he would have to be involved.

On September twenty-first, he was seated in a class, which, in only one week's attendance, he had already learned to hate. He was thoroughly bored. His mind drifted off to the situation in Europe. In Poland, German Stukas were displaying new aerial tactics, dive-bombing defending units that were then being overrun by the armoured Blitzkreig launched by the Wehrmacht. Aviation was spearheading a military advance, a fact he found fascinating. Meanwhile, the professor's voice droned on. Suddenly, Robert reached a decision. He picked up his books and slipped them into his satchel. "Excuse me." The other students stared and some stood to allow him by. When he reached the aisle, a certain electricity in the air caused the lecturer to stop. Robert turned and continued walking.

"Er, Mister Edmunds, is it?"

Robert turned.

"You are leaving the class?"

"Yes sir."

"May I ask why, without my permission?"

"There are more important things to do, sir."

"What can possibly be more important than Euclidian Geometry, Mister Edmunds?"

"The war, sir!" Turning, Robert left the room and ended his university career. He could not, in all conscience, sit there while a major war erupted utilizing airplanes.

He already investigated the means of joining up. The argument with his parents was brief. Margaret was tearful; her motherly fears an insufficient argument to sway him. Tom could find no way to dissuade his son from doing something he himself had done only twenty-four years before. In two days, Robert was gone. He knew better than to get involved with the slower Canadian branch, so instead, he proceeded straight to a Royal Air Force recruiting office. An officer there wasted no time performing his attestation. By the afternoon, armed with a travel warrant, Aircraftsman Second Class Robert Edmunds was on a train to the Saint Lawrence and passage across the Atlantic.

Royal Air Force Hullavington was a pleasant place to be in England's West Country. Permanent "H" blocks and hangars set amongst trees and carefully manicured grounds denied the torments it contained. Dressed in ill-fitting uniforms with the thin ring of 'acting' pilot officers on their sleeves, a couple of hundred young men were being put through the rigours of commissioned officer training. They were harried from morning until night by a group of demonic non-commissioned officers, charged with moulding them into officers. This comprised of early morning rising at six for exercises, followed by a breakfast consisting of porridge, a plate of rubbery fried eggs greasily sliding around with under-cooked bacon, and a cup of tea.

For a month, they were subjected to: Royal Air Force law, King's Regulations, traditions, interspersed with route marches, rifle-firing, spit and polish, parade ground marching and 'leadership' exercises. The latter seemed to comprise of crawling under barbed wire and falling into mudholes while trying to reach impossible objectives. Officers of great wisdom stood on the sidelines and sagaciously scored the performances of these future leaders.

At the end of the month, there was a passing-out parade and speeches, following which, Robert moved on to a training unit. He quickly overcame the elitist and biased opinions of his instructors by proving ample competence in ten hours flying on Tiger Moths. Aerobatics were second nature to him by now. He scored highly on his initial training, obtaining his coveted military wings.

Then he got his wish: a posting to a Hurricane training squadron. Two weeks of ground school and cockpit training, and the day came for his first solo. With the encumbrance of the parachute backpack bumping and jostling behind his knees, he climbed awkwardly onto the wing and into the cockpit. A fitter helped him in, doing up his straps and completing the ground check. The aircraft smelled of hydraulic fluid, oil, and gasoline. He gave the 'all clear' and engaged the starter.

He would never forget that flight. Feeding rudder in against the propeller torque, as he had been taught, he advanced throttle and streaked down the runway. Easing forward on the joystick, he raised the tail wheel, and seconds later, the rumble of the wheels stopped. The sleek machine hurtled off the runway.

Robert selected gear up and adjusted his power for climb. The altimeter soared, as it never had before. Engrossed by the responsibility he carried, his eyes swept the instruments constantly to ensure nothing could go wrong. He was at five thousand feet in no time. He was supposed to stay up about fifteen minutes, trying a series of exercises. The aircraft was a dream! After preliminary approaches to the stall and some incipient spin exercises, he wrapped the aircraft into some tight turns, then rolled it onto its back, and flew inverted.

He was like a horseman trying out a new steed: a nudge here, a full gallop there, a turn and a raking of spurs to test reaction. Twenty minutes later, he felt safe in the aeroplane and brought it home for some practice landings. These were a little trickier than he was used to. For one thing, the Hurricane required a power-on approach instead of the glide he had been accustomed to. With flaps and undercarriage to extend, along with propeller and throttle controls, he had his hands full. Still, the admonishment of Captain Moss Burbridge of the Northern Aero Club in Edmonton held true, 'a good landing is always preceded by a good approach.'

One of the students found this out days later when he forgot to extend the wheels before landing. There was a horrendous shriek of tortured metal. The plane touched down and careened down the runway, its propeller bent back and sparks flying behind it. The crash crews ran out immediately to suppress any fire, while the miserable pilot sat in his seat, as if willing the plane to burst into flame and destroy him and his shame.

Soon, they were out over the sea, firing their guns and engaging in mock dogfights. The 'Phoney War' had commenced. Morale was high in the interlude since Poland fell. Songs like 'We'll hang out our washing on the Seigfreid Line,' accompanied by cartoons of Adolf Hitler at the cinemas epitomized the opinion of the populace that they would soon defeat the Germans, yet again. Beneath the jocularity, grim and frantic efforts were underway to arm the country.

Troops marched and trained. Metal was collected, and ships prepared to face the expected submarine menace. Strict measures of rationing and security began to affect the lives of everyone in Britain. Not a single person seemed to believe the united might of Britain and France, secure behind the Maginot Line, could possible be bested by the Huns. So the pilots trained and drank themselves silly on beer each night, engaging in pranks, which both bound them in camaraderie and obliterated any conscious concerns for safety.

****

Paris.

It was a beautiful sunny day on the Boulevard St. Germain. René took Beth's hand suddenly, tugging her away to one side. "Come, I want to show you my very favourite sculpture."

They turned into the grounds of Saint Severin, crossing a small garden that René told Beth had once been a charnel house. He took her mind off that macabre thought by telling her about it being the site of the first successful gall stone operation in fourteen seventy-four. Louis the Eleventh granted an archer, condemned to death, a pardon if he subjected himself to a surgeon's experimentation to cure him of the ailment.

The happy thought of the archer's survival carried them into the interior of the church. Beth was surprised at its extraordinary width. Once their eyes had adjusted to the gloomy interior, Rene led her down the south side. The sculpture was set in a small recess of a minor chapel and was a sixteenth century rendition of an armed and winged angel, gazing purposefully into the distance, while guarding the tomb of some long-dead merchant. Beth was not particularly impressed with it.

"When my wife and I were at the Sorbonne, we used to pop in here if we missed each other and exchange notes in a little niche behind the legs." Rene giggled. "I used to leave her love poems sometimes."

Beth's estimation of the statue fell another notch. With a surreptitious look in both directions, René suddenly slid his hand beneath the stone folds of the sculpture's skirt. "N'est rien!" He looked wistful for a moment.

"I am sorry." It was all she could think to say.

"Oh! It is I who should be sorry, Beth. You do not wish to hear about such things. Still, it always was my favourite, even before Denise."

****

Verviers, Belgium, May 11, 1940. In the wake of the Blitzkrieg.

Gruppenfuehrer Ewald Kleinst dropped the list on his desk and glared at the man before him. "Herr Schneider, you have failed! I must report this to Berlin immediately!"

The civilian beside the desk blanched visibly and seemed suddenly in need of a seat. "Your men…" He tried to control his dry throat convulsions. "Your men charged on the scene like rampant bulls in a cow pasture! They warned the Jews off!" Emboldened by the lack of interruption, Schneider rambled on. "My men were ready to spring the trap, indeed, we expected to net several other international Jewry bandits." Fully launched now, the spiel of National Socialist phrases flowed from his lips. "We of the Gestapo have long known the efforts of these Zionist swines' attempts to thwart the will of our glorious Fuehrer. Perhaps if the S.S. had not interfered…" His voice trailed off, for his mention of the Shutzstaffel had galvanized the black-uniformed figure behind the desk.

"The S.S., Herr Schneider, has full jurisdiction in these matters, by express order of the Fuehrer! Do not try to tell *me* that your bungling can be blamed off on *my* men! Your job was to infiltrate this group of Jews, so they could easily be arrested when our forces moved into Belgium! Could it be that these Jews are too clever for you and your Gestapo?"

There was sweat on the chubby features of the Gestapo man, and it shone on his bald head. His thick jowly face was almost porcine with deep-set, small eyes, which now glared at the insult. His head snapped back in defiance. The interdepartmental rivalry of the Nazi intelligence units and the secret police was a great weakness in the National Socialist Third Reich and was to remain so until the bitter end. To infer inferior intelligence to the sub-human Jews was the ultimate insult between them.

"All of these Zionists have survived your efforts to liquidate them, Schneider! They have escaped to France and other places to carry on their filthy activities. Now *we* must pursue them there. Twelve of them, worth billions of marks! You will answer for this!"

"What about the others, already in France? What about them?"

"Oh! So you expect we should allow you to let them escape also," sneered Kleinst.

"We have infiltrators in the ring in France. They can keep us advised of the movements and actions of the Jews. Properly executed plans will easily net them for us when our victorious troops have overwhelmed the puny French defences."

"I want the names and contact methods of all these Fifth Columnists this afternoon, Schneider! We shall talk of this again in a few days when I have spoken to Berlin! Brautsch!" The holler brought the door swinging open immediately and an immaculately tailored S.S. Obersturmfuhrer snapped to attention at the threshold. The speed of his entry suggested he had been listening at the door. "Show Herr Schneider out."

Kleinst didn't fail to see the sly grin on Schneider's face as he left. The Gestapo agent knew damned well that Kleinst would not dare to be the bearer of such bad news. As he stumped down the stairs to his car, his agile brain was already working on how to shift the blame to the S.S. Admitting failure to apprehend Jews on the list personally compiled by Reichfuehrer Heinrich Himmler was suicidal. Somehow, he had to get the Jews and take the credit, while blaming Kleinst for the delays.

Upstairs, Kleinst's mind was working on equal and opposite goals. He did not want to be the bad news bearer; there was nasty historical precedent for that. Perhaps if the news was leaked to Berlin, they could work off their rage there before the official report reached them, which would bear better tidings. He was well versed in the political intrigues and manoeuvres of surviving in a totalitarian state; after all, he helped create it.

Not for nothing was Ewald Kleinst wearing the three-star silver insignia of his rank. He had survived the embryonic ups and downs of the Nazi party and steered his promotion through the minefields of unstable superiors. He knew his place in the pecking order and made sure those beneath him knew theirs. His party number was enviably low, his experience and loyalty true.

He was there on November ninth, nineteen twenty-three, when Hitler and Ludendorff marched down Munich's Residenzstrasse towards the Feldherrnhalle for the famed attempted Beer Hall Putsch. When Scheubner-Richter fell mortally wounded in the flurry of shots from the police, he was one of those who helped the fleeing Hitler from the scene. Having helped (and kept intact the fable of Hitler's alleged bravery at the scene), he was favoured, yet cursed with a secret that could be dangerous to him at any time. He was awarded the Blutorden as a participant. The highly prized and very rare insignia on his tunic brought him more respect than any Iron Cross First Class with oak leaves. It made him an exclusive and elite member of a very small group of Hitler adherents.

It was a personal habit of Kleinst's to tug at his collar when bothered. He did so now, staring absently down into the Belgian town square. The apprehension of factions opposed to the Third Reich was well under way, evidenced by the truck below loading a line of prisoners under guard. Logistics were overloaded since the Wehrmacht entered this little town two days before. He and his team of S.S. Einsatzgruppen were hot on the heels of the combat troops. They formed a small, specialized unit of the Ausserordenliche Gefriedigungsaktion (A G Action), which was assigned the task of apprehending important Jews.

Kleinst's special task was to seek out Jews who owned businesses or assets important to the German war effort and seize them. His mandate fell under 'Operation Extraordinary Action' and had been underway since last autumn. He was in Poland for three months effecting the orders of Hans Frank, Nazi Governor-General. In Poland, Kleinst executed his orders, and Jews, with the single-mindedness of a rabid anti-Semite. Now, the conflict had moved into Western Europe. Hot on the heels of the invading German Wehrmacht, Kleinst and his men were charged with seizing richer spoils than Poland had offered.

He resented having to carry documents legalizing the buying of Jewish assets. However, the lack of persuasiveness of the sum offered was overshadowed by the nine-millimetre Luger he wielded. Once the sale was made, the vendor was considered expendable and shipped off to a concentration camp, and with no forwarding address, the money wasn't paid. Those who resisted the proffered purchase suffered Kleinst's preferred treatment for Jews: a bullet in the head. While he hated the required negotiations, someone at the top with a Teutonic sense of thoroughness had deemed it legally necessary. So his success was measured in direct proportion to the number of signatories.

Darkness fell outside. He could see his image in the dirty windowpane. He stood almost two metres in his gleaming jackboots with dirty-blonde short hair and pale blue eyes set in a square face. His cheekbones were high and wide, almost Slavic. He might have been regarded as a handsome man, but there was coldness to the set of his mouth. It brought rejection from many women who looked at him twice.

Around his right eye, a cobweb pattern of white scars marred his face. They were wounds proudly worn, relics of a long ago encounter with a broken bottle in a beer-hall fight when anarchy marched the Bavarian streets. Kleinst was a student in Munich then, struggling against the turmoil of the State and family poverty. His father was wounded in nineteen seventeen, unable to work, even if work was available. With war reparation payments bleeding the country dry, Germany offered little to anyone, except despair. Victimized by the usury of Jewish moneylenders, the Kleinst's slid backwards, evictions, repossessions, and wretchedness piling on them until his mother simply died of overwork.

Young Ewald buried his father soon afterwards. The old man simply gave up. He buried him with his medals on his chest, medals, which bespoke sacrifice and success on the battlefield, and ignored the real battle, the price paid on home soil. Patriotism is a perpetual, ever-demanding extortion of a person's soul, even when you have given all else.

Old Julius Guggenheimer the moneylender waylaid him and demanded his dues on the way home from the cemetery. Something snapped. The old man was without his bodyguard, steered by fate to redirect Ewald's course in life. Before he could think, Ewald drove his fist into the hateful face. Blood and bad teeth erupted from the head. Then he kicked the limp body, snapping ribs, and rupturing organs. Afterwards, he ducked into a beer-hall, fearfully awaiting the police to catch up with him.

Inside, a group of obvious supporters cheered on the impassioned speech of a small man with sideways-slicked hair and a brief moustache. At first, Ewald sat morosely disinterested in the proceedings. Then the man suddenly launched into a tirade against the Jews. When the speaker finished a half-hour later, he had another convert. Ewald Kleinst found his saviour, found a new purpose in life. He grasped the earnest handshake and gazed into the dark, messianic eyes of Adolf Hitler before the evening was over.

The favour he found since that night was now threatened by the lack of ruled lines through names on a list. He knew what he had to do. To out-do Schneider, avoid any blame, he would have to go behind the French lines and pluck a prime Jewish candidate, someone whose assets would be important to Germany. Such success would prove his loyalty and his capabilities.

His stubby finger traced the list of names with assets opposite and stopped at a familiar name. It was that of a family that owned an important armament complex, as well as other assets, since the turn of the century. A family that profited from the sale of munitions used to kill Germans like his father. Double reason then, for choosing this filthy Jew! "Monsieur de Fourquet!" He murmured the name aloud. He looked up again at the image of himself in the window, nodding his head with a self-satisfied aggrandisement. "De Fourquet!" Gruppenfuehrer Ewald Kleinst was looking forward to squeezing and eliminating the de Fourquets.

****

Paris in the spring of nineteen forty was a strange place. Europe once again fell into war in the autumn of nineteen thirty-nine, yet fighting had not come until the past week. The armies of both sides marched, armed, and postured throughout the cold winter in what was now known as the Phoney War. The Maginot Line stood inviolate, an impregnable bulwark against German aggression. The French Army was the biggest and best equipped in the world, therefore France was apprehensive but confident. Government purse strings loosened in the need to re-arm and equip. René de Fourquet worked twenty hours a day to desperately try and increase production, while coping with a loss of manpower as reserves were called up.

Beth saw little of him after being in England for a month with Helen. While there, she saw Robert, who was with a Royal Air Force squadron, flying a Hurricane fighter. Prompted by Tom, Robert tried to dissuade Beth from returning to France but to no avail. It was he who had finally blown the whistle on her plans. It took quite an argument and another telephoned shouting match home to Alberta with her father, but Beth determinedly returned to Paris at the beginning of May. The legalities regarding the Sturdees were proceeding in good fashion and should be finalized in just two weeks. She didn't see how her ex-in-laws could possibly know the way she was spending her time in Europe.

Then the world fell in. The combined treachery and ease of the fall of both Norway and Denmark was a prelude to more recent events. Nobody could have known. Now, the Germans were in Belgium, only a short distance away. The news, while not inspiring, was not too alarming. The French and British armies were moving to repel the Nazi menace.

****

Village of St. Denis-aux-Riviére, Northern France, May 17, 1940.

For a couple of days break, René brought Beth up to the estate near Douai. He still had a mass of work to wade through and was constantly on the telephone, but he made time to be with her. He was busy in the music room when Beth decided to take a walk in the outside gardens.

She had only been here two days and already grew to love this place. It was built in the eighteenth century and was as elegant a place as she had ever seen. The main house was stone-built with slate mansard roofs and leaded windows, set in deep wooden frames. Inside, it contained a wide variety of architecture with dark oak English-style wainscoting, white plaster walls, and low, age-darkened beams. She particularly liked the library. Having inherited her father's love of books, the cosy decor and walls filled with tomes and a massive fireplace had sparked her fancy. Idly, she wondered if the sight of the library would ameliorate her father's vehement opposition to her being here.

Outside, the estate contained a centre-courtyard farm accessible through a front archway with stables and numerous lofts to explore. The garden behind the house sloped down towards a small stream and artificial lake. Stone walls and balustrades terraced the slope, joined by stairways. Trees and shrubs abounded amongst ponds spread with lily pads. Some nineteenth century owner added stone sculptures that helped the sense of permanence, a feeling she was growing daily to associate with René de Fourquet.

She hoped that in a few months, her parents could come to France. She and René could be married in this garden with hundreds of guests. She knew full well that his sophisticated European ways, his style of life, and the aura of power around him was part of the attraction for her. She also knew her family would look upon her love as an infatuation, like a young girl idolizing a prince. Beth knew more was afoot here. There might have been that kind of infatuation with Edward. With René, it was unbounded and unreserved love. She knew that René and her father would get along fine if they could only meet. After all, they would talk business endlessly!

The early bulbs, the daffodils, crocuses, hyacinths, and tulips were finishing now, and a couple of old gardeners toiled to remove the dead vegetation, making way for the burgeoning shoots of the myriad roses. Soon, the garden would be transformed into another of its well-planned seasonal faces. Alphonse, one of the oldest gardeners, was weeding one of the rose beds when Beth decided to try out her strengthening French on him.

"Eh bien, Monsieur, comment ça va?"

The old man huffed and straightened his back. He hadn't heard her coming. He was the epitome of the elderly Frenchman. A pair of worn and cracked boots stuck out from beneath baggy and shiny-worn black suit pants. A matching jacket was thrown across the handle of his wheelbarrow. Held at the neck by a stud with no collar, a blue and white striped flannel shirt lurked beneath a navy blue pullover upon which he now wiped his hands, as if it were unseemly to talk to the mistress with them dirty. The hands, Beth noted, were gnarled and enlarged by physical labour. The face matched, old and wrinkled with wide, pendulous jowls. Its generous white moustache, long stained by the juices of his filthy old pipe and vin ordinaire, quivered. He returned her greeting. A slight bow of respect followed.

"I see you are preparing the rose bed, Alphonse. Do you expect a good crop this year?"

"Oui, Madame. The shoots are as strong as I have seen them. Soon, we shall have buds. I only hope to live to see them."

"You are sick, Alphonse?"

"No, Madame, it is just that soon perhaps, I have to don my medals again and march off to meet the filthy Boche once more." He paused to spit, thought better of it in her presence, and resisted the temptation.

"But you are much too old to join up and go fight, Alphonse!"

"Madame!" He drew himself up proudly. "One is never too old to fight for one's country!" The measured words were spoken with deep dignity. "I have many old comrades, long since dead, whose blood fertilized this very soil in defence of France!" The words died to a whisper on the last word. The faded blue eyes turned reflective as he saw an army of ghosts march across his mind, shrouded in time, yet long remembered.

The full impact of the war came home to Beth for the first time. Less than a hundred miles away, men were dying to preserve her freedom to walk in these gardens. Alphonse's words were a simple statement of faith, a peasant's precis of all the current verbose speeches about loyalty, duty, and honour. Surely, if this was the timbre of the average Frenchman, then she had little to fear!

"If you go, Alphonse, you must take with you my scarf. You shall be my champion on the battlefield!" Beth felt instant remorse at the remark, feeling like some modern day Guinevere, mocking the old man. He was serious and reached out for the theatrically proffered garment.

"I should be greatly honoured, Madame. Rest assured your colours will be carried bravely!"

"À bientôt, Alphonse. Bon chance!" Beth felt slightly foolish at giving away her scarf, a brightly dyed silk one she recently bought at a Paris market. It would be even more embarrassing to now ask for it back. She left it clutched in the gnarled hand.

The secondary thought, as Beth turned away, was if an old soldier expected to have to go back to war, then France was really in a lot of trouble. A chill pervaded her body. She walked quickly back towards the house. As her steps quickened, the sense of dread deepened. She was in a panicky run across the terrace seeking the reassurance of René's presence when the door to the music room opened, and there he was. His face was white and shocked. Beth stumbled to a standstill ten feet from him and froze. Her premonition found substance in his appearance.

"I just heard!" His voice was a croak.

"What, René?"

"The Germans! They almost have Holland! They have also crossed the Meuse and are driving across Belgium in our rear! Brussels will fall today!" René referred to the belated access granted by King Leopold of the Belgians to British and French Army units, whose governments requested positions on his soil to forestall a German attack. After shilly-shallying over neutrality, Leopold finally succumbed and called for assistance when his forces became beleaguered by a superior German onslaught. It would prove an after-the-fact decision and a mortal blow to France and Britain, not to mention his own country.

"But the French Army will stop them, surely? And the British? The British are also in Belgium! René, there is hope!" Beth moved closer to him and placed her hands on his chest as if to hold off his despair.

"I fear not, Chérie. It would seem those units arrived only in time to be encircled and captured. There is little doubt the Germans will make it into Northern France." René put his arm around her shoulders and steered them inside.

"The Maginot Line!"

"…is outflanked and may prove useless. I may lose the factories in Douai!" Tears flowed down René's cheeks. The glasses rattled as he poured them each a cognac.

Beth stared at him aghast. Only minutes ago, in the garden, she was planning their wedding, envisaging a golden day with the guests, her parents, and most of all, their happiness. Now, it was all in ruins. She experienced her first victimization by war. "What can be done?"

"Destroy them!"

"What?" This was more horrible!

"Destroy them! It is the only way." His face was grim. "You know about the stories of the new Nazi Germany. Think of the horror stories from Poland last autumn. What of the barbaric bombing of Rotterdam only days ago? We cannot allow the factories to fall into their hands and aid their war effort. Unless something drastic is done, they could be in Douai in a matter of days." The words brought renewed vigour to René. He tossed back the last of the cognac and strode to the phone.

As Beth caressed his neck to calm him, René spent a fruitless half hour trying to reach Douai. All the lines were tied up or dead. He finally got through to Paris and reached Armand Fournier. He crisply gave orders to co-operate with the government in the event it was decided to destroy the factories and other facilities the de Fourquet's owned. "We must return to Paris immediately! Nothing can be achieved here! Beth, go upstairs and pack. We leave in fifteen minutes."

Almost in a daze, Beth ran upstairs and threw a few things in her bags. When she carried them down, René was already at the foot of the stairs, addressing the servants. There was a deep air of gloom and defeatism as he broke the news. He quickly briefed André, the manager of the estate, on his requirements.

"Come!" Grabbing a large briefcase from the stairs, René seized her hand and propelled them both through to the kitchen. He flung open the door to the cellar. As they hurried down the stairs into the semi-darkness, Beth's curiosity rose.

"Why are we coming down here?"

"There are some things down here I need to take back to Paris. Also, I want to show you this place for the future." They walked swiftly across the stone flags of the floor. The dim light filtering through windows grimed by the years lit their way. Wine racks, derelict furniture, and implements were scattered everywhere. Across the main cellar, a wrought iron grille from floor to ceiling barred their way. René produced a massive iron key and brushing away the cobwebs, unlocked a gate in its centre. Against the far wall was a row of huge wine casks, six feet across and lying on their sides. "The key will lock the gate from either side. We will leave it unlocked. Sometimes valuables can be best protected by not drawing attention with a locked door. Here! If you need to hide, the key is here!" He placed it on top of a stacked barrel where it could not be readily seen.

This further mystified Beth, but René was already over at the huge casks. "One, two, three, four." He counted from the left and then approached the cask behind his pointed finger. "Here!" He checked to make sure she was watching carefully and then pressed a knothole mark just along the side of the cask. "Stand back!" He grabbed her arm and moved her aside. Grabbing the rim, he pulled and the end of the cask swung towards them like a huge circular door. Behind it, the massive wooden structure was empty, like a tunnel. "Come!"

They stepped into the cask. It felt strange to be walking through a giant barrel, but it was a false one, with no end on it. René snapped on a flashlight, revealing the building's stone foundation wall at the rear. Set in the middle was a small wooden door that seemed to lead outside the cellar wall. Reaching into a hidden recess, René produced another key and unlocked the door and pulled hard against some resistance. Behind was a small subterranean room about ten feet square. The walls were lined with cupboards and bunk beds. A table and some chairs were pushed to one side beside a large keg.

"A secret hideaway!" Beth breathed, "This is just like the movies!"

"Yes, a sensible Jew always has a place to hide himself and his valuables. Some of my ancestors hid here during pogroms in the past. As to the valuables, there are few here right now. I will have to tell you later about them. Hold this!" René thrust the briefcase at her and pointed the flashlight. He moved quickly to one of the cupboards and grabbed two bundles wrapped in oilskin.

Outside again, he stowed the key and showed her how to reset the mechanism that latched the front of the cask. They returned through the kitchen to the main hall. The car was ready, and in a matter of minutes, they were gone.

It was a glum journey. Many of the roads were occupied by troops and equipment on the move. They passed several emplacements of heavy guns beside the road. Situated as they were in the midst of apparently peaceful countryside, they provided an ominous reminder of the German menace. In fact, they travelled directly across the main German line of advance. Although they didn't know it at the time, advance Panzer units were only a couple of dozen kilometres away.

There was much to discuss, but the uncertainties caused René's mood to swing from fighting to fleeing. Beth noticed when he spoke in the first person it was 'fight.' Any pronouncements spoken collectively were 'flee.' He felt France might fall. If it did, Spain's Fascist Franco might throw in his lot with Hitler and attack Portugal. With Norway, Denmark, Holland, and Belgium already gone, this would lead to a totally German coastline for Europe. Italy's Mussolini was a Hitler adherent. The Mediterranean would join the Atlantic under Nazi sway. It was a grim prospect.

"René, you must not seek to flee on my account. If you want to truly fight, I shall be at your side."

"This is not your fight, Beth!"

"Oh but it is! I am going to marry a Frenchman, a Jewish Frenchman. Anyone threatening him threatens me and mine. Therefore, I have the right to fight back. His friend is my friend, his enemy is my sworn enemy."

The words were spoken with a quiet vehemence. That made them more convincing, and in the late darkening light of the May night, René glanced across at her. The chin was high. The eyes smouldered. He knew he had chosen wisely.

When they arrived in Paris, it was in turmoil. Communications to the north were out. Messages were being sent by courier. At René's office, documents were signed concerning the agreed fate of the de Fourquet industries, but nobody seemed to be making decisions in the government. Nobody seemed capable of giving an order.

Paris, although in turmoil, had a feeling of underlying confidence. The Republic had faced adversity before and confounded its enemies. The famed Parisian air of supremacy would not allow for defeat. Even so, the news from the Front grew grimmer by the day. The main surprise thrust of the German attack developed out of the Ardennes, slicing across France south of Douai and isolating Northern France from Paris. René was now out of touch with his industries there. The Belgians were gallantly hanging on. There was still hope of a military success with French and British units still holding most of Northern France and access to Britain through the Channel ports.

Events were unfolding in France that would spell disaster. The lack of decision-making in the government, which René had experienced, seemed to go right to the top. Paul Reynaud shuffled his cabinet the day after they returned to Paris. General Weygand replaced General Gamelin as supreme commander. The addition of Marshall Pétain as Deputy Minister of Defence was generally regarded as a stiffening of French resolution. Surely the hero of Verdun from the Great War would give positive leadership!

Reynaud, though, was being severely undermined. His mistress, the Countess de Portes, a high-handed and domineering woman, continuously burst in on his conferences, loudly declaiming her opinions on matters out of her league. Her motives were difficult to understand but were certainly not subordinated to any patriotic considerations. Rather, her behaviour typified the total lack of coherence and will of the government. The switching of army commanders delayed the implementation of counter-attacks and strategic planning, further stressing the command structure.

On the evening of the twenty-second, René told Beth to prepare for an important dinner engagement. They would travel just outside Paris to the home of some friends. It was already dark when they left. Beth would never remember where they went, but eventually, they were shown into a smart house on the outskirts of a village. The party was a relatively small one, about a dozen people. Beth was totally astounded to find the guest of honour was Winston Churchill, the new Prime Minister of Britain.

Despite the desperate times, the dinner was well provided in an elegant, well-appointed dining room. As they made their way through the many courses, the conversation touched on many aspects of the war. Beth was a little disappointed in Churchill. He sat hunched in the place of honour, his elderly features broad and jowly. He frequently scowled. It was obvious he was extremely tired and under duress. Nonetheless, he dominated the conversation, interrupting and talking over people where he chose to do so. Beth thought he was rather peremptory and overbearing. For all that, he was well learned and even exchanged a few knowledgeable words about Canada when they were introduced. Most of the people in the dining room had vested interests, besides patriotic purpose, and it made for an interesting evening.

René was able to recount his problems with the French government in trying to disable his industrial complexes. Churchill muttered misgivings about how the war was being conducted by the French. "When I was in

Paris a week ago," the voice was a deep mumbling growl, "I asked General Gamelin where the mass of reserves were, and he advised me there were none. I was totally aghast." He pronounced the word in the English "agharst" style, which sounded strange to Beth, but a suitable word for all that.

"Mr. Churchill," the speaker was a tall aesthetic lawyer, prominent in the French law courts. "What will Britain do if any more countries fall to the Nazis?" Everyone in the room paused, realizing that, tactfully, the man avoided naming France as the next national victim.

Churchill paused. He was in the act of unwrapping and preparing to light one of his famous cigars. His features creased furiously, enhancing the bulldog-like expression. The host hovered at his elbow with a questioning tilt of a brandy bottle. He gave a small nod of grateful acceptance. "Excellent Napoleon, mon ami...ahem! What will Britain do?" Churchill spoke as if speaking to himself, contemplating his lighting of the cigar with care. The light from the silver candleware on the table picked out the highlights of his face, the deeper creases forming dark abysses. "Why Sir," the words were muttered. "Britain shall fight. Britain shall fight with all the measure of her resources. Britain shall fight with all her might. Britain shall fight with the aid of her Empire and all others who wish to join." The voice was only measurably louder, but the force of oratory seemed to make the voice soar like a gathering hurricane around their heads. "Britain will never stop fighting until this scourge of the gutter, this intolerable Nazi oppression is removed from the face of civilization. Tell one, tell all, that Britain will fight, fight, fight." The force of conviction behind the words and the glint behind the blue eyes caused the lawyer's eyes to drop. There was a long silence in the room.

There was further talk about the sending of more British fighter plane squadrons across the Channel to attack the Germans, but Churchill made it clear that not many planes would be forthcoming. As he pointed out, they were made to control the skies, not interdict heavy armour. That was the task of artillery. Churchill also expounded on his theory of holding each village and crossroads with riflemen, demolishing houses on the German tanks, and killing the crews when they emerged. It sounded more like guerrilla tactics than solid opposition to an invading army and bore the hallmark of expected defeat. The main tactic required to defeat the Germans was to cut off the mile-wide corridor they had cut from the

Ardennes to the Channel. Successful flank attacks to cut this corridor would decapitate the Panzer divisions. Since they would by now be suffering personal exhaustion, lack of fuel and supplies, plus equipment wearing out and breaking down, now was the time. Yet, the changes in command had consumed days of inaction.

They were quickly on their way home again, Beth's head a little dizzy from the experience. She was still a little unimpressed with Churchill as a person but had to admit he bore an aura of leadership. She certainly admired his bravery in coming to France on this second of what would eventually be three daring trips.

The news was no better over the next while. The British rescued thousands of soldiers from Dunkirk. The Germans over-ran Northern France. Holland was theirs and King Leopold of the Belgians surrendered after gallant fighting by his armed forces. Since this was done with no agreement with the British and French, it resulted in the capture and defeat of the very Allied forces that came to his aid. It was generally regarded as almost treachery. On May twenty-seventh, Reynaud denounced Leopold's decision over broadcast radio and vowed to carry on the French cause from North Africa, if necessary.

The rot around him belied the stalwart words. The high hopes for Pétain were shattered. He was senile and began a campaign for a political surrender, while leaving the army undefeated. By the end of the first week in June, cabinet ministers were spread around the country, isolated at various châteaux and trying to run the country by inadequate telephone links. The determination of the front line was often accomplished by phoning a village post office and seeing what language the call was answered in.

On June ninth, the Jewish Society called a meeting. It was held at the home of Abraham Bloch, a prominent junior minister at the Quai d'Orsay. René and Beth jumped in the Citroen just before six o'clock to attend. The mood of Paris was now difficult to define. Many people had fled; others remained with grim determination to confront the hatred 'Boche.' Even though most of the British had left and their armies beaten back, the Parisians, on the whole, believed their government was in firm control, with strong invincible might to back it.

After all, had they not turned aside the German advance, that glorious siege, in eighteen seventy? Had they not done it again in nineteen fourteen, going on to defeat them? The posters that had magically appeared all over Paris overnight enhanced the sense that work was going on behind the scenes: 'Citoyens! Aux Armes!' How splendidly evocative of the glory of eighteen seventy that was!

On the way over to the Boulevard Bineau, where the Blochs lived, Beth saw hundreds of the challenging posters slapped hurriedly on doors and walls. They even appeared on the iron street urinals beside the stern rebuke 'Défence d'afficier.' There was little evidence of the vaunted 'Arondissement by arondissement' defence of Paris. Nobody seemed to question the lack of work building street barricades, mining bridges and buildings to defend the city. With the streets so deserted, it took only minutes to make the drive.

Their destination was up a narrow side street. They parked on the broader boulevard and walked the last fifty metres. The trees were leafed out and ready for the warm days when one could enjoy an aperitif at a bistro and bask in the sun. The menace from the north overshadowed the mood. Entering the large stone-built apartment building, they were confronted by the concierge who emerged from her door with the sentry-like nosiness of her kind. They enquired of the Blochs and were dismissed with a scowling 'Vingt-neuf' and a contemptuous wave of a pudgy hand.

Beth could feel the woman's eyes boring into their backs like hot coals as they ascended the stairs. The stone steps rang with their footsteps. The ironwork railings were cold in the semi-darkness. Beth wondered if the woman was a member of the 'Action Français,' a fanatically anti-Semitic organization that recently merged with other extreme groups. Until recently, Beth was unaware that the persecution of Jews was an old and popular cult in Europe. Once invalid, now resurgent persecution was apparent with the success of Nazism. Many Jews had already learned to their cost not to underestimate the hatred ranged against them.

Down the gloomy passageway of the second floor, they found number twenty-nine and pulled the ancient bell-pull. Abraham Bloch answered and reinforced Beth's apprehensions, by peering around the door and then down the hallway before letting them enter. Inside, they went to the spacious apartment's sitting room and exchanged greetings with eight other people already congregated there. They waited for ten minutes for other expected attendees, exchanging small talk, while Madame Bloch, a tiny woman with a busy nature, plied them with canapés and coffee.

By six-thirty, they accepted the inevitable and commenced the meeting. Many Jews had already fled Paris, while others shunned Jewish organizations, seeking anonymity. Bloch formally opened the meeting. Benjamin Broussard reported on the current situation. Broussard had a personal friendship with Georges Mandel, the great French Jewish patriot and now Minister of the Interior. Broussard claimed authenticity by association.

"Georges phoned me this afternoon. The government is established at Tours." The slim, dark curly-headed Broussard never failed to establish his credentials as a conduit for the most unimpeachable sources. "He told me Paris is safe. The Seventh Army, with part of the Tenth, will fall back to defend Paris. He assured me arrangements are in hand to make any attack on the city by the Germans a very costly business indeed!" A small wave of relief and chatter swept through the people present.

Another man, a banker named Roth now rose. "I am advised the government is in close contact with the British. Monsieur Churchill has been to France twice and promised more aid, including many fighter planes." Startled, Beth turned towards René at this pronouncement she knew to be false but he gave no outward indication of refuting it. Roth continued, "General Weygand thinks we can stop the Germans. With Paris as an anchor for the whole front, the Germans cannot advance further. Also, Reynaud is talking to the Americans, urging them to join with us or at least make unity with our cause. And with Pétain by his side, France will triumph again!" Roth puffed out his cheeks. His wispy moustache quivered as he sat down. Amidst the stir around her, Beth again looked at René, but he was inscrutable.

A Rabbi rose next and advised them all that the Grand Rabbin of Paris would remain in the city as a symbol of solidarity and faith, no matter what happened. After a quick prayer, the meeting broke up into a half dozen conversations concerning escape, rationing, resistance, and patriotism.

René took Beth home after some polite indulgence. Astonished at René's silence at the meeting, they were no sooner in the car when she burst out. "Why didn't you say something? We *know* Churchill won't be sending more planes. *We* spoke *to him ourselves!*" Beth was bewildered.

"Whatever I might have said in there would have counted for nothing. They are all deluding themselves. France is going down in a torrent of rhetoric."

"But they want to fight, René! How can you abandon them?" Now Beth was angry, thinking she could see cowardice at work.

"They won't fight, Beth. There is no plan to defend Paris! I found out yesterday, Mon Dieu! France is sliding towards doom, and Churchill has seen it!"

"Then what are we going to do?"

"Leave. Tomorrow. Early. Pack tonight and head for the vineyard in Bordeaux. I will drop you at the apartment. Start packing and get the servants organized. I must go and tell Mother and Rebecca. It will be useless trying to argue with Mother over the telephone."

Back at the apartment, René dropped Beth off and she went inside to pass the word to the servants.

They were full of questions as what to take, feeding off each other's Gallic panic, until she raised her voice. "Pack only one suitcase per person. Put anything of great value in the trunks, which can be loaded on the baggage racks of the vehicles. Anyone who wishes to stay, you are free to do so. I need to know by nine o'clock who intends to come with us to Bordeaux. Now get busy! The Master will have further orders when he arrives!"

It was almost midnight before René returned. Beth was almost frantic with worry. The insecurity of the whole situation played on her mind. She met him in the hallway at the sound of his key in the latch. His face was grim. "You scared me, being so long."

His stiff anger forced her to step back. "They will not come!"

"What! Why not?"

"Mother wants to show her solidarity with the Grand Rabbin. Like a typical Parisian, she does not believe Paris will fall. It took two hours of violent argument, in which I pointed out the treatment of Jews under the Nazis. Finally, she agreed to leave in three days if the situation 'gets any worse.' She dared to challenge *my* patriotism, just because she is too stupid and stubborn to see that her death will serve France for nothing!"

"René!"

"I only managed to extract that concession from her on the grounds of her major holdings in the de Fourquet complex. I told her it was her responsibility to protect her safety in the interests of the family, our employees, and France."

"So we wait three more days?"

"No, you leave tomorrow for Bordeaux."

"What do you mean *you leave?* Are you not coming with me?"

"No, I will follow in a few days, if I need to get Mother and Rebecca out of Paris."

"Absolutely *not*! I have told you, I stay with you!"

"But Beth, everyone in the household in two cars will make for slow travelling. With Meurice or Pierre, I can afford to wait a couple of days and then make better speed to catch you."

"Better speed? With your mother?"

"Beth, I need somebody I can trust to take all the documents out of Paris to a safe place. I beg you to help me with this!"

"No!" Beth plopped down on the bed and glared at him. "For the last time, I will not leave Paris without you! And that, Monsieur, is my last word!"

René stared at her. He knew she meant it. The confrontation was insurmountable. "Then we must compromise. You have to leave Paris, I need someone to safeguard the documents." He held up a palm to settle the outburst cooking on her face. "I shall accompany you perhaps to the Loire, where it will be safer. From there, if necessary, I shall return, after phoning Mother to fetch her out. In the meantime, you shall travel on to Bordeaux and prepare everything for our arrival."

At this point, Beth realized she had won all the concessions she could get and quietly nodded her head. For the next two hours, they worked hard, finalizing their arrangements, and completing the packing. Under René's firm guidance, both cars were fuelled and packed with valuables, valises, and victuals. The artworks, tableware, and furniture were consigned to a storage warehouse in the care of three servants who chose to stay in Paris. With a large tip and a revolver under his coat, Georges, the concierge's husband, stood guard over the two vehicles, while everyone travelling tried to get some sleep. Cars were becoming scarce in Paris. The urgency of the situation had reduced the scruples of evacuees.

Desperately tired, René and Beth finally went to bed at nearly three in the morning. Almost in moments, it seemed Marguerite the maid was awakening them with coffee and rolls. It was past six now and by seven-thirty, they were on their way.

The first indication that things might not go well happened at the Gare Montparnasse. They turned right off the Boulevard Montparnasse on to Avenue Maine and immediately, the quiet streets gave way to a mob of people milling around trying to get a train out of Paris. Their way was totally blocked. Just as they slowed down, a gendarme stepped out.

"Bonjours, Mésdames, Messieurs." He glanced at the baggage both on the roof of the car and strapped on the back. "I am sorry, but it is impossible for you to get through here. I suggest, if you are leaving Paris, that you go back to Boulevard Montparnasse and then take Boulevard Raspail."

"Are all these people waiting for trains?"

"Oui, Monsieur, but there are no more trains. They wait merely in the hope that one may depart, but there will be none. Some of these people have come all the way from Belgium, and they are quite desperate. I would recommend you leave immediately!"

As if to back the gendarme's words, Beth saw a group of people detach themselves from the crowd and head in their direction. René turned the Citroen around. People began to beg for a seat in the car, some waving money and valuables to indicate their willingness to pay. One woman held out her baby and entreated them to take it with them. Two of the men, seeing them intent on leaving, began to curse and threaten them. The gendarme held the crowd back, while they finished turning. As Beth looked back, she saw several people, led by a nurse in uniform, breaking into a store. There were groups of miserable, starving children amongst the refugees. It was obvious things were starting to get out of hand. It was a further example to her of the miseries of warfare.

Taking the gendarme's advice, they reached the Place Denfort-Rochereau and immediately ran into a stream of traffic leaving the city. Out past the Montparnasse cemetery and the Port d'Orleans, cars, horse-drawn wagons, and pushcarts straggled along. An old man, looking just like Alphonse the gardener, patiently trundled an ancient bicycle piled high with pitiful baggage. Beside him, his stout wife, bundled in heavy clothes, lugged a suitcase. The man's stoic bearing, his resigned plodding in the long crocodile of refugees was to be one of Beth's permanent memories of the time.

It took three full hours to get out of Paris. They were hot and exasperated by the time they reached the outskirts. During one of the frequent stops, Meurice, who drove the second car, jumped out and came forward to René's window.

"Sir, I know this country well. I suggest we turn left at the next turn and try the quieter country roads through Corbeil and Malesherbes." René quickly nodded assent. They were getting nowhere fast jammed in the heavy one-way traffic. Only occasional army vehicles went the other way. Everyone was getting irritable and progress was what they needed. They simply had to get to Orléans and on to Tours as soon as possible.

Several kilometres later, Meurice tooted his horn and waved out the window. While waiting to turn left at the junction as directed, they were dismayed when a soldier riding on a short military convoy yelled out that advance German units were seen at Versailles and pushing southward. After leaving the main road, René was soon able to push down the accelerator. They sped up to about fifty kilometres per hour. A small cheer inside the cars greeted this achievement but their relief was short-lived. Only minutes later, they screeched to a halt at the sound of explosions over to their rear right. Piling out of the cars, they stood at the roadside, rooted in horror at what they saw. Over the highway they had just left, a series of aircraft, decorated with black crosses, swept down on the dense traffic and dropped bombs.

The bombers swept low over the defenceless vehicles. The crump of the exploding bombs shook the ground beneath their feet. Although there was some military traffic, the bombers were obviously being indiscriminate as they turned back, and lining up on the road, raked it with machinegun fire for a couple of kilometres. They could only imagine the full horror of the situation. Each of them visualized the crowded, slow moving picture of the road they had so recently left.

"Mon Dieu, c'est l'Enfer!" The staunch Catholic Marguerite crossed herself fervently.

"Come! We do not wish to share their fate!" René hustled them back into the cars. They gunned the vehicles down the road. Anxious necks swivelled heads above and behind them. They travelled, stunned into silence at what they had witnessed.

Beth was horrified by what she had seen. There was absolutely no doubt about what they had seen the German aircraft attacking; they were too close to be mistaken. "Now we see the Nazi beast at work in our own land!" A tear trickled down René's cheek. She turned to look at him. Slumping in her seat, weak and shocked, Beth wondered where it would all end. Obviously worse was to come. If the Germans could attack in such a manner without challenge, then things were grim for France. For the first time, she found herself concurring fully with René's decision to leave Paris.

Meurice's suggestion proved excellent. They made good progress, zigzagging southward, occasionally crossing other roads choked with refugees. At such times, they nervously watched the sky. It was particularly slow crossing the river at Malesherbes. The exchange of dark humour and truth between groups stirred the ingredients of panic. The occasional report of German aircraft sightings coloured the dire mood.

The second time they stopped in the middle of the ancient stone bridge, Albert volunteered to drive the car, suggesting the others walk to be picked up on the far side. They were sitting ducks if a German bomber came along. The risk was high, since bridges would be prime targets. They climbed out of the car next to the bridge parapet and quickly made their way across. Just after leaving the car, Beth glanced sideways at a large, powerful-looking vehicle revealed between two cars on her side of the road. It was inching along the other way. It was odd that someone would be travelling in the other direction. She supposed that is what caught her attention.

Or was it the sense of being watched? Leaning out of the shadows of the vehicle interior, she saw a large man with dark blonde hair gazing at them intently. His gaze was cold. Beth felt an unaccountable icy ball materialize in the pit of her stomach. He saw her looking at him, and then his attention seemed to focus on René. He turned and spoke to the driver, while looking back in the direction they were walking. In that moment, Beth saw his face was covered with white scars on one side. The big car hesitated and tried to go into reverse gear, but a big military truck loaded with soldiers was close behind it. It had to go on forward as the truck driver leaned on his horn.

By four in the afternoon, they were south of Malesherbes and by-passed Pithiviers by side roads. They intended to cross the Loire at Châteauneuf-sur-Loire. It seemed like a good proposition to overnight there. Stuck in the cars all day, they were stressed, stiff and tired, and needed the break. Further reports said the Germans were bombing as far south as the bridges on the Loire. This news sent them down a series of endless lanes, passing east of Châteauneuf, and taking them to the tiny village of St. Germaine-des-Prés.

Here, where the Loire cut a deep valley before swinging westward towards the Atlantic Ocean, the steep slopes were dotted with picturesque, almost fairy-tale châteaux and elegant estates. Such was their urgency, the passengers of the two cars had little interest in tourism, and they sought only shelter. The population of St. Germaine was swelled fourfold by refugees fleeing the north like most of the surrounding area. There were, consequently, no regular accommodations to be had. Several enterprising farmers and homeowners capitalized with certain peasant canniness on the misfortunes of the travellers.

It was eight in the evening before René waved enough francs under the nose of a farmer willing to accommodate them all. Due to their number, he grudgingly consented to their using a disused stable out behind the other farm buildings. Hiding the cars behind the barn, safe from other refugees, they carried inside the necessary luggage and food Jeanette had brought along.

An old forge stood in one corner. They quickly lit it to provide illumination, heat, and a means of cooking. Within the hour, they sat around, feasting on a peasant's stew, washing it down with a couple of bottles of Troplong Mondot. The presence of wine in such surroundings was entirely incongruous. Washing down stew with a Grand Cru Classé Première under other circumstances would be sacrilegious. Yet, their adventures called for a celebration. Only the best wines were brought along anyway.

The night was cold, but the forge gave them some comfort. There were several holes in the roof. The brick and beam walls were crumbling. It was obvious the farmer considered the building unsuitable for his animals but suitable for rent-paying refugees. They sat in a building-wide open area where horses had once been shoed and saddled. Further in, a central passageway led onto stalls on each side. They looked in ill repair, but a large pile of straw in one corner promised the means of cosiness. Albert had already spread some in each of the stalls they would occupy. In deference to René and Beth, he gave them the place of honour: the best stall, keeping several unoccupied between them and the next people.

After the previous short night's sleep and such a stressful day, the stew and wine caught up with Beth. She started to doze. "I must phone Paris." René's abrupt statement and his rising caught her unaware. "I must find out about the status of Paris."

"I will go with you, Sir. I need to phone my mother also!" Meurice leapt to his feet and walked to the door before René could reply.

"I will not be long, Beth. Meurice and I will drive into Châteauneuf and find a telephone and perhaps fill up the cars at a garage." Beth nodded, now too sleepy to really care. The two men left.

They returned an hour later with the news that made millions of Frenchmen cry. Paris was declared an open city! The news totally flabbergasted everyone present. The decision was made two days ago. Beth now realized René must have had inside information. He had told her, more or less, what was to happen. Not even General Hering, appointed commander of the forces to defend Paris, had been told about this horrendous decision. Seemingly, General Weygand pushed for this decision, a total betrayal of the French people's faith in their government. It was a national shame. The idea of the hated Boche marching without opposition into the capital was anathema to all.

While the Germans had not yet occupied Paris, all communications were severed. René was unable to get through to his mother. He took Beth to their stall. "I have to return to Paris!"

"No, René, you cannot! You'll never make it in, and you certainly will not get back out!"

"I *have* to go! Mother and Rebecca have to be got out, and there are others who need help."

"None of them heeded you when there was time."

"But I *must* try!"

"And how are you going to get a procession of Jews out of Paris under the Nazis' noses? My darling René, it is suicidal!"

"I have to do it Beth! You don't see?"

It hit her then. Thousands of years of persecution – Jewish blood – made to resist and fight in the face of overwhelming odds. It didn't matter how much you watered the blood, it never lost its stubbornness. In the final analysis, no matter how he declared his non-alignment with Hebrew ways, you scratch a Jew and you uncover a stoic lineage running right back to Solomon and David.

"Then I'm coming with you!"

"No!"

"Don't you 'no' *me*, Mister! I'm coming!"

"No, Beth," his tone was soft. He framed her face between his hands. "I need you to do what is an equally important task. The documents *must* be evacuated to safety. We agreed." He touched his fingers to her lips to still her protest and rushed on. "As a family member, it is your duty to do this, against all your feelings and all the odds. Yes, my darling Beth, you are a family member." Her eyes opened wider as he plunged on. "There is one more thing we must do before we part. Beth, will you marry me?"

She gasped both at the surprise and the audacity. "René?"

"Tonight! Now! I have made the arrangements. You told me your Decree Nisi has come through, and you are free to do it. Please Beth. I love you. I want you for my wife. I need the strength of knowing you are waiting for me in Bordeaux!"

Beth was lost. She always figured she had a romantic view of life. She already knew that she and René would one day be married. These circumstances of the formal act were straight out of some novelette. But that knowledge did nothing to reduce her feelings. "How can we get married tonight?"

"I have made arrangements in the village, helped by a sizeable donation to a certain church. We can do it now!"

"Oh René, *yes, yes, yes!*" They talked for a few more minutes, and hand in hand, they walked out to tell the others their good news. There was anger in the air, now that the initial shock of Paris had sunk in, but the mood became almost festive at their announcement. They quickly bundled themselves back into the cars and drove down to the village.

The church, shrouded in darkness, loomed only as a large square tower. They pulled up before it. René discovered its roots went back to the year eight hundred six. They were standing in history. Inside, the beauty of the old church was breathtaking. It was built in the shape of a Greek cross. They were to be married in the east apse where a magnificent mosaic decorated the roof. The mosaic was composed of thousands of coloured glass beads and depicted the Ark of the Covenant of Our Lord, surrounded by cherubims and angels. Charlemagne reputedly brought the glass from Italy.

René actually lied to the priest, telling him they were both Roman Catholics. The father, at first, protested the irregularity of the request but eventually agreed to proceed in view of the war, particularly when René made a sizeable donation to the church for its renovation fund. Despite the hurried nature of the wedding between a Jew and a lapsed Catholic in a Roman Catholic Church, the ancient building – the apse – lent a sense of dignity and continuity of sanctity, especially under the circumstances.

René and Pierre, who was appointed best man, took their position in front of the venerable Father Alain. As the eldest man, Albert was to give away the bride and stood ready for Beth to take his arm. In a flurry of activity, the women bustled around Beth, quickly brushing her hair and thrusting into her hand a posy of wild flowers picked outside in the darkness. They were all closed up and the dim candlelight of the church did nothing to open them, adding to the impromptu nature of the proceedings.

Albert proudly handed Beth to the altar. The nuptials were dealt with fairly quickly. A hastily summonsed choirboy, Alphonse, sang a Te Deum, while the others, more familiar with the Catholic dogma, helped with prayer responses and allayed any suspicions the old priest may have entertained or conveniently ignored concerning their faiths. Three of the servants signed the register as witnesses. They returned to the farm after profusely thanking the old priest and tipping the choirboy.

Pierre and Meurice volunteered to accompany René back to Paris. Albert, who also drove, would take the rather overloaded second car to Bordeaux. They expected few delays once they crossed the Loire the next day, so they should have a relatively smooth ride south. The men had earlier planned to leave for Paris at three a.m. to get a jump on the traffic. René and Beth retired to their stall after a toast from the bottles extracted from the wine trunk and well wishes from everyone present. Extra blankets were laid on a bed of straw. Everyone removed themselves to the far end of the stables out of respect. It had been a wedding far from the expectations of both of them, but René promised Beth a proper one, once they were together again. For better or worse, they were now one.

Spending their wedding night in a stable was certainly different. In some strange way, it enhanced the basic feelings they held for each other. They discovered no need of luxurious trappings and came together with a simple lovemaking that seemed earthier, more basic. The soft yielding straw beneath her seemed more appropriate to Beth than silken sheets. She responded lustily to René. Finally spent, they clung to each other and whispered endearments, punctuated by concerns for the hazards ahead. Soon, they slept, curled up together.

Awake early, René decided to leave. Meurice protested, but his master was adamant. Complaining and taking his time, Meurice went to start the car, loaded with their needs. Re-entering the barn, René knelt down and embraced Beth, carefully kissing her. "See you at the estate, my darling."

She smiled sleepily, exhausted by the past few days. "Hurry home safely, my love." But he was gone, afraid to prolong the moment.

After his departure, Beth came fully awake and was unable to sleep. She was terribly worried about René and knew she would not rest until he joined her again. An hour's restlessness told her that activity was the only way to alleviate her anxiety. Deciding to follow René's example, she roused everyone to get on the road. The sooner she got settled in Bordeaux, the sooner all would come well. Yawning and grumbling, the party packed the car and climbed aboard. Carefully checking to see the valise containing the valuables was nestled next to her, Beth took her seat, and they pulled away.

They were rounding the corner of the stable, when a bright glare of headlights bathed them in light. A car swept up in front of them. With a wave of relief and elation, she thought René had changed his mind and returned. Her thoughts were dashed in the next moment. Four men leapt out of the car and rudely wrenched open their doors. A pistol was thrust in her face, and a harsh voice told her to get out.

The bewildered party was herded roughly out of the car and back inside the stable. Beth was suddenly shocked to see a familiar visage in the criss-cross of flashlights. The leader was the man with the scarred face she saw on the bridge at Malesherbes. They were all lined up against a wall. One of the men covered them with a submachine gun. A woman, she couldn't see who, had readied a scream, but it was cut off by a brutal punch. She could hear the woman crying softly in pain.

Their assailants spoke few words, but Albert identified them. "Mon Dieu! Les Boches! Ils sont les Boches!" He opened his mouth to shout something and one of the men quickly stepped forward to strike him across the face with his weapon. The sound of the impact made a horrible wet thud. Blood streaming, Albert slumped to the ground. Jeanne knelt beside him and muttered imprecations at the men.

"Silence!" the scarred man barked. "Now, which one of you is Monsieur de Fourquet?" The accent was thick and harsh from the German tongue and with poor vocabulary. There was a long defiant silence. "Answer me, you French swine!" He waved his pistol menacingly. Beth shuddered. She realized there was no bluff here. He would really kill one of them if he so chose. "Who then is Madame de Fourquet? You?" He waved the pistol in Beth's direction.

Beth was startled. She only shared the name for a few hours and to hear it said under these circumstances was shocking. How could he know who she was so soon? She nodded her head dumbly.

"Where is your husband?"

"Il n'est pas ici, il a..." she groped in her confusion for the proper French word, but it would not come. "He is not here..."

"Englander!"

"No, I'm Canadian, you ignorant bastard!"

The words were lost to Kleinst, but he recognized the defiance creeping into the woman's voice. He knew how to deal with that! He quickly stepped forward and slapped her across the face. The force of the blow spun Beth around. She fell to the floor, clutching herself. As she rolled onto her buttocks, back against the wall, Marguerite was thrust into view, her arm twisted up behind her back. The pistol was held close to the maid's temple.

"Vere husband iss, shoot girl." The voice was low but full of menace. Beth gasped at the sheer callousness. She did not need translation to understand the poor English. Marguerite mewled in pain as her arm was twisted higher up her back. "Schnell!" The pistol was cocked and ready.

"Paris! He has returned to Paris!" Chalk white and with an apologetic look at Beth, Marguerite blurted out the words and was flung aside.

"Pourquoi Paris?" The defiance of the French was building. Silence met his question. There was little time to extract the information and gunfire at the farm would unquestionably bring the local gendarmes to investigate. Kleinst pondered that for a moment. He was eighty kilometres ahead of the German forward units, and besides Berlin's displeasure, if he failed, he had to consider the further risk of being apprehended or killed by the French. What he needed most was a telephone. "Ou-est Meurice?"

"Meurice?" Beth gasped. The full significance of the question hit home. Meurice vanished once or twice during the journey. He had done so after the wedding. *That* was how this man knew she was married! Seeing him just yesterday was not a coincidence. Meurice was guiding him onto their trail! René didn't announce his intent of returning to Paris until after Meurice was back at the farm. He obviously was unable to telephone again without arousing some kind of suspicion. He led them here. These men caught them by the narrowest of margins after they left. Only his earlier departure had saved René from falling into their hands already. Now she understood Meurice's determination to go back to Paris. He played the faithful servant to his master, but he had other reasons to be with René. He was ready to betray him!

"Meurice est totem!" Albert propped himself up, sitting against the wall. He knew the German word for "dead."

"When? How?"

"As soon as I see him, sale Boche." The mixture of English, French, and German conveyed meaning but would have been comical in other circumstances.

"You talk too much, Frenchman!" Ignoring the insult, Kleinst turned to his men and issued rapid orders in German. Two of them roared away in their car moments later. Satisfied the word would be passed back to his people in Paris to find de Fourquet, Kleinst waved the pistol again at Beth and told her to go to her car. The others made to accompany them, but he gestured to his other man, who barred their way with his submachine gun. "Nein, ve haff no use of stupid French. Vith the kleine fly trapped in my web, the Jewish spider vill soon come to see, if mein men miss him in Paris." Kleinst laughed at his own analogy.

Realizing his intent, Beth could have wept. The timing of her marriage to René was hastened by circumstance and a protective convenience. Within hours it had instead become a potential and deadly liability to him. She was a hostage now, an Achilles heel to the strength he must find to extricate himself from the clutches of the Germans.

She was roughly handled out the door and pushed into the back seat of the car. Kleinst slumped next to her. With a shock, she realized he was sitting right next to the de Fourquet documents and valuables, probably the very things he sought! She was dazed that Meurice was a traitor and terrified he would turn in René to the first German patrol they met. Stuck without transport behind her, her household staff could be of no assistance. She was a refugee in an adopted land, out in the middle of nowhere: in the dark, married, and possibly widowed in a matter of hours. She was now kidnapped by the ruthless secret police of a conquering invader! Drained of all her strength, she slumped in the seat as the car moved off.

An upper window shot open as they passed the farmhouse. Fed up with the nightlong comings and goings of his impromptu guests, dressed in his nightshirt, the farmer leaned far out of his window, shaking his fist and haranguing them for their thoughtlessness and big-city noise.

René made a gallant but unfortunate miscalculation in returning to Paris. The advancing, victorious Wehrmacht drew pincers around the capital. Troops were turning back everyone who tried to leave. It was still possible for a small trickle of despondent and hopelessly demoralized refugees to return with proper identification. That was their only hope if they continued.

The three men in the car were unaware of this. One of them sat with a quiet satisfaction that René was playing directly into his hands. Meurice had been a member of a pro-Fascist group for ten years. Anti-Semitism was as natural to him as breathing. He looked forward to the rewards he would receive when this arch-Jew, de Fourquet, was delivered into the hands of his Nazi masters.

The refugee traffic was a little lighter now. Since they were travelling the opposite direction to most, they found it faster on the main roads north. That is where the first morning flight of the Luftwaffe found them. There was little warning of the attack. There were few people around to see the aircraft and panic off the road ahead of them. The Junkers swooped in behind them and directed a hail of machine-gun fire along the road. The windows on the right side of the car, without warning, disintegrated in a hail of glass shards. Curious gouts of redness exploded on the inside. René, sitting in the back, barely had time to register the passage of an express train through the back of the car. He saw people and horses slumping to the ground ahead before the car lurched to the left, rammed a wagon filled with family goods, and plunged into the ditch.

He must have hit his head, for he awoke to hear screaming and cursing all around him. A dozen crumpled figures lay sprawled outside in the ditch and across the road. Relatives tended the wounded and wailed over the loss of loved ones. The Germans were gone. A horse, shot through the neck, neighed in agony and terror, careening around on the road, pulling a light cart behind it. It kept smashing into other vehicles, while people jumped out of its way. Suddenly, a great coughing gout of blood erupted from its mouth. It flopped to the road, twitching and jerking.

Turning, René found Meurice, who was sitting next to him. Half of his manservant's brains were spread over the intact left window of the car. Blotches of red and white tissue were splattered over all of them. Pierre was moaning in front. He was grazed by another machine gun round. His shirt was sodden with blood. Turning to himself, René found cuts from broken glass. After another bile-wrenching look at Meurice, he climbed from the car and helped Pierre out. They were lucky. The speed of the aircraft had spread the bullets just enough to spare them.

They worked on Pierre's wound, and with help from other refugees, got the car back on the road. Rather than abandon Meurice at the roadside, they decided to take him back to Paris. They covered him with an overcoat and delicately avoiding the spattered upholstery, climbed into the front seats, René behind the wheel. Pierre emptied the dead man's pockets and placed his belongings on the floor by his feet. They set off and the smell of feces from the back provided them further discomfort.

René was now doubly determined to reach Paris. They passed the sixty kilometre sign just before the attack. It was not far. The car did not seem to have suffered any mechanical damage, aside from the bullet holes. They made quick progress. As he drove, René was depressed by the mass of abandoned belongings at the side of the road. It was amazing the kinds of things people tried to escape Paris with. Enormous mattresses, rolled like unwieldy Swiss rolls, chests of drawers, probably family heirlooms, had been unceremoniously dumped in the ditch as survival and escape eclipsed their value. More depressing by their absence was the lack of French military units.

They came across a Wehrmacht barrier fifteen kilometres further on. A steel-helmeted German military policeman stepped forward with a white, semi-circular paddle with which he waved them to a halt. Three infantrymen stood wide apart, Schmeissers cocked and ready and pointed at the car. A fourth soldier sat in a motorcycle combination. A heavier calibre weapon was aimed right at them. A Feldwebel stepped forward and demanded their papers.

Perhaps it was their demeanour or maybe a Jew's first encounter with the 'Master Race,' but René's hand, with a mind of its own, sought amongst Meurice's belongings until he found the wallet and presented it instead of his own.

"Meurice Desladiers? Achtung!" Three submachine guns were thrust into the car. "Where is the Jew, de Fourquet?" The French was halting and poor, but the words took their breath away.

René, heart in his mouth, could only jerk a thumb to the back of the car. The German moved to the rear door and pulled the coat aside to view the mess beneath. "Ah! He has already been dealt with! Excellent!" Retreating, the man distastefully tried to wipe off some brain tissue that adhered to his trousers. "There are orders for you to report to the Hôtel Crillon in Paris. They are the express orders of S.S. General Kleinst." The hard German consonants accentuated the authority. The Feldwebel fumbled in a leather pouch strapped to his belt and extracted a form.

"This is a pass for you." He scribbled his signature on the bottom next to another. "It will take you through all roadblocks to Paris. I will phone to say you are on your way. If you are late, you will have to answer directly to the General! He is with you?" The man waved at Pierre.

René nodded. He did not trust himself to say a word.

"Then be on your way. It looks like he needs a doctor! Heil Hitler!" The Feldwebel's arm shot out like a piston in the Nazi salute. Before he knew what he was doing, René replied in kind and let in the clutch. He promptly stalled the car in his anxiety to be gone and muttered expletives under his breath. He got it going under the shadow of the Feldwebel. The engine revved and they shot away towards Paris.

Arms akimbo, the Feldwebel watched them go. He was a mild Bavarian, not a Fascist, but happy for the victory of German arms. "Schweinehund!" he muttered scornfully as they vanished up the road. No good German would behave like the *schisenkopf* French traitor Desladiers, whom he would as soon have shot, given his choice.

There were long stunned moments of silence in the car.

"What the hell was that all about?"

"They are looking for me, Pierre, specifically for me."

"But why, Sir?"

"Because I am a Jew, but mainly, right now, because I am a rich, industrialist Jew. They want me and my armament factory, Pierre. When they stopped us, I suddenly decided to pretend to be Meurice for some reason, and it worked."

Pierre did not comprehend. He never had to cope with being a Jew. Why René was important, alive to Germans, was beyond him. Despite that, he knew where his loyalties lay. "How can I help you, Monsieur de Fourquet?"

"Merci, mon cher ami! Merci!" René reached out and squeezed Pierre's arm. "You can best help by getting yourself medical attention, Pierre. It is too dangerous for you to be seen with me. I will drop you off." He waved off the coming protest from the wounded man. "I will drop you off. We will arrange to meet later. I must hide as soon as I can ascertain the situation with Mother and Rebecca. I suppose I could permanently adopt the identity of Monsieur Meurice Desladiers, but I suspect he will become a much sought-after person before today's end!"

"But, Sir!" Pierre's old face creased with horror. He finally understood. "Meurice was a traitor, a Fifth Columnist, a...a Nazi?"

"Yes Pierre. The Germans are very thorough. I suspect they may have targeted me two years ago, when old Jean died and Meurice took his place.

It was all carefully planned to drop me in their hands. We were very, very lucky. Thank God the others are safe!"

"C'est diabolique, Monsieur!"

Pressing the accelerator firmly down, René sped on for Paris. Armed with the military pass, he had little doubt about getting into Paris. He hoped they did not meet any French battle units that might prove hostile. With Paris an open city it was not likely. It was too late to turn around. He had a grim foreboding that Beth was right. Once in, he would have great difficulty in getting back out of Paris.

A French farm field, June 1940.

Bearing a steaming mug of tea laced with sugar and condensed milk, the Aircraftsman Second Class stooped to the entrance to the tent, jiggling the heavy fabric. Having given the equivalent of a knock, he pushed his way inside. "Morning, Sir, here's your cuppa. It's almost five now."

The only occupant of the tent stirred in the wood and canvas camp bed and rolled over, immediately awake. "What news?"

"They say the Jerries are driving on Paris. We'll be going back to Blighty pretty quick."

Robert Edmunds grunted and grabbed the mug. A rancid wave of body odour and dirty clothing assailed his nostrils. He moved out from under the blankets to sit up. He had not washed for three days and had been in the same clothing, awake and sleeping for more than a week. The smell seemed to fit the times. The Germans were winning. Two Forty-two Squadron was sent over to Northern France at the beginning of the open warfare as part of Churchill's promised fighter aid to France. They were in the thick of the action ever since the Germans invaded Belgium. Now, having abandoned almost all its equipment, the British Expeditionary Force was mostly evacuated from Dunkirk in the past week. France seemed lost. In the past five days, the squadron had been chased by the Wehrmacht and harried by the Luftwaffe. It was forced to retreat and fly to safer airstrips continually.

The Hurricanes could fortunately take off from grass strips, so any farmer's meadow, which was long enough, would suffice. Their ability to fight effectively was crippled by the abandonment of vital equipment, sometimes only minutes before German units overran the field. Tools, spares, ammunition, petrol, and men were lost either by destruction or separation from their units. Three times already, Robert had flown off to new airstrips, leaving behind his ground crew 'erks' to try and catch up by truck. On one occasion, he flew with an aircraftsman fitter sitting in his lap. So desperate were they. He flew repeated sorties to attack Luftwaffe bombers and claimed two Junkers Eighty-seven Stuka dive-bombers, although they were unconfirmed 'kills.'

Now, clutching the mug of tea, he stumbled from the tent, dishevelled and weary. It was just past dawn. It was cold and damp in the early morning light and his glance skyward revealed broken stratus cloud backed by a clear sky. There would be aerial combat today. His second reflex was to look to his aircraft. 'F' for 'Freddie' with the Two Forty-two Squadron letters "LE" painted on its side stood about two hundred feet away. It stood drawn up tight to a copse of trees and shrubs. Raised engine cowls distorted its distinctive hump-backed shape. Flight Sergeant Bob Brackenridge and two erks were working on the Merlin engine.

Robert turned and walked slowly towards another copse in front of where a canvas screen had been erected on some posts. Behind it was the latrine, a slit trench hurriedly dug in the ground. It was a sign of the desperate times that this one was totally communal and did not separate 'officers' from 'other ranks.' He had trained his bowels to function on his awakening each morning. Trying to go later was usually impossible. The cramping pains of urgency were totally unwelcome in the cockpit of a fighter plane.

Unbuttoning and lowering his trousers, he sighed as the cold air struck his naked groin and buttocks. A quick flash of sensuality was eliminated by the smell of his body, hardly better than that which was emanating from the trench. He crouched, carefully holding his garments away from his stream of urine. He rubbed his heavily whiskered chin and reached for his tea, as a soft stool slid from him. He fell to wondering about Beth. He was still annoyed with her for returning to France over his arguments. He could only begin to guess what kind of man this René fellow was she was involved with. It looked like Paris would fall soon, even if heavy fighting stopped the Germans for a while. Surely Beth would get out in time?

The whine of a starter, followed by the coughing misfires of a badly timed engine, came from a short distance off as fitters readied an aircraft.

The noise continued for almost a minute, an ill-timed and unfortunate event, for the Luftwaffe was prowling early today. The sound of their approaching engines went unnoticed. Before Robert or anyone else was aware, a strafing pair of Messerschmidt One Hundred Nine fighters jumped them.

The first came from almost tree level through the opening used by the Hurricanes as final approach. It passed directly over Robert. The sudden blast of sound and air blew him backwards, almost into the latrine trench. Its guns opened up at the same time and added to the din. With a curse and a grimace at his undefended state, Robert yanked his trousers up and blundered into the open. His one thought was to get into 'Freddie' and take off. Foremost in his mind was not combat but survival for his machine. On the ground, as it was, it was a sitting duck.

An explosion from his left and a gout of orange flame bespoke the fate of one of the aircraft caught on the ground. It spurred him on. Brackenridge and his men frantically fastened the engine cowls. One of them was jumping in the cockpit, ready to crank it up. Robert knew the plane was fuelled and armed. He could be off in moments.

A crescendo of sound behind him announced the approach of a second German aircraft. Just to his right, the ground seemed to erupt in a turmoil of grass and earth, showering him with dirt. At unbelievable speed, the boiling inferno streaked past him and sped at 'Freddie.' Robert watched. He fell to the ground dismayed. The gunfire seemed to pause at his plane, hammering at the shuddering airframe, puncturing and slamming it until it was a torn wreck. A glow appeared amidships, and suddenly it exploded. The flaming high-octane petrol spewed out like a blossoming peony rose, full of death. The blast swept over his prone body, hot and hungry as a childhood monster. The Hurricane, broken-backed, folded in upon itself while throwing shards of aluminium all around.

When Robert looked up, a pool of fire surrounded his plane. Brackenridge and his men were gone. Only blackened heaps in the flames revealed where they had fallen. He beat his fists on the ground and cried at the horror. His crew chief had three children back in England. Ammunition in the blaze began to cook off, further hazarding the area.

He staggered to his feet and took command of three nearby airmen, helping to organise aid to the wounded. Two Hurricanes made it into the air. It was unlikely the Messerschmidts would return with the element of surprise gone. With a snarl of distaste and discomfort, he realized his recent ablutions were not properly concluded. His underpants had reached a new sticky low in hygiene.

****

French farmhouse, 20 kms east of Orléans.

"Ja, Herr General, they reported de Fourquet dead in the back of the car and directed the driver to the Hôtel Crillon as you ordered"

"They were sure it was him?"

"I don't know how they made the identification, Herr General. They said half the head was shot away, and the car had been machine-gunned. Perhaps they took the driver's word."

"That is what I am afraid of! For what reason would Desladiers shoot de Fourquet? The fact that de Fourquet may be dead I find disturbing rather than comforting. Get a description from the officer and men at the roadblock on all the people in the car. Do it at once, Brautsch!"

With a click of heels, the aide left towards the short-wave radio in the other room. Kleinst moved to the doorway and tugged at his collar in frustration. The world would not miss one filthy Jew, but he would be comforted to know it was the right Jew. If de Fourquet slipped through their hands again, Berlin would extract retribution. "And reinstate the order to identify and arrest de Fourquet on sight!" he yelled after Brautsch.

He furiously stamped down the stone hallway of the small farmhouse where they were hidden and waved a hand at a sentry standing guard over the room where Madame de Fourquet was imprisoned. The sentry opened the door and stepped aside. She sat despondently in one corner, bewildered by events. Kleinst looked at her without expression. She had medium length dark hair and an elfin prettiness that was attractive. The thought of forcing his attentions upon her came easily, but she had a determined set to her face. He knew it would cause more trouble than it was worth.

The time to tell her of her husband's death was not yet, Kleinst decided. She must suffer a little more. Perhaps the knowledge held a trump hand for him. Keep her scared. He merely glared ominously at her and then turned heel and left.

His rapid visit had the required effect. Further confused, Beth dissolved into suppressed sobs. She was being held on a tiny farm east of Orleans.

The Germans obviously prepared carefully. The place was isolated. They had a powerful radio they used to stay in constant contact with their superiors. Beth could not know it, but the rightful occupants of the farm lay dead, stacked like cordwood in the barn. Kleinst had introduced himself to her, quite freely, declaring his purpose with a grandiose superiority. So much for him! If they had indeed caught René, she thought, he would have been quick to gloat. The obvious conclusion was that René was still free, no thanks to that bastard Meurice! This thought stiffened her. She scraped her forearm over her teary cheeks.

The hours slid by in the semi darkness. Her isolation unnerved her. It was meant to. The war raged on miles away. Unknown to her and with equal despondency, a battered Anglo-French Army licked its wounds in Britain, fresh from Dunkirk, while German units occupied the Channel coast. Her brother Robert, exhausted and filthy, took off in his borrowed Hurricane fighter less than a half hour flight away from her to make his own escape to England. Finally, she was sent for.

They took her to the room where the radio was. One of the men was bent over a microphone, turning a dial on the set. His face was a mask of concentration. Wires went through the open window and were connected to an antenna strung between the house and one of the barns. "Adler, ein, trei, acht." The man kept repeating the message, keying the microphone, and then listening.

The radio heterodyned, and another signal tuned across its frequency. There was a staccato of Morse code. The tone dropped to a mournful squawk, like a broody hen as it slid away off tune. Under the circumstances, it sounded to Beth like a defeated military unit pleading for help, sliding away to its fate, mocked by a plaintive cry.

Faintly, tip-toeing through the ether, a reply came back. "Adler...Zie totem... nich ... "

Beth could not make it out, but the Germans obviously could. Kleinst lurched forward as if he had been bitten in the seat. He scowled at the radio. Beth saw the operator cringe as if expecting to be struck.

"Kommen zie!" He sprang to his feet and strode through into the kitchen, dragging Beth by the arm. He went around the kitchen table and sat in the wooden chair. The guard pushed her forward from behind, positioning her before her captor. Retreating, he backed against the wall, machinegun across his chest.

The German was furious. The scars on his face glowed a livid white. Beth knew she was in for trouble. Kleinst just received the bad news regarding the identity of the driver. "Vere your man, in Paris go?" He wasted no time, though communication was difficult without a common language.

Beth found that encouraging. It meant René was still at large and thought to have reached Paris. She shrugged, precipitating a barrage of questions from Kleinst. Between genuine and faked facility with the French language, Beth managed to avoid most of them, while increasingly infuriating the German.

"Who he in Paris knows? Who he go to? Not family! Ve haff zem vatched und haff *plans* for zem!" The menace dripping from that statement made Beth shudder. Already she had witnessed the atrocities the Nazis were capable of. She knew full well how ruthless this man was.

"Je ne compriendo." Deliberately, she mangled the language they half shared.

Kleinst had reached the height of frustration. He wasn't sure, without common language between them, just when she was avoiding the question. He swore, cursing his lack of English and her's of French.

"My father shot a whole bunch of you bastards about twenty-five years ago," Beth offered helpfully. Kleinst ignored her.

"Get her bags!" The guard nodded, and stepping forward, propped his weapon against the wall behind Kleinst's chair. Turning, he disappeared into the passageway. In the meantime, Kleinst appeared to come to the boil. He walked around the table and stood in front of Beth. "Vere..." he slapped her across the face. "Would…" The backhand came in recoil, snapping her head around. "Your husband…" Her nose was bleeding. "Go?"

Beth shook her head. She was stunned by the suddenness and pain of the attack. Seizing her by the neckline, he suddenly ripped her blouse down the front and punched her in the breast. Gasping with pain and embarrassment, Beth slumped to her knees. He grabbed her by the hair, his other hand fumbling at her right breast. The thumb and finger found and tweaked her nipple. She screamed in agony. She was brutally hauled to her feet by her hair and nipple. He pushed her away. "Vere?" He yelled, stepping in towards her.

Beth had had enough. Her scalp screamed with the pain he inflicted. Her mouth was swelling and the salty taste of blood ran over her upper lip. As he stepped towards her, she straightened up and kicked out at him as hard as she could and got lucky. The pointed toe of her boot caught him in the left testicle. In a howl of pain and rage, Kleinst doubled over, clutching himself.

Beth heard a loud thump from the passageway. The returning soldier dropped the bags he was fetching. Heavy feet started to pound towards the door. She quickly leaped to the heavy oak slab and slammed it shut. There was a bolt on her side. With a strength born of desperation, she shot it home, just as the man hit the door. Turning, she found Kleinst on his knees, face contorted, fumbling to unholster his pistol. He was swearing a blue streak in graphic-sounding German. He seemed now determined to kill her. A row of pots and skillets hung from a rack over the ancient-looking stove. Beth swept one from a hook without thinking. Kleinst tried to duck as she swung it, but she caught him with the edge, right on the cheekbone. He went down, as if poleaxed, and the pistol skittered across the floor.

The sound of pounding boots faded down the passageway beyond the door and grew louder in the next room. Beth heard the man crash into a piece of furniture and swear with pain. Any second now, he would appear in the other doorway, and she would be lost. She desperately cast around for help. Her eye fell on the machinegun the man had laid behind Kleinst's chair. She leaped to it, scooping it up, and pointing it at the doorway. The man appeared and gasped when he saw the muzzle levelled at him. He leaped out of sight again and lunged for his sidearm holster. Beth squeezed the trigger, but nothing happened. Fumbling and cursing, she tried to find what might be the safety on the weapon. She found it just as the man reappeared flourishing his pistol.

The Schmeisser erupted in a hail of bullets. A look of surprised anguish froze on the man's face when the first half dozen slugs ripped into him. He slumped backwards, dead. Unused to the force of the magazine spring, Beth was unable to control the weapon's aim. A stream of bullets stitched their way up the doorpost, across the wall and into the ceiling. The wall was whitewashed stone, and with spitting howls and screams, the remainder of the magazine ricocheted around the room, destroying windows, shelves of preserve jars and cupboards. Her finger was frozen on the trigger. The weapon did not stop until the last round was gone. The howl of bullets and falling debris came to a halt. Beth realized with horror that she had almost killed herself.

Her attention was refocused by Kleinst trying again to get to his knees, blood streaming from his opened face. Beth pointed the machinegun at him, realized it was empty, and dropped it to the floor. Quickly, she grabbed his pistol from the floor. He had slid behind the table for protection and she knew, with other Germans around, it was time to flee. She had to get away and may yet need the bullets in the gun. Heading quickly for the back door, she cursed, turned back, and grabbed the bag with the documents. She slipped to her knees in the blood of the dead man and saw Kleinst get to his feet. It was a bad moment, but he was half unconscious and slumped back, giving her time to make it outside.

The Germans' car was still parked where they left it. The key was inside. She threw herself in. Desperately sobbing now, she turned the key and pumped the gas pedal. It wouldn't start! Kleinst appeared in the doorway, hand to his head. Beth pointed the automatic pistol at him and squeezed the trigger repeatedly. With a yell, the German fell back through the doorway. Chips cut him again, as she pumped six rounds at him, unsure but hopeful she hit him. None of the other Germans had appeared.

She returned to the ignition, and with a gratifying cough, the engine fired. Flooring the gas pedal, Beth slammed the car into gear. With a roar, the Renault dug in its rear wheels and skated sideways across the yard like a frenzied crab. Clouds of dirt and dust obscured its departure. Wrestling with the wheel like a madwoman, Beth brought the car out onto the main road. Almost before Kleinst could get back to his feet, the sound of escape dulled to a faint hum down the French lane.

It was ten minutes before Beth stopped the car. Terror drove her this far, slamming down the road at over a hundred kilometres per hour. Finally, the shock took over. She had just killed a human being in the most desperate circumstances and she began to tremble uncontrollably. She barely managed to safely stop at the side of the road. She was afraid she would totally lose control. The car slewed to a stop in the welcome shade of some chestnut trees. She levered her muscle-tight hands off the wheel, put her head down, and wept.

It was a desperate situation she found herself in. She was thousands of miles from home, in the middle of a war, sought by a bunch of murderous thugs who, she had no doubt now, would kill her and her recently espoused husband on sight if they found them. Her scalp was on fire. The pain in her breast made her want to throw up. And then she did. It came suddenly, explosively, with barely enough time to open the car door.

The taste was horrible, but the vomiting seemed to put her back on track. Placing both hands on the steering wheel, she pushed herself erect and gazed distantly down the road. She absolutely had to get moving. Somehow, she had to get to Bordeaux, catch up with the servants who must be almost there by now. The car was low on gas, and she had no money. She leaned over and dragged the document valise over beside her. There were a couple of heavy manila folders, tied with string and full of documents. A leather pouch contained an amount of gold and jewellery that took her breath away. Another smaller wallet contained a wad of banknotes. That solved one immediate problem.

She was hungry. It hit her suddenly. She reached into the back for a cardboard box that contained some canned food in it. Peaches: energy, sugar, and refreshment all in one! A can opener was there. She opened a can. Lacking a spoon, she used her fingers to eat, drinking the sweet syrup straight from the can. It was marvellous, just like a morning coffee. A serviette did a job on her face, which was a wreck in the driving mirror.

She spilled juice on her blouse, and that drew her attention to its ripped state. Gently, she extracted her right breast and examined the damage. Several blue welts converged on the nipple. It was scratched and bled a little. She rubbed saliva over it, hoping it would help. She did her best to restore her dignity and began to feel slightly better. She wondered grimly how Kleinst was alleviating the pain he must be feeling.

"Hope he never walks again!" she muttered. Perking slightly at that thought, she turned again to her routing. She must travel south and west, cross the Loire, and head for Bordeaux. It may take the Germans a little while to get organized, but the sooner she crossed the river, the more difficult it would be for them to track her. Turning the key in the ignition, she got the car in motion again, confident the shaking had stopped.

As she got going, an old man appeared coming the opposite way on a horse drawn cart. The horse was plodding along with a ponderous boredom. The man sat on the side of the cart, legs dangling, reins held loose, and contentedly smoking a pipe. He was dressed in the ubiquitous shiny black suit, cloth cap, and shirt with collar missing but the stud in place. The war may have been taking place on another planet. He was Albert and all the other old Frenchmen together; the timelessness of the scene seemed to overwhelm the brief aberration of a German invasion in Beth's mind. Drawing abreast, the man turned and nodded a polite greeting, bobbing his head, while he removed the pipe and mimed a word. She waved back with an exuberance that almost startled him. She shot off, bound for Bordeaux.

Before crossing the Loire at Blois, she picked up a refugee family, relishing the protection and company they afforded. She dropped them at Angoulême, no longer worried about one woman in a car being prey to desperate people. She soon made Libourne, her turn-off for the vineyard. She put enough distance between herself and the German Army that she felt, surely, the French Army would hold them at bay.

Pausing only for directions, Beth struck out westwards towards St. Emilion. She could see the limestone ridge against which it nestled and soon found herself in ancient streets with red-tile roofs and shady trees. Only kilometres now – suddenly, she saw it – a stonewalled driveway entrance with the sign 'Château L'Église D'Artou.' The name was a long way from mid-Atlantic onboard the 'Queen Mary,' where she first saw it on a wine bottle. Still, it provided hope, continuity. She turned in, sobbing with the sudden desperate thought that René might have beaten her here. She drove past the tidy lines of green vines, marching row on row over the slope of the land. She finally reached the gravelled circle before the ochre-washed limestone château with its tall windows, steep dark slate roof, and the round turrets. The other car from Paris was here, parked to the side, still dusty from the trip.

Merguerite answered the door and shrieked upon seeing her. Within seconds, they were all there, weeping their relief and exclaiming at her appearance. They dragged her inside, talking all at once until she suddenly burst into tears. They all stopped dead, startled.

"Le Mâitre...René...he is here?" They shook their heads and looked one to the other, none wishing to be the bearer of bad news.

For five days she fretted at the Château. She went for walks, but only short ones, in case news arrived. Combined with the two days the Nazis kept her, it had been a week since she saw René. She returned from such a walk on the eighth day, and Albert was all smiles through his bruises. "He has sent a letter to you, Madame."

"Where is it? Give it to me, quick! He is safe?"

"I believe he is Madame. A young man delivered the envelope an hour ago."

Beth tore open the letter and held it in one hand, while grasping a proffered glass of cognac. The liquor burned warmly, stopping her tears, and bringing focus to the reading.

My Darling Beth,

I am safe in Paris. By the time you read this, the Germans will have occupied Paris and we shall all be under the Nazi jackboot. Meurice turned out to be a traitor. I am happy to say an enemy aircraft strafing killed him, which was poetic justice. He was a member of some French Fascist organization and was trying to deliver me into the hands of the Nazis. Pierre was slightly hurt but is recuperating with friends.

I will have to assume another identity. If you ever receive a message from 'Albert Defarge' or mentioning that name, it will be genuinely from me. If the letter ends 'love and kisses,' do the exact opposite of any instructions. Also, disregard anything that might be signed by me; it will have been done under duress. If any rendezvous dates are given, subtract five days from the date. Sorry to be so mysterious, but I cannot know what will happen.

As soon as you read this, get passage to England, and take the special valise with you. If you love me, do not stay in France!!! The Germans are bound to occupy Bordeaux and you cannot hide. I have your Aunt Helen's address in England and will try to contact you there. If England is endangered, go back to Alberta.

Once the Germans relax a little, I hope to get out of here. Mother and Rebecca have been taken and I cannot find out where. Too many questions are dangerous. With this letter is a will, properly signed and witnessed, which names you my legal heir. There is enough in the valise, if you haven't already looked, to get you by until we meet again.

I love you and long to be with you again. Please carry out my instructions to the letter; it will make my ordeal here more endurable knowing you are helping in this way. All of us rely on you to help rid France of these Nazi murderers.

Take care and wait for me, I love you desperately.
René

Beth sat long, gazing mistily at the scrawled signature. It was an enormous relief to know he was safe, yet the dangers were colossal. She wished she could write back to tell him she had kicked one of the 'Nazi murderers' in the balls, but she couldn't. She did, however, receive immortal status with the servants when she described how she had escaped.

Francois Dubeq, the manager of the estate, was a short fat man with a frog-face and bulging eyes. He was totally unsympathetic to their plight. His only wish was to be free of them. The last time this part of France was invaded was during the Hundred Years War in the fourteenth century, so a fracas up north meant little to these people. After what she saw and had been through, Beth was exasperated to see people knuckle under so easily. True, there was insufficient accommodation, but Beth was annoyed with him and was tempted to fire him.

Albert and Jeanne calmed her and volunteered to stay as a poste restante, in case messages or René himself showed up in Bordeaux. Some of the others wanted to wait and see how France fared before making their choice.

Albert and Beth went to Bordeaux the next day. The place was in total confusion. Some of the French government departments had set up there, but they were chaotic and close to panic. The military news was grim, with heavy defeatism prevalent amongst everyone. The Spanish Embassy was being mobbed for visas but in vain. The Spaniards were only issuing clearance for people travelling through Spain to other international destinations. They were refusing refugees.

Through the British Consul, Beth managed to obtain passage on a ship leaving in three days. They returned to the vineyard to make ready for a teary farewell with the staff. Before she left, Beth took Dubeq aside and told him in no uncertain terms what she expected of him and what she would do to him if he deviated one iota from her instructions. She surprised herself, realizing afterwards that as Madame de Fourquet, Chatelaine of the family, still in pain from a half torn-off nipple; she didn't have to take any stick from an employee! Dubeq was eating out of her hand by the time she was through.

The Bay of Biscay was rough, and with submarine scares, it was a trying voyage. Two days later, she was alighting from a train into the arms of Aunt Helen. They telegraphed Edmonton to announce her wedding and safe return. Helen was agog at all that had happened. She was worried sick about Beth and more so when Robert checked in after getting back from the Continent and described conditions across the Channel.

Despite her worry for René, Beth settled in at Reading with Helen. She went for long, restful walks that helped ease her stress. A few weeks after her arrival, she felt queasy one morning and vomited in the toilet.

The second time it happened, she counted back, realizing that the momentous events leaving Paris had eclipsed notice of a monthly non-occurrence.

She stood in front of the mirror, dress raised and knickers down. Turning sideways, she could see no obvious bulge above the pubic hair. She didn't look any different, yet! Her hand went to her belly where René loved to lay his head. Her hand spread wide and gently stroked the soft swell of her abdomen. Well, he had better make it out of Paris; he was going to be a father!

TWELVE

THE QUEEN'S HEAD

Dawn stole into the sky with the peculiarly greenish haze of a south of England morning. It would only stay this way for a few minutes. The light of the sun refracted through a thin layer of almost-mist, flushing colour from the lush grass and trees. The heightened angle of the sun and its increased heat would soon combine to evaporate the phenomenon.

The blackout curtains were drawn back. They did that before retiring last night. Snug beneath the heavy bedclothes, they had savoured the stars in the late night sky, flaunting the blackout rules. Now, only the sky and green haze were visible from the bed. A pair of thrushes sang nearby and a distant but distinctive blackbird answered. The dawn chorus had awakened him.

The yellowing sun changed the hue of the sky. He turned his attention to the ceiling of the room. The ancient plaster was cracked in a dozen places and suitable for long-term contemplation with its myriad scars and interesting stains. The low oak beams were likewise a veritable road map of interest. The colourful counterpane on the four-poster bed had at first been thrown back to facilitate their lovemaking, snatched back over them again by individual nocturnal discomfort at the chill night air. He smiled at their conjecture the night before as to how many couplings had occurred in the four-poster bed, since its ornate oak carvings divulged its date of origin as sixteen hundred five. Oh, what stories it could tell!

She lay, back towards him, curled up in a deep sleep. Dark hair tangled over her pillow hid her face. He raised the bedclothes with an elbow and eased over towards her. His eyes drank in the whiteness of her upper back and the descending curve to her waist. Below there, her hip soared up from the mattress with a totally womanly roundness. He felt the first symptoms of arousal as the sensuousness of her bare buttocks and their cleft were revealed to him.

He snuggled up to her, matching her contours, positioning himself. Disturbed by the cold waft of air, then the heat of him near her loins, she gave a low moan and rotated her hips, further moulding them together. He felt her languid arousal from deep sleep heightening his awareness. His arm reached out, his left palm slipping over and familiarly cupping the hard round dome. His fingers hovered over the centre of power as he felt her rising up, up to meet him as one. The moment was here! He would respond totally to it...now, now, now.

"Break." He pulled his right hand over and pushed hard on the rounded dome with his left. With a rumble of power, the Rolls Royce Merlin delivered its full rated horsepower. The Hurricane rolled to the right and dived at full throttle. Oh God! He was dreaming! Dreaming of sweet Anne's body at a time like this!

Glued in an echelon right of the tail of his section leader, Robert Edmunds changed his thoughts explosively. Flights of Heinkel One-eleven bombers were passing like ugly dark crosses several thousand feet below. He could clearly see the distinctive greenhouse-style noses. Slightly behind and above the bombers, a shark-like school of Messerschmidt One Hundred Nine fighter escorts kept guard, ready to do battle with any British fighters that might dare to attack.

Screaming out of the sky behind the enemy machines, the flight of Hurricanes lanced in front of the German fighters and opened fire on the bombers bound for London. Robert had only subconsciously taken the first transmission on the radio because of his daydreaming, but that was behind him now. Smitty opened fire, making a long, raking burst over the rear pair of Heinkels. Robert could see the first deadly dimples appearing in the wings of the second aircraft as a dust of metal fragments flew off under the impact of the heavy rounds. The other member of the section, Les Markham, also opened fire on a bomber.

Quickly glancing in his rear view mirror, Robert saw small black specks behind winking bright flashes at them as the Messerschmidts dived in pursuit of them. "Here they come, Red Leader, five o'clock and closing fast."

"Red Flight, break right, now...now...*now*! Okay, chaps you're on your own. Good hunting!" Somehow Flight Lieutenant Eric Mitchell's voice always seemed calm.

Three miles ahead and below the bombers, Red Flight wheeled around to defend themselves against the German fighters. The manoeuvre gave them a possible second crack at the bombers, but they had scattered after the first pass. Two bombers poured smoke and would likely be counted as 'probables.' Although slightly inferior to the Messerschmidt fighters, these early-Mark Hurricanes were bolstered by the knowledge that Blue Flight had started down soon behind them. The Germans were about to be caught in between. Several bombers had jettisoned their bombs and turned for home in light of the danger, while three closed formation and carried on towards London.

The outline of Smitty's 'Hurribox' went grey and fuzzy. The turn tightened. Robert's blood drained from his head under the increased gravity forces. They were barely through the turn when the Messerschmidts were upon them. With a head-on presentation, Robert's gun-port canvas covers shredded when he pressed the firing button on the joystick. He felt the familiar shudder go through the airframe as he fired a one-second burst.

The enemy aircraft slashed by him, and they were off into another vision-greying turn. He quickly analysed the situation. Smitty was about halfway through his ammunition; he was about one quarter through his own. The German fighters would run for home any second now. They did not have enough fuel to escort bombers beyond this point. They must already be using up precious reserves in this dogfight.

The talk on the radio was cacophonic with orders, warnings, exultant yells, and expletives being sounded all at once. Smitty rolled quickly right. Robert checked his mirror swiftly and followed, catching sight of a black shape close in behind. A hail of gunfire swept over his wings. He could see strikes on Smitty's wings. He pulled back abruptly on the stick, directly into the path of the German fighter. Baulked by the imminence of a collision, the Messerschmidt pilot skidded away.

With the power chopped and a brutal reversal of controls, Robert's Hurricane went from a climbing, positive gravity-force turn and flipped over on its back. The murderous negative force he now pulled was more than the plane was built to take. Pinned in his seat, while soaring upside-down, he spotted the other fighter below and to his left. The Hurricane shuddered and creaked alarmingly. He kicked in left rudder. With a sickening lurch, it slid, wing-down, behind the receding Messerschmidt. Robert had time for a one-second burst before he had to add power and neutralize the controls.

As propeller and wings bit the air again, he realized the sky was suddenly empty. The Messershmidts had fled, light on fuel. A flaming Hurricane corkscrewed its way to doom off to the south. More smoke trails denoted what he hoped were bomber kills. The action seemed to have taken hours. He knew from experience that only minutes had gone by. The Heinkels should not be too far away. As if reading his mind, the sector controller came on the air with his imperturbable tones. "Red Leader, Red Leader, this is Whistler. Three Bandits now vector two eight zero, twelve miles. Buster."

"Let's go, Red Seven!" Robert spotted the enduring cowl of Smitty's Hurricane appear on his left. In response to the 'Buster,' they redlined their engines and dove after the Heinkels. Robert saw they were over the Thames Estuary, so the target would appear to be either London Docks or Hornchurch RAF airfield. Southend Pier stuck out like a narrow plank from the coast just ahead to the right. He saw black puffs appear as the anti-aircraft batteries based on it opened futile fire on the raiders. However, the Hurricanes could not catch them now. The bastards were through and a few more Londoners would die today.

Having failed to catch the Heinkels, the Hurricanes turned northwards and set course for Duxford on the orders of Woody Woodall, the Sector Controller. The fighters had to be refuelled, re-armed, and readied for the next possible enemy attack. Robert's mind drifted again. The raid on London reminded him about Beth. They saw quite a bit of each other since the Germans made them both flee France. The rest of the family in Canada was forced to follow the drama of her escape by mail. While he had not met his new brother-in-law, Robert hoped fervently that one day he would. It was good to see Beth so happy, even if it was modified by René's absence.

On the general scene, Air Chief Marshall 'Stuffy' Dowding, Chief of Fighter Command, fought off his critics as well as the Germans. He correctly saw that the Luftwaffe needed to destroy the Royal Air Force as a viable fighting force in order to control the skies. This was a prerequisite to the invasion of Britain. The Royal Navy, despite its superior numbers, could not be caught manoeuvring in the narrow confines of the English Channel trying to destroy a German invasion fleet, while enemy bombers circled freely overhead.

Logically, the Germans sought attrition of British air power by bombing and strafing their home bases. It was a cardinal sin to be caught helpless on the ground, hence the present return to base for refuelling and fresh ammunition in order to be instantly able to take-off again. Dowding also resisted those who would have swarms of RAF fighters meet the Germans head-on. He felt the Germans would encourage such encounters, seeking to destroy his precious fighters in the sky. The trade-off was the German bombers that got through but without a reserve of fighters, Churchill's vaunted 'Island Fortress' would be devoid of combat capability.

New aircraft were being rapidly built from the aluminium pots and pans donated by a cognizant British public, under the urging of Mr. Beaverbrook, a fellow Canadian. The real problem was the shortage of trained, especially experienced pilots. Many were lost in the Battle of France against German pilots battle-hardened in the Condor Legion, in Spain's Civil War. Other irreplaceable equipment and ground personnel was also lost or abandoned in France when aircraft rarely returned to the field they departed from.

The retreat and evacuation from France took on the appearance of a rout with crews scrambling to keep aircraft flying against increasing odds. Two Forty-two Squadron was hard hit. Almost as soon as the Germans took Belgium, their spares, armaments, personnel, and tools could not keep up with the rapid redeployment moves they were forced to make. Unserviceable aircraft were frequently torched minutes before advance German units over-ran their aerodrome.

Frantic scrambles ensued, as Stukas dive-bombed their aerodromes and casualties grew. Robert still too vividly recalled the loss of his first Hurricane, 'Freddie' in Normandy. Grimy, unshaven, and utterly exhausted, the Two Forty-two Squadron personnel retreated via Chateaudun, Le Mans, Nantes, and finally crossing the white cliffs of England to land at Tangmere. From there, the system passed them to Coltishall, where they were still based, and commuting daily to join the 'Wing' at Duxford.

Dispirited, defeated, and with most of their eighteen Mark I Hurricanes in a marginal state of preparedness, the pilots, still short of personnel kit and clothing, hung around and rested in this lull. Morale was low; Coltishall was terrible. Wing Commander Leigh-Mallory visited them there. He departed, it was later said, 'with a certain look in his eye.'

Soon after, word came down that they would receive a new squadron commander. To a chorus of groans and disbelief, they later learned their new leader was to be a Cranwell college graduate and that he had no bloody legs!

It was thus, around late June that the 'Ready Hut' was filled with a collection of scruffy pilots, waiting with complete disinterest, for the arrival of their new commander. The door banged open to reveal Flight Lieutenant

Peter 'Boozy' MacDonald, Honourable Member of Parliament for the Isle of Wight and present Adjutant for Two Forty-two Squadron. Beside him, a look of deepening horror suffusing his square face, stood newly promoted Squadron Leader Douglas Bader. Already a man of tremendous vitality and enthusiasm, perhaps the promotion heightened Bader's sense of duty and military expectations. His initial shock of meeting such a group of subordinates must have been deep. Through the dust motes suspended in the light through the window, the shadowy interior of the hut seemed to be filled with a despondent and motley crew of the most unmilitary and ill-clad ruffians he had ever witnessed.

"Who's in charge here?" The snapped question, more a command for revelation, had a nasty tone, which, coming from a ranking officer, would have caused more-military personnel to view with trepidation. Not the crew of Two Forty-two. The dust motes continued to float tranquilly, undisturbed by the customary greeting for a superior officer. Despite the inaction, eyeballs slewed left and right, awaiting the voluntary sacrifice by one of their number admitting to being 'in charge.'

Bader's temperature was churning to a boiling point before Flight Lieutenant Stan Turner rose laconically. "I guess I am, Sir." He added a lazy salute as an afterthought, his obstinance and rebellion showing.

Bader immediately launched into a fearsome tirade about pride, appearance, military preparedness, et cetera, salted with an originality of phrase, which perked the interest of more than one in the crew. It was during a rare pause for breath that Turner interrupted.

"Sir, these men have lost everything in the retreat from France. They are good fighting men, but we have lost machines, men, spares, not to mention our personal kit and clothes. We are ready to fly and fight, if someone topside will give us the necessary means. Nobody in charge has seen fit to be the slightest bit of help to us."

There was a pregnant pause at this insubordinate offering. Bader thought deeply. He finally had opened his mouth, not to deliver another berating, but to apologize. Abruptly, he turned away, stumping off with a butting, rolling gait on his tin legs. There was a Hurricane parked nearby. He climbed onto the wing then snugged down in the cockpit. Moments later, he taxied away and took off. Bemused by his mercurial behaviour, not sure whether they had even scared him off, the pilots trooped outside to watch the departure.

For the next few minutes they were treated to one of the most faultless flying displays they had ever seen. The Hurricane roared back at them at low level to ensure their attention and pulled up into a vertical climb. Rolling off the top and proceeding into a loop, Bader advanced into a series of acrobatics before pulling off a perfect landing. Taxiing up to the group of men, he shut down. Sliding off the wing, as the hot engine ticked behind him, Bader issued a series of executive commands. They were obeyed with alacrity. Two Forty-two had a new commander!

Miracles were wrought in the next few days. 'Boozy' (who was named for his slow and slurred speech, rather than his imbibing habits) had his considerable intelligence stretched to keep pace with Bader's insistent orders. Warrant Officer Bernard West, responsible for keeping the planes on line, was given full ear to his needs.

Between the end of June and the first weekend of July, the whole squadron buckled down to serious training exercises. No respecter of tradition where it did not serve, Bader abandoned the inept 'line astern' fighting tactics and adopted the Luftwaffe's 'Schwarm' (Five Finger) and 'Rotte' (Trio) formations. New flight commanders were appointed, and the squadron appeared to be coming along.

However, West still had not received the necessaries to keep the Hurricanes flying. To a 'doer' like Douglas Bader, it was inconceivable that, especially in a time of war, such obstructions and boneheadedness should prevent him from getting at the enemy's throat. After a particularly galling telephone call, where a senior supplies officer berated his staff for overzealousness in ordering parts, Bader exploded. He composed and sent off a signal to Fighter Command. It read: 'Two Forty-two Squadron now operational regarding pilots, but non-operational, repeat, non-operational regards equipment.' He was immediately summonsed to Headquarters. Evidently, he made little bones about the situation. The reaction was swift and terrible. Within days, the urgently required supplies were showered on the squadron. Numerous supply staff wore red faces.

With others, Bader later become a proponent of the 'Big Wing' strategy, but it ran contrary to 'Stuffy' Dowding's policy and merely became a contentious issue rather than a cooperative effort to preserve the RAF fighter numbers.

THIRTEEN

THE WOMEN'S VOLUNTARY SERVICE

London, 1941.

Beth Edmunds-Sturdee-de Fourquet mouthed a most unladylike curse and jammed on the brakes. The old Daimler ambulance lurched and bucked, stopping just short of the rubble lying in the street. In the blackout, with the air laden with dust, the debris was invisible when she sped around the corner. Flames licked high above a row of houses further down the street. She could see a number of fire appliances blocking the way. A searchlight stabbed the sky from a few blocks away, and the distinct patter of shrapnel from anti-aircraft fire could be heard on the surrounding rooftops. The Blitz was over, but Herman Goering's Luftwaffe still visited London regularly enough to deal death and destruction.

She gave birth to a beautiful baby boy in late March. Despite the joys of motherhood, she rapidly became bored and felt helpless at no news of René. She had not produced much milk for the child, so he was rapidly weaned, leaving her free to join the Women's Voluntary Service. She was warmly welcomed, since she had a driver's licence – a rarity for women in Britain. On normal shifts, she spent five days in London, driving an ambulance, dressed in a pair of dumpy coveralls, and then getting a day or so off. The war was now a more direct, if sickening, fascination she could not shake off.

She enjoyed the days off to go to Reading and visit Aunt Helen, who looked after baby David for her. Off-duty action in London was better than sitting around enduring the long silence from France. It was preferable to socialize with some of the girls and have fun, to let off some steam in one of the crowded and colourful London pubs. Anything else was frustrating and unendurable. Some nights, she cried herself to sleep, missing the man who had so taken her devotion and filled the void all other men seemed to leave in her. She wanted her life with René de Fourquet back.

Anything she could do to shorten the war and be reunited with him, she would do.

In the frenzied social whirl of a war-torn capital, it was natural she would meet lots of young men who propositioned her. But her favourite was Roland de Fonce-Pelligard, a Free French officer attached to the staff of General de Gaulle. Contact with him improved her French. She cultivated the friendship, shrewdly forging links with the powerful and well placed in order that she could find out more about René. So far, she had not slept with him, despite his urgency and her own needs. For now, it was simply René.

Her duties in the meantime, did not harden her to the death and destruction. She frequently helped scrabble at bombed buildings, loading injured into the ambulance and speeding them to the nearest hospital or first aid centre. On other occasions, it was done more leisurely, for corpses, pieces of corpses, and charred bodies no longer required the urgency. It could get quite grisly, now that war had put civilians in the front line.

Cranking furiously at the wheel, Beth jerked the awkward gear lever into low and ground her way back onto Stepney Road. It was still a mile or so to the hospital, and the old man in the back was bleeding furiously. The other two passengers were beyond help.

Nurse Ethel Martin, her partner, stuck her head into the driving cab. "More blocked streets?"

"Yeah! How's the old man doing?"

"Cursing the Kaiser's offspring for trying to get him in this war, too! He's getting very weak though. Better step on it, luv!"

"Well, here goes." Swinging out of the corner, Beth floored the accelerator, and the big vehicle lurched forward.

Behind them, only a block away, a flash of blinding light blossomed up, lighting the whole scene momentarily. The entire street stood out starkly, the rows of drab houses and properties photographed on their retinas. A thunderous roar of sound followed, and the ground lurched beneath their wheels. A growing patter of broken masonry, roof tiles, and shattered glass announced another bomb strike.

"Missed me by 'arf, Adolf, yer bleedin' barstard!" Ethel's Cockney tones crowed to nobody in particular in the back.

Mindful that bombs rarely dropped singly and the aircraft might be overflying them, Beth slipped the ancient clutch, rammed the shift into high, and with knuckles white upon the wheel, careened down the street as fast as she could go. Seconds later, two receding detonations behind them did little to still her racing heart.

She had been a married woman for fifteen months on this autumn night of nineteen forty-one. Her son David was born on time and healthy. He was six months old. She spent only one night as the wife of the husband she yearned for. No news came out of France from René since she left Bordeaux. She was unable to communicate with Albert at the vineyard either. It was totally frustrating. She ached to place the baby in René's arms.

She was free the following night and went with her roommate from the Bayswater flat, Elspeth, to a pub just off Piccadilly. Roland promised to meet them there. They were tipsy on beer and arm-in-arm, singing, 'Roll out the Barrel' to the rolling thunder of a piano by nine that evening.

Years later, she could never travel to London and see its characteristic brick and stone architecture without visualizing that scene: the ancient polished woodwork of the bar, its grimy ceiling plastered with posters for variety shows and warnings about spies. 'Loose lips sink ships.' 'Is your journey really necessary?' was a particularly poignant one, as it always reminded her that David would be waiting for her in Reading, in the care of Aunt Helen, who elected to stay in Britain.

The cigarette and pipe smoke billowed thicker and thicker. In the dwindling oxygen level of the crowded place, they sang at the top of their lungs, daring the frosted glass panels in the top of the partition between the 'Snug' and the 'Public Bar' to shatter. The feeling of togetherness, the solidarity, was a shared intimacy in such places during these uncertain days of the war that would forever hold a place in the hearts of all who were there. At midnight, they staggered out onto the pavement and arm in arm, carolled their way to the Piccadilly Underground and home.

Roland extracted a promise of a picnic with Beth the next day. He showed up next morning in a commandeered car about ten o'clock. It was a beautiful day. He took her up past Chelsea and Sunbury until they found a perfect spot, not far from Virginia Water. They were under a canopy of weeping willows, right on the bank of the river, and the sun streamed down through the leaves like a golden shower.

Roland was a fascinating enigma to Beth. He was a tall, gangling man, with a flowing mane of corn-blonde hair and a moustache to suit. He had hawk-like features with a nose to match de Gaulle's. He was an enigma because while he featured the hauteur, the careless leadership of the rich and privileged with their droit de seigneur, he came across as an idler, almost a buffoon. Beth could never figure out whether he was just a hanger-on at de Gaulle's staff or someone really important who hid his abilities behind some kind of smokescreen.

She easily pictured him as a medieval troubadour, riding around France with his lyre, rescuing maidens, and charming the general populace. Then, the hair sometimes flashed a golden-red, hinting perhaps at Jacobite or Frankish ancestry, confusing the image yet again. Now, that red flashed as he leaned over her and refilled her glass with the champagne he had somehow found. They filled themselves with pork pies and cheese. How Roland found the picnic ingredients with all the rationing, Beth could not imagine. She could not imagine also why he was suddenly over her, his lips pressed against hers, his hardening body pressed across her thigh.

She seemed to watch from a great distance as his hand slid inside her dress and fondled her breasts. Without a refusal and without consent, she let him take her there, beneath the willow bower. In his anxiousness, Roland failed to note her lack of passion; her's was just a dull response. She began to cry, soundlessly, as he entered her. The tears welled up, fogging her vision until the whole act became a blur.

Not until it was finished did Roland notice her distress. He held her closely, horrified by what he had done, horrified not by the act, which he wanted, but the terrible realization that he'd committed an act of self-gratification rather than mutual love.

"Ah Cherie! Si vous plais, m'excuser! Je suis un chien, un cochon. Ah, ma pouvre petite. Beth, how could I have done this?" He wept openly and held her tightly, achieving more closeness with her then than he had by his physical attentions.

They both wept, for different reasons, although both for betrayal. He felt he betrayed her trust, and she felt that in that moment she had betrayed René. For at the moment when Roland penetrated her, she realized she had given up on her husband. From this moment on, surely René would be a fading memory. She could hope and pray to be reunited with him, but the act with Roland was a physical first step of separation from his memory, an irrevocable step towards acceptance that he was gone, perhaps forever.

****

Canada.

Like most men his age at university, David Williams signed up for the Territorial Army. It was a reasoned, rational decision for an educated man. Trained as an officer, he was able to satisfy his patriotic fervour, yet retain a certain bargaining power as to where he may be posted in the event he was drafted.

He sported a head of light brown hair and a straight nose with a fine yet firm mouth, which women found attractive. His eyes were a clear light blue, favouring perhaps his mother's Celtic genes rather than the darker colouring his surname suggested. He stood a little less than six feet with a slim yet muscular frame toughened by a love for rugby. He was an easy-going individual, popular with his peers and the local girls. Academically, he shone, achieving high marks with a minimum of effort.

David had an excellent knack of finding his way incisively to the core of a matter, peeling away layers of disguise and camouflage with ease. His law professors marked him as having a rare investigative talent. His love of Sir Arthur Conan-Doyle's hero ensured he was nicknamed 'Sherlock,' an appellation that was shortened to 'Sher' and stuck.

The various news items of the war were closely followed by the students in the Territorial ranks, from the early, desperate years, to the increasing gains from nineteen forty-three on. It was at the end of that year that David graduated with his law degree. He was now faced with joining the military after receiving a call-up date with the army. Through a chance contact, he discovered the navy was looking for lawyers. He volunteered as a result.

His mother and father were furious with him; no sooner had they finished celebrating his success, he was off, volunteering for the navy of all things! The fact he seemed assured of a cosy legal appointment swayed them not at all. The fickle nature of postings and duty assignments proved them right. By the time David reported to Toronto for duty, his posting was changed to Halifax, Nova Scotia. He was assigned to sea duties on a corvette. With the German submarine 'Wolf Packs' at their peak of activity in the North Atlantic, his chances of becoming a naval casualty had now far outstripped those of the infantry.

After six weeks of intensive seamanship training, King's Regulations, heavy porridge, greasy food, and cocoa, David graduated as a sub-lieutenant, Royal Canadian Navy (Volunteer Reserve). The year nineteen forty-three was wearing out. The experiences the navy gained over the previous three years of escorting convoys was beginning to show. Despite the tardiness, lack of understanding, and built-in inertia of higher authority, new equipment and adequate training were beginning to creep into the light of day.

In the initial days of the Battle of the Atlantic, as it was now being called, the rush to provide rudimentary ships as escorts was paramount, equipping them with the simplest of armament. Often, even with a German U-Boat in sight, the corvettes lacked the armament to sink it. Prodded by the heavy losses of shipping and men, the British Navy had been critical of the Canadians, as indeed had its own naval staff.

Anti-submarine warfare was coming into its own. Warships now carried 'radar,' a form of radio device that transmitted a high frequency signal that bounced off targets and came back, giving the distance and bearing of an object. 'Asdic,' another British device did the same thing underwater, sending out a strong 'ping' of sound that bounced off submarines and revealed their position. High Frequency Direction Finding (HFDF) enabled ships to tune in and find the direction of radio signals transmitted by U-Boats.

David was sent to an anti-submarine warfare school to learn the tricks of all these black boxes and how to successfully track down a U-Boat. Aircraft played a major role in detection. Their mere presence often kept U-Boats down and stymied their efforts to stalk and sink ships.

Another month passed by, and January dawned before David was assigned to a ship. The British-built corvette HMCS (Her Majesty's Canadian Ship) 'Peace Hills' was acquired from the Royal Navy in exchange for some Algerine class minesweepers built in Canada. It was the most modern of the corvettes, built with increased endurance for long patrols. The warship was just being commissioned, so David was one of its original crew. Men were transferred from numerous other ships to form a hard-core, experienced crew to offset the newly trained, like David. He found himself reporting to a two-year veteran of corvettes, Lieutenant Johnnie Symes.

'Peace Hills' was berthed at Jetty Five in the Halifax dockyard when he first set eyes on her. With a more rakish bow, longer forecastle structure, her lines were sleeker than the early model corvette on which he had trained.

Her number, K508, was painted in a stark black contrast to the grey splotches of camouflage paint along her sides. He quickly took in her other lines, the dominant four-inch gun on the foredeck, the bridge with twenty millimetre cannons, and the afterdeck with the depth charge rollers and the 'Squid' mortar, which could throw depth charges. Despite the same type of squat funnel on this latest class of corvette, she still looked suitable to him as his first assignment.

Although any ship was big to a prairie boy, David learned in his short naval career that the corvettes were tiny compared to other warships. Only two hundred and fifty feet long and thirty-six feet wide, they were little more than corks in a maelstrom when it came to mid-ocean swells. Even so, his heart swelled with the pride of ownership. He walked the gangway to amidships, saluted the quarterdeck, and requested permission to board from the young officer of the watch.

The lieutenants and the lieutenant commander, who was captain, claimed higher priority, and soon dissuaded him of personal ownership, but he was allowed to retain his pride. The working up of the ship took place southwards into American waters. While it was hotly rumoured they might make it to Bermuda and get shore leave, instead they found themselves making a quick courtesy visit into Norfolk, Virginia. Recent losses and other escort ships taken for refitting mandated their debut on the North Atlantic stage a little sooner than planned. As a warship, they left Halifax fully armed, and after oiling at Norfolk, they stood out to sea and set course to meet a westbound convoy.

Transiting alone, they were able to continue their training, while maintaining a war patrol footing. The older hands had lots of tales for all occasions, including ones concerning solo ships that had been torpedoed because they had no support. The natural wariness of being in a war zone for the first time raised the consciousness of everyone. The captain, Lieutenant Commander George Wright, Royal Canadian Navy (RCN), had every reason to feel pleased with the apparent efficiency of his crew.

****

On January tenth, nineteen forty-four, Edward Sturdee Junior entrained to Ontario to join his father's old family law firm. An announcement in the newspaper concerning his departure quoted his father as lauding his decision. A scoutmaster in Edmonton, Edward patriotically joined a part-time militia group but was mysteriously assaulted by two fellow soldiers only a week before his sudden departure. As Sturdee Senior put it: "The tainted reporting of one Nathan Connaught had impugned his family's reputation and polluted this court-martial offence case. In quoting certain *unreliable sources* concerning *implied sexual perversions with young boys*, the reporter would reap the full legal wrath of Sturdee's law firm."

No such lawsuit was launched. The Alberta Premier quit visiting Sturdee's home. Edward Sturdee Junior was never heard from again.

****

Northern Italy, Appenine Mountains.

The piece of steel that flew across the Italian field had killed before. It contained a high proportion of iron from a sword that had been wielded by a Roman legionnaire at the Battle of Actium. Buried for centuries, it was eventually unearthed and smelted into a cooking pot in the Middle Ages. For many years it was part of an Italian Count's iron railings surrounding his Florentine home. The shortage of raw materials for the munitions industry caused the Italians to rip it out and smelt it anew into an artillery shell. The German Wehrmacht seized the artillery piece it was designed for when the Italians capitulated. Now fired at an advancing Allied unit, the steel was released when the shell exploded.

The pulsating hiss of the madly rotating shard was lost in the din of battle. The roar of engines of an advancing line of Sherman tanks crossing the alluvial flats of the Italian river valley was punctuated by the whine of artillery shells overhead and their explosive termination of flight. The German line was trying to halt the tanks' advance.

One tank stopped and threw a track when hit by a shell. The exploding round temporarily deafened the crew with its massive clangour. The vehicle slewed around helpless and broadside to the enemy. Two more rounds were dropped into the breech and were rapidly fired by the gunner over open sights at the ground ahead. Then, since immobility made it a target of easy opportunity, the tank was abandoned by its crew, which ran doubled over, to seek the shelter of one of the stout stone walls that divided off the fields.

The young driver was crouched low. He ran, cringing under the imminent impact of enemy fire, fully conscious of the vulnerability of his flesh. The deadly steel shard caught him through the left shoulder from the front, straightening him up like a puppet. A spray of pink droplets exploded around him, like a halo. His collarbone and upper ribs were smashed. The hydraulic shock of the impact destroyed three of the ventricles of his heart, ruptured countless venous valves, and tore open the aortic arch. Blood vessels in his head erupted, causing a massive and terminal stroke. With his torn upper arteries pulsing blood, he was dead before he hit the ground.

******

Mid-Atlantic, June 10, 1944. Dogwatch.

A wall of dark water, higher than three houses, loomed out of the twilight, green phosphorescence of the breaking wave glowing eerily. The small ship jammed its prow under the monster with a white splash of spray, followed by a hum, like a tuning fork. Its backbone was bent and the whole ship quivered. Swallowed by the water, she creaked, groaned, and plunged deeper. Just as the smooth mass seemed to totally ingest the foredeck, a welter of spray shot out. The ship bobbed like a cork.

With a mighty slap and a crash of white water, the ocean beat against the bridge windows, blowing spray above the masthead. The ship rose up the flank of the wave, like a crazy roller coaster, canting impossibly on her beam. The rogue wave slid beneath her like the liquid caress of some infinitely powerful and nightmarish creature. Great spreading pools of light green water, filled with air bubbles, smoothed the top of the wave like oil, as the ship crested and righted. They poised on high, like kings of the entire domain around them. And then the sickening slide and plunge down the other side.

"Third wave, Number Four." The Skipper's voice was matter of fact. Merely that he spoke at all told Sub Lieutenant David Williams that fear was not his alone.

It was the second day of the nor'wester, and the 'Peace Hills' was showing scars. Two lifeboats were gone and a section of the rail with them. Several windows were staved in, their hollow stares blinded by plywood nailed over them. The convoy they were escorting was scattered hopelessly, each ship fighting singly for survival against the elements. Tomorrow, according to the coded radio forecast, the storm should blow itself out and then the hard part would begin.

Rising from their safe smooth haven beneath the sea, any U-Boats in the area would find easy prey. Twenty merchant ships and four corvettes covered about twenty-five to thirty square miles before the storm. That was a tight, well-protected convoy. By dawn tomorrow, they could cover hundreds of square miles, making them easier to find and scattered so badly, they would be unprotected.

The 'Edwin C. Drood,' a Liberty ship, would be particularly easy. The steamer broke radio silence only hours ago to report two hatches staved in and down at the head by five degrees, taking on water. It was impossible to instill in these merchantmen the need for radio silence at all costs. A message intended for a friend ten miles away also reached an enemy a thousand miles away. A radio direction finding could pinpoint their position. German radio stations in France would be happy to broadcast the information to any listening U-Boats.

There was little the 'Peace Hills' could do until the sea subsided. She hung back in case she could offer assistance to the 'Drood,' such as a tow or taking off her crew. There was nothing else anyone could do in this storm.

It was David's fourth voyage. He was now a seasoned corvette officer. He expected to see his listing to full lieutenant when they got back to Halifax; if they returned to Halifax. In the past six months, he saw sea warfare in its crudest form. He lost count of the number of ships he saw sunk; their prows or sterns canted crazily to the sky, as they slipped beneath the waves, blowing boilers and groaning horribly in their metal death throes. Many were the tankers that exploded in a ball of flame after being torpedoed. The cold relentless sea snuffed the short illumination.

Worst were the number of men he witnessed dead in the water, injured, drowned, frozen to death, or horribly disabled by the thick bunker oil that hardened to a tar-like consistency when it met the cold water.

****

Edmonton.

When he was old enough, Danny Edmunds joined the Alpine Club of Canada and began a life-long romance with the mountains. His rock hammer became his key to revealing mysteries. He was an expert on any rock to be found in an Alberta streambed in no time.

He was into advanced theory by the time he was accepted into university and was an honour student the first two years. His performance only faltered when his research got in the way of study for routine exams.

It was in late nineteen forty-three when Danny met a man who would change his direction in geology. Doctor J.C. Sproule was a guest lecturer at the University of Alberta. He was, in later years, described as the 'father' of petroleum geology in Canada. It was sufficient that he awakened a further interest other than theory in Danny Edmunds. The challenge of unlocking the mysteries of petroleum deposits beneath the ground fired Danny's imagination.

Cameron Sproule laid a lot of the groundwork for the petroleum industry in Alberta. He was a leading proponent for exploration of the Arctic in later years. The Turner Valley oilfields, active since the early years of the century, were the public's only visible evidence that his theories and foresight had any foundation. Speculation, such as what Tom Edmunds had seen destroy his friend O'Hanlon, coloured oil exploration with a risk venture bordering on gambling, in some people's eyes.

Yet, the oil seemed to be there. The presence of oil was acknowledged since the first white man sailed down the Athabasca and saw the tar sands. The first well in Alberta was drilled at Pelican Rapids in eighteen ninety-four by the old cable tool method. Medicine Hat used gas wells to heat itself since nineteen twelve. Turner Valley had been producing since nineteen fourteen. The problem was that Edmonton had not had a local strike. Its citizens, after the numerous financial collapses of drilling enterprises, gave up any interest.

Still, the proliferation of the internal combustion engine demanded increased supplies. The expertise gathered in the Oklahoma and Texas oilfields was spreading. Sproule saw Western Canada's turn arriving.

Finishing university with honours, Danny decided it was time to learn the oil drilling trade right at the bottom and signed on as a roustabout for a drilling company out of Calgary. Right off the train, a roughneck named 'Smiley' Evernden met him.

Smiley had worked in Oklahoma. His accent was almost as broad as his stomach and belt buckle. At some point, he had suffered a lash from a steel chain across the face. The makeshift stitching of the wound and subsequent healing puckered the side of his face in a grimace, which resembled a smile, hence his nickname. He stood nearly six feet tall and had shoulders like a bear. Tufts of dirty blond hair sprouted from the neck of his shirt.

Smiley laughed like a bull moose, but generally, he was pretty cool and calm. Occasionally, something like a bellow of laughter or an outflow of cussing revealed the turbulence that lurked beneath his exterior. There was a story about him being hit by the chain while running pipe, but that was too ordinary for oil patch legend. The other story was he was in a fight over the right to land on a West Texas lease. One of the opposition used a chain on him in the dispute and had been killed for his pains. The police were still looking for a suspect. Supposedly, Smiley appeared in Calgary not long after.

Danny Edmunds found himself in Smiley's company, conducted to the tailgate of a mud-caked and dilapidated Chevrolet half ton. He threw his bag in the back, and they were on their way in moments. They hit the trail to Vulcan after stops at a couple of stores. The now heavily laden vehicle bucked and twisted on the dirt road, trailing a heavy plume of dust.

Danny didn't know how long this stint with drilling would last. Now that he was out of university, he was eligible for service in the military and could be called up any time. He might have toyed with the idea of volunteering, but after James' death in Italy, he knew one more member of the family at risk would kill his mother. She made it clear that after her husband, Robert, and now the sacrifice of James, she figured the Edmunds family had 'done its bit.' She aged visibly since the loss. James was a volunteer. Going with Tom's unspoken consent had widened the split between his parents. Margaret still spent most of her time in her room and overtly blamed Tom for the loss of James. With her wishes in the matter made clear, Danny decided to carry on and see what fate dealt him. If the army called him up, then he could not be directly blamed. He had been told that vital oilfield workers were not subject to military service, so it remained to be seen what would happen.

"Hey!" With a start, he realized it was the third time someone had tried to get his attention. "If you're deaf, sonny, I can't use you on the rig!"

"Sorry, I was just thinking about the war."

"Well, you'll have a war for sure, if you don't pay attention when I talk to you!"

******

Mid Atlantic, August, 1944.

On the night of August twenty-fifth, nineteen forty-four, a convoy of ships called SC One Thirty-seven was headed eastbound across the Atlantic, ploughing through a light sea with low rain clouds obscuring the sky and making visibility difficult. Station-keeping in the planned positioning of ships was not such a problem as it had been in earlier years. The 'Peace Hills' had the latest British-built Two-seventy-one P-type centimetric radar to ensure the freighters kept station in the convoy. Their positions were clearly delineated on the screen in the radar room, snug inside from the weather.

Even in good weather, collisions were not unknown between merchantmen unused to sailing in formations. Any adverse weather or attacks by U-Boats totally scrambled any sign of order. It required everyone to be alert. An attack could come at almost any time, for as it proceeded, the orderly movement of the convoy and its escorts was signalled around them by the steady turns of their propellers beating against the cold waters of the North Atlantic.

This combined tympanic signature spread as sound waves in the sub sea, easily heard by listening ears many miles distant. In the grim cat-and-mouse of convoy and escorts versus the U-Boats, circumstances and needs dictated opportunities for encounters for both sides. Contrary to popular opinion, submarines spent most of their time at the surface. This was because, when submerged, they worked from batteries that fed electric motors. To be able to submerge and stay down, a submarine had to frequently recharge its batteries. This was done with generators attached to the diesel engines that also propelled the submarine on the surface. Since the diesels needed air to run, the submarines had to surface to run them.

The submarine was also faster on the surface than submerged, meaning they usually transited enroute and chased to intercept ships in this mode. Because the submarine's effectiveness and its survival lie in its being submerged, the attacking Germans would choose to be submerged. By aggressive patrolling, the Allies also chose to keep the Germans submerged. Not only did it hinder their operational ability, but when their batteries ran low, they were forced to the surface no matter what the risk. By forcing a low battery situation on a submarine, the sub-hunters ensured its attack potential was limited, short of a suicidal attempt.

On the surface, a submarine lost its edge of opportunity and more frequently became the hunted, not the hunter. The Germans had very inventively introduced the 'Snorkel,' a kind of breathing tube that extended up beside the periscope and drew air down to the diesels. They could then be run with the submarine barely submerged. This made for a much smaller visual or radar target than the surfaced submarine drawing air.

One of the cat-and-mouse truths about listening on hydrophones for noises was that near the sea surface, a lot of interference destroyed the clarity of the signal and drowned out the fainter sounds of distant targets. Thus, a submarine deep enough to hear a far away ship might then have to surface to go fast enough to intercept it. If already on the surface, it might not hear the ship at all due to the surface interference.

For this and other reasons, the Germans were ingenious in trying to place numerous submarines, called 'Wolf Packs' astride the paths of possible convoys. By attacking in larger numbers and sharing the detection workload, the havoc they could wreak on a convoy dramatically increased. The finding and tracking of a convoy could be achieved in many ways.

Spies who saw the ships sail and knew the convoy's course and final destination were the first source. Sightings by other U-Boats, who then signalled position course and speed back to Germany by high frequency radio, were the second. Although the Messerschmidt Condor, the biggest plane in the German Luftwaffe still patrolled the Atlantic to seek convoys, its effectiveness was reduced by increased Allied air superiority. Two other methods, both slaves of radio, could betray a convoy's position. One was a HFDF or direction finding bearing of a high frequency radio transmission source. From the known position of two finders, combined with their relative bearings, a cross on a map revealed the source's position. Radio silence was the only protection. Because of the need to track and perform rendezvous at sea with escorts, position reports were necessary. Besides the direction finding betrayal, the text of these messages, if known, were very revealing to an enemy. For this reason, they were sent in secret code. But the Germans and the Allies worked very hard, and often successfully, at cracking each other's codes.

Whether it was betrayal or chance mattered not. The end result of a Wolf Pack and a convoy meeting spelled disaster and death. Even though the tide of change now lay with the Allied escorts, the Germans usually had the edge of surprise on their side. The year nineteen forty-four revealed an astonishing decline in ships sunk under escort. Improved equipment, like the Two Seventy-one P radar, the One Forty-four Q Asdic sonar, Hedgehog ahead-throwing depth charge mortar, and better tactics took their toll on the German submarines. Still, they were a determined foe and only vigilance forewarned of an attack.

Only miles ahead of SC One Thirty-seven, the last foamy trace of three diving submarines disappeared. Hereafter, the occasional short wake of a periscope alone would betray their positions. They tracked the ships for any change in course and worked up their attack intercepts. Eastward, a faint glimmer of dawn leaked beneath the breaking ceiling and streaks of a watery sunrise penetrated the layers. Soon it would be light.

It was five in the morning when the presence of the U-Boats became known in dramatic fashion. A tanker, prime target for the Germans, erupted in a sheet of flame. One torpedo slammed into her engine room seconds before another took her amidships. One moment the sea was an inky drizzle, the next a yellow and orange sun blossomed outward. Typically, the tanker was in one of the inner lines of ships in the convoy, theoretically safer. The fact that it had gone up first told the escorts at least one submarine was loose inside the convoy lines.

The commodore of the convoy, aboard the destroyer 'HMS Wolfenden,' instantly made light signals for the convoy to adopt the avoidance routine published in their orders. As usual, there was a delay due to lookouts' inattention, poorly manoeuvrable ships, and other reasons, resulting in a frenzied, poorly coordinated scattering of freighters. Before hardly a ship had turned, a column of water shot up the side of a steamer near the right front of the outer line. She was stricken by another torpedo. Now the escorts knew they were up against at least two submarines.

The corvette 'HMCS Clear Hills,' along the right flank, heeled hard to port. The sea boiled from her stern. Making maximum revolutions, she cut between the starboard line of ships and drove in upon the suspected position of the first submarine. Within two minutes, she ejected depth charges in the area.

Meanwhile, the 'Wolfenden' changed course to attack the second submarine. The sounding of action stations aboard 'Peace Hills' had brought sailors tumbling from their bunks and hammocks. As David Williams burst into the wheelhouse, one of his ratings called a radar contact – possible submarine – on a relative bearing of zero six zero degrees.

Captain Wright paused a moment. If he chased this target, he could be failing, by his mere lack of presence, to suppress a threat from the north side of the convoy.

"Hard starboard, increase revolutions to maximum, steer course one two zero."

"Hard starboard to one two zero, aye sir." The helmsman's answer was automatic. Even as the ship heeled, the beat of the engine increased.

"All positions manned, Captain."

"Aye that."

All eyes turned to the area of sea towards where they were headed. If the radar target was another submarine, it would have to lie between the columns of ships now frantically scattering around them. Since the commodore's evasion signal required a turn to the left away from the suspected danger, the 'Peace Hills' should have a clear passage to the spot. However, the lookouts with binoculars glued to their eyes were just as interested in the position of other ships as in spotting the submarine.

"Last range?"

"Three thousand yards, Captain."

"Very well, we'll set a wide pattern at five hundred short, a single off the rail at four hundred. If that submarine saw the convoy turn, he'll be trying to keep station. Set them for seventy feet."

"Aye, aye, Sir." The weapons officer seized his chance to give orders to the detail handling depth charges. On the aft deck, several pairs of hands quickly set the primers in the charges to detonate at the prearranged depth.

"Torpedo impact near off the port bow, Captain, approximate range six thousand yards. Merchantman." The port bridge lookout sang out the information without taking the glasses from his face. David saw George Wright give a faint sigh of relief. The latest victim was still diagonally across the convoy from them, so his decision to leave protective station was, so far, justified. They would do a good job if they could harrie the submarine so it couldn't launch more torpedoes. Rather, they would prefer to sink it.

Hitting her stride now at fifteen knots, 'Peace Hills' bore down on the contact. The order to fire was given. The sharp cough of the Squid mortar on each side was almost simultaneous. The last depth charge rolled over the stern and splashed into the sea only seconds later.

"Starboard about to three four zero, ahead two thirds." The instructions were echoed and complied with. The corvette, which could out-turn a submarine, slewed around in a bid to pounce on any U-Boat that the depth charges might bring to the surface.

"Asdic contact, bearing one four zero, range one thousand...aaaah!" The sonar operator waited too long to get the information. The sound of the exploding depth charges tore at his eardrums. David quickly jumped to the position and pulled the man out of his seat, taking the headphones for himself. He grimly crouched over the equipment. So now, they did have a positive contact! The submarine was aft of them on their starboard quarter, heading after the line of ships they had just penetrated in search of it. The foaming white subsidence of water, where the depth charges exploded, was south and east of the U-Boat.

"Very well, starboard to three two zero, maximum revolutions. Plot, how do we look?"

"Range is approximate, Captain. Your steer looks good."

Again, the little corvette heeled, as the rudder went over and the propeller thrashed the sea.

"Torpedo track amidships, heading three one zero away from us." The starboard lookout now had the best view.

"Position of the torpedo source?"

"Slightly starboard of dead ahead, Captain."

"Continue to three three zero, ready full pattern depth charges. Plot?"

"Concur, Captain, range estimated seven hundred yards."

"How does that torpedo look?"

"It may just..." A gout of water from the stern of the freighter erased the lookout's hopeful words. The torpedo aimed at it struck home. With its propeller, rudder, and most of its stern disintegrated, the freighter wallowed like a bulldog running in mud and began to slew sideways as it lost way.

"Shit!"

"Belay that!"

"Aye, aye, Sir. Sorry Sir!"

"Range?"

"Two hundred yards."

'Peace Hills' already signalled she was hunting a positive target. The 'Clear Hills,' her sister ship, was turning her direction to join the hunt. This time, the Squid fired again, then again, and another ponderous depth charge rolled off the stern rack. The distinctive fountains of water and shock waves strummed up through the depths, killing and stunning fish for a mile around.

In the reverberations following the explosions, David sought desperately for a sonar signal. He anxiously watched the trace travelling on the cathode ray tube. Not only would he hear any higher-toned return 'ping,' but the quivering spot of light travelling across the screen was a time trace, graded in distance, so he could determine the range. A blip would appear to show the distance to the target. The Asdic was also rotatable. The round dial on the equipment would show him the relative bearing the signal was received back from. There! There came a sharp tonal increase in the sound and a faint blip on the scale. There was a brief grinding, like giant teeth, followed by a sustained snoring noise from their starboard rear quarter.

"Bubbles bearing one six zero!"

All eyes focussed on the giant air bubbles bursting the surface, not far behind their starboard rear.

"Undetermined sonar noises, Captain, weak Asdic contact bearing two zero zero, range five hundred yards."

"Starboard to one five five. Engines half ahead. Set pattern of two for five hundred feet over the bubbles. Plot?"

"Concur, Captain. It may be sinking."

Again, the 'Peace Hills' closed on its contact and dropped depth charges. The 'Clear Hills' was only a mile away, but they signalled her to stand off. There was no further evidence of a submarine.

It was now fifteen minutes since the tanker had been attacked. There was little doubt it was gone. The freighter nearest 'Peace Hills' was sinking rapidly by the stern. Its blunt bow reared higher and higher as she prepared to plunge to the bottom of the sea. Faintly on the wind came the sounds of bulkheads breaking and the crash of her precious cargo moving aftward, hastening her demise. Through the binoculars, men could be seen desperately rowing away from the hulk in lifeboats. The slower amongst them abandoned ship by throwing themselves into the sea. They wanted to avoid being sucked down into the vortex when their ship sank. The good news was, no further attacks had taken place. Under orders, the two corvettes plied a line across the wake of the retreating convoy, trying to keep the submarines from following.

They could not be sure aboard 'Peace Hills,' but they thought they had damaged, if not destroyed, a U-Boat. Captain Wright ordered the information into the ship's log.

A flat grey light now reigned over the scene, sufficient that ships could be seen more than five miles away. The convoy was scattered, but mainly in the same direction. Soon, they could resume herding them across the ocean. 'Clear Hills' steered slowly over to pick up survivors of the freighter, which had finally disappeared ten minutes before. Two lifeboats could be seen bobbing up and down on the waves. The heads in them bowed low under the stress and misery of being blown off their ship into the icy grip of the ocean.

David was vigilant on the Asdic, listening to the monotonous shimmering sound that went omni directionally through the water, alert for the returning 'ping' the Doppler effect caused when it came back, having bounced off a sub sea target. He noted the sinking freighter and rotated his passive listening receiver away from it. This way, the noisy interference caused by the sound of the dying ship was greatly reduced. Then suddenly, back from the direction where the submarines surely lay, there came a faint, maximum range return, hardly perceptible.

"Possible Asdic contact, Captain. Range three thousand yards, bearing one seven zero. No depth indication."

"Damn, just when we want to pick up survivors! Right turn to one zero zero, two thirds ahead. Signal 'Clear Hills' we have a target that position. Tell him we want to conduct 'Operation Observant'." The corvettes would now operate as a hunting pair. Since 'Peace Hills' had the target, 'Clear Hills' would turn off her active sonar and be guided by 'Peace Hills' over the target and told when to depth charge it.

"'Clear Hills' acknowledges, Captain. Her Asdic is down."

"Excellent. Now, let's see if we can nail this blighter!"

It was time to be nervous. In blocking any U-Boat pursuit of the convoy, the little corvettes made themselves targets. Everyone knew how badly they fared if they took a torpedo. Very soon, they would have to stop and pick up survivors and then be sitting ducks. In the meantime, the sight of being ignored by the corvettes, which they were expecting to save their lives, magnified the suffering of the floating survivors. A signalman on the 'Clear Hills' was semaphoring them, trying to explain the need for the ship's apparent callousness.

"Asdic?"

"Nothing, Captain. We may have a temperature inversion here." The boundary between two layers of water with differing temperatures tended to block the Asdic's efficiency, a fact submarines made use of at every opportunity. David felt the captain's eyes, burning with accusation, boring into his back. Men were perishing in the sea all around them, their fate hanging on how long the corvette should spend pursuing a possible target. The guilt was eating the captain up.

"Last range?"

"Three thousand one hundred, Captain."

"Plot for 'Clear Hills' to drop one depth charge eight hundred short on that bearing, set for one hundred feet."

"Aye, Captain."

David tried to will a return on his screen, but nothing. The Asdic sounded through the depths, fading away into the distance. The signal was sent to 'Clear Hills' to drop her depth charge. David removed the headphones to protect his hearing. Moments later, the sea erupted two miles away.

"Left to zero six zero, let's try a wide sweep."

The sun broke out ahead of them halfway through the turn, and the lookouts strained for the sign of a periscope wake. Nothing.

"Further left, three six zero."

A mile and a half to their left, 'Clear Hills' was now slowing, men lining her sides to throw lines and assist the torpedoed merchant mariners onto the safety of their ship. There were about twenty-five awaiting rescue, some bobbing around Carley floats, grimly hanging on against the horrible grasp of the cold water, others safer but still dismally ensconced in lifeboats. Oil covered the water in a black sheet, coagulating into gobs on anything it touched. It smoothed the waves like some grim cloak.

From stories told, the crew aboard 'Peace Hills' knew that men out there were dying from being covered in the viscous black oil. It would coat them, blind them, and ingested into their lungs and stomachs, choke them and poison them into death.

"Asdic?" The captain's voice was pleading, laced with accusation.

"Nothing, Captain."

"Sir, 'Clear Hills' is signalling. *Must stop now!* Too many survivors in water."

"Acknowledge!"

"Aye, aye, Sir!"

The signalman's light clattered. Captain Wright stalked the bridge in a tight display of nerves. His hands were clasped behind him. He looked like a worried Horatio Nelson, fretting that his shot was falling short at Trafalgar. He stooped over David's shoulder, lurched away to the bridge screen, and peered out, as if by some supreme effort, he could divine the whereabouts of a submarine. The sea, shadowed by the last of the cloud, undulated darkly past, like it was deliberately mocking him.

Suddenly, a high whine came into David's headset. "Torpedo running!" he roared. Madly, he swung the azimuth wheel for maximum volume and glanced down at the dial. "Bearing zero niner zero."

"Signal 'Clear Hills.' Tell her to get out of there!" Even as the captain spoke, they saw water boil at their sister ship's stern She heard the torpedo too. "Maximum revolutions! Steer one seven zero! Range, Asdic?"

"About two thousand yards, Captain. He was masked by the sinking ship!"

A mile away, 'Clear Hills' thrashed the sea madly. She was almost dead in the water with boarding nets streamed when the torpedo had been fired. She inexorably quivered and shook as each frenzied revolution of her propeller took her out from the path of the torpedo. Survivors of the sunken ships screamed at the terror and disappointment of being abandoned, but there was no choice. Two life rafts were drawn against the corvette's side by the vacuum of her passage and turned turtle, spilling terror-stricken men into the icy clutches of the sea. Only yards away from rescue, three men were instead drawn screaming into the thrashing path of the propeller.

The torpedo struck only seconds later. 'Clear Hills' was blown sideways, heeled over hard to port by the force of the explosion. A gout of water shot up over her aft quarters, which canted up crazily. The transmitted shockwave of the detonation travelled through the water and killed every swimmer in the immediate vicinity. Part of the boilers exploded moments later, blowing plates off the ship's side. The mast toppled and fell, the last image before steam blocked the view from 'Peace Hills.'

Passing a quarter mile away, 'Peace Hills' was travelling at full speed for the source of the torpedo. She was like a wolf hot on the heels of a rabbit.

David had a full active return on his Asdic. The submarine tried to slide westward across their path. It was obvious the Germans were diving hard, trying to escape. In the meantime, 'Wolfenden' was summonsed and sliced the water only a quarter mile abeam and slightly behind, angling in behind them. David knew this only subliminally from listening to the orders and spoken messages between the two ships. His attention was riveted to the Asdic set, tracking the submarine.

The U-Boat turned again, corkscrewing its way desperately towards the depths. David wondered at the men who had just taken such a risk when they could easily have escaped. Were they reckless fools or just brave, duty-bound sailors? At this juncture, they could not fire back. They were at the mercy of the attacking ships.

"Pattern." The laconic observation was his cue. He removed the headset when he heard the splashes of the depth charges. They were all around the submarine. Anxious moments ticked by. They waited for the charges to reach their fused depth. Seconds later, the loud explosions ripped through the water, reverberating off the sides of the ship. 'Wolfenden' fired a full pattern in her turn, set for a lower depth, and soon, they too hammered at the sea.

In the wake of the sonar disturbances, David heard the sound he had been trained for at the submarine warfare school: the unmistakeable sound of a break up in the sub sea. The submarine was collapsing, sinking. He listened to the grating and shrieking of tortured metal, as bulkheads and hull imploded. He pictured the men inside, dying in this horrible fashion, and felt bile rise in his throat. Then he thought of the poor merchant seamen and the crew of the 'Clear Hills.'

There being no further sonar contacts, the two warships gave way. Each launched a lifeboat to search for survivors and bodies. 'Clear Hills' was gone. The lookouts reported her sinking in two minutes. The corvettes were lightly built, so slight a citadel against the power of a torpedo. As the deck watch was doubled to help survivors board, some went down the nets to assist men who were too frozen, too exhausted, too injured, or coated in fuel oil to manage it themselves. They came up on deck, spluttering, cursing. Some cursed out of frustration, some cursed the dead captain of the 'Clear Hills' for abandoning and killing some of them, but most were silent, shocked beyond belief.

They were helped or carried below, stripped of their clothes, and wrapped in blankets. Gallons of hot milky tea were dispensed, laced with sugar and rum, where requested. The top deck and companionways were slippery with oil and water. Coughing and spluttering, blinded and vomiting, men who had been soaked in the bunker oil suffered horribly. Blood, vomit, and water covered the floors, tables, and chairs of the seamens' messes and bunks of the ship, as first aid was administered. With no doctor aboard, they did what they could with compression pads, bandages, and immobilizing slings. 'Wolfenden' had a doctor, and as soon as they were able, they would transfer the most critically injured over to her.

Thirty-nine men and eighteen bodies were picked up by 'Peace Hills.' Happily, 'Wolfenden' managed forty-three more, plus thirteen victims hauled from their watery graves. Ultimately, a further forty-seven men were lost from all the ships, a terrible day in the Battle of the Atlantic. Three precious merchantmen were gone and one tiny corvette. The cost in lives and shipping was bad enough, but the cargoes destined for the troops now ashore in France since D-Day were also lost.

Three more men died in horrible distress as a result of ingesting the oil before they made port. It was an awful experience for everyone and totally quashed any thought of celebrating a 'maybe' U-Boat kill and one shared with 'Wolfenden.' The fact they had graphic evidence onboard of how the German crew had also died helped make the mood no less sombre.

****

East Germany.

The first indication the guards had left was the absence of morning roll call. It was a daily ritual ingrained in the detainees, a time of dread for the duties allotted to them. To be sent to the quarries meant being dead within days, worked literally to death. Release was found only in a merciful bullet. Now, as the morning chill oppressed the rising smoke of the campfires into a pall around them, they sought reassurance. They sought the familiar security of their captors' presence to tell them a new day had begun. Was this a trick? Was it some new game of humility and degradation the guards were playing?

There was nothing. No Kapos. No guards. No officers yelling at them. No sign of any kind that life was as it had been the day before. Peering out the filthy windows, they beheld no guards behind the wire or in the watchtowers. They had seen strange aircraft flying by the past week. A very distant rumble of guns or bombs kindled a hope so tenuous that the effort to merely believe was too traumatic for their battered bodies. Bewildered, anxious, and insecure, they filtered out of their filthy, lice-ridden, and frigid bunks, exiting in growing numbers as the unspoken word spread. Each of them still capable of thought were visited by the sense of a change, convinced through the numbness of their existence that some radical, though not unwelcome, change had come upon them.

A brave soul – filthy and emaciated to a pile of bones encased in a pitiful sac of skin – staggered to the main gate. It remained barred. No warning cry came from the high towers. No burst of machine-gun fire cut him down. Only the shrill cry of a jay pierced the cool morning, echoed by the distant idle squawking of a crow. Leaning against the wire of the gate, the figure passed its hands through the strands and curved its spine back. It strained upwards against the horizontal beam that secured the gates.

A drift of smoke obscured him, while the collective watchers held their breath. It was like the rolling back of the Messiah's tomb, or the moment when Moses parted the Red Sea. When the smoke cleared, the bar was inches above its resting point, and in the absence of gunfire, four more figures scuttled to his aid. A sigh, like a religious ecstasy, went through the throng. The bar was lifted and cast to the ground, releasing the gates that slowly swung open.

The crow stopped its raucous sound and a great silence fell upon the camp, fraught with a revelation. The line upon line of huts wavered in the air. Untended fires smouldered down. Even more smoke drifted and sank around them. The watchtowers stood like immobile bayonets pointed at their hearts and hopes, while the high barbed wire fences posed a still-ominous threat. Was it true then? Was Germany beaten? Why else would the guards disappear?

The low sun glanced off the shaven head of the stick person poised in the gate opening, creating a halo. His ball and socket knees moved him between the gates. He stopped as if he had seen a revelation, stopped like a Prophet of the Old Testament and raised his arms. In Hebrew, he whispered, "Freedom." With a rumble of astonishment and acceptance, the mob within the camp moved forward and headed for the road outside.

Some stopped just outside the gates, looking up at the sign above them: 'Arbeit macht Frie.' 'Work makes Free' was a terrible cynicism for what had been done beyond these gates. Behind them, the squat and blackened chimneys of the dreaded ovens were dead and cold. No ugly black smoke curled from their parapets. All was still.

Only about ten percent of the camp population was fit enough to travel. They quickly split into small groups. Fearful of any kind of authority, any person in uniform, they shrank into the ground at the first sign of confrontation. Equipped only with a sense of survival, they walked, keeping the sun more and more to their right as it rose. They walked, painfully headed east, away from the Nazis.

FOURTEEN

SCARLETT O'HARA

The summer of nineteen forty-five was a bewildering one for the people of Europe. One by one, they stuck their heads out of their doors to see if the storm had truly passed. Despite the exultation of liberation, the darkness of the previous five years of Nazi occupation was a slow-clearing pall of dreadful grey. 'Nacht und Knebel,' Adolf Hitler proclaimed over the people in his thrall. Today, the Paris weather seemed to echo that call. 'Night and Fog.'

An inversion trapped smoke over the city. The sky was a murky, sunless canopy that threatened drizzle. Life had changed for these grey people lined up before grey buildings to receive grey, yet precious, rationed food. Life had changed irrevocably. Many people, friends, relatives, and loved ones, were gone: dead, missing, or fled. Familiar sights were destroyed: houses, factories, churches, bridges, and railway stations were ruined. It did not matter whether it was friendly or enemy warfare that rained upon them. These objects were gone from the European continent.

Beth entered France through Bordeaux in March. Getting into France with a British passport was easy. She was yet to discover that getting out was tough. The French were relentless against Nazi collaborators. Some were murdered in the streets. Many a young woman, who had consorted with German soldiers, was stripped naked, shaven of her hair and beaten through her town. Anyone leaving France was automatically suspect.

Warned of the shortages and lack of coherent order, Beth came prepared with tins of salmon, cigarettes, several cases of scotch, and other trading goods plus a good supply of ready money. The further north she travelled, to the most recently liberated areas, the more bewildered the people were. They dwelled in fear of that midnight knock on the door throughout the Occupation. The habit was born of mortal terror. They could not yet risk that it might return.

Beth left David, now four years old, in Reading. In Bordeaux, she spent almost two months with her staff at the winery. She already knew they heard nothing more from René. Hearing it from them in person destroyed some of the hope that still flowed through her veins. The winery had not suffered in any way, even though the Germans nominally seized it as part of René's estate. They merely lost that part of stock they were forced to declare to the Germans. The staff cleverly hid a large portion of vintages in stock and thus preserved lineage of their wines.

The train to Paris was full and the journey tedious. Refugees and demobilized soldiers filled every station as yhe nation tried to shake itself back into normality. From the Gare de Montparnasse, a taxi took her to the apartment, where she found the Wehrmacht had seized it as a billet for soldiers on leave. The walls and hallways were scarred and dirtied. What furniture was left had been smashed. No restitution was made. Any damage done by the Germans was made worse by indigent refugees who claimed squatter's rights until she had the concierge throw them out.

She hired a couple at a very cheap rate to tidy up and seek some furniture. They were willing to be servants for a roof over their heads. This second day in Paris, she arrived at the office of a lawyer, Claude-Francois Langret, who was mentioned in some of René's documents, the ones she took to England.

"Madame de Forquet?" The elderly secretary with the unruly white hair poked her head around the door and looked questioningly at the full waiting room. Beth climbed to her feet and entered the lawyer's office.

Langret proved to be an erect old man with a pink pate shining through a thinning mane of white hair. He peered over a pince-nez at her and then rose to his feet. He wore an ancient, though, well-kept black suit, with high winged collar. Beth was struck by the image of an elderly Neville Chamberlain waving his useless peace document.

"Madame de Fourquet, I am delighted to meet you. I received your letter some while ago." The diction was slow and precise, but whether from age or the need to find the English words, Beth could not be sure. Certainly, his voice was firm, considering his desiccated state. Beth wrote to him several months before to outline her needs and introduced herself through an English lawyer.

"Madeleine, le thé pour Madame, s'il vous plait."

"Oui, Monsieur Langret." The secretary bobbed back out of sight.

"Now then, how may I be of assistance?" The long pouchy face wrinkled into an inviting smile, but Beth noted how his eyes maintained a coldness she couldn't determine.

"This could take some time."

"Madame, the Boche have gone. I can take life at my leisure now!" His arms rose expansively and a wan smile began to touch his eyes.

"Well, my primary business is to locate my husband."

"That is Monsieur René de Fourquet?"

Beth wondered for a moment, why the formality? "Yes, he disappeared in nineteen forty, and I have had no word of him since. He...he was...is, Jewish, of course, so that is a factor." A deep silence fell between them. The disclosures concerning the death camps run by the Nazi S.S. had shocked the world.

"And where exactly did you last see your...er, see Monsieur de Fourquet?"

"In a little village on the Loire. We had just been married and..."

"Do you have any identification, Madame?" The lawyer interrupted her and suddenly, Beth realized with a cold chill down her spine why he was being so formal.

"You...you, think I am not who I say I am?" The direct stare with the stern eyes answered her question, and she pushed back her chair. The horror in her recoil moved the old lawyer.

"Madame, I am sorry if I cause you any distress. However, you must realize that all over the continent, people are trying to put their lives together. Many unscrupulous impostors are trying to inveigle their way into dead persons' shoes. You must realize that if you are truly Madame de Fourquet, then I am protecting your interests by correctly identifying you and not someone else." He paused. "There is a lot of money at stake here. All I have is a letter from a British solicitor to tell me who you are. I was aware that Monsieur de Fourquet was in love with some young lady before the war, but I have no evidence of a marriage between them."

The logic was insurmountable. Beth felt the initial chill dissipating. "I can give you my passport. That should dispel most of your doubts as to my identity. I can relate certain facts about René, his business affairs, and his property that should allay your fears. I can also present witnesses to the marriage, and while I do not have a written certificate, I know where to find the record book. I have a letter signed by my husband naming me as his legal heir. There is also..." and here Beth smiled. "There is also a matter of Monsieur de Fourquet's son and heir to be acknowledged."

Langret sat stonily for a moment. Beth wondered if she had only fuelled his suspicions. He suddenly sat forward. "Madame, on a personal basis, I believe you. However, it is my duty to the estate to determine your claim. Once this is done, I shall be entirely yours to command."

Two days later, Beth entered St. Germaine-des-Prés for the second time in her life. It was quiet. Doubtless, it returned to the sleepy timelessness it enjoyed before the war, but she remembered it differently because of the urgency of the times on her last visit. Langret had provided her a car and a reliable older man named Albert Descaries to escort her.

They discovered a small pension in the village and inquired of the way to the church. Within an hour, Beth found herself gazing up at the Arc of the Covenant of our Lord again, in the company of a young priest. "It is a great pity that the Reverend Father Alain did not live to see France liberated, but he has gone to a greater reward." He made the sign of the cross and genuflected towards the altar. "Here is the book of registrations!"

Eagerly, Beth turned back the pages until she found the right one. "There!" she pointed, signed by husband and wife, the priest, and witnesses, including Pierre. "There was someone else present! Another witness. A choirboy. Alphonse! That was his name!"

"Yes, Alphonse! Of course, he was a great hero with 'le Résistance!' But he was wounded, you see." Beth's face fell at the thought that the young, sweet-voiced kid she had so briefly known could have been harmed. "But, he is fine, Madame, and I know where to find him, if you wish."

Alphonse appeared at the pension later that evening and remembered Beth well. He was wounded fighting with the Resistance, losing two fingers. He was at a loss for work, a husky eighteen years old and free for hire. Since she had to take him back to Paris as a witness, she hired him. His dark brown eyes beneath the tousled dark hair lit up at the offer. He became her chauffeur, a position he was to faithfully fill for many years.

Within a month, with necessary documents and sworn statements, Langret filed Beth and David as the rightful heirs of the estates of the de Fourquet family. René's mother and sister were recorded in captured Nazi files as having been sent to Buchenwald concentration camp, where they were victims of the gas chamber. There was no other immediate family to take precedence. Nearly all branches of relatives had been decimated. The day the papers were returned acknowledging Beth's hereditary rights, Langret invited her to lunch at a stylish restaurant on the Bois de Boulogne. He handed her copies of the documents, and with the panache only a Frenchman could muster, had two gift boxes brought to the table over dessert.

He made her open the larger first. It turned out to be a magnum of nineteen thirty-two Bollinger champagne. "You must save this very special wine for a very special occasion, Madame: The day your husband returns." The smaller ring box contained a silver necklace chain with a matching locket, elegantly engraved with two hands reaching towards each other, and the word 'Hope.'

He made them both cry. Langret swore his total fealty to her, a promise he diligently kept until the day he died.

****

Village of St. Denis-aux-Rivière, July 1, 1945.

Beth stood in the driveway to the house. She told Alphonse to stop while she climbed from the car. It had been five years since she fled from here with René when the Germans were making Blitzkrieg across Belgium. She had loved this place, more so because she expected to visit it often.

Three shell holes breached the upper walls and numerous pockmarks showed where small-arms fire had been directed. Bivouacs had been made by large numbers of troops. Excavations marred the once pristine gardens the other Alphonse had tended. Several tracked vehicles had manoeuvred through the grounds, tearing out trees and shrubs. They passed a pillbox on the way in, guarding the approaches to the top of the ridge, where the road climbed passing the entrance gate. It was smoke-blackened and deserted. Weeds grew up around it, as if they wished to hide it from sight.

Her mind went back to the book, 'Gone with the Wind.' She remembered prophetically buying the novel at the beginning of this odyssey. Now, feeling like Scarlett O'Hara at Tara, Beth gazed at the devastation and felt tears flow down her cheeks. Alphonse came up behind her and placed a hand on her shoulder. Well! If Scarlett could do it, Beth could do it!

"I'll walk from here, Alphonse. Bring the car to the front door."

The gravel of the driveway felt good beneath her feet; its rustling crunches sounded like a welcome. Boards were nailed over several of the windows, which appeared broken, so at least someone was trying to care for the place. She possessed a key for the huge oaken door and stepped into the foyer with its tiled floor. None of the furnishings she remembered were there. The carved oaken banister was splintered and holed by automatic rounds. The once-polished and pristine treads of the curved staircase were soiled and dirty. The whole place looked forlorn.

She quickly toured through the place. There was little left upstairs. What hadn't been looted was wrecked. Alphonse joined her in the kitchen, shaking his head, more in sympathy for her expression than actual understanding of the amount of devastation.

"I truly love this place, Alphonse. It was my favourite of all the places Monsieur owned."

"You will restore it to its former glory, Madame. I know you will."

The cellar! Beth sprang up and strode to the small door in the wainscoting beneath the stairs. It was open. With Alphonse close behind, she gingerly made her way down the stone steps. She remembered there was a faint light through the basement windows, probably less now with the dirt of neglect. She moved around heaps of debris and items which five years of searching looters had left, and found the iron grill. Of course, the gate was open. Knocking on the barrels as she went, she received hollow responses, speaking of more pillage and possibly, drunken celebrations.

"Alphonse, please go back to the kitchen. I need to be alone here for a few minutes."

As soon as he was gone, Beth reached behind the fourth cask to the secret knothole and pushed it. There was a faint click and she pulled the end of the cask open. Inside was as she remembered it and she quickly groped for the key. The small wooden door she remembered well. What would be behind it? Likely nothing; René would not have hidden here, and unless he had subsequently left something, it should remain as they both left it more than five years before.

The door was a little stiff and the light poor inside the cask. In the room, the air was a little dank. Beth drew to one side to allow light in to see inside before she entered. A couple of feet up one wall, a gleam of white drew her attention. She narrowed her eyes, trying to focus and identify it. When she did, her screams brought Alphonse on the run. Slumped against the corner of the room opposite the door was a skeleton, clad in ragged clothing.

"René! René! Oh my God, René!"

Alphonse clutched her tightly, more terrified by the depths of her distress than the sight of the bony relic in the room.

The local gendarmes were very interested in Beth's find. Obviously rats had managed to enter the place. Otherwise the figure would have been mummified. They found a yellowed copy of a Paris newspaper dated July nineteen forty. That helped them map the time of death. The skeleton was that of a man about six feet tall, so it was not René. No wallet or other documents were found with it, and the identity of the man was never determined.

Speculation was he had been injured and hidden there, probably by René, since nobody else knew of the secret room. René had not returned to feed or rescue him. It was a theory with good probability, but Beth knew René would not have abandoned anyone. The morbid extension of the theory was that something dire and unknown happened to René to prevent his return.

****

Calgary.

David Williams had the typical emotional letdown of many young men when he returned to Calgary from the war. The world was rid of evil. Now it was time to rebuild – rebuild a land of justice and social reform, where the underprivileged were to be redeemed by a new wave of consciousness. War could never be allowed to return. His parents moved to Calgary early in the war. He moved back with them once he got himself established.

There was a certain amount of backbiting and finger pointing concerning profiteering by industrialists, much as there had been after the first war. A fiery journalist by the name of Nathan Connaught attacked several Edmonton companies. In a series of articles David read, it turned out they were owned by his father's old nemesis, Thomas Edmunds. Restless and unfulfilled, he felt compelled to do something worthwhile, so the old investigative talents of 'Sher' Williams went to work. Working his way into a law firm took most of his time and energy, but eventually, late in August nineteen forty-seven, he came home with a smile.

"I've done it, Mom!"

"Done what, dear?"

"Got Edmunds by the tail, dead to rights!"

"Tom Edmunds?"

David missed the quick turn of his mother's head. "Yes, that old bastard who has been such a jerk to Dad all these years. I have unearthed a whole bunch of evidence that will ruin him. Maybe even put him in jail!"

"But he's an honest man!"

"What? How can you say that?" David rushed on, too immersed in what he had to say to see the look of chagrin on Jeanne's face. "Back in the early twenties, there was a group of city councillors who got greedy and bought land in expectation of a huge development, a civic centre. It was all planned and everything. Someone blew the whistle on them and in the panic to get out, they sold off cheaply to that someone."

"So what? That doesn't sound very illegal to me."

"Ah, but it gets better! You see, the individual lots were not bought by one person but by several. Edmunds bankrolled a lot of poor people to become the buyers and carefully foisted wills on them to ensure he became the beneficiary. Others, he bought out. The end result was he owns two whole city blocks downtown, and nobody but me knows about it."

"So, where is the illegality?"

"Well, as a conspiracy, it is enough of a dubious nature to severely taint him. The kicker is that two people, who seemingly tried to change their wills, died."

There was an audible thump. Jeanne slumped into a chair, her face as white as chalk. "You say..." The voice was a whisper. "You say Tom Edmunds killed these people?"

"I have no proof of that, yet. Still, it needs more investigating. The bastard probably got somebody else to do it anyway."

"What are you going to do with this information?"

"Nothing yet, not until I have finished the whole thing. Don't you think Dad will love this?"

"You're not going to give it to him are you?"

"I don't know yet. I may want to confront the old bastard myself or let that journalist, Nathan Connaught, get the big scoop."

"But you'll do nothing until you are sure?"

"Yeah, Mom. I can't afford to be sued by a man that rich!" He gave her his special dazzling smile. She always melted under it but he frowned now when he saw her gazing at some object far away and beyond his comprehension.

Two days later, the postman delivered a registered mail envelope for him. Jeanne signed for it. It came from an Edmonton address. She stood in the hallway after closing the front door. The envelope burned her fingers. For the past two nights, she had lain awake, wondering what she should do. She refused to believe Tom Edmunds was crooked. Like most businessmen, he probably had some enemies; her own husband was a handy example. She did not, above all else, believe Tom would be a murderer, even by association. Twice she picked up the phone to call him to ask him outright if what David said was true, but each time, seized by doubt, she hung up.

It felt like a betrayal to even ask; at the same time, she knew she would have to look into his eyes when she asked the question. It was straw grasping to hope that David would fail to get the final evidence he needed. She still did not know what that might be or how he intended to make use of what he knew. She had little illusion that if he succeeded, he would try to bring Tom Edmunds down. He was brought up in this household to hate the name.

Before she knew it, the kitchen knife was under the flap of the envelope and it was open. She lacked the courage to read it immediately, and placing it on the kitchen table, went to brew some tea. It was still waiting there, mocking her, when she returned with a steaming mug, gloating with an arrogance she could not ignore.

In that envelope, she knew, was information that might change her life forever. She lived a greater part of her life with a lie. The fact it had been comfortably accommodated and caused little anguish was now a thing of the past. She could destroy the envelope, but she knew the thoroughness of her son would foil that. Sooner or later, he would find out.

There was only one way to see! Inside the thick envelope was a sheaf of land title mimeographs. Sifting through them, she could see they were for the same area of Edmonton, only a handful of blocks from where she had lived with her mother, Lillette. Different names occupied the purchaser entries, although numerous ones listed companies and names she recognized as being associated with Tom Edmunds.

There was a letter attached from an investigative agency. Quickly scanning the page, Jeanne learned that David's correspondent failed to find solid proof of complicity in murder. More investigation would be required to establish guilt by Tom Edmunds.

David came home from work at six that evening and sat down at the kitchen table for supper. Jeanne was thankful that John was out to a late meeting and would not be home for a while. After placing his plate before him, Jeanne silently slid the letter beside it and moved softly into the chair across the table.

"Oh! It came! Good!" David reached for the salt and then frowned, noticing for the first time that the letter had been opened. "Why has this been opened? Did you...?"

Jeanne was nodding. "Yes, I opened it."

"But why? Mother! You have never done this before! What right...?"

"Every right: a mother's right!"

"I think you had better explain! How dare you open my mail!"

"What are you going to do with the information in there?"

"Well, I don't know. I haven't seen it yet!"

"Then look at it and tell me. Now!"

After a long and curious look at his mother, David opened the envelope and studied the contents. He gave an occasional grunt and nodded his head but gave away little as to his opinion. Finally, he looked up. "Well, it is not as tight as I thought, but still enough to make that bastard really squirm. Maybe ruin him."

"That's what I was afraid you would say. David, you cannot do this."

"Cannot do this? What the hell are you talking about, woman?"

"Don't you dare speak to me the way your father does or I'll slap your face!"

"Mother! What the hell is going on here?"

"I am asking you not to do this to Tom Edmunds!"

"Why not? He's been a pain in the ass to this family for years, and now I have him nearly dead to rights!"

"Please, David, you cannot do it!" Tears were streaming down her cheeks and Jeanne looked at him beseechingly.

"Again...why not?" The cold lawyer was coming out now.

"Because he is your real father!"

The air went out of the kitchen like some enormous external vacuum had drawn it out. The tenth anniversary clock on the shelf ticked away as if trying to fill the void. David Williams sat and stared at his mother like a coiled spring that suddenly suffered a total loss of tension.

"How?"

"We were lovers."

"You mean you went out and betrayed Dad, after all the hatred between them? How could you?"

Jeanne was shaking her head. "No, David." Now the secret was out. She found a great calming peace descend upon her. "Tom Edmunds and I were lovers before the Great War. After he went away to fight, I met your father and got engaged. You were conceived in Edmonton when I went there to bury your Grandma. It wasn't supposed to happen, but it just did."

"So you betrayed both of them. All three of us!"

"Oh God, David, please don't see it that way!"

"You still love him don't you?" It was an accusation, not a question.

"How could I not love a man who treated me as he did?"

"Do you still talk to him? Does he know about me?"

"No. I have not spoken to him since then, and he doesn't know about you."

"And Dad?"

"I could never tell him." Her statement made it clear that she never expected David to, either.

To her complete astonishment, Jeanne saw David burst into tears. She moved around the table and wrapped herself around his shoulders, while he cried like a child. She expected rage, and still did, yet he cried liked someone absolved of a deadly sin. Finally, after several minutes, he pushed back his chair and gazed at her through reddened eyes. "I suppose I always knew. Not that it was Tom Edmunds, but more that there was always something between Dad and me. I thought it was just his nature, but I never felt the closeness I saw in my friends and their fathers."

"He has always loved you."

"Yes, but it was something – indefinable."

****

Edmonds Building, Jasper Avenue, Edmonton.

"Yes, I am David Williams."

"Son of John Williams." The voice was flat but held a low menace.

"Yes."

"Then you are the son of Jeanne!" The face softened into a look of almost delight, and with a jolt, David realized his mother had told the truth. In that one revealing moment, the smile for his mother, he knew the truth. Almost as quickly, Tom Edmunds' face closed again. He was in the presence of the enemy.

They were in Tom's office, high in the Edmunds' Building. It was a corner office with two sides of windows looking out over the city from the fifteenth floor. The furnishings were simple, yet tasteful. One whole wall was taken up by bookshelves with copies of classical literature. In the blind corner of the room was a sitting area around a low table with comfortable chairs and a sofa. In this area, photographs recording the history of Edmunds' businesses hung on the wall. In the centre, was an enlargement of a First World War battlefield: the mud, shellholes, and barbed wire a mute testimony of human suffering.

David was impressed with the modern outer office and the young, shapely blonde lady who had shown him inside.

"Coffee? Let's sit over there, more comfortable." They moved to the sitting area. Tom poured coffee for both of them at the wet bar to the side. "Now, what can I do for you?"

"Actually, nothing. I just wanted to meet you."

"Well, David, I don't see..."

"*Sher*. You can call me *Sher*." It was said on impulse.

"*Sher*?"

"Yes, after Sherlock Holmes. I got the nickname in law school because I like Conan Doyle, and I have a talent for investigation."

"Ah! You are a literary person?"

"Not really, but I see from your shelves that you are."

"Taught to me at sea by an old sailor."

"So you were in the navy?"

"No, I ran away from home and went to sea, years ago. The chief engineer on a steamer taught me the value of books."

"I was on corvettes in the North Atlantic."

"See any action?"

"Perhaps too much." They were silent a moment, reliving memories and weaving the first faint threads of familiarity between them. David reflected that this man had a kinder face than the one that often stared out from articles denigrating his actions. The face was creased by hard experience and the greying hair and capillary-reddened nose were a route-map of the man, just like the photographs beside him.

In turn, Tom saw he was taking a shine to the young man. Hardly surprising, since he was Jeanne's boy, yet there seemed something oddly familiar about him: his demeanour, his looks and posture. Jeanne!

"Now that it is behind you, you intend to practice law?"

"Yes, but I am smitten by investigation. Not the 'private eye' type of thing, but documentary tracing of dealings, history of contracts, that kind of thing."

"Well, it sounds very obscure to me, maybe even boring, but a man has to do what a man has to do." The smile was warm. "What example have you done along these lines?"

For an answer, David reached for the briefcase beside him and put it on the low table. He gestured with his hand for Tom to open it.

"What is this?" The question related to the purpose of the visit, not the object on the table. Tom opened the briefcase and pulled out the sheaf of documents inside. His frown deepened as he read them. He looked up occasionally at the young man.

Finally, he tossed the bundle on the table. "So, young man, what is this? Some kind of threat? Blackmail?"

"Two people who owned lots in that area died under *mysterious* circumstances. Did you have anything to do with that?"

For a moment, Tom Edmunds looked at his visitor with a mind to throw him out of his office. It seemed like this pup was a true offspring of that hyena John Williams. Rage surged through him like a tide. He had to know what the motive was here and where it was all going.

He sighed. "There was a rather clever scheme to buy up those two city blocks and keep the owners discreet. In itself, there was nothing illegal in what was done. Some people were well paid to ensure the lots they legally held were directed back to me when they died. Again, that is not illegal. The two people who died, I am not familiar with. How and why they died, I do not know, but their deaths were not caused by me or any of my companies."

'Sher' was watching the man before him like a hawk. There was no discomfort, no subtle body language of deceit, and he wanted to believe it.

"We arranged a similar deal through the Depression. It enabled us to acquire land holdings we otherwise may not have. You have done your homework well on this, and I would wish you were working for me on similar deals, except you have still not told me why you are here."

David felt his resolve to ruin this man dissolving like a snowball on a hot griddle. "You may have those. They are the only copies, so your secret is safe with me."

That's when David made the decision to join Tom Edmunds' company.

****

East of Edmonton.

The North Saskatchewan River is the most northerly river shedding water from the Great Divide into the Atlantic Ocean. Its nearest neighbour to the north, the Athabasca, flows from the same source in the Rocky Mountains, but empties northward to the Arctic Ocean.

Maps show the Saskatchewan makes tantalizing bends northwards after leaving the Rockies, seeming to toy with the idea of spilling over the intervening ground and draining down the great, tilted plateau of the Canadian Plains towards the north instead of the east. From the air, ancient abandoned riverbeds are visible, tracing such previous attempts over the thousands of years since the last Ice Age retreated.

About forty miles northeast of Edmonton, north of the fifty-fourth parallel, the river makes its final last effort to flow north, coming within forty-eight miles of a sympathetic southerly bend of the Athabasca. Thwarted by its high banks, the river succumbs to its fate and mutters off, meandering east by south into Saskatchewan. The character of the river here, just south of the communities of Smoky Lake, Bellis, and Edwand is much like that of Edmonton, high banks with occasional outcroppings of rock. Heavily wooded, its main character is a steep slope of ochre and brown coloured glacial till, furrowed by thousands of rivulets.

In the late fall of nineteen fifty, Danny Edmunds made his way towards this last great northward sweep of the Saskatchewan. Earlier in the summer he was canoeing with a friend, Henry Smith, when he chanced upon a geological key. Henry was well accustomed to Danny's frequent stops to scrutinize exposed rocks and patiently waited by the beached canoe, while Danny landed with his rock hammer and took some samples.

The rock in question was the last outcropping before the river turned southeasterly. A mudslide obliterated most of it, but near the waterline, an area of rock protruded where the water piled up. It was obviously limestone. The interesting fact was it appeared to be tilted. Laboratory tests and scrutiny in Edmonton revealed nothing of any great importance to the sample Danny took back, except the limestone was Devonian. This, especially coupled with apparent tilting of the rock, was what interested Danny.

The Devonian reefs of ancient limestone were the classic reservoirs for oil reserves. Alberta was crazy on exploration ever since the nineteen forty-nine oil strike at Imperial Oil's Leduc Number One signalled a new era of prosperity. A tilt in the strata of these rocks was an added key that oil might be found. Such a tilt may well prove to be an anticline and add to the opportunity to find oil.

An anticline is the slope of stratified rock downwards from both sides of a crest. Initially, limestone strata are formed horizontally from the skeletons of billions of sub-sea creatures that fall to the seabed. Layer upon layer of skeletons and silt accumulate into reefs, the weight compressing the calcium remains into rock strata. Through millions of years, the seabed becomes land and the death and decomposition of flaura and fauna atop the rock forms the oil. By some geological means, the layers of rock are then forced upwards to form a crest. This can often be accomplished by an expansion of salt deposits below the formations and is known as a salt dome. Once the dome is formed, oil seeps downhill along the strata and becomes trapped in porous sub-layers of different rock and pockets that were originally reefs millions of years before. It is these subterranean Devonian limestone reefs that became the mother lode of Alberta oil well drilling.

Danny had decided to test his hunch of a possible anticline near the river bend. Now, he drove east along a minor road with a long plume of dust rising behind the wheels of his Ford half-ton truck. It was a dry, cool afternoon. The sun was high in a blue sky that seemed to reach forever. Crops were ripened in the fields. In some places, tardy farmers made huge dust clouds cutting and combining their harvests. Wheat stubble stretched out from the very roadside as far as the eye could see, interspersed by blocks of trees, where poorer land had not yet yielded to a determined settler.

Joe Cardinal sat quietly beside Danny, taking in the scenery while chain-smoking. Joe was a Cree Indian with a strong back and, conveniently, little knowledge of what Danny was up to. He liked to work for a few months each year and then vanish the rest of the time into the bush somewhere west of Rocky Mountain House. That's where he had trap lines and a family socked away.

They turned north at a weather-beaten sign, skidding in the uneven ruts of the new road that seemed to contain no gravel at all. More trees clustered around their path. It looked like they were headed into bush country. The place Danny was looking for was on the south side of the river and about a half mile from the riverbank. He had checked out the ownership of the sections of land around the area and made a careful list of them in a notebook.

The first person he needed to see was Josef Goszynwycki. He owned the property on the corner of the riverbend. The land suddenly dropped away, shelving down where the river had at some time altered its course northward and then moved on again, creating a wide step in the land. A break in the poplars and scrubby spruce indicated a driveway. He slowed down. The dust plume caught up to them, like some elastic shadow, drifting over them with its nostril-twitching dryness.

In the back of the truck, Danny had some rudimentary instruments to investigate his hunch about the anticline, but he drove here without prior notice, since Mr. Goszynwycki had no telephone. They reached the farm a short way down the rutted track. It was a ramshackle collection of weathered boards and reflected decades of dawn to dusk toil. A shaggy dog of indeterminate breed announced their arrival, careful to stay his distance from strangers. A gnarled man with grey hair appeared on the stoop of the house. He wore railway engineer coveralls that were stained and torn in a dozen places. He stood motionless, not unfriendly, but wary of infrequent company.

"Mr. Goszynwycki?"

"Yeah. You fellas from the bank?"

"No."

"Then I guess I won't be needing this." From behind his back, the farmer produced a single barrel shotgun and laid it against the wall. "Coffee's on. I'm just having a break."

The oblique reference to tough times was reflected inside the house. It was dilapidated and well used although clean as a new pin. A bulky woman wearing an apron over a cotton dress with faded flower print poured coffee for them without so much as a greeting. Danny recognized the style as one from his childhood. The woman knew her place and immediately retreated to let the men folk talk.

They started out with the inconsequentials of the weather, the government, and the economy. It was obvious to Danny from the start that he could probably buy any cooperation he needed, but he was canny enough to realize he could not insult the man's pride. There came a lull.

"Mr. Goszynwycki, Joe and I have come out here to do some tests, which I would like to seek your permission to do."

"You government men?" The question was shot like an accusation. Goszynwycki leaned back sharply as if he had been suddenly confronted by an aroused rattlesnake.

"No, no, I am a geologist, and Joe is my helper. I was canoeing down the river a few months ago and saw some rock formations I was interested in. In order to check them out, I need your permission to spend a day or so on your land setting up some instruments. I would be happy to pay you something for access." Danny thought he saw an opener to offer to hire the farmer, but his second thought was if he told friends what he was doing, word might get to the wrong ears. It was better he maintain confidentiality. Despite the old-country male dominance obvious in the place, the old man's eyes slid around to his wife, working in the kitchen.

He spoke in Polish and after a moment, she replied. "Dwardzies cia dolarow za dzien i moga spac w stodole..."

"Would twenty dollars a day be okay and you could use the barn to sleep?"

Danny smiled and offered his hand. Two days of humping the heavy equipment through the bush was now his to endure. He just hoped he could keep the gravity pattern constant.

****

Calgary.

When David Williams broke the news to his father, his bags were already packed and loaded in his car. He would drive up to Edmonton and work for the Edmunds organization. Recognizing his talent, Tom Edmunds offered him a job. With total detachment, David had analysed what the job would bring and what he wanted of life. The two meshed. They had danced around each other, both inexplicably anxious to collaborate, their relationship tenuous because of Tom and John's history.

He knew the news would devastate his father, but it had to be done. He discounted the fact of his birth. As he had told his mother, he always felt there was some indefinable distance between him and his father. Both John Williams and Tom Edmunds might never know the truth. Better that way, perhaps. At the words, John Williams sat, stunned in his seat. His colour deepened and his fists clenched.

"You would betray me by working for that rotten, profit-grubbing bastard?" He lost track of words. The rage caught him. He leapt to his feet and confronted David. His arm swung and an open-handed slap took his son across the cheek. Jeanne screamed and rushed to his side to restrain him, but it was over. "Get out!" The words were softly final, a bitter residue of defeat.

David remained stationary and made no reaction to the assault. His mother looked at him, guilt and sorrow flavouring her tears. She shook her head imperceptibly, and he took the cue to leave. Behind him, John Williams broke down and cried disconsolately. He had lost so much to Edmunds. Now he lost more on a personal basis. He aged visibly inside his wife's sympathetic arms. Both of his children had walked away from him and he could not fathom why. He vowed never to speak to his son ever again.

****

Sylvie de Fonce-Pelligard.

Roland de Fonce-Pelligard's wartime service to France served him well after the German defeat. The high connections he shrewdly forged and the credit he fostered for himself helped insert him in high position in the French government. Roland was too shrewd to involve himself in politics. In the decade that followed the war, with its volatile environment of short-term governments, it proved him right. He sought and was given a fairly high position in the French Foreign Service at the Quai d'Orsay. His duties included liaison with the Deuxième Bureau that handled   security matters. Through those years, in the power struggles for control of France, he was privy to a great many sensitive secrets. This made him a powerful man.

Because they kept in close touch, Beth was invited to his nineteen fifty-two wedding to Sylvie Daigneault. It was held in an ancient church with the bride in white, surrounded by the attendant splendour of medieval pomp. Roland's tall figure towered over the group at the altar, his fine head of golden hair shining like an aura in a shaft of leaded-window light. Beth could not help but see him as she always fantasized, like some Middle-Ages troubadour, stately and chivalrous. And chivalrous he had been, never once mentioning their sexual encounter, never once making any other advance toward her. Indeed, he was a devoted and faithful friend.

He had tried to help her seek news of René, but nothing had come of it. It was a blank wall. Despite his reserve with Beth, Roland was as hedonistic as ever, and in this regard, Sylvie outdid him. It is perhaps typical that people bearing great secrets take risks of compromise in their habits. The sexual peregrinations of Roland and Sylvie, even after their marriage, would have been cause for social ostracizing and even blackmail, were it not for the closed circles they moved in.

In short, they slept with whomever they liked, whenever they liked, and neither of them seemed to care or display jealousy. They were happy together, childless and carefree. Between them, their pillow talk with others led them into new secrets. These in themselves were of little interest to Sylvie, but she liked to help Roland. Roland was not above a little arm-twisting. His career flourished further as a result.

Sylvie was a tiny, slim woman with little for breasts and pale white skin. She habitually wore her black hair short and straight, emphasizing her pixie-like appearance. At a time when many women tried to emulate Edith Piaff, Sylvie was way ahead. Her urchin looks were more a model for Piaff than the other way around. She had a straight nose, high cheekbones, small mouth, and dark, dark eyes that could smoulder. Although she was not beautiful by a model's standards, she mesmerized men and gobbled them up voraciously. Once ensnared in Sylvie's sexual web, they became clay, doting on her and lavishing her with presents. Aside from an occasional peccadillo and helping Roland, Sylvie did not use her power for personal gain. She was, perhaps, that perfect gift to men, a woman who loved sex.

Her admirers were legion. Only those who displayed jealousy were discarded out of hand. It was astonishing to Beth, and abhorred by other women, how she did it. One night, years later, passing time at the weekend estate the de Fonce-Pelligards kept out near Versailles, Beth asked Sylvie how she became such a magnet.

"But I adore sex, Beth. I would have sex with you, if you liked. I live to feel the flush of blood, the slow build of passion, and then the frantic movement of bodies against mine. It is time. It is history. It is the universe, the stars. Would you *like* to have sex with me?"

"Well, I like sex, but er...I'm really not sure I want it with another woman."

"Ah, but women can be the best lovers for women. They *know* just what to do and how to do it. Some men are just so ignorant!"

"Yes, but..."

"Never mind, the offer is there if you ever want. I know about you and Roland." The remark was made quickly, taking Beth off guard. "It's all right, Beth." Sylvie's palm came up to still her. "I am not put out by it. It happened so long ago, and as you know, Roland and I go our separate ways freely when it comes to our sex lives. Still, you would be the only woman I could ever be jealous of when it came to Roland." Sylvie smiled and laid a hand on Beth's arm.

The admission came as a total surprise to Beth. "But how on earth did you ever talk of this?"

"Ah, he loves you dearly, Beth. He would give his life for you. He always regretted being a pig on that day and has placed you on a pedestal from which you would need a parachute to get down. Just never use the poor dear for anything but friendship; he would probably die if you offered him sex!"

They laughed, but it came home to Beth that the power of love and sex were tools in the hands of some people, as long as they were the objects of adoration. It brought her to the question of *how* Sylvie wielded such power.

"Ah, it is true that men think with their penises. Yet they can be so sweet while trying to slide their brains into the warm, dark, and wet fantasy they are seeking. Afterwards, some try to be kind and rewarding, often from latent guilt, but to have the real power over them, we women have to know how to give them everything and then even go beyond their imaginations. I have no shame. I will do anything a man...or men..." she chuckled, "want."

"You mean you…"

"*Mais certainment, Cherie*! I have had up to three men working on me at the same time, and there was still too much of me for all of them!"

"But what makes them want to keep coming back?"

"Many things. There is allure, a sense of danger. There is risk and abandonment. No wife would consent to some of the things I've done with her husband. If you want *practical* advice, after he has experienced *le petit mort,* as they say, send him to heaven! He will never forget it. He may only have devotion to give, but there is more if you wish it."

That advice was a revelation of a new path for Beth. Day by day, the possibility of René's return grew dimmer. She had established discreet but fairly regular liaisons with men the past year or so. An elderly businessman was presently courting her, pressing for marriage. He was rich, and Beth now knew how she could captivate him. He had already taken liberties with her in his chauffeured car. She knew the sexual urges he displayed were beyond his abilities to perform. Still, he was vulnerable to her needs.

The talk with Sylvie opened her eyes to certain facts in life. She was rich but wanted to be richer. Rich elderly men would plead for her hand in marriage. She could easily dazzle them with her sexual prowess, while taking her satisfaction elsewhere with abler, younger men. So it was that she married seventy-year old Francois Laboiret, who owned three hotels and several apartment blocks in Paris. The old man was kind to her and genuinely liked David, whom he doted on. He did a good job of being a husband and father. The lust displayed by his young wife on their honeymoon in Cannes surprised and thrilled him. While he admitted inwardly that he was not quite up to it, outwardly, he laboured valorously to fulfil his duties.

In two years, he was dead. Beth and David, now twelve years old, lived on in the private suite of the Hôtel Paginard, four blocks from the Louvre. Not only had their estate grown, so had the circle of acquaintances fostered by Laboiret increased Beth's influence. At the age of thirty-three, she was now a millionairess several times over.

Two years later, she took another older husband, Jean-Pierre Touillisant. He had extensive dealings in French Africa and the Far East. There were legal tangles with his surviving relatives after his death five years later. Old Langret was dead but her new lawyer from the firm, Tissard, made short work of them, armed with a will. Beth's fortune increased again. Shrewdly, knowing little of the overseas trade, she was magnanimous in her victory and cut in Jean-Pierre's son, Louis, for a quarter of the profits. An expert in his business, Louis did famously. Beth only had to attend directors' meetings to keep in touch with her profits.

******

Edmunds Building.

The silence stretched out in Tom Edmunds' office. Across from him, Danny stared at his father. He was determined not to get upset at this juncture. All his life, he and his father fought where they might co-operate, criticized where they might have praised. Some similarity in their make-up had abraded their relationship. Some deep-rooted stubbornness caused neither to yield.

Now he seethed with anger. After all the arguments he mustered, all the evidence and enthusiasm, his father refused to invest in the well he wanted to drill. Only miles away, Leduc, Devon, and Redwater were punching wells and pumping oil, and here, his father stubbornly refused to reap the reward of a sure thing.

"Well, I guess I had better go and find my financing elsewhere." The pause dragged on. Danny hauled himself to his feet and left the office. No sooner had he left, Tom was on the phone.

"Alex? Drop everything! I need to see if I can purchase a piece of land. I'm not sure of its legal description, but you should be able to find its location. What? No! This is *extremely* important. Danny thinks he has found a new oilfield. I want to see if we can get control of the land. What! You're kidding! When did *that* come into effect? In the thirties? You must be joking! At all events, find the legal description. Yes, bye!"

Tom had no reason to note that in the nineteen thirties, the provincial government passed legislation decreeing every mineral beneath the ground as belonging to His Majesty. Only the people who owned the land prior to the Act had ownership over the mineral rights on their properties.

"Alex!" He was on the phone again like a plummeting hawk. "Get me a list of all the properties we bought prior to that Minerals Act. We could be sitting on a goldmine! Yeah, I should have known you would already be on to it. How many, roughly? Very well, bring them around tonight."

It was a Thursday, and by midnight, they plotted all the properties on a map. Cumulatively between them, they owned almost ten thousand acres that qualified under the grandfather clause of the Minerals Rights Act. Many of the properties were remote and covered with timber. Tom bought them cheap in order to supply the lumber mill. Some were nearer to Edmonton. These properties could potentially be oil-rich.

Alex defined the property Danny was interested in and discovered Josef Goszynwycki owned it. Under the Act, only Goszynwycki could claim the minerals beneath the land as his own. The obvious tactic was to offer him a great deal of money in a partnership, but the terms of the Act prevented this. The only way they could get his co-operation was if he was paid a right-of-access to carry out the exploration. The province would only lease out exploration rights to licensed companies.

And now, Tom discovered, the Alberta oil rush was the genuine article. Major companies were buying up land rights by the thousands of acres. Smaller investors were in on the act too, subleasing potentially hot land they themselves had leased to a higher bidder and making a quick profit.

He sat back and reflected on the negative influence Tim O'Hanlon had made with him regarding the oil business. The Irishman made and finally lost a fortune in the land deals surrounding the oil patch. It was the main reason why Tom evaded involvement with Danny. The stakes were high in an industry he knew little about. Now, he began to reconsider his first gut-reaction. The evidence rolled in of a determined boom, backed by solid oil finds. If the investments paid off, millions of dollars would come flooding into the economy, boosting business in all quarters. People would have more money to buy his cars. They would want homes built by his construction company. More people would flood in demanding land and services of all kinds.

Infrastructure was the key. He should provide everything people might need from cradle to grave. Lumber, concrete, gravel, entertainment, travel, furnishings, medical treatment, transportation, sports facilities, and even funeral directors – the whole gamut of human needs would break loose. Yet the main challenge was the oil. It looked like there was going to be an Edmunds Oil Company!

"David," (Tom had never called him 'Sher') "I have a very important task for you. Can you come up right away?"

"Money!" was his opener when David strode into his office and flopped in a chair. "Money is going to come flooding into Alberta in the wake of this oil boom. I want you to execute a study of how cities grow. Commission some university types if you have to. Give me a historical breakdown of how cities grow and prosper, allied with the oil business. Concentrate on the areas where careful investments have yielded good results."

David nodded. "What's the plan?"

"I want to have my finger in every pie in town when this thing really starts to roll. There will be some investments in the oil patch itself, as we are starting an oil company. However, the real spin-off will be land and infrastructure."

"I see where you're coming from. How much can I have?"

"You can have a budget of twenty thousand for now. Go to Texas and Oklahoma. Take a month. Find out how they have coped with this thing. Come back with ideas. Make it work."

As he left Tom's office, 'Sher' Williams was remembering how he had once likened himself to 'Saul on the road to Damascus.' Well, now the revelation had arrived. His strange calling to work for Tom Edmunds was finally becoming his miracle.

****

Paris.

Beth was walking along the Quai Saint Michel, looking across the Seine at the twin towers of Notre Dame when, suddenly, she felt René. He was there, beside her, tugging at her hand, the bright sun of the nineteen forty afternoon washing over them. She stopped and turned, looking off to her right, where the high, pointed tower of Saint Severin showed between two buildings.

Sometimes I left love poems! Again she heard his giggle. The hairs on her neck prickled. The stupid statue and his hiding place! She stepped out, cut across the street, and walked rapidly along Rue Saint Jaques until she reached the curved east wall of the double ambulatory. By the time she reached the entrance, she was running headlong and a church functionary clucked and murmured admonishment at her headlong, irreverent entry. She plunged to her left and then back to her right, as memory corrected her.

There! She stepped over the rope meant to keep visitors out of arms reach of the statue and plunged her hand into the gap behind the feet. There! It was there! She waved an envelope under the drop-mouthed stare of the robed man who had followed her. "He left me a message. Eight years. Oh, René."

Beth left the church and sat on a wooden bench out in the sunlight. She looked at the envelope, terrified to open it, petrified not to. Her hand shook and a cold wave of shock ran through her body. She could feel the chill run down through her diaphragm and drain down her belly and legs to her ankles. The old paper tore easily, and she removed the letter inside. It was in Rene's hand.

July 18, 1940.

My Darling Beth,

What a terrible thing I did leaving you! The fury of the Germans is terrible to see. After finally beating France, yet the revenge of the Wehrmacht is minor compared to this Nazi horror, which Germany has spawned.
I love you.

They have rounded up prominent Jews and shipped them off to camps. Mother and Rebecca disappeared before I could get back, and there is no trace of them. The Nazis are looking for me specifically, and I weep to think what they may have done to make my family betray me. They wish to "legally" take over the family holdings by capturing me. Please, oh please, Beth, use all the resources of the de Fourquet family to free France of this monster, Hitler! No matter what happens, do not give them anything, even if it means my death!
I love you.

Many loyal Frenchman, including Albert Defarge, are banding together to fight on under this oppression, but it is early days and will take some time to organize. I desperately want to join them, but I fear my prominence will not only concentrate attention on them, but also betray them through me. My one intent, now, is to get away and join you. It may be I can achieve more to free France with my wealth at a distance than to stay here, hobbled by having to hide constantly.
I love you.

It will be desperately difficult now; there are frequent spot checks for identity purposes, and it is hard to trust anyone.
I love you.

Almost by definition, if your hand ever finds this, France will be free, but I will not be with you to celebrate. But know I will always love you. So, you should wish me "bon chance." I die a little each moment I am away from you.

I love you.

Your loving husband,
René

The church grounds blurred beyond her tears. She recognized his writing, but it all came home to her with the name, 'Albert Defarge.' Her jewellery case contained a tattered letter. *If you ever receive a message from Albert Defarge or mentioning that name, it will be genuinely from me.*

****

East of Edmonton.

Recognizing his father's predatory nature, Danny Edmunds had contacted Beth in France and offered her a partnership in the well. He was determined to keep what autonomy he could. The only way was to keep Tom Edmunds out. After checking with her experts in the matter, Beth came through with one hundred thousand dollars. They drew up partnership papers for the endeavour.

Now, Danny hung over the mud separator and watched the slow ooze of the drilling mud across the tank to the pump inlet. His left hand supported a small shovel resting on the side of the tank. In the shovel lay a pile of drill bit cuttings, scooped from the shaker tray. The pile of cuttings was furrowed where his fingers had sorted through them, looking for clues to their character, looking for that initial show of hydrocarbon deposits that would tell him the well might actually be profitable. The stress of financing, managing and actually being here was exhausting him.

These small fragments of substratum, gouged out by the drill bit, took about half an hour to make their way to the top of the hole, carried by the drilling mud. They were through glacial till again, almost three thousand feet down and into a Devonian limestone formation. Sometime, today or tomorrow, they would penetrate the typical pay level of the formation. Then, the stress level would rise. He ached to see the first cuttings to show a sandstone layer, which would indicate porosity sufficient to contain oil or gas. Each passing hour would bring a new expectation. He felt like a gambler watching a roulette wheel that wouldn't stop and reveal the moment of truth. Sighing, he tipped the contents of the shovel onto the growing heap of geological evidence by his feet. It bespoke of the ground far beneath his feet.

He looked up and around at the clear blue sky. The drilling derrick rose like a phallic symbol above the surrounding trees. The normally quiet mutter of its diesel engines crescendoed, as a string of drill stem was withdrawn from the hole. Truckloads of gravel and sand had been dumped, but the surrounding area was like a quagmire after the recent rains. Pipe and equipment sat on logs that were largely sunk into the ooze. Nearby trailers were splattered and splashed with mud. A half-ton truck sat mired to the axles. Only the weight and dogged gears of a water truck propelled it towards the rig.

The stack of drill pipe in the fingerboards beside the rig, secured at the monkey-board, grew as they pulled pipe to change drill bits. How often Danny remembered these trips in and out of the hole when he performed the crunching hard work on the drilling platform under the watchful and critical eye of Smiley Evernden. In another hour, they would be able to put a fresh bit on the string and run back down the hole.

The next shift could be critical if they finally penetrated the expected oil-bearing zones. Danny reminded himself to check with the mud man that there was a plentiful quantity of the needed materials to control any kicks that might happen when they got down to that depth. It was always prudent to have a thicker and denser mud mixed and ready to pump downhole to control any untoward pressure. Half a mile down, the average pressure in the hole was over three hundred pounds per square inch. Penetration of a layer with high hydrostatic pressure could negatively affect the fine balance between well pressure and mud pressure. If that hydrostatic pressure ever got loose, they would have a serious problem, maybe even a blowout. As a proper precaution, they needed a barite slug mix ready to go, to increase the mud weight.

Drilling was a dirty, hard, and often gruelling business, but it had been mostly routine, so far. The rig was an old Hammond and Eaves type, leased from a company that fell on hard financial times. It was trucked from Texas seven years prior and showed its age. Still, the price was as good as Danny could get. The crew was reasonably experienced and the budget, so far, survived his concerns. Now that they were getting down to the typical drill depth of Devonian deposits in the Edmonton area, he was living on the drilling platform.

Slowly, he climbed the steel steps and looked into the mud man's cubicle. Charlie Krebbs was not there, probably on a coffee break. A quick look at the logs showed Danny that Krebbs was not on top of the job. The drilling fluid was still the thinner type circulated for normal drilling rates. The Marsh Funnel readings that defined the mud density were too light. There was no denser material batched up. Danny picked up the phone and cranked the handle to reach the cook-shack.

"Krebbs there?"

A delay. "Hello."

"Krebbs, how come there is no barite ready to go in case we need it?"

"What, at this depth?"

"At any depth!"

"Swabbing pressure and recovery rates were all right ten minutes ago!" Krebbs was cross. He hated being disturbed.

"Well, the guys only have about three strings left to pull. I want some twenty ppg mud readied along with a barite slug before they finish. Better get on it!"

Krebbs hung up on him. Angry now, Danny wrote a notation in the mud log concerning the situation. Krebbs would be really pissed off but to hell with him. It was Danny's hole. Danny's cheque was paying his wages.

Sighing again, Danny shifted his weight in his muddy rubber boots and moved on to the driller's shack. Fred Kaminski was at his station, looking out. His crew chained another length of five and a half inch drill pipe and unthreaded it from the string in the hole. Two of them held onto the pipe with a length of chain, while the derrickman, up on the monkey-board swung the lifting block sideways from the rig's vertical axis.

The crew lowered the butt end of the triple string of thirty-foot long drill stem, alongside its brethren that now numbered seventeen. High above them, the monkey-board man secured the vertically stacked string to the bundle in the fingerboards and disconnected the hoisting block. Disconnecting the clutch, one of the hands let the heavy block descend, dragging the hoisting cable behind it. He braked it deftly just above the

Kelly platform. Three men stepped in to secure it to the next string to be pulled. Into the threaded end of the drill pipe protruding from the floor, they deftly spun a plug, which was swabbed with dope to prevent the threads from binding. It had a large steel loop on top. To this, they would attach the crown block. When this next length was raised out of the hole, they would clamp on to the top of the string below, so it could not fall down the hole and then they would spin off the joint between them.

While they hoisted and stacked the next string, the last two remaining would hang suspended from the rotary platform, clamped at the top by the powerful tongs at the Kelly platform. The drill bit was hanging over a twentyeight hundred-foot plunge to the bottom of the hole. Only another three lengths and they would be able to change the blunted bit with a fresh one. That was their reason for tripping out of the hole on this occasion.

While the drill stem was suspended inside the hole, there was not an empty space between it and the bottom. The whole bore was filled with drilling mud. Drilling mud had several important purposes and was specially formulated. Primarily, it provided weight to help seal in the tremendous subterranean pressures. Augmented by compressed gas, these pressures were capable of throwing tons of steel out of the hole like peas from a peashooter. Then, anything in the hole: gas, oil, water, or mud would blow out like an express train. In order to seal these pressures from escaping, the weight of the mud, pumped under pressure into the hole, was critical in this regard. It was the reason Danny was annoyed with Krebbs. The mud also acted as a lubricant, pumped down inside the hollow drill stem pipe. It prevented the drill bit from overheating and becoming blunted. The mud was then allowed to come to the surface, via the annulus, carrying tiny chips of rock that the drill bit had gouged out.

The rock chips were screened out. The mud passed through large settling tanks before being recirculated. Geologists, like Danny, haunted the screens. This was where they were able to study and analyse the strata types beneath the ground as the bit penetrated them and the mud brought them up for observation.

Circulation was a vital part of the mud's role. If the rig lost circulation, underground pressure would begin to rule and bad things could happen. Circulation was usually lost through fissures in the rock, where the mud would leak away into the formation instead of returning to the surface. This was fairly common in limestone, which was often fractured or eroded. At times when circulation was lost, cement and other materials would be pumped down the hole in an attempt to seal it off. Drillers were known to pump anything they could lay their hands on, including sawdust, to clog up fissures and get circulation back.

All the time the density and weight of the withdrawing pipe was being lost in the hole, Kaminski was compensating by turning up the pressure of the mud. The pumps strained to maintain the pressure. When the business end of the pipe was withdrawn, only mud and the blowout preventer would oppose the forces below. The blowout preventer was an enormous type of valve. It allowed access to the hole for the drill pipe with separate access for the mud circulation and rams. The hydraulically actuated rams were like doors, which could be inserted to seal off the well in an emergency. It was attached to the thirty-inch diameter steel pipe, called a surface casing, which led into the well from ground level. The casing, a hundred feet long, was sunk into the rock and cemented to it.

Danny looked out for a minute at the mud-splattered men on the platform. They wore rubber boots and hats and stout coveralls. Their leather-gloved hands moved surely around slippery tons of moving steel, which could crush them in an instant of carelessness. They were thoroughly grimy and wet from the sprays of mud and water. He thought again of Smiley and how he had learned this trade of a roughneck under that old taskmaster.

Kaminski, a man of few words and much chewing baccy, grunted with an inflection of concern and pointed to the pressure gauge beside his station. The outlet pressure of the mud was falling. They had a loss of circulation somewhere. He grabbed the phone beside him and punched the intercom for the mud man. "Hey, Krebbs, I need some more weight. Got any of that bentonite?" He listened briefly. "All right, soon as you can!"

He hung up the phone and cranked open the mud pumps a little more. Still, the pressure showed a faint decline. Suddenly, there was a bump from below them and steel decking jumped slightly before clanging back into place. Far beneath them, a bubble of gas was moving up the hole, accelerating, as the squeeze of great depth forced it upwards.

"Stop the pull!" Danny issued the order urgently and seized the controls himself. Kaminski leapt to the door and yelled at the crew to stop breaking the pipe. They had a length of drill pipe tight in the jaws of the tongs and were preparing to unscrew it and sling it to the side of the rig with the rest.

There was a deep rumble beneath them, like the slow belch of a giant. "Looks like an induced kick, Fred!" Madly, Danny upped the mud pumps to their maximum output, but they still would not hold the bump in the well below them. The rig derrick suddenly sang as a massive pressure outbreak turned loose below them. The drill stem, like a giant piston, strained against the grip of the Kelly tongs and stretched the steel derrick by an inch. A high-pitched whine of tensile torture commenced. It was joined by another scream of torment as the drill stem was forced between the Kelly jaws, smoke pouring off it, the frictional heat burning off lubricants and melting the steel.

"She's gonna go!" Kaminsky roared the words and leaped to the Klaxon to warn the crew. The hoarse, urgent bursts of the emergency alarm swamped the site, almost an unnecessary adjunct to the alarming sounds coming from the bowels of the earth. Echoey hiccups of sound were coming from all around. Tortured metal approached its tensile limits. A burst of mud exited the rotary platform. Such was the force behind it that it squirted forty feet into the air before twisting like a demented thing and smashing in the window of the drilling shack.

"Choke it, Fred, choke it!" Frantically, the driller leapt to the lever that controlled a lateral valve on the blowout preventer, opening an exit for the spray of gas and mud to exit. Danny was hoping to reduce the initial pressure and get some heavier mud in the hole.

"Nothing, Danny. Goddamned thing don't work! No hydraulic power!"

"Blowout preventer?"

"No-go! Hydraulics are gone!"

Horrified, Danny stared at the driller. "Get into the hell hole and crank the manual. That bloody Krebbs. I'll have his balls for not being ready for this! Sonofabitch didn't have any barite mixed, and we won't have any kill rate to control this!"

Kaminski gave him a look of wild disbelief and then fled to the stairs. Danny knew what was happening. Loss of circulation was bad enough at the best of times, but loss when you were tripping out of the hole was disastrous if the well kicked. And this one had. With the sudden loss of mud pressure, with no mud weight to throw down the hole, he was going to have to rely on blowing off the excess pressure and then sealing it in with the blowout preventer. The speed with which it was happening was unusual though.

The roughnecks raced down the stairs from the decking to the ground and ran like hares. High above them, the derrickman on the monkey-board swung around to hitch his lifeline onto his escape line, the 'Geronimo.' It would be a terrifying slide down to the ground on the line secured at about forty-five degrees, but a better chance than staying. As he swung around, he kicked a couple of tools, including a two-foot long monkey wrench over the edge of the platform. They fell awkwardly, bouncing off the lattice girders of the derrick, creating sparks as they went.

With a screaming tear, the drill pipe shifted, once, twice, and then let go. Mud shot from the open hole, evacuating at tremendous speed and bubbled with gouts of gas. The wrench fell right into such a bubble, sparking off a girder as it went, and in a moment, the gas was ignited. The last two strings of pipe went through the top of the rig like a runaway piston, tearing out the top works and creating enough friction and sparks to ignite further pockets of gas.

There were a series of "whoomps" as flammable gas ignited. The whole derrick was a fireball in seconds. A sound, like a hundred runaway steam trains now dominated everything. The ground shook. Mud was blowing almost two hundred feet in the air, drenching everything around it, except the fire. And then the oil came.

It exited with a mighty cough, momentarily cutting off the gas that fuelled the flames, but then, it too ignited. A shock wave of superheated air blasted over the site. Beneath the water truck, a hundred feet away, half submerged in mud, Danny felt the clothes on his back begin to smoulder. Conscious of the fuel tank on the vehicle, he crawled as swiftly as he could through the mud to the rear of the truck. Rolling over to coat himself well with insulating mud, he clambered to his feet and ran as fast as he could.

Normally, when a well 'comes in,' it is stem tested. A throttled pipe from the blowout preventer is led to a flare pit, and the escaping gas or oil is ignited. By measuring the pressure at the beginning and at the end of the test over a lengthy period, an estimate of the reserves of the well can be made. The well, pre-named Edmunds de Fourquet et al Number One blew for weeks before it was capped, and the pressure never seemed to let up.

Barely had the calls for help been made when other problems began to arise. Within hours, the press was on the scene. This was the biggest blowout in Edmonton's new oil patch experience. The newspapers, radio, and movie camera teams had a field day. They were not only a public relations nightmare, but they plain got in the way, pressing in dangerously close, demanding interviews and cluttering up the area, making access poor for heavy vehicles.

Government officials were close behind, making the point that Danny and his business associates were responsible to 'put the fire out and clean up the mess.' The cost would be enormous. A team from Oklahoma would have to be flown up to extinguish the blaze and re-cap the well. For two bits, Danny would have walked away, but something in the sight of that well fired up his resistance and awoke in him a feeling as strong as the power of love. Undeniably, the flow showed a rich well that would more than compensate for the expense.

Kaminiski was in hospital suffering from burns. He was unable to close off the well in time, but being down below the jet of flame and smoke, protected by the draw works, he managed to crawl away and live to tell the tale.

The thick black smoke and the red tongues of flame were visible for miles around. Passenger aircraft remarked about it from far away. What was even more awesome was to be up close and hear that ear-crushing roar of high pressure gas escaping and feel the ground tremble and shake beneath your feet. It was nature in the raw.

The bank didn't want to know. They were neophytes to the oil industry, and to them, a blowout was an indication of a business that was failing, rather than a spectacular demonstration of success. They only saw the down side of the ledger and refused to make any further loans. Desperately, Danny phoned around but could find little encouragement. He got himself into this predicament and the message was he had to get himself out.

The vultures gathered. Two major oil companies called and offered to take over management of the well for an eighty percent share. 'Northern Alberta Petroleum Associates' or NAPA, a group of merchant investors, joined them looking for easy and quick profits. They obviously had inside information and offered to take only a seventy percent share. Their greedy interest only told Danny one thing; he had a winner on his hands.

The Oklahoma people wanted cash, a down payment, transportation pre-paid, and ready money to lay their hands on necessary equipment upon arrival. They did not take shares in oil wells; they were too risky. Danny could still hear the 'y'all' belly laugh, as the man hung up laughing at his own joke. He was accommodating and neighbourly enough, he just wanted guaranteed payment.

In desperation, Danny turned to Beth. He found her in Bordeaux after running up a fifty-dollar phone bill.

"How delightful. I saw this in a movie not long ago. Big, hulking men fighting somewhere in the States, being rained on by black oil. Some big movie star. Winning against all odds. Are you getting any movie footage, Danny?" The line was poor and he could only hear her half the time.

"Beth! This is serious! We could lose the whole thing. I'm sorry, but your investment could be at risk here. Can you let me have more money?"

"How much?" The delay on the line was incredible. It was difficult to talk in the usual cadence.

"At least two hundred thousand – for starters!" The pause was long, and he thought the line was dead, except for the hiss and pop of static. "Beth?"

"Yeah, still here. I'm thinking. Danny are you *absolutely sure?*" The question came out of the headset suddenly clear like the ether had underlined its importance.

"Yes! If you mean sure about the well, yes, yes, yes! It has been burning like an inferno for two days now and might burn that way forever. We have to cap it and then it will be profitable. Imperial and Shell and others have tried to buy me out, so it must be attractive. Beth, the Imperial Leduc well has been pumping at a rate of three hundred barrels of oil per day. This well has to be at least as big, so even at only half that rate, with oil at two dollars fifty-three U.S., it comes to…"

"About four hundred dollars per day." Like her father, Beth was quick with numbers.

"Yeah, that's, hmm, one hundred and forty thousand dollars, plus, per year. And we still have step-out drilling to increase production."

"So why not take the money offer and run?"

"Because I'm madly in love, Beth. Do you remember when I fell in love with the mountains on that holiday? Well this is ten times as strong. This is the mother lode. Besides, this is *huge money*, Beth.

Do you know what the odds are of drilling a producing well, this big, first try?"

"It is only money if you can ship the oil, Danny." She was way ahead of him. "Who will be doing the refining, and what will they pay for the stock?"

"Details, details, Beth. Even at a few pennies per barrel, your investment will be returned with interest. We cannot yet evaluate the yield on this well, but the experts are saying it is big. The locked-in value of the reserves will give us collateral with the banks to drill step-out holes and properly test the field."

There was another long pause on the line. "I will invest one hundred and fifty thousand dollars more in exchange for *preferred* shares at the common rate. Also, I want another seat on the board of directors. If you need more money, there will be further terms."

"Beth! This is your own brother!"

"Sorry, little brother. This is business and big money at risk. If it were anyone *but* my own brother, I wouldn't entertain it, certainly not at the end of a telephone! Come to think of it, send me a telegram immediately confirming those terms."

"All right, all right, but you sound like Dad!"

"Is he in on this?" It was an exclamation as much as a question.

"No, at least not yet. But I don't know if I can keep him out, now."

"Well try!"

"What about the money?"

"I'll have my lawyer wire it over to Uncle Alex. Get yours to make up an agreement. No agreement, no money. Talk to Uncle Alex."

"You *are* your father's daughter!" He broke the connection and stared out of the window. Five miles away, a light wind took a large smudge of black smoke and spread it out towards Saskatchewan. Money on the wind! The sooner it was tamed, the sooner the money would be his – theirs. Sighing, he reached for the phone.

When the Oklahomans or 'Okies' arrived, they took residence in Danny's trailer, now towed a quarter mile away from the raging inferno of the rig site. The derrick crashed down in the first hour after the blowout, its lower extremities melted until it could not support the upper weight. Now, it lay crumpled and twisted beside the hole.

With an exaggerated casualness emphasized by their drawls, Jed Ferguson and his two comrades quickly planned their attack on the runaway. Ferguson was a tiny slip of a man, wiry and quick, with a face like old shoe leather. His young helpers, Tom Alworthy and Jim McIlthwaite were enormous, broad-shouldered men with huge hands. They could drive bulldozers with the tender touch of a child's mother.

Fortunately, the blowout preventer was still intact. Closing it was the main road to success. Wearing huge white flame-resistant suits and breathing apparatus, they were able to get close enough to estimate its viability. They would attach dynamite to strategic parts of the fallen derrick to break it up and then haul it off out of the way. Water hoses would be played on the draw works and other areas both to cool the man who would go in to crank the manual blowout preventer and to douse possible hot spots, which might cause re-ignition once the flame was extinguished. Before the man ventured in, a charge would be set off in the fire-stream. The momentary vacuum would deprive the flame of oxygen and put out the blaze.

To the disappointment of the movie camera crews present, the dousing of the flame and the subsequent shut-in of the well went in textbook style. The well fire made national news at every movie theatre across the nation, but the fight to control it was too mundane and drew little but terse announcement by way of attention.

Danny was delighted to wave Jed Ferguson and his gang off only a day later after a mind-cracking night of hard liquor to celebrate their success. His hangover barely faded before he went after the owners of the drilling rig. Survey of the wreckage revealed the engine driving the primary hydraulic pump failed due to a broken crankshaft, robbing them of the ability to quickly shut-in the well from the driller's shack. Evidence showed the engine was reported questionable numerous times, and shoddy maintenance had left it unreliable. It had chosen the worst possible time to fail.

Krebbs, the mud man, was also an employee of the drilling company, Beatton Brothers Drilling and Mud Inc., known to its employees as 'Beaten, Buggered, and Damned Inc.' Beaten, Buggered, and Damned they were by the time several disgruntled employees and a police seizure of their records finished revealing the facts. In September, their reports carefully marshalled, Alex McFarlane and Danny paid a visit to the corporate offices of the Beatton Brothers.

Alex was implacable, making the strongest case for a lawsuit of immense proportions. In view of the incompetence of its employees, the disregard with which it had leased ill-repaired equipment that was responsible for unleashing a catastrophe of immense proportions, costing his clients several hundred thousand dollars, he proposed to pay Beatton Brothers not a dime while suing them for five million dollars.

Their lawyer was present, but aside from a brief rally to apportion some of the blame to Danny, he had little to stand on. Bolstered by the knowledge the Beattons were deep in debt, Alex went for the kill. After a half hour, the Beattons went into a huddle and made a counter offer. They were prepared to surrender their entire assets to Edmunds' Drilling Inc., provided their debts were also covered, in exchange for a statement of non-liability. They also asked for fifty thousand dollars 'get lost' money, which was rapidly bargained down by half.

The agreement was drawn up and signed immediately. Danny left the yard owning a drilling company, two rigs, and about sixty employees. His cost was about three hundred and fifty thousand plus the two hundred thousand to Jed Ferguson. He made immediate plans for step-out drilling to prove the oilfield he found.

****

Edmunds Drilling Inc. had yielded three producing oilfields east of Redwater. At least two take-over bids for the company were thwarted, mainly by the family influence. It had proven impossible to keep Tom Edmunds out of the picture when he saw the opportunity. Danny was in a quandary. He did not want to sell the company but the temptation to take the money was immense. He was also not well versed with raising money through shares and the small issue that he offered was gobbled up by Tom. Badgered now by his shareholders, his ownership position was severely threatened.

Danny finally met Tom at his office with Beth on the telephone from France. "I have land with mineral rights. I have money. I can raise more money. I want financial control of what I see will be an oil company. You are backed into a corner where I can call a shareholders' meeting and take over your company. I am willing to place Edmunds' Drilling into the Edmunds Enterprises consortium. I am willing to allow you, with your expertise, to continue to explore and drill for oil and finance your efforts. This seems to be your main desire, so why deal with the financial headaches? Should you choose not to accept these terms, I will ally myself with another drilling company and achieve the same end. You, in turn, will wither without the financial backing I can give."

Miserable, Danny agreed. Beth insisted on keeping her share. Both of them took Edmunds Enterprises stock in exchange for the Edmunds

Drilling shares. Thus Edmunds Oil was born with Danny as Vice-President of Exploration. With their enormous block of shares, Tom, Danny, and Beth were able to defeat any kind of motion in the boardroom. Alex McFarlane, like a grey eminence, held proxy rights for over ten percent of the shares through a network of contacts. They never used his block of votes, and instead, kept them as a secret weapon for the time they were really needed.

Four more finds eastward towards the Saskatchewan border promised good results. With Tom's patent formula for flow-through involvement, he pushed to build his own refinery, followed by the establishment of a network of gasoline filling stations. The construction industry was gearing up for massive residential additions. City council granted new commercial building applications. The car dealership was healthy, and the trucking company also braced for increased business, much of it oilfield -related. The research that 'Sher' had conducted in the United States paid off. Independent oil companies could thrive if they carefully handled their share ownership and refused to sell to the majors.

Capital investment money was a problem, but they carefully floated share issues in their own selected businesses and cross-funded the project. The banks were interested; they had done their homework too. Everything was mortgaged to the hilt, including the house on Ada Boulevard. The flow of money from oil sales became a steady beat. The Chinese from Vancouver were always interested in injecting capital. Through their help, Edmunds Enterprises' interest in trucking, car sales, and construction businesses, plus oil drilling, production, and marketing remained inviolate to outside interference.

****

Eastern Poland.

Vladimir Ashkimovich Keremov paid great attention to his duties as a political commissar. He wielded considerable influence in the area of his responsibility and had also learned to steer the safest political path by the most brutal methods. In nineteen forty three, attached to a unit of the Twenty-fifth Guards Brigade that was overrun by a German SS Motorized Regiment, he had known the quick fate assigned to Soviet political officers. German soldiers had orders to shoot them on sight. Only moments before the Germans arrived to take prisoners, he discovered a Soviet infantryman begging for help with one of his legs shredded by shrapnel.

There was little blood on the brown tunic, and drawing his Makarov pistol, Keremov finished the luckless man with a bullet in the head and took his uniform. With no time to dress the corpse, he stuffed his own tunic with its telltale sleeve markings and identifying papers under the body with a primed grenade. He quickly dashed under fire into the area occupied by another surrendering unit where nobody knew him. Many Soviet soldiers would willingly denounce a political to the Nazis to gain decent treatment. Keremov knew to hide his identity well.

The ruse worked. Keremov survived a short but dangerous captivity of several days before the Nazis were counter-attacked and driven off. Since then, he also survived expediencies of the political arena because he both knew his place and exercised the survival cunning of the peasant. None of his experiences, including the indiscriminate purges, had deterred his total dedication to the Communist Party. Nowhere could the Supreme Soviet have found such blind faith as his. This made Keremov a very dangerous person.

Keremov, in keeping with the latest five-year plan from Moscow, contemplated the political security of his assigned territory, extending east from Lublin, in Poland, to the Bug River. It was a remote area in the southeast of Poland, isolated by marshes to the north and supporting numerous scattered and impoverished farms. He could not accept the ingrained and stolid indifference of the local peasants to political correctness. Ignorant of history, he was not aware that for more than a thousand years, they lived basically the same lives, while successive waves of invaders rolled over them. They were still here although the invaders were either gone or assimilated, a statement of historical durability lost on the political commissar.

The peasants had only survival to occupy their thoughts. Since they lived their lives within a few kilometres of their birthplace, they knew and cared for little outside their own existence. The only ideology that penetrated their basic subsistence was Christianity. They accepted with bovine grace, that the latest invaders – the Soviets – would persecute this, while they themselves blithely continued their faith in a clandestine fashion. In other words, it was so ingrained it could not be changed in any short period of time.

While not understanding this, Keremov was still dedicated to improving the lives of his bucolic charges by turning them into good Communists. His latest peeve was the small groups of squatters who took over abandoned Polish farms at the end of the Great Patriotic War. He knew most of them masqueraded as Poles. They were actually a polyglot of renegade Russians, Germans, and others. There was a predominance of men at these farms. Some had taken up with women who were widowed or forcibly taken, and with the serene indifference of cattle, were now producing snotty-nosed brats not likely to serve Soviet plans.

Keremov had a solution he could work with because of the announced five-year plan to boost farm production in the Soviet Socialist Republic by Collective Farming. Daily, he harangued the local army officers and the NKVD – The People's Commissariat for Internal Affairs (Secret Police) with the need to remove these people and replace them with proper Soviet farmers. They posed a security risk and a possible threat to Russia. Finally, someone had listened to him.

He stood at the railway siding and watched in satisfaction as the first wagonloads of miserable creatures were herded into a train. They were bound for work camps far beyond the Ural Mountains, where they could cause no harm. Within days, selected Soviet citizen farmers would arrive to replace them and march, arms linked, towards another victory for the proletariat. Keremov would be there to ensure they maintained and strengthened their faith.

FIFTEEN

JEANNE WILLIAMS

By the spring of nineteen fifty-two, Jeanne Williams came to the conclusion that she was in a marriage that had run its course and no longer mattered to her. For more than thirty years, she faithfully dedicated her life to John Williams, but she came to learn that in return, she received nothing from the relationship.

John was totally engrossed in his work more than ever. It was as if it was the only driving force, the only important thing in his life. He barely touched her anymore and seemed to find any reason to avoid intimacy with her. She felt like she was drying up, shrivelling like an autumnal leaf too long on the ground. Her very nature rebelled. Every day, she felt the need for an outlet for her frustration and the sense of failure she felt.

Her children were gone. Jennifer was almost a shadowed memory except for the occasional letter. The arrhythmic Christmas cards had finally failed. Love squandered to disinterest. John hated the husband and resented his daughter for the feeling of betrayal he nurtured. A couple of visits by train were all Jeanne had to remember of her two grandchildren, who were growing to maturity while being deprived of grandparental love. David was in Edmonton and working for Tom Edmunds – an even greater betrayal in John's mind. There was no hesitation, no forgiveness possible for that particular Judas.

And John drank too much. The union work was full of stress, too intense for a man of such rigid and unyielding principles. She realized now that the initial fascination with him, the joining with a holy crusade, had been a false premise. Life brought to her the truth concerning the natural course of the distribution of wealth. Some would always have it; many would only crave it. Yet, John Williams was an evangelist of sorts, an unyielding rock of righteousness. The tides and winds of life broke around him and over him but could not erode the staunch principles of which he was built. An armour of self-protection girded him: a layer of plates contrived from self-righteousness, selfishness, denial, contradiction, and egotism. Jeanne was on the outside.

She joined women's clubs, became a school trustee – anything to get out of the house and establish an existence for herself. John saw her activities only as a suitable adjunct to his public figure, allowing her faint applause for supporting him. He was once asked to give a speech to a women's organization and launched a cutting diatribe against big business. The speech was so close a call for Communism that, given the political atmosphere of the times, Jeanne was embarrassed. Looking around, she saw women shifting in their seats, too polite to demur, yet, obviously irritated. She resigned the next day.

She gazed out of the window of the little house they had bought in Edmonton. The ongoing crusade had brought her back to her roots. John had accepted a regional vice-presidency with the United Construction and Catering Workers Union, a fairly new but powerful group. As always, it was not the money but the 'principle' and the 'people' that perked John's interest. To Jeanne, it was just another cul-de-sac of failure.

The only uplifting feature was she would get to see David more, though it would have to be surreptitiously. It annoyed her immensely that the years-long schism between father and son had remained. It was as bitter now as the day it happened. She failed to see the irony that her son had actually formed a permanent relationship with his true father. So long a time had passed living the lie.

****

Canadian Arctic, October.

The Douglas DC3 cargo plane rumbled through the sky. Its cockpit was a warm cocoon in the freezing endlessness of the Arctic twilight. The plane lurched frequently in the turbulence, throwing the propellers out of synchronization, and sending rippling waves of vibration through the airframe. A gentle hand from one of the pilots crept out frequently to caress the propeller levers into harmony. There was no formal responsibility for this; the act merely fell to the first person sufficiently irritated by the sound.

In the reflected glow of the flight instrument lights, Robert Edmunds sat with one foot up on the panel, fingertips nursing the plane along its way. They were on a flight from Cambridge Bay (Cam Main) with a load of building materials and supplies.

The Cold War was in full swing. The Americans were the driving force to establish two lines of radar defence across the Canadian Arctic to defend against any possibility of a Russian strategic airborne attack through the backdoor of the North. With ranges of thousands of miles, aircraft no longer had to fly the traditional easterly or westerly routes to attack enemies. Now, they could fly the shorter distances of the great circle polar routes, where Russian and Canadian landmasses were less than a thousand miles apart. There was nobody to see them or warn of their coming, but the Americans hoped to put a stop to that.

Millions were spent on a chain of sophisticated long-range radar warning sites, known as the DEW line, meaning 'Distant Early Warning.' This line was being constructed from Greenland to Alaska. Further south in Canada, the Mid-Line did not provide the kind of distant insulation the Americans desired. In theory, jet fighters would rise from northern airports and rush to intercept any Russian incursion into Northern Canada. Since these bombers would be carrying thermonuclear weapons capable of massive destruction, the chance of detonating one while shooting a bomber down was considered. In the event, the destruction of some stunted trees, a few hundred miles of tundra, some polar bears, and caribou were considered more preferable than a nuclear burst closer to populated centres further south.

The Americans provided construction money, senior personnel, and overriding command. It was amusing for some Canadians to watch a few of the on-site individuals trying to adapt to Arctic conditions. A Texan's first time experience of minus forty degrees was an amusing sight to behold. Billy McGuffy, Robert's irreverent Irish co-pilot, did not help matters. McGuffy pried the red star off a bottle of a popular brand of whisky and stuck it on his fur hat. He gloried in opening the aircraft door, and saluting at attention, addressing any American army officer who was waiting as 'Comrade.' As the initial consternation, relief, and then fury of these gentlemen subsided, it rose again in renewed doubt. They discovered a Deep South accent versus a Derry brogue left very little means of communication in their common language. McGuffy might as well have been a Russian.

Heavily loaded, the DC3 pounded on westwards into a darkening sky. It was late October. There were still great areas of the Beaufort Sea free from ice. Cold high-pressure weather systems born in Siberia swept eastward, trying to fill low pressures spawned in the Alaska Gulf, bringing winds over the water that scooped up the warmer moisture steaming up from the sea. Borne aloft, these super cooled water droplets lurked in clouds, ready to splatter and instantly freeze on unwary aircraft flying into them. The North was already littered with wrecks of aircraft that failed to complete their journeys after encountering severe icing conditions.

Robert Edmunds bought three of these DC3's from war surplus. They were contracted to the Americans for flying supplies east and west along the DEW line chain. Tom Edmunds underwrote the loan in return for a significant share. There were dozens of aircraft being used to support the closure of the northern airspaces to the Russians. It was very lucrative. Crewing the fleet was easy. There were many ex-servicemen, both pilots and engineers, who were trained to operate this stalwart workhorse of the air.

A faint whiteness began to dust the windshield. Robert checked again to see the carburettor anti-ice was working. This device directed warm air into the throat of the carburettor to ensure ice did not build up and limit the engine's greedy need for air. The downside was the warm ingested air caused a reduction in power. The two pilots started a constant sweep of vigilance from engines to wings to monitor the build-up of ice.

"Looks pretty wet, Boss." McGuffy's irreverence was not limited to American soldiers. His relentless urge to ruffle feathers was only limited, in Robert's case, by a margin of pure respect and recognition of the signature on the bottom of his paycheque each month. "Try the boots, will ye." The wheeze of air, as the pneumatic system tried to inflate the rubber boots on the wings to break the ice off, rose to an adenoidal whine before giving up. McGuffy once likened the sound to 'cowboy singing' and narrowly escaped a thrashing from an irate Oklahoman wearing cowboy boots. Not designed to compete against the extremes of the Arctic, the de-ice boots often became too brittle and ruptured at the application of air pressure, rendering them useless.

"We'll try higher." Reaching forward, Robert pushed the mixtures up. He selected a higher rpm and cracked the throttles open a bit more. The aircraft slowly crept higher. They were overloaded, as usual on these trips, and ice was the last thing they needed. At the application of power, a figure stirred in the back and came up forward to see what was going on.

Al Denman was a skinny, diminutive man with dark brushed-back hair and piercing blue eyes. A chain smoker, McGuffy always insisted he would disappear if he turned sideways, except for the lighted cigarette. Denham was certainly worthy of more obvious respect. He had the ingrained oil stains of a Pratt and Whitney radial engine mechanic's skin and clothing. He was worth double his weight in gold for he was a genius at keeping aircraft running. With the minimal amount of equipment, he would spend hours in the freezing cold, long after other mechanics gave up, went for coffee, and telephoned to order replacement parts. Such unworthies were invariably subjected to Denham cranking over an engine hours later and bringing it to a thundering, melodious roar.

The flare of a Zippo lighter at the cockpit door announced his arrival. "Trouble?"

"Yeah, we've started to pick up some ice, and your bloody boots arn't working." The Irishman pronounced 'bloody' as 'bliddy.' It was always difficult to tell whether McDuffy's pronouncements were serious or teasing, but Denham always seemed to ignore both, and the opportunity to hit back.

"Yeah, Paddy, but I was referring to the cylinder on the left engine." Neither of the pilots could hear it yet, but Denham's tuned ear detected the faintest possible arrhythmic sound.

"Cracked?" It was the obvious guess, as cold air striking the array of hot radial cylinders frequently caused cracks in the metal, exposed at the front of the engines. Denham always carried a couple of spares. He could magically replace cylinders in an engine in a few hours, even under the most primitive conditions.

"Ah-ha."

The plane plunged on and up, swimming through the turbulent air. The turbulence was, in a way, a clue to better flying conditions as it indicated a boundary between two air masses, one warmer and wetter and one colder and drier, battling together. Climbing would probably put them into the wedge of warmer air aloft, but there should be colder air further above. If they could get into the warmer air, they would be in better circumstances. Both pilots knew the colder air of a cold front was pushing south easterly below them and could be a better choice, but if they went down and did not get out of the ice, they would never be able to climb up again. They would also get an undesirable increased headwind. It was best to try high first. They peered out into the growing murk; anxious to see a lightening of the sky that might indicate they were between layers of cloud.

Robert checked the relative bearing of the automatic direction-finding needle, tuned to the radio beacon at Lady Franklin Point, a DEW-Line site. Switching frequency to the beacon at Cape Parry, he scowled at the weak response of the needle. If they were on track for their destination, it should be straight ahead. Any change of course to the right to maintain track would tell him he had changed air masses. The outside air thermometer stood at twenty degrees Fahrenheit. A change in that reading would also be a clue. He always marvelled at how water droplets did not freeze into chunks of solid ice at temperatures so far below the freezing point.

The oil pressure on the left engine flickered. The first discordant sound emanated from that side. The oil temperature stood steady, for now.

"How far to our destination?" It was a casual question but betrayed Denham's concern.

"About a hundred miles." Three pairs of eyes swept the airspeed indicator. They were down to one hundred and twenty miles an hour because of the ice, and with a growing headwind, it translated into about a one-hour flight.

Without prompting, McGuffy tuned the radio to the DEW line high frequency and called for weather at Cape Parry, Lady Franklin Point and Cambridge Bay. "All obscured, less than a mile in snow and blowing snow. The wind is two ninety at twenty-five miles and hour, gusting thirty. Altimeter twenty-nine point six five. Tuytoyaktuk is no better, but pressure rising."

Robert moved his altimeter knob from the two nine nine two inches of mercury it was set at. There was a good pressure gradient developing with, probably, clearing weather ahead. However, somewhere out to the north, a nasty low pressure was dragging this weather behind it.

"So much for forecasts." With little for reporting stations to mark their progress, Arctic storms could sweep down almost anywhere along the Arctic coast without warning. Both pilots sat and reflected on the skills they would have to bring to nurse the DC3 to a landing on one engine in such conditions.

The oil temperature and pressure gauges were going slowly in opposite directions. It was imperceptible to an unpractised eye but obvious to pilots with a problem. The pressure was dropping. Oil leaked out of the cracked cylinder, and with lubrication lost, friction began to overheat the components. Robert levelled the aircraft and reduced power slightly on the left. They did not dare open the cowl flaps to lower the temperature for fear of cracking more cylinders. Besides, the increased drag would slow them even further. They were stuck with few options.

McGuffy increased the mixture slightly to help keep the cylinder head temperature cooler, but it was a losing battle. Ten minutes later, the oil pressure hovered just above the minimum allowable and engine temperature had reached maximum.

Denham said it for them. "Better shut it down."

The two pilots exchanged looks. Both of them would prefer to run the engine until it actually quit, in order to cope with shooting an approach under such low visibility conditions. However, the reality was that this engine was going to seize very shortly and would not last them to any safe destination.

Robert nodded at McGuffy's glance for concurrence. He increased the power slightly on the right engine, and they started the shutdown procedure. If they ran the engine until it seized and they could not get the propeller feathered, it would windmill, causing enough drag to make for control problems.

McGuffy got on the radio again and gave a revised time of arrival, warning them of their status and the possible need for rescue assistance on landing. Looking out, Robert made the call. Indeed the propeller had feathered and was stationary. Without a word, they watched as the aircraft slowed. Underpowered on one engine, overloaded and smeared with ice, they began to settle from six thousand feet, back towards the ground below.

****

Tuesday, October 1955.

The accident on the highway to Jasper was almost a freak one, except accident investigators always confirm there are circumstances leading up to such events. The logging truck was on its fourth run of the day with a load of spruce logs to a sawmill just east of Edson. One of the chains restraining the load, which weighed twenty tons, chafed continuously and had worn to the point of failure. The highway was quite tortuous along this section, twisting and turning left and right through the forest. Many of the bends were blind.

The truck was on the inside of the bend, going east, when the chain finally failed. The truck slowed to forty miles per hour, but as the front of the logs came loose the centrifugal force carried the tail end of the lumber across the opposite traffic lane, dragging the rear boogies with it. There were four unfortunate occupants of a Chevrolet car that was traveling west. It was headed for a conference at the Jasper Park Lodge. Through the dust on the road, the driver had no time to see the danger before the sweeping cascade of logs, part way off the sliding boogies, loomed like a massive tumbling wall before him. The vehicle was impacted in a split second, pulverized and peeling apart under the destructive power. Two logs went end-first through the windshield, instantly killing all four men. Another log went under the front end, scooping the car and flipping it into the trees beside the road. The tortured sound of the truck's arrest went on long after the grisly car rolled one last time and came to rest.

Jeanne Williams learned of her husband's death about five hours after it happened. The Edson RCMP called to confirm he was in a car traveling west that day. Proper identification was impossible. Only the wallets retrieved at the accident site pointed to the victims' names. The closed coffin funerals were held jointly with the union making a big deal in memoriam of its four executives who had died. After the church service, several hundred well-wishers filed past the four widows to express their condolences. Jeanne was numb, mostly with disbelief. She had nothing in common with these people, and she regarded the service as nothing more that one last duty to John to mark some strange transition into a new world.

David was there, of course. Jennifer sent a card and letter, regretting her non-attendance, but opening the door for the re-establishment of a relationship. Then, it was over. A meagre insurance policy, paid by the union, provided money she could bank and draw a pension on. At fifty-five years of age, she was now a widow and without any kind of employment that would bring her an income.

****

It would not have been at all appropriate for a wreath from Tom Edmunds to appear at the church where John Williams' funeral was conducted. Tom pondered the matter, torn by his own feelings for Jeanne. David 'Sher' Williams surprised him by appearing back at work the following day as if nothing had happened.

"I thought you would be away for a few days." He hovered in David's office doorway when he discovered it occupied.

David's head snapped up as if he had been accused of something and made to speak, then kept quiet. An odd look came over his face as he looked at Tom. It was almost as if he was choking on words.

The pause went on for too long. "I don't suppose you know, but I knew your mother slightly, before they were married. Under the circumstances, I cannot contact her, but would like her to know she has my sympathy. Your father and I were, er, enemies, I guess, for lack of a better word." David's stare went on, and Tom was starting to feel uncomfortable.

"Well, you know, he and I did not see eye-to-eye on many things either. He never spoke to me again after I came to work for you."

"I'm sorry."

"No. Not at all. I made my choice, and he did not like it. Simple as that." David paused again. "If you like, I will tell her you send your sympathies."

"Yes. Yes, please." Awkwardly, Tom left, feeling like he had been shoved blindfolded into the midst of an on-stage drama without lines or a role to play.

Arctic.

At three thousand feet, the DC3 broke layers. They picked up ice all the way down, despite repeated tries of the wing deice boots. Every prominence of the aircraft now sported an inch of rime ice, opaque white growth that built outwards and forwards with an implacable deadliness. A vibration in the airframe told them the wire aerials of the high frequency and direction finding radios were also festooned. Radio reception was attenuated, closing them in further, isolating them from the sound of a friendly voice. The automatic direction finder was now almost useless. Only the slow increase in volume told Robert they were getting closer. He flew on the last reliable bearing he had. They had to hope they were still getting reception when they got close. He could do a manual loop approach when they got there. It did not rely on the automatic function of the direction finder. He gave a wry thought to how they were helping get a radar net installed that could eventually steer them direct to their destination. As of tonight, it was not yet working. They were on their own.

The directional compass precessed due to internal friction of its gyro. A rate of change of fifteen degrees per hour was acceptable and manual resetting was possible with reference to the magnetic spirit compass in the cockpit. If they did not reset the compass, by the time they got to destination, they would be steering about fifteen degrees off course and might well miss seeing the runway. Resetting by referring to the magnetic compass was notoriously unreliable this close to the Magnetic North Pole. It was only a few hundred miles away. Normally, crews used the astrocompass to get a bearing from the sun, the moon, or a star. In cloud, this was impossible.

A snowstorm with ground visibility of one mile was not as bad as it sounded; there was usually some visibility from the air. They should see Cape Parry if they got within a few miles of it. McGuffy already had spread a map by which he could navigate their way visually if they saw a ground feature they could identify. A view of the coastline would provide them with a route to follow.

Even though they were not picking up any more ice, the load, the loss of lift due to ice, and the power of only one engine brought the undercast layer closer and closer. At twenty-eight hundred feet, they went into the tops and immediately, the icing returned.

"I'm going lower, Paddy. What's the highest ground around?"

"About six hundred feet." McGuffy was ready for that question.

"Better suit up. There may not be time later." On by one, taking turns at the controls, they donned heavy trousers and parkas, laying thick mitts to hand. If they had to force-land the plane, they had better be ready to face the Arctic conditions if they survived the impact. It would be a shame to get knocked out and then freeze to death before they came around.

They peered anxiously through the only space left on the icy windows, seeking the ground. McGuffy had his stubby finger pressed to the map where he best figured their position to be. Anticipated features were memorized, yet what he might see could be entirely different.

"Got it!" Through a broken layer beneath them, dimly visible in the low light, a dark object with definitive edges slid by beneath them.

"Where are we?"

"Fucking lost!" McGuffy was at his best. "Let her down some more.

Looks like we have room below." Gradually beneath them, the land took faint form. They knew in this area long ridges ran east and west with escarpments and rocky outcrops. They were helpful for visible reference of the ground but hardly conducive to safe landing.

They were out of cloud. To the right, a dark reflection on the underside of the cloud suggested open sea. Flurries of snow whipped by the windshield, obscuring vision. Fate was teasing them, for just as McGuffy's body language suggested he was getting somewhere with his map reading, another new shudder ran through the aircraft. All eyes went to the gauges.

"What was that?"

"Don't know." The engine definitely missed. It surged again, yawing the aircraft against the rudder trim that was keeping it straight on one engine.

"Oh, Lordy!" They juggled with the carburettor-icing lever, trying it off, then on, then off again. The engine speed increased with it off, as it should, but they had to put it back on again. Moments later, the engine surged again.

"I think it's the magnetos." Denham's analysis sent Robert's hand to the switches. He tried running on one of the two for a few seconds. As soon as he tried the second magneto off, the engine stopped then backfired. He quickly went to the other one again. The engine missed again and again. Airspeed decayed, and the altimeter began to unwind.

"Okay, Paddy. Looks like we're going to have to put this thing down. Al, you better go in the back and brace yourself."

"What amongst all that freight? No way! I'll jamb myself into the radio compartment here."

Robert was too busy to argue. With some power on the engine, he was able to give them time to get ready, but he knew he would have to shut the engine down before they hit the ground, before the one-sided power made the plane uncontrollable at low speed.

"See a good spot?"

"Yeah, looks like a flat area at one o'clock. Turn right about twenty degrees and you'll see it."

"Give me half the flap and we'll shut the engine down at about a hundred feet. Gear up, of course." Robert slowly eased the speed back and pointed the nose at a white area bordered by dark objects. They could only be large boulders or worse.

Uneven ground was invisible with the low-light or 'white-out' condition. Only the dark spots gave any depth perception of their height and the nature of the terrain they were approaching.

"Shut it down."

McGuffy quickly pulled levers. The engine snorted and was stilled, leaving only a curious hissing of air around the nose. The DC3 was back less than one hundred miles an hour now. Robert was careful the combination of weight and loss of lift due to ice did not contribute to him stalling the aircraft before they were flared for the landing. McGuffy hit the landing lights and ground relief sprang at them. The grey snow area revealed itself as rippled hummocks, perhaps three feet high. They applied full flaps, confident their point of impact would be early in the clear area.

"Eighty-five." McGuffy's speed call was accompanied by a buffeting from the tail. One wing began to drop as the aircraft prepared to stall. Unsticking slightly, Robert let the nose drop. He began to ride just the onset of the buffet. "Hang on, Al!"

The first impact was surprisingly gentle and came from the rear. Robert used the last of the lift to raise the nose. There was a harder bump, and the nose pitched downwards, resulting in a hard slamming deceleration. The fuselage ground through the snow crust into the terrain beneath. A huge bang from the right announced the wing meeting a rock. They were violently slewed in that direction. McGuffy almost put his head in Robert's lap. Robert felt his head hit the side of the cockpit and greyed out after an initial flash of red pain, aware vaguely that the aircraft was skidding sideways now. The bumps were becoming more and more deliberate and persistent. His effort to keep the aircraft straight with the rudder pedals was instinctive but futile.

In a shower of snow and dirt, the DC3 finally ploughed to a stop. For a moment, nothing happened. Then McGuffy leaned over and started hitting fuel cocks and battery switches. "Are you okay, Boss?"

"Yes, but my ankle hurts. Think it may be broken."

"Al, you there?"

"Yeah, I'm fine. Just a couple of bruises."

"Phew!"

The outside silence had a profundity bordering on a presence. It closed around them like a shroud. Robert shuddered. He thought of all the great explorers who faced this circumstance with no promise they might live to recount their experience. Only a faint soughing of wind and flurries of snow told of the breeze outside. The gusts had helped them, lowering their speed over the ground when they landed and shortening the distance the aircraft had slid, thus reducing any encounters with unyielding objects. Robert gingerly wriggled the toes of his left foot and gasped with pain. He simultaneously felt the crepitus of broken bones.

"Hurt lots?" A demonstration of sympathy from McGuffy was as alien as the elements outside.

"Not too bad. It can wait. If we still have battery power, why don't you try the high frequency and see if you can tell them we are down. Did you manage a position?"

"Not really, but I think I saw the Gulf shoreline, so it should not be too bad for search aircraft to find us."

"What makes you think all the American friends you've made will want to come looking for you when they hear you're down?"

"I'm going to take a look around." Aloof from the bantering from up front, Al Denham opened the door to the main cabin. "Goddamn!"

"What's up?"

"Well, some of the cargo broke loose. Gonna be difficult to get through. Looks like there are some fuselage holes back there too." Denham's voice faded away as he crawled over the tangle of crates and boxes.

McGuffy found some life in the batteries, but there seemed to be no action on the radio. He attempted a broadcast in the hopes of it being picked up. Then he shut the master switch off again. The antenna was probably ripped off. A creeping cold already began to steal into their bodies through the fur-lined leather jackets and heavy clothing.

Assured that Robert was comfortable, McGuffy went to the back of the plane and started to move cargo around, selecting items that might be of use to them. He found the heavy tarpaulins used as engine tents and the survival gear stowed aft. He came back to announce the right wing was gone and the aft fuselage badly wrinkled and holed.

Denham, ever practical, returned minutes later with a can of oil he drained from the engine before it congealed and became impossible to obtain. It would burn with a black smoke to make signals. He also drained avgas from the wing tank into a small jerry can. They could use it to run the pressure stove packed in the survival gear.

"Right wing is gone, most of the tail, too. There's not enough snow out there to build a shelter. The left wing is too close to the ground to make a roof for us, so I think we should stay in here. We can insulate ourselves a little at the back end with the boxes of cargo."

"Very well, let's do that. Sorry, I can't help."

"Okay, Boss, just sit here and review your landing technique, while we take care of it."

For the next hour, Robert sat and endured the onset of the cold, while the other two toiled. There were a great deal of bumps and scrapes, punctuated by cursing, before they came forward again to help him out of his seat. It was a tenet of survival that staying in the aircraft was not a good move. Its metal hull would act like a giant freezer. However, there was no other shelter available.

Robert eased out of his seat using McGuffy for balance. Every knock and bump of his foot caused him to bite his lip in pain. Bending his knee up, he raised the lower limb and slowly hopped through the cockpit door into the cabin. His crew had built an igloo out of boxes in the back of the plane with tarpaulin doors front and rear. Further aft, the pressure stove hissed under an old can filled with snow. Denham was creating water.

Concerned that immobility would lead to frostbite, it was necessary to remove Robert's boot, inspect his injury, immobilize, and insulate it against the cold. Trying to remove the boot caused too much pain, so they resorted to cutting it off. McGuffy produced a wicked looking knife from a sheath sewn to his coveralls. When exposed, the ankle looked puffy and was turning purple. Fortunately, it was a simple fracture. No bones protruded through the skin. It just needed immobilizing. Using a couple of small pieces of wood, McGuffy skilfully wrapped the ankle, preventing rotational movement. He checked that Robert could still wriggle his toes for feeling and promote blood flow. A huge fur-lined mitten was then pulled over the foot. An outer wrapping of tarpaulin provided cushioned insulation.

By the time he was finished, Al produced enough melted snow to provide a tin mug of coffee. He threw in a cube of chocolate and stirred it with a screwdriver drawn from his pocket before they passed it around.

"Coffee and chocolate together?" Even though the brew tasted delicious under the circumstances, McGuffy could not pass up the chance to criticize.

"Sure. Very big in Austria and Switzerland. They call it mocha."

"Aye, well, you won't find it down any Belfast street!"

"I think we will have lots of gas, so maybe I can rig up some kind of heater using the pressure stove. We'll need some ventilation though, so we don't asphyxiate ourselves." Denham showed interest in neither the fare offered in Belfast cafes, nor criticism of his innkeeping.

Robert felt useless under the circumstances, but he recognized the hot drink staved off any shock reaction he might have suffered as a result of his injuries. The ankle problem was typical of pilots doing crash landings. They tended to rigidly stand on the rudder pedals, and when they thrashed back, the ankle gave way under the force. His crewmen worked quickly and effectively at getting him into suitable shelter. His head ached from the bump it had taken. Various joints throughout his body began to complain of the abuse they took. At least, they were alive and in good shape with a few hundred pounds of groceries to feed off. All they could do now was wait for rescue.

They were subjected to a ferocious Arctic storm for the next three days. The temperature hovered about fifteen degrees Fahrenheit. The winds blew out of the west at thirty miles per hour, gusting to over forty. While the Arctic is a semi desert, they were now getting one of the batches of snowfall that made up for the annual accumulation. Moisture off the open water was picked up by the winds and dropped as snow.

Drifts began to pile up on the windward side of the DC3 almost to the top of the fuselage. The snug living area McGuffy and Al had constructed served them well. The two other men made Robert's lot easier. They brought him an oilcan when he needed to relieve himself and helped him to a five-gallon oil pail at the rear of the aircraft for more serious toilet needs. To expose bare buttocks outside in that wind would have invited quick frostbite, so the toilet at the back of the aircraft was a welcome facility. Eskimos had flaps sewn in the back of their polar bearskin pants to enable this need, but ordinary trousers exposed too much flesh.

Frost-hardened snow blew like a fine dust upon the wind and entered every crack and hole in the fuselage. Even a tiny pinprick allowed drifts inches high to accumulate. A huge wall of snow began to fill up the aft fuselage near the door due to the large hole in the rear end of the plane. The fine particulate nature of the snow made for a dense and deeply frozen consistency. It froze almost as hard as rock. Amongst the cargo, they found canned food, toilet paper, paperback novels, and other small items to assist them. Most of the electronic equipment was of no help at all, but cases and crates helped the construction of their bivouac.

Despite all their efforts and Denham's ingenious rigging of a heater, the cold still percolated to their bones. It was particularly hard on Robert. He could not move around like the others. The inside of the aircraft frosted up like the inside of a freezer from condensation. They spent turns sleeping, one person was always awake – who had the job of waking the others every couple of hours to ensure they did not suffer frostbite. The two men on sleeping shift huddled together for warmth under all the material they could find.

The ankle throbbed and ached with a dull monotonous pain. It wore down Robert's morale, even though McGuffy inspected it and declared it as well as could be expected. In some fashion, the ankle provided a distraction to the onset of the cold. The way it crept into them was stultifying. Robert again marvelled how the early explorers coped. Sweat, shed skin, and dirt accumulated on the inside of their clothing, reducing the insulating qualities of the material.

With the responsibility of carrying the watch and with his partner's lives in his hands, Robert found he had to concentrate hard to stay awake. The chill of his body gradually crept to his brain. Had he been alone, he knew, he would have drifted off into an endless sleep. While awake, he constantly thought of his wife, Anne, and little Elizabeth. Of course, the two men under the tarpaulins were not asleep all the time, so they told stories and chatted about inconsequentials. McGuffy's abrasive nature underwent a miraculous metamorphosis. He was amicable as could be.

On the third day, while Robert was on watch, the wind began to abate. A couple of hours later, stiff and labouring with cold limbs, he toiled his way up to the cockpit. A snowdrift had built up outside right to the seat on the co-pilot's side. The thermometer read only five degrees now, a drop of ten, and the altimeter showed them at a lower elevation, meaning the pressure had risen. Grabbing a stiff binder off a flight manual, he laboriously scraped the layer of frost off the inside of the side window, finishing the job with bare fingers, which instantly tingled and froze. Peering through the small hole, he could see a faint patch of blue sky to the south. The colder, clearer air of the high-pressure system had arrived, bringing skies that might promise rescue.

It was so uplifting that he awakened the others. Their sleeping during the day was not strange. Their whole life rhythms now revolved around a place in the bed. The welcome news demanded a celebration. Al brewed up a batch of his mocha coffee. Afterwards, he and McGuffy went outside to ready the signalling equipment they had assembled.

Being immobile, Robert was assigned the 'Gibson Girl,' a hand-cranked emergency radio that would put out a signal on five hundred kilocycles. Denham readied a length of wire, which he would string outside as an antenna. They fashioned large panels out of boxes that could be laid out in the snow to attract searching aircraft. Some of the books were soaking in avgas. They would be set on fire at the sound of an aircraft, oil to be poured on to provide a more visible black smoke. They also drew a design on paper that McGuffy would tramp out in the snow. All they needed was an aircraft to come by.

Only a day later, a faint drone of aero engines announced their salvation.

****

SIXTEEN

EDITH CAVELL

At eleven thousand and thirty-three feet, Mount Edith Cavell is a major peak of the Canadian Rockies. The mountain stands squarely in view from the Jasper town site. It is clearly visible from the Jasper Park Lodge, where Danny Edmunds first saw it. The summit ridge is aligned roughly east west, giving an almost flat appearance, although it enhances rather than detracts from the mountain's appeal.

Striations of snow and rock on the north face caused the Indians to name it 'The White Ghost.' It was a fitting name to its presence, hovering over the valley on low-light nights. The more pragmatic voyageurs knew it as 'La Montagne de la Grand Traverse,' a signpost on their journey announcing portage of their canoes over the Rocky Mountain watershed. It was eventually named for Nurse Edith Cavell, who was executed by the Germans in nineteen fifteen after she was captured and accused of spying. Nestled in the central upper corrie of the main face is the Angel Glacier, so named because of its winged shape, hanging above the valley below. Gravel paths run up the massive moraine on the opposite side of the upper valley from the main mountain face. It was up one of these viewpoint accesses that Danny now trudged with a climbing pack settled on his back.

There were five men in the party: Danny, Wayne Smith, Neil McCubbin, plus Jim and Tom Hunter, the latter three all Scotsmen. It was the day Danny fulfilled a wish to climb Edith Cavell. It was six in the morning when they parked their cars at the old teahouse. Danny remembered it from his visit with his parents. The teahouse sat almost at the tree line, accessible by driving up a switchback gravel trail, which put the traveller above the shoulder of the hanging valley through which the Athabasca River flowed. It saved a lot of strenuous climbing through the trees and bush by being able to drive that far. Cavell was within reach.

Off to his right as he plodded on, Danny had a clear view of the Angel Glacier and the dark frowning walls of the north face. Near the top, the rock appeared both lighter brown and dark with the characteristic grey of the limestone also showing. Looking back over his shoulder, he could just see a sliver of Cavell Lake, which collected and briefly calmed the rushing waters of the stream below. It shone aquamarine, boasting its glacial-fed nature as the first of the day's light struck it.

Below to the right, another lake, still in shadow, sat grey and sullen looking. Miniature icebergs dotted its surface. The upper edge of the lake comprised a wall of ice twenty feet high where another glacier lurked, mostly hidden by detritus that had fallen from the wall of rock above. This glacier calved the icebergs dotting the lake's surface and kept it at an extremely cold temperature. The valley above it was characterized by bergschrunds, tapering steeply down into the depths of the valley and feeding it snow and rock. Rock falls and avalanches fed the jumbled pile at the foot of the face, while simultaneously eroding the mountain.

As he walked, Danny's practised eye picked out the features of the mountain; the typically glaciated walls, the hanging valleys, the huge moraine piled along the east side of the valley. High above, the permanent snowcap of the mountain peeked over the precipice – a massive cornice looking almost like a wig.

They were heading for an ascent up the East Ridge, the classical route. Like the feet of previous users, theirs began to trace individual routes across a huge expanse of enormous boulders. The path on the moraine tapered out and became indecipherable. The trees off to the left were fading, becoming stunted as they approached the true tree line. The head of the valley loomed above them, shutting off the sky, and closing in tighter. A wide bergschrund swept across the entire basal wall right down from the col to the right.

It was a further sixty minutes heavy haul up the steep slope before they came out on the col proper. A fairly easy slope led to the rounded and inferior heights of Cavell's easterly neighbour to the left. To the right, the East Ridge took off upward in steps and disappeared high above. They stopped for a break. Alternately looking at their route and the eternal false crests it would present to them, they gazed down into the deep valley to the southwest.

A keen wind blew in their faces. It was with some dismay they saw the weather boiling in around the peaks to the west. A quick council did not change their plan to proceed. With Wayne Smith, the possibility of turning back was remote. A short, stocky man with thinning hair and bright blue dancing eyes, his massive legs made him a formidable mountaineer. Danny always described Wayne's rhythmic and indefatigable step-kicking up a steep snow slope as a 'clockwork soldier.' He was a tough, resourceful, and daring climber who let very little defeat him.

The three Scotsmen were not about to let 'a little wee weather' get in their way either. They got to their feet and began to tackle the ridge. The rock climbed in short vicious steps and did not require roping up but challenged their scrambling techniques and their stamina. Like most limestone, the rock was badly fractured and weathered, often yielding to a planted foot, robbing the slithering climbers of progress and energy.

In the thinning air, they gradually began to feel the cost of their efforts, although it hardly showed on Wayne. Splatters of thin rain droplets began, and pausing for a brief breather, Danny took his last look from his vantage point before the clouds closed around them. It was a disappointment in this mid-July to be dogged by rain, but in the mountains, only a fool did not expect the worst. They broke out and donned their waterproofs and continued toiling upward.

Around eleven o'clock, the rain turned to sleet and soon thereafter, snow. Visibility was down to yards. Progress was laboured and miserable with heads down. They were onto permanent snow now, crunching into it about a foot before the compacted layers beneath supported their weight. Danny could feel his legs becoming heavier and heavier. He plodded on and the others were slowing, too. They stopped for another brief break, ate chocolate and raisins, swigging orange juice from an old army water bottle.

It grew colder in their light clothing, but as long as they kept moving, it was not too bad. Flakes of snow started to stick to their faces, eyebrows, and lashes, hampering their vision. The ground snow, cloud, and swirling flakes joined to create a whiteout. There were no shadows to give any depth perception. Danny sometimes found himself tracking sideways a little. It was on one such occasion that Jim called out mildly from just ahead. "Mind the edge!" He looked up from his labouring and saw, only feet away, the yawning openness of space, a terrifying vista of nothingness between him and the valley floor below. He could see quite clearly down through the clouds to the valley bottom half a mile beneath his feet. He felt a brief moment of terror, understanding that without Jim's warning he could have easily walked over the edge and fallen to his death. Without a doubt, he was standing on the very cornice atop the north wall he had seen hours before from below. He was treading on an overhang of snow only a few feet thick, secure only because wind compaction and the freezing of the individual snowflakes was strong enough to support him. Sobered, he turned more to his left, keeping as far from the edge as he could.

The recognition of his whereabouts told him they must be on the summit ridge. He stepped out with renewed resolution. The going got easier and just minutes later, he found Wayne sitting in the snow declaring this spot, for lack of a better reference, to be the summit.

It was a disappointment to them all. Instead of the endless vista of mountains as far as the eye could see, their world was limited to twenty feet in the greying whiteness. Poised so high, they could feel the relentless force of nature around them. The wind swept up and over them, creating and lifting snow over their elevated position, and then plunging it over the precipice nearby into the limitless depths. Even without the summit scenery, the exposure was palpable.

The thorough dampness quickly reached them, and after a quick snack, they cinched their backpacks, shrugged deeper into their clothes, and marched off through the gathering snowfall. The slope quickened. They slithered and kicked their way downwards until rock began to reassert itself from the snowy slope. It was now two in the afternoon, but it looked like twilight. The adrenalin high of getting to the summit had passed. Now, they had the drudgery of getting back down safely. Descents were always risky. The very nature of the exercise was such that you faced outwards from the rock with gravity tearing at your feet. Climbing up, the toes could flex upward, giving you the thrust and balance to work the rock. Going down, it was mostly the heels, since the toes could not dig in, especially through stout leather boot soles.

Going down, you could not fall face forward and clutch the rock as you could ascending. You would merely fall on your butt and perhaps glissade or twist and clutch the vicious sponge-like texture of the limestone if you slipped. The calf muscles cramped. The knee joints impacted when you arrested your descent continuously with a hard-placed boot. Your toes slid forward against the inside toe of the boot, exquisitely teasing blisters conjured up by hours of friction with woollen socks.

They came out above black brooding cliffs that offered no way down either by climbing or rappelling, since they disappeared hundreds of feet below, still plummeting downwards. It was a bad moment. Wayne admitted they were lost. Neil led another quick council. He advocated climbing backwards and cutting to the left to avoid the cliffs. Nobody questioned why they had not merely retraced their tracks through the summit snow back to the East Ridge. They were too good a team to apportion blame. However, tiredness and hypothermia were playing their parts. It crossed Danny's mind he would like to sit there for a few hours and rest, but the others were off.

For hours, they toiled downwards, circumnavigating impossible cliffs and slithering down steep ravines on scree. The falling snow began to thin and turned to sleet once again, wetting their legs and increasing the misery. Water seeped down into their boots and clothing, chaffing their worn skin. They were out of the wind. Sleet turned to rain and visibility began to increase. Able to pick better routes, they found a long scree slope and whooped their way down, running and sliding like crazy men. Danny loved the scree. It was a little like skating on gravel. By digging in the heel of his boots and taking very quick, short shuffling strides to maintain balance, it was possible to go down impossibly steep slopes in the upright position without falling. Every so often, however, an unyielding hidden boulder would arrest a foot. One of them would pitch over, rolling down the slope until a spread-eagled poise stopped their plunge. It was great fun.

Trees began to appear, and the slope started to flatten slightly. A faint game trail crossed from left to right, contouring the slope. They took it gladly, striding along the flattened pockets of earth amidst stunted willows and wildflowers. Foliage became more prevalent. The occasional rounded rock protruding from the ground caught a toe, eliciting grunts of discomfort. The pace increased uncomfortably. Then before Danny realized it, his partners were jogging along the trail. He could not believe it! They were out all day slogging up a bloody mountain, and now they were running! He ran with them.

The trail was tantalizing. It grew more defined by travel-wear. It boasted horse droppings. It oozed the promise of civilization nearby. Yet, still it went on. While the descent was mostly a gradual slope making for easy going, once in a while, a shoulder of the mountain (which Danny was beginning to dislike) descended from the clouds. That would necessitate a brief interval of climbing to reach the other side. The reversal of climbing instead of descending and its effect on tired muscles and raw feet made for hard going.

Danny was slogging now, no doubt about it. The others strode on like it was an afternoon Sunday stroll. But he was still with them. A row of horizontal and parallel poles looked strange to him until he suddenly realized they must be the corrals for the packhorses, just below Cavell Lake. Sure enough, they reached the bridge across the outflow and made the steep climb to the road on the other side. Swinging along, they marched the slow slope upwards to the teahouse.

It was nine thirty and almost dark when they finally returned to the cars in the parking lot. They were gone for fifteen and a half hours. They had come down on the wrong side and had to walk all the way back to their starting point. The rain thinned and visibility was now much improved, but it had obviously been a poor-weather day at the teahouse.

They were unlacing their sodden boots and stripping off grimy, horrid socks when a middle-aged man stepped out of a car nearby and strolled over towards them. "Have you been far?" The drawling accent was impeccably upper crust Englishman.

"Up to the top." Wayne's voice was typically noncommittal.

"You've been to the top of Edith Cavell in *this*?" The man's voice expressed astonishment. "Well, I *do* congratulate you!"

Danny felt like he had climbed Mount Everest.

****

Nathan Connaught did not consciously choose to come into conflict with the Edmunds family. It was a fate, an equation of time, space, gravitational pull, or some other phenomenon. Mostly, it was largely due to the way the family loomed on the Edmonton horizon and were always being pushed under his nose.

He knew Tom Edmunds by reputation before his first encounter with the family, which was Beth's wedding to Edward Sturdee. The opulence, the sheer expensive splendour of the event offended his nascent socialism, especially after a decade of economic depression. That the bride was rich, beautiful, and vivacious was sufficient insult to him. That she should marry the handsomest man in the city was an overkill of colossal magnitude.

Nathan escaped his home at an early age, a survival of the spirit necessitating the severing of his family ties. His parents were a lost cause financially, socially, morally, and congenitally. He worked in an Edmonton grocery store for the first few years. It financed his progress through night school and a college course in journalism. Despite his considerable writing skills, he could never enunciate why he chose the profession, even though his skills and enthusiasm were obvious.

Indelibly, the print of his dysfunctional parents was upon him. Providing an adequate screen for the elusive Nathan persona were a homburg hat, a voluminous, flapping raincoat, and rancid old cigars. It was a hard-bitten Hollywood image, fostered by tough journalists and detectives of the silver screen. Some people avowed it was compensation, for Nathan was a skinny man, unlike his heavy-bodied father. The clothes were obviously theatrical props, bolstering a feeling of inadequacy. If anyone ever believed Nathan Connaught was inadequate, however, they had never been on the receiving end of his caustic typewriter.

At the other end of the scale, Nathan had the touch. He could come upon a story of human interest, of human suffering and reduce his readers to tears. Many times, his stirring narratives brought donations to families and individuals in need. He built up a loyal following of readers and editors, who faithfully subscribed to his words, no matter how puerile. So established was his readership, he could almost do no wrong. His column became a fixture in the local newspaper, a soapbox pedestal from which he jousted with dragons of his own perception without being truly called to heel.

The Edmunds family became such a dragon to him. An early interview with Tom Edmunds was disastrous. They had such opposite views on life; the interview's chance of success was roughly equivalent to a skater with red-hot skates trying to cross a ten-mile lake covered with a quarter inch of ice. At the first wrong word, the skater's boot went through the ice, cracks spread in every direction, and the frigid water beneath was thrashed to white foam.

Nathan went back to his office and opened a file on the Edmunds family. As the business empire grew over the years, he carefully indexed it and so he never lost the opportunity to launch a barb. From Tom's perspective, Nathan became 'that skinny little squint-eyed turd.' His ability to seize on a suitable literary quote was defeated by the power of Nathan's vitriol.

In the middle of the turmoil surrounding unionising of the oil plants in the very early fifties, Nathan helped John Williams with a continuous barrage of innuendo and steered the newspaper perilously close to slander in promoting the union's efforts to franchise the plants. In the process, he came up with one of his pearls. It was perhaps an obvious recall of historical precedent that he raised, but it also unearthed an embarrassment John Williams might have preferred left unmentioned. He wrote:

In assisting in the struggle for union enfranchisement for the workers in the Edmunds Enterprises oil plants, the United Construction and Catering Workers' Union seeks to help raise the lifestyle of the common employee to a decent level. How long must people labour like blind, subservient slaves under the oppressive dreams of self-serving capitalism? This nation, this province, this city were founded on the sweated labour of the common man and woman and it is time they were recognized and rewarded for their contribution.

In opposing this inherent right of democracy, Thomas Edmunds is determined to trample on the hopes and dreams of his employees. How will he achieve his ends this time? In nineteen twenty-one, his company, Edmunds Transport, closed its doors overnight, throwing out of work two dozen faithful employees who only sought union membership for themselves. Will he do the same this time? How can he? We are talking about hundreds of people now, and they will not knuckle under to such high-handed action.

Thomas Edmunds wields too much power, economically and politically in this city, and if he is not stopped, we may as well rename our cherished home "Edmundstown."

The article caused uproar of rather limited proportions dependent upon people's views and sense of facts, but it polarized a lot of thinking. In a few short paragraphs, Nathan Connaught denied the history of Western Canada, ignoring the fact of entrepreneurial endeavour from the beaver fur trade, the CPR, and every investor who ever lived. He also distorted the facts of the previous labour dispute. But for his power of influence, the union, especially John Williams, would have severed all association with him for dredging up their defeat and embarrassment of thirty years before.

Only one of his words was perpetuated: 'Edmundstown.' It became a catchphrase, just as 'go picket a for-sale sign' had after the Edmunds

Transport affair. Visitors to Edmonton would use the word jokingly, as did Edmontonians, describing where they were from when they travelled. The effect was to only spread Tom Edmunds' name further around Canada.

****

Siberia.

The town of Upskayoyve-Ostravenyesko, on the Trans-Siberian Railway, was a mere clearing in the vastness of the forests of middle Russia. It owed its existence to the xenophobic character of the Soviets who wanted it kept away from prying eyes. The hatred of foreigners was not a direct product of Josef Stalin or the peasant's natural abhorrence of outsiders. The Germans and the Japanese had invaded Russia, and briefly in the early nineteen twenties, the Western Allies occupied some of the sacred Rodina. There were lots of reasons for mistrust.

Upskayoyve-Ostravenyesko was also a military secret. It built vital parts and electronic equipment for the Mikoyan Gureyevich aircraft company. Technically inferior and lacking the scientists to challenge Western military advances, the Soviets established many towns similar to Upsakayoyve-Ostravenyesko to exploit the harvest from industrial espionage they waged worldwide.

With the help of sympathisers, the Soviets stole other nations' secrets wherever they could. Avoiding the time, research effort, and cost of devising their own atom bomb, they succeeded in stealing enough secret information to build their own, closing the gap on technology. The same efforts yielded more mundane advances in all fields. In nineteen fifty-three, with the help of a sexually compromised technician, their spies managed to steal a complete guidance system for a French-made air-to-air missile.

Enclosed in an outer crate with Cyrillic script, the boxed guidance system was loaded in Marseilles onto a Soviet ship. It sailed east through the Mediterranean. It passed through the Bosporus and crossed the Black Sea to dock in the Crimea. Within a week, under the eager eyes of several scientists, a work party from the local prison camp in Upskayoyve-Ostravenyesko was levering the wooden crate open. Having revealed the inner French crate containing the prize, two of three prisoners, dressed in the grubby blue coveralls worn by all the inmates, hacked at the lid with their crowbars.

"Non! Ce n'est pas la manière d'ouvrir la *boîte*. Regardez, lisez les mots. Ce devrait être ce côté vers le haut!" Agitated, the third prisoner grabbed the shoulders of the two men attacking the box and drew them back. In the shocked silence, he stepped forward and lovingly traced the foreign words stencilled on the box with a finger, crooning their pronunciation. Turning, suddenly acting mute, he indicated by signs that the box should be inverted before being opened. Inside were papers the prisoner seized before he could be stopped. The scientists present, none of whom could speak any other language, had no difficulty in recognizing that the man was avidly reading the contents and saw for themselves a great opportunity to curry favour.

They immediately told the camp commander the man must be assigned to them as a translator and given preferential treatment. This produced a first-class row. Prisoners were not to be accorded special treatment. Besides, the Commandant did not like a bunch of Apparatchiks telling him what to do. Under considerable pressure, the officer investigated the background of the prisoner, fearful that if some future act of sabotage came to pass, he would receive the blame.

The prisoner in question was shipped from Poland two years before. Emaciated and stooped, he sported a head wound of grotesque proportions. It ran from above his right eyebrow and was visible across his balding scalp. He responded only to the name he had been given: Mikhail. He had no knowledge of where he was or who he really was, a fact that aroused all the suspicions of the Commandant. Either this man was a monumental liar or incredibly stupid, both of which could be a threat to the Commandant's future.

The camp doctor suggested the man suffered from gross amnesia, caused by the obvious head wound. Dragged in quivering for interrogation, fellow prisoners were quick to tell all they knew about the man. He communicated little but was known to speak a little Russian, a little Polish, and a little German. Some nights, he suffered torturous dreams and spoke in a language none of them understood, although it might have been French. The prisoners had a mutual bond of survival but made few friends, so no confidences were shared. They all learned the lessons of vulnerability to betrayal, where a man might denounce another for a crust of dried black bread.

With no recourse, the Commandant reluctantly released the man to the Apparatchiks, salving his pride with dire threats to everyone of the consequences if things did not go right. He need not have worried. As though a door opened to him and reawakened his intellect, the prisoner Mikhail became a quick study for the electronic technology. He became a valuable asset to the laboratory.

Mikail showed a talent for technology, not as an engineer, but from the organizational standpoint. He had a talent for managing the various departments necessary to achieve success and bringing them and their products together at the appropriate time. He quickly became fluent in Russian and also disclosed fluency in English. The flood of worldwide technological information pirated by the KGB and GRU spy agencies passed largely through his hands.

Although the amnesia he appeared to suffer did not abate, he was rational and intelligent enough to realize that wherever he had come from, the Soviets could not possibly allow him to ever go home and reveal the extent of their espionage. He was a prisoner of the Soviet Union for life. He was allowed certain privileges; his own small apartment and a card to purchase commodities at the local Communist party store that were unobtainable to the common people. This was eminently preferable to being in one of the gulags. He accepted it gratefully, if with a slight resentment. He knew he was watched constantly, so he was still in a prison, albeit one more comfortable and tolerable.

Almost a year after he was allowed the apartment, a dark-haired woman in her early thirties came to work in the complex and very quickly made it clear she would entertain advances from him. Within a month, the attractive and well-endowed Alissa Markovich Davidova moved in with him. The sexual diversion was welcome, but his long incarceration with the Germans had blunted his prowess. Alissa's occasional overnight visits with her 'aunt' confirmed his suspicion that she was a KGB plant. She was both a reward and a jailer. Her absences suggested a lover she appreciated more than him.

A batch of smuggled microfilm documents crossed Mikhail's desk in nineteen fifty-nine. It caused him great excitement. Depicting parts proposals for a radically new propulsion unit, it was not the technological implications on the prints, but the mention of certain companies and places that prompted thoughts that had been dormant for years. He was seized by restlessness and had to take great pains not to betray his mental state to those around him, particularly Alissa Markovich. At night, his dreams became more vivid with the same people filling them. He was determined to leave and carefully plotted his escape from the complex. Knowing he would require some kind of legitimate trading goods to assure acceptance outside the Soviet Union, Mikhail stole paper copies of the propulsion plans he saw. They would not be noted as missing for several weeks when they were not returned to the central registry. By then, he hoped to be long gone.

****

Millicent Barnes.

Millicent was flattered by the attention of such a famous person as Nathan Connaught. He was being his most charming self as they lounged in the corner booth of the Starlight Lounge, just off Jasper Avenue.

Easily swayed by alcohol, Millicent had been well plied by the cunning Nathan, who was now picking her brains about Edmunds Enterprises. She was employed there for three years, graduating from the typing pool to a senior secretary, thanks to some well-planned evening classes. For all that, she was a silly girl, prone to flattery and vain about herself. It left her vulnerable to someone of Nathan's character.

Millicent liked to emphasize key words for effect. "Well, I know for a *fact* that there was a connection between Mr. Edmunds and some *Chinese* businessmen. There was a little Chink who used to come with a *briefcase* several times a year and spend a *lot* of time in his office. It was all *very* hush-hush. I know that because he used to arrive by the *private* entrance, as if *we* were not supposed to see him. Once, one of the girls had to take a document into Mr. Edmunds' office, while the Chink was there. She said *he* was giving *Mr. Edmunds* what-for! Can you imagine *anyone* telling off Mr. Edmunds?" Millicent pursed her lipstick-bright lips at the mere thought and reached for her cocktail.

She looked up again, her ample cheeks flushed with self-importance, and Nathan suddenly realized he might have to bed this fat little trollop, if only to keep her quiet about their meeting. "Everyone *knows* that Mr. Edmunds *eats* at that Chinese restaurant. Er, what's its name?"

"The Mandarin Duck."

"Yes, that is *it!* So, if he eats there, there *must* be a *connection!*"

"Oh, everyone knows he is connected there and eats for free." Nathan's comment was dismissive, but he was playing her like a fish.

"*Yeah,* but, I *know* something else!" Millicent leaned in, conspiratorially, and Nathan waited for the pay dirt. He had a bottle of vodka at home, a tape recorder, and a packet of condoms.

****

Germany.

The tattered and emaciated figure crouched in the alley. The rain increased its steady downpour from a night sky. A piece of oiled paper held overhead merely deflected an increased soaking, since he was already wet through. A beard, mostly white, masked facial bones stretching the man's parchment skin. Where there was no hair, blackheads and dirt-lined skin told of long neglect and lack of opportunities for hygiene. With twenty-five hundred kilometres behind him, the man was on his last lap of a carefully planned trip.

A torn and battered cloth cap kept some vestige of heat in his brain, which still operated on a survival level learned long ago. The railyards were close by. They funnelled trains towards France, and even now, railcars with the familiar French National Railway signage were shunted into a siding ready for dispatch. For two days, the man watched, assimilated, and calculated the departure time, as the stationary rolling stock grew in number. There was one flatcar with tarpaulins he figured he could stow away on, based on his experience of the past six months. Beneath the tarpaulins was a grain harvester with a driving cab he could shelter in.

By his reckoning, the freight train would leave around dawn. He would have time to scavenge restaurant trashcans for food to take along before getting aboard prior to first light. Meanwhile, his eyes grew heavy. It was time to get some sleep.

****

By nineteen sixty, the Edmunds financial empire reached a new plateau. Oil was still coming out of the ground as fast as it could be pumped. Feedstock to the petrochemical industry began to grow enormously. More plants came on line near Fort Saskatchewan. Drilling and refining supported the OmniWest gas stations that proliferated across Alberta. They were also spreading into Saskatchewan and British Columbia.

Trans-West Transportation and the Ford franchise blossomed as if unstoppable. AllWest Lumberyards and Home Improvement Centres had reached fifteen branches. Thomas' stores were in every major city in Western Canada and had opened food floors. Two more radio stations came on stream. Negotiations were underway to franchise in a new national television network. A new major construction company, BuildWest, habitually found itself the successful bidder on projects associated with Edmunds, including three hotels.

Although the word 'West' tacked onto a name was usually a giveaway of Edmunds ownership, it was not exclusively used, since announced ownership was not always advisable. Careful study was made of businesses before naming them to see whether the Edmunds financial umbrella would accord trust and consumer loyalty or whether discreet ownership better served commercial ends. Many bought-out companies retained their original names, effectively masking ownership. Much of this was accomplished with the brilliant input of 'Sher' Williams who had risen to the position of Vice-President, Research and Development, with Edmunds Enterprises.

The financial empire was worth an estimated one hundred and ninety million dollars in total. This was augmented by share capital in other enterprises, seeded by the Edmunds'-owned Rupertsland Trust Company, a major depositor of whom was a certain Chinese organization. In nineteen fifty-five and nineteen fifty-nine, major oil companies tried to squeeze Edmunds Enterprises out of the petroleum business. Price wars at the gas pumps, the most vulnerable point of attack, accompanied by hostile bids for shares constituted the main strategy.

The first attempt failed because of the astonishing loyalty of Western Canadians to one of their own. While most people would have welcomed lower prices, a clever ad campaign helped consumers decide that in the long term, an independent, locally owned establishment would perennially challenge the hegemony of the multinationals. The oil came from Alberta and by golly, Albertans would have a say in it. The certain loss of jobs attached to such a sale also contributed to the quick defeat of the ploy.

The second attempt foundered when 'Sher' Williams filed a lawsuit in federal court, charging conspiracy, unfair practice, and price-fixing. Since price-fixing is normally a complaint about elevated prices, it was considered strange by some observers that price reduction would prompt such a charge. However, 'Sher's' careful research graphically showed that the predatory behaviour of the majors, when successful, inevitably resulted in higher prices due to a monopoly. He held a press conference, and after describing his complaint, unveiled two easels beside him. One showed a gas station price sign before a price war involving a take-over in the United States. The other showed the heavily inflated price six months later. Despite it being clear evidence, there was a certain cynical rumble throughout the room. Unaffected by this, 'Sher' calmly signalled two assistants who, several times over, removed the signs to reveal several layers. As he intoned the names of companies similarly victimized, they finally revealed six different cases where take-overs were not in the consumers' best interest.

It all went on television. A couple of members of parliament were interviewed and blustered their intent to have a bill presented in Ottawa. Several days later, gas pump prices returned to normal levels with the propaganda message that *a temporary glut on the market created "storage" problems and had been resolved by increased consumption.*

Both attempts were stymied by the refusal of shareholders to sell at any price. Since the vast majority of voting shares resided with the Edmunds family, the only beneficiaries were people who had made a quick dollar on shares that could not influence control of the company. Edmunds Enterprises actively encouraged its employees to buy company shares – matching their costs – so loyalty to the company helped defeat the strategy. The three escalating offers were also topped by offers from an unknown entity that wound up buying shares. Opinion was that this was Tom Edmunds buying back shares, but it was not. Buyers were going to lose because it was inevitable the share value would soon return to lower and more realistic values, whatever the outcome. Share sales fell to a dribble.

The whole colossal enterprise still cleaved to the 'flow-through' principle, wherein each supported and complimented the others. Few citizens went from birth to death without being touched by Edmunds Enterprises. Endowments to hospitals, schools and universities, loans, car purchases, gasoline, food, house construction, consumer goods, and even a funeral parlour figured in the list of businesses.

This was obvious to Nathan Connaught when he embarked on as thorough an analysis as he could muster of Tom Edmunds' holdings. The driving force behind this particular effort was the recent news that Edmunds Enterprises had won government taxation exemptions and a low interest loan to develop new oil exploration. There was a howl of protest from many quarters, coming as it did on the heels of other major tax concessions. It took three weeks and the efforts of two research assistants to compile the information. Despite his already jaundiced opinion, even Nathan was surprised at the number of threads sown throughout Canadian society by Edmunds.

He had already sketched out the heady text of his new attack. The figures placed on his desk drove him to new hyperbole: *"The residing of such wealth and power in the hands of one family, guided and controlled by one man for his own self-aggrandisement can only be seen for what it is, an all-out assault on the welfare of the ordinary citizen. Government legislation must be introduced to restrict the overbearing and all-pervading influence this group of companies has both on citizens and the government, which seems singularly helpless at negotiating reasonable terms for public monies thrown to it."* Nathan went on to chastise, *"...a Social Credit government that lost its "social" soul and responsibility to the common man by being corrupted by wealth. Power tends to corrupt, and absolute power corrupts absolutely."*

The article was headed 'Alberta on a million dollars a day. Can you get by on it?' and laid out in graphic detail the various companies and values controlled by Tom Edmunds. He went on to question why one man should be allowed to exercise his ambitions, hiding behind the screens of corporate intrigue and barriers. *"Men do not become tyrants to keep out the cold,"* he thundered. *"Corporations have neither bodies to be punished, nor souls to be condemned; they therefore do as they like."*

Ever ready to take a swipe at the leader of this enormous wealth, Nathan climaxed his attack by paraphrasing William Shakespeare's Julius Caesar: *"Why, Albertans, he doth bestride the narrow world like a Colossus; and we petty men walk beneath his huge legs, and peep about."* The implicit threat of reprisal in ancient and inflammatory words was carried forward to the present day with a haughty sniff of distain and dismissal, wherein Nathan referred to Tom as *this ' Emperor of the East Slope.'*

It was a good article, factually correct, and providing an exposé suitable to inspire jealousy or admiration. That it also served as a vehicle for Nathan's virulent anti-business attitude was of little importance to most people. The article might have almost gone unremembered into the newspaper's archives. Tom Edmunds instantly disliked it for the exposé, yet loved the sprinkled quotes of Aristotle, Shakespeare, and others. He gave mute tribute to Nathan for the incisive remarks about socialist governments. It did not matter how virulently left wing a government might be in Alberta; the amount of wealth coming out of the ground would corrupt its methods. The millions of dollars filled their coffers, dragged their ministers into corporate boardrooms, where the penurious political style of socialism, always looking for funds to dispense, was totally swamped by them.

Two days after the article was published, however, the energy minister was interviewed by reporters and specifically questioned as to why the government so slavishly granted the tax concessions to Tom Edmunds. Needled mercilessly and finally exasperated by a cutting accusation from Nathan Connaught, the minister grinned facetiously and replied. "Well, maybe it's because *you* have told us all he is the *Emperor of the East Slope*."

It was a faux pas of tremendous import, taped for television viewing, and it almost cost the minister his job. For days, the press thundered for his resignation. The government back-pedalled in a full retreat. Initially ignored, Nathan's article was now being studied.

It ultimately backfired on him. The quote 'Emperor of the East Slope' out-did the 'Edmundstown' gem that Nathan dropped on the public in earlier days. Despite widespread dislike of Tom Edmunds, based mostly on envy, like most cities, Edmontonians had a sneaking pride in any of its citizens who did well, especially if they scored victories over outsiders. Any Edmontonian who grumbled about having to buy from an Edmunds company would chortle with team complicity at the thought of sales coming from an outside source, which in turn complained about its lot.

In short, Edmontonians loved the quote and basked quite happily in the reflected glory.

****

Paris.

The streets made sense. There were crowds of people, but since leaving the marshalling yards, they had not bothered him on his walk towards the centre of the city. He knew where he was going. He could not have voiced the address, could not have said why he marched, but the compulsion that began in Siberia was as strong as it had been more than half a year before. It took careful planning and the setting up of a day's alibi to gain a head start on his jailers when he escaped. But escaped he had, eluding them on two separate and close occasions, crossing borders against all odds.

He fed from garbage cans, eschewed company, and avoided uniforms like the plague, like the Gendarme who now looked at him curiously then ignored him. He held his head high and pretended he belonged. The scarecrow marched on. There was a growing feeling of accomplishment accompanying each step. A building anticipation kept him moving, despite a steadily nagging fatigue. As he passed Les Invalides and reached St Francois Xavier, vivid flashes of recall battered him. He staggered as if punches were being inflicted upon him. The street sign on the ornate iron lamp standard mocked and teased him as he turned onto Rue Oudinot. So familiar was it.

He stopped beneath the shade trees and turned to face the apartment block across the street some fifty meters down the road. Faces leaped at him, faces of the dead. A girl-child's giggling blonde innocence, framed in a white lace dress under a summer sun, a parasol over her shoulder. Her mother, blonde and beautiful was smiling on. Then they were bloated, drowned, and dead.

An elderly woman, face wrinkled, held up heavily bejewelled hands, beseeching him to some task, while a timid and darkly-trussed daughter clung to her arm. Gone. Gone to the Nazis. Killed in a concentration camp. The fatigue swelled to irresistible proportions. He wondered why he was here. And then another face, dark hair again, with an elfin carelessness swam into his vision, coming out of the apartment opposite.

It was twenty years, but he knew her in an instant. It was reality – his journey's end – atonement for all that had gone before. With a cry weakened by his pitiful condition, the tramp darted from between two parked vehicles, straight into the path of an approaching car.

The screech of brakes from across the street startled Beth. The dull thud finding its way to her ears through all the other city noises had an ominous sound. A babble of voices quickly arose from nearby, and she turned to her liveried chauffeur who was with her.

"Alphonse, what has happened?"

"I don't know Madame. Perhaps it is an accident."

"Well, please go and see." She opened the limousine door herself and climbed into the back seat with her attaché case.

Alphonse was back in moments. "It was just an old derelict, Madame. He has stepped in front of a car and been knocked down."

"Oh, is there anything we can do?"

"I fear not, Madame." A Gallic shrug. "He is quite dead."

****

Edmonton.

It was a Thursday evening. Tom was running late for his regular meeting, hosted by Alex McFarlane tonight. For some inexplicable reason, on his way out of the house, he backed up after passing Margaret's door to say goodbye. Just as he raised his hand to knock, he heard a voice on the other side of the door. "…know why you put up with it. He is out and about with women all the time. It is a disgrace. He obviously does not care about the hurt he causes you. You should sue him for divorce; it would be worth millions of dollars to you. We could move away, live somewhere nicer. I would never let someone like Tom Edmunds treat *me* like that!" The voice moved away from the door and faded.

Tom stood shocked. Margaret's long-time companion, Gladys Smith, had left a year ago and been replaced by a bony little slip of a woman named Mary Isbister. A spinster, with tiny glasses and greying hair tied in a severe bun, Mary had the constant sour squint of the disenchanted. Various negative changes to the household since her arrival began to fall into place. Margaret had become even more distant, if that were possible. Demands had been made, exasperating him. He recalled how Mary's sourness seemed to deepen whenever she encountered him. Now he knew the cause.

He went back to his study and wrote a cheque for a thousand dollars. Returning to the door, he knocked and waited until Mary answered. Her face fell at the sight of him, lips pursed in open distaste. "I need a word with you, please, Mary."

She muttered something to Margaret and then stepped outside, turning to close the door. When she turned to face him, he grasped her by the front of her frock, physically lifting her off her feet. He pushed her back against the wall as her mouth fell open in a gasp. His face came up close to hers, glaring into her frightened eyes. His voice was low, the words for her alone.

"Listen to me carefully, you sour, ungrateful, back-stabbing witch. You were entrusted with a special task in my house. You have betrayed that trust. I have never hit a woman in my life, but if you are still here when I return, I shall personally throw you out in the street and call the police. I will then use all means at my disposal to sue your sorry, skinny, rotten ass. Here!" Depositing her back to the floor, Tom stuffed the cheque into her nerveless fingers and strode away.

Not until he was three blocks away did it hit him what he had done. At the same time, the real anger swept over him and he had to park the car for a few minutes while he caught his breath.

****

Paris.

Like most major cities, Paris has an ambulance system that copes with the majority of daily emergencies in an efficient way. Medical attention is paid for by the recipient. However, without proof of ability to pay, life may hang by a tenuous thread for the injured. At times of overload, the system may cynically, but not accountably, provide precedence to the more affluent members of society.

The ambulance with the blue flashing lights and insistent klaxon screeched into the hospital emergency receiving area. It was transporting a challenge when the caseload was only of average size.

Doctor Louis Chaguille, an overworked intern, got caught up in the adrenalin of the moment and had the pitiful contents of the stretcher placed on an emergency bed in moments. While his staff fulfilled his urgent commands for equipment and drug infusions, he palpated the lower limbs of the traffic victim and determined he definitely had a fractured femur, possibly a distal fracture of the left tibia, and some internal damage, accompanied by a broken pelvis. His first task was to arrest the effects of severe shock. This he initiated promptly with fluids.

The traffic victim was a despicably clad vagrant who reeked of ill kempt clothing and body odour. He ordered the garments cut from the body. These would, of course, be kept for possible identification, especially the contents of the pockets. The thought of billing was suppressed beneath the sure knowledge that here was a high-risk patient who may never be able to pay. However, he may have relatives who could be dunned for the bill. Chaguille shrugged. It was not his concern.

Nurse Emily Deschamps found the piece of folded paper in the dirty clothing, and hopeful of some kind of identification on this only find, opened it. The word 'secret' took her by surprise. Although the drawing beneath made no sense, it looked official, so she thought she should show it to Doctor Chaguille. Chaguille, an amateur mechanic, immediately saw the significance of the find.

"This man must have some worth to someone if he is carrying this around. Was there any means of identification on him?"

"No, Doctor. This is all there was."

"Then, please get administration to contact this company immediately, and get one of their personnel over here to identify him."

It took several hours before a junior security guard reached the hospital. To him, the document shown was possibly genuine, but he did not have the expertise to make a judgement. Refused custody of the paper by a determined Emily Deschamps, he returned to his supervisor and showed him the project number he scribbled down. A call to the contact person for that department produced a panic of the first degree. Within hours, a team of experts descended on the hospital, and the Deuxième Bureau had been advised. Since the documents bore the stamp of France's Bureau pour le Procurement des objets Militaire, a national security breach was declared.

Concerned the tramp may be liquidated to protect his contacts, the Deuxième Bureau whisked him into a private nursing home, where he was guarded day and night. There were important questions to ask this man as soon as he was fit to talk.

The vice president in charge of research and development at Societé de Fabrication des Militaires was shocked. "They found this design on a *tramp*?"

"Yes Sir. I checked myself at the hospital, and the nurse who found it said it definitely came from his clothing. She herself removed it from his jacket."

"Then who is this man? How does he come to have a closely guarded industrial secret of ours in his pocket?"

"I do not know. It is a mystery."

"Solve it! Get back there immediately with some security men. Spare no effort! Find out where he got it from!"

Despite the most urgent questioning, the Deuxième Bureau received nothing from the old derelict. While he seemed to be recovering from his injuries, mentally, he retreated into some inner state they could not penetrate. The only thing they learned was his name. Yet, comatose on drugs and restless in his sleep, he murmured two names. The attending nurse reported them to the agents, and they sat in shocked silence. One name, that supposedly of the tramp, meant nothing. The other was something else to them. A chief officer of an armament company, a rival to the one penetrated, named by someone carrying secret plans for military hardware suggested espionage at the highest level. They decided to set a trap for that person, moving the derelict to a less exclusive bed in the nursing home and bugging the room.

****

"Pardon, Madame. Do you remember the old derelict who was knocked down a week or so ago?" Alphonse peered in his mirror, anxious not to disturb his mistress working in the back of the car.

"What's that, Alphonse?"

"The derelict, Madame, who was hit by a car."

"What of him?"

"It is strange, Madame, but Maria says a nurse called from the hospital to say he was asking for you."

"But you said he was dead! He survived and is asking for me?"

"Yes, Madame. It is inconceivable, no?"

"Well, it is nothing to me, but I wonder how he knows my name."

"Perhaps he just learned it and hopes to sponge off you."

"Perhaps. Does he have a name?"

"Maria says he calls himself Albert Defarge."

In the back of the vehicle, the clipboard Beth was using to sign documents slid from her nerveless fingers to the floor. The front of the car interior blurred through tears. Her life force ran down through her body like sand out of an emptying timer. A dark veil crept over her, a cold sweat threatening to lubricate her slide into unconsciousness. "Alphonse!" She struggled not to faint, her voice a croak.

"Madame! Are you ill?" Anxiously, Alphonse peered in the mirror, watching his mistress teeter in her seat. To an accompaniment of irate horns, he cut off four other cars and swerved into the curb. In an instant, he was leaning over her in the back, grasping her icy and clammy hands like a sea anchor restraining a ship in peril, striving to bring her back to him.

"The hospital..." The words were a thin replica of her normal voice, squeezed by the enormous boulder in her throat.

"Yes, Madame, the Hôpital Université is nearby. We can be there in minutes. What is wrong?"

Beth shook her head dumbly, unable to speak. "It is not me, Alphonse; it is *him*! I am just a little shocked. Give me a brandy!" The fiery spirit in the glass Alphonse proffered loosened her throat. "You must take me immediately to the hospital where this man is, Alphonse!"

"But your meeting this morning, it is extremely important!"

"Call the office and tell Raymond Armandier to take charge. Find out from Maria where this man is."

"Yes, Madame." Bewildered, Alphonse climbed back behind the wheel and used the car phone. "The nurse was particular, Madame. The man is at a nursing home off the Cours de Ballard."

"Take me there immediately!" Now that her heart had restarted, Beth felt it running uncontrollably wild and poured herself another brandy. Watching in the mirror, Alphonse shook his head. He knew his mistress did some strange things, but this episode beat a lot of them. Crossing the Seine, he wheeled around the Bastille and headed east towards Vincennes.

It had to be a coincidence! Beth's mind went back to those dark days at the Château L'Église D'Artou years ago. France was beaten. The Germans had conquered, and animals like Ewald Kleinst had free rein to hunt her and her family. A letter arrived, its contents now dissolved by time, instructions as to how to conduct herself in her husband's absence, coded to preserve their integrity. That letter now reposed in a wallet amongst her treasured possessions, but she had not forgotten the content. *If you ever receive a message from 'Albert Defarge' or mentioning that name, it will be genuinely from me.*

"*René!*" She finally voiced the name inside her mind. Was it possible after all these years?

Alphonse wheeled them into the forecourt of the nursing home twenty minutes later. In her state of mind, it did not appear strange to Beth that a mere tramp should be afforded the convenience of an exclusive clinic set back from the street in a building of such elegant appearance. Nor had she bothered to consider why he might go to the trouble of contacting her. With dogged determination replacing her earlier trepidation, she sailed up the front steps into the reception area with Alphonse struggling to catch up.

"Albert Defarge. Where is his room, please?"

"Room deux cent seize, second floor, but you cannot see him immediately." The dark-haired receptionist was told to stall this visitor. She gave a discreet signal to two men sitting in the waiting area.

"I wish to see him right away." Turning away, Beth headed for the stairs.

"Madame, please, the doctor is with him. You may visit in about two minutes. May I have your name?"

"Elizabeth de Fourquet." The name came out without thought. Alphonse gaped at this unusual declaration. "I am going upstairs, *now!*"

One of the men nodded, and the receptionist made no further resistance.

Upstairs, the hallway took them to a plain white door halfway along. "Alphonse, wait here!"

Momentarily, Beth put her hand to the door and leaned to rest her forehead against it. She felt like opening the door would be like one of the television game shows the Americans had popularised. Behind the door was either her heavenly desire or some black fiend from hell. Perplexed, Alphonse watched her enter the room.

It was light and airy inside. The leafy presence of outside trees lent a sense of relaxed security to the two occupants. Both were asleep; the nearest a hummock in the bed, head buried invisibly beneath the bedding. Nearer the window, the second man was lying on his back, a placid look on his face. His head was mostly bald, thin white tufts of hair straggling onto the pillow. A horrible scar disfigured the upper part of his face, but she recognized the hawkish beak of a nose pointing straight up to the ceiling. With legs growing weaker by the step, Beth staggered to the bed and sank to her knees beside it, gazing at the man's profile.

She could not bring herself to touch him, not yet ready to be reassured or disappointed by a puff of smoke that may take him away. A feeling she would never define crept over her, something akin to relief, and something like despair at the loss of time. The complications René's return would bring to her life had not yet registered. All she saw was René. A tear rolled down her cheek, joined by another, and she began to cry soundlessly. Sightless, she reached out and took the gnarled hand resting on the counterpane. A line from Robert Louis Stevenson, learned on her father's knee, rolled through her mind: '...and the hunter, home from the hill...'

The knock on the door was emphatic and only broke into Beth's world like a faint echo. The presence of two Duxième agents blundering through the door came like a cavalry charge, pillaging her thoughts. "Madame, we are agents of the Duxième Bureau. You must accompany us to headquarters immediately to answer to charges of the gravest nature!"

"What?" Bewildered, the realization of their identities came like a dark cloak, threatening to obscure the vital nature of her discovery.

"Madame, we need to question you immediately concerning this man. There has been a major breach of national security!"

"He…he is my…husband!" Beth was still groping with the reality.

"He was found with secret papers on his person, and you are accused of complicity!" The speaker was a gaunt man with stern features who brooked no argument from law-breakers.

"What? He is injured. I must take him away and care for him!"

"You cannot. He is in the care of the Securité. You must come with us or be arrested!"

It was Kleinst all over again! Beth looked momentarily at the two men. "This man is in my care. Nobody! Nobody will prevent me from protecting him!"

"Madame!" The other agent made the mistake of stepping aggressively forward and found a small automatic pistol thrust into his face. Beth kept it in her purse ever since she received a threat several years before.

"Now, gentlemen. You have not been paying attention! This man is my husband. He is a French national hero and has been missing since the war. I do not know what your reasoning is here, but he is in my care, and I will not be separated from him, not for one second! Do you understand?"

Helpless, backed against the wall with the muzzle of the pistol thrust up his nose, the hapless agent nodded. "Alphonse!" Gaping at the scene, the chauffeur entered the room. "Alphonse, the man in the bed is my husband, René de Fourquet, whom you remember. Confirm for these men who he is!"

Dumbly, Alphonse moved to the bed, looked down, and drew a hiss of breath. Pale beyond description, he crossed himself and then nodded at the two agents.

"Cover these two. If either of them moves, shoot them both!" Startled, the two agents stepped back, their apprehension reinforced by the enthusiasm with which Alphonse took the firearm and waved it at them.

With one quick look of affirmation, Beth left the room and went towards the stairs. A third agent came up to meet her and harangued her at the top. She brushed by him, ignoring his tirade. When he reached out and grabbed her shoulder, she cried out. "Alphonse!"

"Oui, Madame?"

"One round into the ceiling. Now!"

The crack of the pistol stopped the agent in his tracks. "One more word and he shoots to kill! Come with me! Now!" She screamed the last word, her voice reverberating up and down the hallways. "You fucking bastards think you are going to mess with me? You really think I have waited all these years for some useless limp-dick morons to get in my way?"

Downstairs, she physically ejected a doctor from his office and dialled Roland's number. Waved to a chair, the agent with her could not believe that an accused person could phone a person of such authority with such ease. Sparing Roland nothing, shamelessly playing on their relationship, Beth made him release René to her safekeeping. Holding the phone out to the shocked agent, she could hear Roland tearing a strip off the man, ordering him to afford Madame his full protection and courtesy, while promising him access to the accused.

Within the hour, they left the nursing home. Still encased in casts, René was carefully laid across the rear seat of the limousine, Alphonse at the wheel. Relenting slightly, Beth let the senior agent ride along in the front seat.

The reappearance of René de Fourquet after so many years was a sensation in France. That he survived the war was incredible enough. That he endured the captivity of the Nazis even more so. To have been abducted into Russia and finally escaped to return after all these years was beyond belief. Especially newsworthy to the tabloids and the sordid interests of their readers were the numerous marriages and affairs of his wife, which had taken place in his absence. Beth was devastated by the attention she received, but fortunately, René still lived in a state of semi comprehension. She was able to whisk him away to the house near St. Denis, a place of seclusion, where only trustworthy staff supervised him.

It was the staff at the nursing home that lined their pockets by giving details to the press. Few of them were aware of the Deuxième's interest and found themselves in deep trouble for exposing a national security issue. The agents themselves were deeply perturbed at the circumstances. All their police instincts were aroused against René and Beth. Because the bearer of the secret documents turned out to be her husband, to them, it was too much to swallow as happenstance. The Russian part of the matter, the shame of René's incarceration, and above all, the revelation of espionage against France were in the open before diplomacy could corral it. A full-blown diplomatic incident ensued with France recalling her ambassador and expulsing half the Russian embassy staff as declared KGB operatives.

To Beth, it all meant little. The first time René opened his eyes and looked at her, nothing else in the world mattered. His first recognition was guarded, a half smile like a child acknowledging an accomplishment scarcely understood. Beth hired a Swiss psychiatrist who supervised his care and directed the means of nursing him into the present. It was a long and never-to-be-completed task. The head injury and years of self-preservation induced an introverted psyche that could hardly be penetrated. Several doctors diagnosed severe amnesia and early Alzheimer's disease. Beth sat with him for hours, showing him photographs and reminding him of places and names. There were occasional brief flashes of the man within, but he did not fully acknowledge her. While this was painful to her, she had at least known him in the past. To David de Fourquet, the father he finally met for the first time was a hollow shell, the substance of which could only be provided by his mother's narrative. It was bitterly disappointing to both of them in the same and separate ways, but they lived in hope.

One spring morning following his return, he snuck out of the apartment, while the help was in the kitchen. A frantic search of Paris ensued for three hours before Beth had a sudden hunch and went to Saint Severin. Dressed only in shirt and pants against the chill, René stood before the winged stone figure in the side chapel. "René!" He ignored her motherly admonition. Stepping forward, he reached beneath the stone skirt, withdrawing his hand empty.

He turned with a smile. "She got the message."

Somewhere in the frail figure, the need to seek out a phantom endured. He gave no hint of his history for the past twenty-odd years, so they had no clue to his malady, no hint of restitutive care. The physical damage from being hit by the car in Paris endured. He walked painfully with the aid of a cane. One night, contrary to the psychiatrist's advice, Beth undressed and got into bed with René. Naked against him, she felt only the slackened limbs and palsied body of an old man. She placed his face between her breasts and willed their bodies to be as one. She received only a whimper of protest at the suffocation. Later in the night, he rolled over and snuggled against her, an act that typified the following nights.

****

Edmonton.

Alex McFarlane awoke with a terrible headache. Frowning with the pain and pondering the cause, he stumbled out of bed, reflecting that a good pipe of Balkan Sobranie and a couple of drams of Glenfiddich were his only indulgence the night before.

Donning his robe, he left the bedroom, crossing to the bathroom, circling the banister at the head of the stairs. A tornado of red flame swept behind his eyes and impinged on the back of his skull like a hammer. Poleaxed, he fell sideways. As his eyes dimmed forever, his last sight was the flight of stairs yawning before him, the first bounce a nerveless jerk of fading vision.

Beth took the first flight to Edmonton to attend the funeral of her beloved Uncle Alex. The news that he had been found dead of a stroke at the foot of his stairs was a terrible shock, ameliorated only by the mercy of its suddenness. The service was a simple Presbyterian one, followed by cremation. At the reading of the will, Tom was found to inherit all of Alex's shares in the Edmunds group of companies. Beth received the Edmonton house and its artefacts, worth some five million dollars. The legacy best left by Alex to Beth, however, was his love. She kept the poem he had written at the time of her first marriage, and somehow, he found his way into her affections to the point where it seemed he was a second father. It was not quite a father-and-daughter relationship, and they both knew it.

Only one request in the will laid any burden on them. That Tom and Beth should jointly spread his ashes on the waters of the river at Kingussie, his birthplace, in the heart of the Scottish Highlands. And so it was that one warm July day. They held the urn together and upended it over the silver play of water rushing towards the Moray Firth. The grey dust fell out in a thick clump, thinning to a sprinkle, as they gently shook the container. Swallowed quickly by the turbulent waters, the last remains of Alex MacFarlane blended with his heritage and were re-assimilated. They looked out over the broad valley with its rounded mountains of greens, browns, and purple heather, sharing a moment.

Later in the small hotel, they sat in the quiet of the bar lounge, determined to spend one night more close to their departed friend. The peat fire glowed and smoked. Tom started a fat cigar. A single malt from the distillery just a stone's throw away completed the ambience.

"Why did he never marry? Have children?"

"I can't truly say, Beth."

"Was it Matilda Brown?" A confirmed bachelor, Alex had a housekeeper for years, the spinster Matilda Brown. On the rare occasion when there was little else to focus on, gossips would talk of them, but it was a dry and speculative discourse.

"I think Alex was afraid to marry. Whether he and Matilda were involved that way, we shall never know. He was wounded in the Great War. You would not know, but he lost a testicle to a piece of shrapnel. I think it was always a source of great embarrassment to him, something he could not bear anyone to find out. I would never have known, but one of our old comrades knew and told me. Alex sometimes hinted around the subject, but being the private person he truly was, he never brought the subject up."

"How can a piece of shrapnel do that without other wounds?"

"Well, exploding steel has strange habits. There were many unaccountable wounds." The mention of exploding steel brought other thoughts to each of them simultaneously, and their minds went to James, long dead in an Italian field. The double loss hit hard. They held hands, while silent tears flowed for separate reasons: one for the loss of a son and promise denied, the other for redemption never granted.

Edmonton, MacDonald Hotel.

"Hello, Tom."

He hated these canapés and white wine functions. They always exposed him to people who wanted to promote their own agendas by kissing his ass, or more directly, sticking their hands in his wallet. Surrounded by sycophants, assaulted by the ambitious, beguiled by the beggars, it was always the same.

Now, the low voice over his shoulder took him spinning back forty years to a dimly lit and dilapidated church. She stood behind him and he spun around to see her, his senses stumbling onto a dance floor, the first time they had come face-to-face. The freckles were still there. The hair was streaked with grey. Framed by creases tempered by the wisdom of passing years, the eyes still had the same sparkle.

"Hello, Jeanne." He reached out a hand and the touch was like throwing a switch. A flood of warmth went through him, and he saw her pupils dilate as she experienced the same. "It is so nice to see you. How are things?"

"Oh, I am doing quite well. I spend a lot of time fundraising for various organizations, which is why I am here at this library function." Tom was reminded of his purpose here. His own literary interests made him a natural contributor to the library. Still, he detected wistfulness in her comment. It sounded hollow.

"Mr. Edmunds? Sorry, it is time for the speeches." City councillor Debra Evans, Edmonton's chief supporter of the library, was at his elbow.

"See you in a few minutes." Tom grimaced at Jeanne, and she smiled.

The speeches droned on for about twenty minutes before Tom rose to speak. A polite round of genteel applause met his introduction. He was always good for a touch and the assembled supporters knew it.

"Ladies and gentlemen. It was my intent tonight to make a gift of twenty thousand dollars to the library fund on behalf of Edmunds Enterprises. I believe that was known to you all beforehand. How these secrets get out, I have no idea." A titter of laughter swept the room. "However, that plan has changed." He gazed sternly at the room and backbones froze, expecting the worst. "My company comptroller is not here to write up or authorize any change, so I have to take it upon my own purse to double this amount to a total of forty thousand dollars." Cheers and hearty applause dispelled a moment of silence as Debra Evans went to the large fundraising board and indicated it was now over the top of the target.

Tom sought out Jeanne again soon thereafter. "That was a very nice thing to do," she smiled.

"Let's just say I was persuaded by the diligent efforts of a certain library promoter!"

They were surrounded by a sea of well-wishers. Relief and gratitude crowded in on them. Debra Evans was close by, strutting and preening at the attention she was getting. The crowd flowed by them, thinning, until they stood alone.

"Before someone from the paper writes a speculative article about you and me, can I offer you a ride home?"

"Yes, I'll just get my coat from the counter."

Outside, they climbed into Tom's Ford. He had several vehicles, but always used more modest models around town to escape attention. "Giving away all that money has made me hungry. Do you like Chinese food?"

"To tell the truth, I have hardly tried it."

"Well, here's your chance."

There was a parking space close to the Mandarin Duck, and they walked in the front door. A handsome Chinese man in his thirties, obviously the manager, intercepted them at the door. "Ah! Uncle Tom, how are you? Are you going to honour us by eating tonight?"

"Jimmy!" Tom stretched out his hand. They shook vigorously. "Can we get a back room, please?"

"Absolutely! I will just throw out the people who are in there now." Tom made to object, but the man laughed. "Just joking! You know I have better manners than that!"

"Jimmy, I would like you to meet a very old and dear friend. This is Jeanne," Tom choked on the last name, "Williams."

"Hello, Jeanne. If you are a friend of Tom Edmunds, then you are family to us. Welcome!" Jimmy waved a hand and escorted them to a small cozy back room. "I will be back with the usual wine."

Tom raised a questioning eyebrow to Jeanne, but she nodded her consent to wine.

"Uncle Tom? Family?"

Tom settled in his seat with assurance and a comfortable air. "Jimmy is my God-son. I did a favour for his father, years ago, and they have poured familial blessings on me ever since. I eat and drink here for free and have done so for the past twenty years since he went into business. It is a strong bond."

"Favours to Chinese, personal donations to the library, this is not the face of Tom Edmunds I read about in the paper!"

"Yeah, well that snotty little bastard Nathan-bloody-Connaught and his ilk know nothing."

They played catch-up for the next several hours. The restaurant closed for the night and the staff cleaned up. As they left, Jeanne noticed three people besides Jimmy had stayed behind, respectfully waiting to serve any need they had. Not sensing the distracted demeanour of his departing guests, he cheerfully shook their hands again and babbled on about them returning soon.

"Do you feel like going for a walk?" It was the next day, and it had taken a lot of courage and the conquering of doubt to make the call.

There was a brief bowel-churning pause. "Sure. When?"

"How about I pick you up in fifteen minutes?"

"But, I'm not dressed for..."

"Don't worry, neither am I."

It was the same Ford that pulled to the curbside. They set off across town, and Jeanne soon realized where they were bound but said nothing. They murmured inconsequential talk along the way. Tom parked on a street at the upper end of Mill Creek. They set off, strolling down the deepening valley.

They reached the tree in five minutes. They stopped thirty feet away, taking in its splendour. It stood tall amongst the other trees, one of a half-dozen clump of spruce surrounded by poplar. Darkly sleek, the new growth had almost completely changed to its permanent colour. The trunk was strong and sturdy. For a long minute, they stood, isolated by mere feet, yet cemented together by a decades-long bond. Then Tom took her hand.

They stopped beneath the spread of branches, and in a simple mutual act, embraced. Tom could feel her tears on his cheek and his own eyes filled.

"Time...so much wasted time." Her voice choked.

'Hush." He patted her back and stroked her hair. The smell of spruce resin, like a catalyst on his senses, mingled with that of her skin.

"Do you come here often?"

"Yes. It is like a church to me. Like a confessional, a place to come and pray."

"I have been here too. Is it too late for us?"

"No. I think we are immortal, destined for each other."

She pulled away from him and looked up into his face. Her woman's perspective, her own personal empathy, and that primordial sense of the female told her this was right. Like a revelation that lurked just beneath her consciousness from the very beginning, she knew she had always loved this man. He had aged, as had she. His eyebrows were bushy, variegated with white, and the hair had thinned. The same blue eyes spoke the same love declared and rejected years before. She felt...yes – *comfortable at last.*

For his part, Tom felt battered by waves of emotion. So many times had he been close to Jeanne, so many times fate had intervened. Even as his arms greedily devoured the offering of her, his mind went back to 'sensibilities' and the obstacles in their way. He had established himself in an apartment in the Edmunds Building, but Margaret lived on as a recluse, still ensconced in the Ada Boulevard house. She would never set him free. Her late fanatical devotion to Roman Catholic dogma ensured they could never divorce. David 'Sher' Williams; how would he respond to a relationship between his mother and the man his father so hated? David was almost like a son to him. Losing his respect or losing him altogether would be terrible. What would the media say when the story broke? He could almost see Nathan Connaught's column now.

Jeanne's hand went to his cheek, smearing a wet rivulet. "Could you still love me, Tom?"

"God help me, I never stopped."

They cried together, Jeanne's back against the rough bark of the tree. Stalwart, it kept guard over them, its branches shielding their emotions as it had for the long years since they planted it. They kissed, and a faint rustle through branches above seemingly applauded them.

****

Tom had traveled through the Caribbean several years earlier. He fell in love with Tobago, in particular. There, he befriended a local plantation family who had fallen on hard times with the dwindling fortunes of the sugar cane industry. The area on the north end of the island was remote, but tourism was a growing opportunity. In partnership, they had built a small resort hotel that turned a profit. Tom was granted a small plot of land to build a house on, as part of the deal. He had commissioned a builder to commence work but once the main concrete foundation and a few block walls were up, he had lost interest.

Now, he was ready and determined to journey south and finish that house. Some kind of retirement was in his future, now that Jeanne was with him. He had spent forty years slavishly tied to his business interests. His marriage had failed and despite numerous dalliances with various women, they had been passing fancies. Jeanne was the only one he had ever truly loved. Now she had come back into his life, it was like a miracle, a revelation that turned his life upside down and disclosed a happiness he had hitherto never known. It made more sense to make plans involving happiness, rather than just working forever. They were cautious about their relationship over the weeks they'd been together and tried to be as circumspect as possible. Every aspect of a permanent relationship was discussed in detail, yet they were tentative, especially about making love. It seemed to grow like a barrier between them, a challenge they were afraid to face.

The latter dysfunctional sex between Jeanne and John and the passing of menopause left her with a form of resignation that her sexuality was somehow over and behind her. She evaded his advances with subtle negative messages. He began to feel that history would repeat itself, and they would not have a consummated partnership and perhaps drift apart.

He realized he needed some distraction, a catalyst to break through her doubts. His imagination soared when he suddenly remembered Tobago.

He had sketches and half-baked plans for the incomplete project. He pulled them out and involved Jeanne, encouraging her to match his enthusiasm. In a matter of days, she was fully engaged. He phoned Dwight in Tobago and sent him the new plans, authorizing the start of construction. Upon the project's completion, thinking it would only take a month or so, they could have fun furnishing the place and setting up a love nest, away from the daily distractions of Edmonton.

They left Edmonton and flew to Miami, then onward, leaving Edmunds Enterprises in David's capable hands. Never having been on such a luxury holiday, Jeanne was astounded by what she saw, and her natural vivaciousness came out. Their happy arrival in Tobago was tarnished when they discovered the construction of the house was only half complete, mostly due to the island's laid-back lifestyle. Nothing was ever done in a hurry. Dwight was apologetic, but since he ran on island time himself, it was hollow repentance.

Tom was upset because it fractured his plans. However, he quickly plunged into the project, enlisting more help, and physically working on it himself. He helped lay cinder blocks and erected walls. Jeanne helped too, mixing cement and shopping in the small town for groceries to feed them. She quickly developed a liking for the hot and spicy Caribbean food. The house site was on top of a high ridge overlooking the bay, set amidst tropical trees and shrubs. It was only a few hundred yards from the main road, an impossibly narrow track with blind hairpin bends that plunged up and down grades as steep as one in three.

It was really like another world. Vivid blossoms amidst the greenery of the trees made a foreground to the deep blue sky. A yellow beach curved around the bay, a demarcation line between the greens and browns of the land and the aquamarine colour of the sea over submerged reefs and the deeper blue of the ocean depths. She loved every minute of it. She also fell more in love with the man she was with.

Tom was baking to a deep brown tan. Every morning, they left the hotel and took a ride up the ridge. Stripped to a pair of shorts, he laboured daily on the house, supervising, assisting, and cajoling the men along. He could tell as they both pitched in that they were establishing a bond that strengthened by the day. The day the roof was finished, Dwight told them a friend would be visiting. The friend had a sailboat. Would they like to go for a short sea trip?

The few hours on the water revived old memories for Tom. It was a hot clear day, and as the yacht put out, he felt the movement of the sea beneath his feet. It brought another inner peace to him. The view of the island heights was spectacular from the sea. They went thirty miles down the coast before putting about. For a while, they hove to and drifted on the waves, while diving into the water. It was warm and clear, and although she did not swim well, Jeanne saw brightly coloured fish swimming around the nearby reef. Tom amused everyone with his tales of the sea from his youth on the way back.

They thanked their hosts and were put ashore by dinghy. They walked hand-in-hand back over the beach. "I want one." Jeanne made the statement, never having asked for anything, and the look in Tom's eyes was enough.

"Let's grab some bedding and food and stay up at the house tonight."

They rode back up the hill. The building site was deserted. Part of the design was a cantilevered deck that straddled the whole front, giving an unobstructed and spectacular view of the bay. Opening a bottle of wine, they sprawled on the mattress they had purloined from the hotel and gazed out. Munching on the food, the wine bottle was half empty when the sky began to darken.

Jeanne was still baffled at how quickly day became night in the tropics. It was only minutes from broad daylight to an amazingly brilliant starlit night. Below them, the cicadas began their brief twilight noise. Their cumulative chorus sounded like a small, ill-tuned gasoline engine.

"I love you, Tom Edmunds." She gazed at him, reaching for his hand. He stared back before leaning over and kissing her briefly.

"I'll be right back." He rose, taking with him the remainder of the wine and the two glasses. Inside the house, he found the rum bottle he had hidden and mixed equal quantities of rum and wine in each glass. Stripping off his shirt, he returned to the warm velvety air outside.

"Here." He proffered Jeanne a glass.

"What's this?"

"Near as I can come to the drink we made in France. Rum instead of brandy, but this place is definitely not an 'Amiens Hut' substitute either!"

She looked at him, remembering the night she buried her mother, remembering a night of sorrow and passion. She saw the old scar over his heart. It all came together. Sipping, then putting the glass down, she stood up and faced him. Deliberately and slowly, she removed her clothes. By the time she was naked, so was he.

They stared at each other unashamedly, some mysteries being preserved by absent moonlight. Wrinkles, thickening of waists, and the unkind force of gravity had altered their bodies but not their minds. They stepped against each other, moulding perfectly. In the warm darkness of the night, in the warm comfort of their love, they joined.

John Warner

Like the main character of this novel, John
Warner was a Canadian immigrant himself,
and drew upon some of his personal
experiences in writing it. Starting in aviation
with the Royal Air Force over forty years ago,
his 22,000 hour flying career forced writing
into second place for many years.

Currently, he is working on two more novels.

warnerjohn753@gmail.com
www.ilthynproductions.com